CHAPTER

13

For Pete's sake

for pete's sake

"Pete, who will you challenge?" Jade replied turning to Pete.

The words were like a punch in a chest. I turned to Jade blown away. Pete was my closest friend outside of Sai. To hear his name sent a shock through me. Judging by his demeanor Pete had better things on his mind. He didn't even bat an eye. He was out of it. He stared out the window in a funk. It was the battle with Beth. I knew Pete. He rarely put his own affairs over others, and this was no exception. He felt he let Beth down, and it was written all over his face. She asked him to not give up on her and he was a second away from doing just that.

"Pete," I said catching his attention.

Everyone stared at him as he finally seemed to notice the attention was on him. I thought before he didn't care, but it was obvious he was so focused on his regrets to hear Jade's question.

"What?" He replied oblivious.

The rest of the legion continued to stare him down surprised by his demeanor.

"What's going on?" He continued.

I hesitated not sure how to say what it was I needed to say.

"You're….You're the next up," I replied pointing at Jade.

He tilted his head slightly showing a bit of shock before shrugging his shoulders in a submissive manner.

"Whatever," he uttered turning back to the window.

A moment passed as everyone tried to be understanding of what he was going through, but after he didn't' speak for a minute or two, Jade was forced to finally press him.

"Pete," Jade pressed. "Who will you challenge?"

He stared out the window pausing for a second before responding.

"Sean," he replied catching everyone off-guard.

"Sean?" Zech replied. "That kid's a monster. Why pick him?"

I turned to Pete seconding Zech's words with my expression. If this kid was the strongest fighter on their squad, he had to be ridiculous. Looking at Herschel and Kadmiel up-close, they were beyond anything I could have imagined and if this kid was better, I didn't even want to think about the possibilities of the danger Pete could be in.

"Yeah, do you like losing or something?" Jo continued.

Pete lowered his head in anguish. Something was written on his face that he wasn't saying. There was a method to his madness.

"It's the only way," he replied. "Jacob is a sure win. With Tim, Sai, and Uriah already out of the equation, we have Luke, and Zech as major competitors…the rest of us are great pieces, but I don't know how we match up. It's a gamble. If I take out their top guy it'll even things out and give us a better chance going forward. Nobody is stupid enough to call Jacob out, and with me out of the equation, the only match-up handicap would be Sam, hypothetically, the rest of you will factor well against their remaining legion."

I gave him a simple look. Everything he said went over my head. He already had this planned, but the truth was I didn't care. After seeing the brutality of Beth's trial, I didn't want to see my best friend fighting the top recruit of their squad.

"You decided on this from the beginning," I replied pressing him.

He nodded still obviously effected by Beth's match. He was paying attention yet half sulking in his response.

"It was a deduction I made soon after Sai was put out," he replied. "Besides, I think I can take this guy. I have a plan. I'm not going down without a fight."

Jade stared stiff and emotionless. It was obvious he wasn't a fan of Pete's strategy, but it was his decision. There was nothing any of us could do about it.

"I disagree but it's your decision to make," Jade asked hesitantly waiting for him to change his mind. "This kid is probably the best recruit the Alpha House has ever had."

Pete nodded stubbornly acknowledging Jade's words. We were still wrestling with the emotions of Beth's last match. The rest of us feared another lopsided battle. Beth had shown us the difference in their experience in ours. As talented as Beth showed herself to be, it was her experience that hurt her the most. Pete was brilliant, but so was this kid. The possibly of another one of our matches ending with a legion member in the hospital was weighing heavily on the minds of everyone there.

"Yeah, are you sure?" Jacob asked.

He nodded solemnly.

"It's for the team," he replied. "Whether I win or I lose, I still pick off their biggest asset. I'll put up a fight. I'll make the academy. The rest falls on you guys to win your match. It's a win-win situation."

Beth's last match and the brutality of it replayed vividly in my mind. Beth made it into the Academy as well, but the cost was heavy. I couldn't stomach seeing Pete go through the same thing. These trials weren't a game. I couldn't let him do it.

"Pete, I get it," I replied choosing my words carefully. "You want to help the team, but this...you're not ready, none of us are. We're not ready for this kid. You saw what just happened to Beth. I don't think I can sit by and watch it happen to you."

Pete shrugged his shoulder.

"What do you want me to do?" he replied. "I don't want to do this anymore than you want me to, but it's the best strategy."

He turned to Jacob and Uriah to back him up. They both hesitated then regretfully acknowledged his words with a nod.

"You're a fearless kid," Uriah replied. "...And one of the smartest kids I know. You'll do fine. I'll make sure of it. Jake, what do you think?"

Jacob nodded signifying he understood what Uriah was hinting at.

"Yeah, we got you," he responded. "We'll be your advisors during the next trial."

Their words filled me with optimism. Putting those two in Pete's corner gave him a chance. I was confident. Pete looked unfazed as he nodded appreciatively.

"Thanks," he replied. "I'll come by your room to train after I visit Beth and Sai."

"Okay. Tim, you and Sam can join in," Uriah replied.

Jade nodded and turned with a smile as he headed downstairs.

"Well, then, there it is," Jade replied. "I'll go and inform the council of your decision. I'll let you know your council scores later via BAU."

As Jade walked off the bus Pete turned to Max.

"I also want an undertaking as well. I want it whether I have the ability to omit it or not" Pete replied sitting down and staring out the window.

Max acknowledged his words with a nod before turning to the rest of us.

"We'll meet you guys tomorrow morning," he replied. "But understand that these competitions can be brutal. Even savage at times. Like I said when you arrived, we may be better, but the beings in this realm are not perfect. They are not evil. They have the ability to make bad decisions, and at times they let pride overtake them, but they are still good people. You guys have the unfortunate disadvantage of fighting in your Earthborn bodies. They don't heal as quickly as the prospects bodies here do. A injury that would take a couple of hours, now takes days, and injuries that would take a day, now takes weeks. It's something these people aren't used to. They aren't going to take it easy on you guys because it takes longer for you to heal. I'm saying this to ask you guys to be careful. We were lucky that Sai's mother gave us invaluable information that is going to speed up the Beth's injury process. She still should be out for a couple of days, but she'll be back before the trials end. That's not always the case…so please, fight valiantly but protect yourselves."

He stood awkwardly waiting for a response before we all acknowledged his words with nods. He fidgeted uncomfortably for another lasting second then hit the side of the transport as he headed off out of it. The transport sputtered for a second than began to move.

"Phew," Zech replied. "I'm happy that we're finally going to get to see Sean up close, but I wish it wasn't against Pete. I kind of like him. I don't want to see him get hurt."

I ignored the boys and stared out the window.

"Yeah, I like Pete too. Sam would have been better," Jo poked with a laugh.

WHOOSH! Sam let off a harmless flamed toward the boys. They playfully dodged as Sam playfully shot it toward them several more times.

"Will you two sit down and be quiet?!" Danielle replied agitated.

"C'mon, there just kids," Sam replied. "They have to be bored by all this."

Danielle turned to Sam with a blank look.

"Well, take them in the simulator if you want. I need a break. They're driving me crazy," she replied.

"You guys up for it?" Sam question. "I could use the practice."

The boys lit up at the sound of his words. They trotted to the back as he followed them and disappeared into one of the portal rooms.

"Finally," Luke replied exhaling as he turned to the window.

The ride lasted a couple of minutes. We arrived in front of the hotel with most of us still in a haze. I was happy to see no press this time. I grabbed my bag and trailed Pete as he and Eve trotted rushing to get to the Medcorps as soon as they could to check up on Beth.

"I'll meet you guys in a little while," Pete replied to Luke, Jacob, and Uriah.

They nodded still corralling their bags. It seemed like everything was topsy-turvy. Before Beth's match we couldn't take a step without the media putting a camera in our faces. Now our trail was bare. Was the media really that fickle? With one loss we were already back page news. I couldn't say I was sad to see them go.

"Eve slow down," I replied trying to keep up with her.

Our trail to the elevator seemed to take seconds.

"Well speed up," she replied not slowing for a second.

"It's not like she's going to be there," I replied a insensitively.

She gave me an exhausted stare.

"I don't care, Tim," she replied. "I just need to see her."

I nodded trying my best to eat my earlier words through my actions. Pete sat silent as the elevator finally arrived.

The elevator opened revealing M-Delta 412 and his robotic smile. We all stepped aboard with a wave as he greeted us with the same robotic response, he greeted us with each time we boarded the elevator transport.

"We need to get to the Medcorps," I replied as Pete and Eve leaned against the elevator walls sulking.

As the door pinged signaling we made it to our floor we all filed out. The med guys zoomed past us as we headed for Sai and Beth's rooms. Shy met us as we approached Sai's room. She wore a sympathetic demeanor.

"Hi, Tim," she replied walking toward me.

"Hi, Shy," I replied. "This is the Med specialist that watches over Sai. These are my friends, Pete and Eve."

She greeted both of them with a smile and handshakes.

"Of course, it's nice to finally meet you," she replied. "Tim still is kind of overextending my credentials. I'm more like a glorified assistant. You know, checking vitals and BAU feeds, nothing special. Although things around here have been pretty busy over the past couple of hours."

I surveyed the hospital as the workers zoomed around.

"Yeah, are all the injuries from the trials," I pressed.

She shook her head irresolutely.

"Well, yes and no. They are the reason for the volume of patients, but they aren't the only patients," she replied looking around.

Eve stared around surveying the layout looking for Beth's room.

"Excuse me. I don't mean to interrupt or be rude, but do you know where my sister is?" she questioned looking for her sister.

Shy scratched her head as if to be pondering then pointed just behind her.

"Room…1…49," she replied. "She's prepped. You can head right in."

Eve nodded with a timid respectful smile.

"Thank you," she replied walking into the nearby room with Pete on her tail.

"Thanks, Shy. I'll be in to see Sai in a couple of minutes," I replied following them.

She smiled acknowledging my words.

"There still hasn't been much of a change since last night, but I understand you're need to see your little friend. I won't bother you. I just make sure you close the door when you exit," she replied staring at a chart as she walked away. "Don't want anymore wind gusts knocking things over."

When I finally made it into Beth's room Eve was sitting at her side holding her hand. She looked so peaceful.

"I'm so sorry," Eve replied tearing up.

She began to tear up as emotion overtook her. My heart went out to her. I was ashamed to admit it, but I couldn't work up sympathetic feelings for her. After the mean things she said to Beth before the trials, a part of me felt like she deserved to feel bad. I wrestled with the convicting self-righteous feelings before coming to my senses. Eve was taking it hard enough. It was obvious she was condemning herself with a conviction I didn't need to match. Guilt was written all over her face as she stared at her battered sister.

"It's not your fault," I replied speaking words my heart didn't truly feel in the moment. "You couldn't have known."

I turned to Pete for help, but he looked spaced out. He stared out a nearby window playing with the blinds. It was weird. I knew the demeanor. He was holding back emotions. I saw him act that way once in his life. It was around the time his mother died. In my life never saw him so much as tear up. Whenever something bothered him, he either disappeared, clammed up or became distant. There was no doubt in my mind. He was hiding emotions as he stared out into the beautiful Heaven Realm evening sky.

"Pete, are you okay?" I replied turning to him.

He continued to stare out the window before turning to me solemnly. He barely showed emotion as he nodded.

"I'm fine," he replied readjusting his backpack.

He diverted his focus trying his best not to look at anyone. His stare went from the floor then to the ceiling. He would peak at Beth from time to time, but it was obvious he was afraid staring at her too long would stir up emotions in him.

"Are you sure?" I pressed.

Eve's gaze turned to him seeming to be the straw that broke his façade.

"I'm fine, Tim!" he snapped sighing angrily. "I'm just fine. Why wouldn't I be? C'mon, you know me. You know, what I'm feeling. Why do you keep asking me a question you know the answer to?"

I raised my hand in a relenting manner that caused him to show regret.

"I'm sorry, Tim. I know you're just looking out for me. It's just…I…I know how to deal when I pay for my mistakes. It's hard to reconcile someone else paying for them," he uttered removing his glasses in a frustrated manner. "Beth trusted me, because I asked her to trust me. I made her believe she could win. I told her that if she believed in herself she had a chance to win, because I'm smart enough to know the risk. I did everything in my power to prepare her. I crossed ever T and dotted every I. I had to be right. Or at least that's what I had her believing."

He smiled blocking an otherwise chilling gaze as he stared me in the eye. I didn't know how to respond as his words exploded from him like a plugged-up dam which was suddenly opened.

"Why wouldn't I be, right?" he replied in a dry sarcastic manner. "I might as well have said to her…if you give up you don't believe in yourself."

"No way," I replied blown away by his take on the situation.

"No way," he chuckled facetiously. "Fact, I told her to trust me, fact, I told her that it didn't matter how much we believed in her, it didn't matter unless she believed in herself. You see me as a pretty intelligent guy, don't you?"

I was taken back by his words not really sure about how I was suppose to respond.

"Of course," I replied.

"Well then you should know that I have gone over this scenario from every angle," he replied angrily. "Beth didn't protect herself and didn't give in because she believed if she did she would have let me, Eve, and most importantly…she felt she would have been letting herself down. She felt she had to prove something. That's all Eve's and my doing. There's no getting around that. So, no Tim, I don't want to be fine right now. I can't forgive myself for that. I don't want this guilt I'm feeling to go away…so please stop trying to make me feel better about failing Beth. Neither of us deserve it right now. You told me to be cautious about overextending her, but my arrogance caused me to ignore your advice and Beth paid for it."

Eve's face fell into her hands at the sound of his words. She began to sob at the sound of his words. I felt like I was caught in a brush fire and I had no way to put out the flames. My head was spinning. I wanted to say they were wrong, but it would just be my take on the situation. That wouldn't be enough to change what they already believed.

"I…I…" I replied trying to cover two bases at once.

Pete stormed past me stumping out of the room more than noticeably agitated. I reached out to grab him. He snatched away from my hand and continued his path out of the room.

"I deserve this…," he replied under his breath catching my attention as he slammed the door behind him.

I wanted to trail him and press him on his words, but Eve was breaking down. I couldn't just leave her. Pete's words had torn the girl apart. First Sai, now Beth. We were dropping like flies, and Pete was on the chopping block. He had a huge task ahead of him. I failed Beth and Sai. I wasn't going to let another friend end up in the same position. Pete needed to focus. This situation was coming at the wrong time. We also needed Eve, but she looked like a shell of herself. What a difference a day made. Yesterday we felt invincible, now, I wondered if we would even survive these trials in one piece.

"Eve," I replied comforting her. "Yes, you made a dumb mistake this morning, but the first thing your sister said was she knows you didn't mean it. You can apologize for those words later. That is not what you should be feeling guilty about right now. What you should be feeling guilty about is demeaning what your sister just did. Your sister deserves more from you two. So, what. Who cares that she lost? She was awesome out there. She showed more metal than anybody thought she had and went toe to toe with one of the top prospects in the trials. If they thought she was weak, I guarantee you they don't think she's weak after that. You're crazy if you think that wasn't worth it to her. She'll go into the Academy with her head up and she'll be fine in a few days."

Eve dried her tears as she stared up at me in an appreciative manner. Just two months ago I would have been stuttering making a mess of things, but now words seemed to come effortless. I wondered if my ability to decipher abilities gave me keener insight. Either way it seemed to come to me like a six sense.

"Eve, she proved she was smart, courageous, and a beast of a remnant," I replied rocking her playfully. "She showed your not the only one in the family that we don't want to get on the wrong side of."

She chuckled wiping the remaining tears.

"She blew me away," she replied clinching Beth's hand and looking her over. "She was always so timid. I've never seen her like that. She rarely competed and avoided most confrontations like the plague, but what I saw tonight. Tim, I wish you could feel how proud I was of her. I never knew she had it in her."

I stared at the door wondering how far Pete had gotten. Eve could see it written on my face.

"Go," she replied ushering me forward.

"What?" I replied trying to play it off.

"I understand you're worried about Pete. I'm fine," she replied. "He has a big day tomorrow. He needs your help more than I do, and I can tell you're worried about him. Go look after your friend. I'm just going to sit here for a while."

I shook my head finally relenting and heading for the door.

"Thanks, Eve," I replied turning back to her.

"Thank you, and don't worry. I'll stop by and tell Sai you said hi," she replied with a chuckle.

I nodded with a smile.

"Okay," I replied awkwardly almost closing myself in the door.

She chuckled once more as I closed the door behind me. I trotted down the hall and impatiently tapped the elevator key. A minute or two passed before the floor bell signaled and the elevator door opened revealing M-Delta 412.

"I detected a slight disturbance in Peter," he replied. "Is everything okay?"

He seemed to be searching and struggling to use mannerisms that were foreign to him. It was weird to see him try and act human. He was still understanding things and his pitch fell somewhere between creepy robot and innocent child.

"Yeah, I'm sure you heard about the trials by now," I replied. "We're all a little on edge is all."

His face went blank as he processed my words.

"On the edge of what?" he replied innocently.

I winced on the inside fumbling looking for an easier way to translate.

"It's a human term. It means we're a little stressed out," I replied as the elevator door binged.

"I'm sorry to hear that?" he replied trying his best to imitate empathy.

It was a terrible attempt, but he tried his best and it was a nice gesture considering the circumstances. I turned to him with a smile as I exited the elevator port.

"Thanks, but we'll be fine," I replied.

His trademark robotic smile appeared as he returned to a place of comfort.

"I'm sure you will," he replied. "It's like you said, you humans need to feel as if you're fighting for something, and even if you have a slim chance at success, it's enough for you to believe in the impossible…They have you and you have a an ability to redefine the realm of possible, I have no doubt that you and your legion will do well."

A smirk showed on my face at the sound of his words. I felt like a big brother realizing his younger brother understood his words for the first time. I nodded acknowledging his words.

"Thanks, I really appreciate it 412," I replied.

He once again showcased his trademark smile as the doors closed. It was eerie that with all the humans around me, it took a synthetic to speak such humanizing words. It filled me with optimism as I made my way to Luke and Jacob's room. I walked a couple steps and turned not confident that I was at the right room door. I stopped backtracking trying to remember exactly where the older boys' suite was. I singled down the choice to one of the two doors, but I still wasn't sure.

"Eenie, meanie, minie, moe," I said thinking out loud randomly picking a door.

A light enveloped me and before I knew it, I was standing in the middle of a room similar to ours. I surveyed the layout looking for the guys, but I couldn't see anyone. I heard faint talking so I followed the sound.

"What do you mean?" said a voice that sounded unfamiliar. "Herschel is gone now. That makes me leader."

A mocking laughter echoed at the sound of his words.

"What's so funny, Abby?" the voice replied angrily.

"To be honest I can't decide," a female voice replied. "The fact that you think you could feel Herschel's shoes, or the fact that you are giving advice to a kid who is smarter and more powerful than you are."

"Well, you've been useless since Herschel left...we need somebody to step up," he replied more arrogantly.

"There's a reason why Herschel chose Abby to be the General instead of you, Kel," said a voice that I recognized immediately.

It was Kadmiel. My heart jumped into my throat at the sound of her words. I accidently entered into one the ABA suites. I started to back out, but a part of me wanted to listen. Maybe there was something I could pick up on that could help me and Pete train. I racked my brain thinking of a power I could use to help me in this situation. It only took me a second to remember Sai's invisibility trait. It took me a second to rewind her actions in her mind but soon my eyes lit up as I could feel the light bending around me. I took a deep breath and walked into the room full of our adversaries.

"Abby's only good at thinking stuff," a voice replied.

The boy talking was the kid Kel from the beginning of the trials. He was lounging in a chair while two girls paced back and forth in front of him. I crept silently next to a chair and hid myself against a nearby wall. The BAU training I received in the simulation showcased itself as I barely made a sound.

"That is literally the stupidest thing I've ever heard," Kadmiel replied cutting her eyes at him.

The girl I assumed to be Abby chuckled at the sound of Kadmiel's words. She was a beautiful girl with wavy dark black hair. She like the rest of her team was clad in a Light Trial robe.

"Speaking bout' stupid. Why did you do that in the last battle?" he snapped. "Go ahead and beat up the media darlings. That's bout as stupid as stupid gets. You're just taking sponsors out of your own pocket. You think that look good."

He had a thick southern accent that made everything he said sound like his mouth was full of peanut butter. He wore a cowboy hat the hung low over his face as he sat back with his feet on a table that sat in front of him. He scratched his chin and chuckled as a toothpick hung loosely out of his mouth.

"That Nazarene bloodline is about as chaotic as tornado," he replied. "You never know what's going to happen…but it sure is fun to watch. I'll tell ya."

Kadmiel stared at him with a look of disdain.

"You're an idiot," she replied flippantly. "Besides, I practically begged that kid to invoke paradosis. That's on them."

She turned to Abby as if to be getting conformation from her. Abby's gaze danced as if she was intentionally avoiding eye contact.

"Still, you need to control that temper of yours," Kel replied.

Abby stared at the corner right next to me as if to be checking for someone. I crept closer sure she wasn't looking at me but still being cautious in my approach.

"Where's Sean? He's taking forever," she responded looking at her watch.

"Knowing him, he's probably still signing autographs," Kadmiel replied.

She chuckled to herself falling back exhaustedly into a chair behind her with a slouch.

"How do you like that? I'm the one who gets the win and they spend the night talking to him," she replied playfully bitter.

Abby smiled as she walked a couple of steps and peaked around the corner.

"Yeah, the only people close to that kid are those two Eli boys," Kel replied.

Kadmiel took a deep breath as if to be picturing something in her head.

"Speaking of close. I'd like to get closer to that Jacob," she replied pulling Abby's robe. "That kid is too hot."

Abby chuckled shaking her head humorously.

"Are guys all you think about?" she replied checking her watch.

Kel sat up and began to tap on the table like a drum as he did light alternated from the tips of his fingers causing his fingers to make a bell like tone with each tap of the table.

"You know Kaddy, romance and fighting. Those are her two favorite pass times," he replied placing his fingers together and separating them causing the light at his finger tips to play and look like an accordion.

"Oh c'mon on Abby, are you seriously saying that those kids from the Theta Delta Legion aren't hot. Not one, I understand the older kids, but that Tim, he's a little young for me, but he still should be on your dream list," she replied leaning back.

Abby cut her eyes and crossed her arms in front of her shaking her head.

"My gosh," Kadmiel replied casually.

"Kaddy, unlike some people, Abby is mature enough to focus on analyzing her opponent to pick them apart. You're too busy analyzing how kissable their lips are," Kel intervened.

"Well excuse me for noticing a work of art when I see one," she replied propping her feet on an ottoman that sat in front her.

She placed her hands behind her head as she lounged backwards.

"Besides, Abby's too focus on her new improved little friend Danielle," she replied looking peripherally at Abby as she spoke. "It's hard for her to think about anything else."

Kel chuckled as Abby ignored the comment.

"My gosh. Now that was a coming of age," Kel replied following it with an infatuation filled whistle. "Talk about hot. I didn't even recognize her."

Abby's demeanor was visibly different as she shuffled uncomfortably as an irked facial expression slowly covered her face.

"You think you could put in a good word for me," Kel continued to poke insensitively.

Kadmiel let out a provoking laugh.

"With the way those two fell out you're better off speaking to her yourself," she replied.

Kel turned to Abby at the sound of Kadmiel's words.

"What do you mean?" Kel replied sitting forward. "What happen with you two?"

Abby ignored his comments and began to walk toward the front door. As she did I turned to see a light emanating in the center of the floor in the shape of a door. Slowly two light bodies began to form until I could finally make out who it was. Sean stood standing with a kid half his size as the light dissipated.

"Well, bout time superstar," Kel replied rising to meet him.

"Yeah, Sean, where were you?" Abby seconded approaching him.

Sean patted the head of the short kid standing next to him. The kid looked even younger than the twins. He wore a back pack that was seven times the size of his whole body. He wore big glasses that covered most of his face.

"Christian wanted to learn the 'Ebeh Kaph technique I learned a couple of weeks ago," Sean replied.

They all stared at the kid as he sniffled and dusted himself off. The kid gave awkward a new meaning. He didn't say hi or even acknowledge the rest of the people in the room.

"Is he supposed to be here?" Abby asked.

"Like they would even find out," Kel replied patting the kid on the back. "This kid is probably the best wormhole conductor at his age level in years. This kid could pinpoint a position on a plane flying at G-force speed."

The kid was dry as dry could get in his demeanor. He didn't even look at Kel as he spoke. He just stared at Sean focused on the boy.

"Alright Chris, I'll see you in a few days, and I'll continue to show you the finer points of the technique, okay?" Sean replied.

The kid didn't say a word. He just vanished as the rest of the legion continued like they were accustomed to his weird behavior.

"That kid is so weird," Abby replied. "He gives me the creeps."

Sean shook his head with a chuckle and tossed his bag on a nearby chair.

"He's a cool kid. He's just a little eccentric," he replied sitting down.

He relaxed then stared at them as if something had just come to mind.

"Why are you guys here?" he replied in a matter of fact type tone.

Abby shook her head in a half-hearted manner.

"The trials with the Selli kid," she replied. "We're here to figure out a strategy?"

He rolled his eyes playfully exhausted.

"Alright then, lay it on me," he replied throwing his hands up jokingly.

They all stared at one another not really knowing what to say.

"Well, we haven't exactly thought of one," she replied. "We were hoping you already had one."

He laughed at the irony.

"So, what's the meeting for then," he replied sarcastically.

Abby shrugged apologetically.

"Well, we do it for everyone else. It's just weird not to do for you too," she replied in an embarrassed tone.

"See, I told you, Abby," Kel complained. "This is a waste of time."

Sean grabbed his backpack and tossed it over his shoulder as he stood up.

"Well, this has been productive," he poked.

Abby shot a sarcastic grin.

"Well think of it this way, we have the utmost confidence in your ability to take care of yourself and do what's best for the team," she replied.

"Well, apparently you're the only ones who think so," he replied stretching.

"What do you mean?" Abby asked caught off-guard by his words.

He shrugged nonchalantly cracking his knuckles.

"I only got a 11 out of 12," he responded casually.

They all sputtered at the sound his words.

"What?" Kel replied. "Are they serious? What did they dock you for?"

"Yeah, what could you have possibly done wrong?" Kadmiel replied
in snarky tone. "Oh, great Sean the second coming."

"Be quiet Kaddy," Abby responded. "We're just saying, if anybody
deserved the first 12 out of 12 in trial history, it should have been Sean. I
mean there has never been a recruit like him in…possibly ever."

Kaddy made a playfully sour face. Abby returned her gesture with a cut
of her eyes before turning back to Sean.

"It's no big deal. That one guy. The counselor from the Zebulun House
felt I lacked a solid sense of loyalty," he replied. "I guess he's right, I
mean, I tend to be a loner in a lot of our missions, outside of Abby. I hate
the Alpha House, and I'm a part of it. I wouldn't exactly call that being
loyal. Let's be real, if it wasn't for Herschel and Abby, I probably
wouldn't be here."

I listened and he was the complete opposite of what I pictured. He reminded me of well, me, except he showcased more maturity and a level head. They all nodded signifying they could understand the point he was making.

"Well, regardless, what are you going to do about the Selli kid?" Abby pressed changing the subject.

"I don't know. I still got a lot of studying to do, you know. Looking at his techniques, habits, flaws," he replied. "I'm just getting in, but you guys are welcome to join me if you want."

Kaddy and Abby grabbed their bags and went to follow him. Kel exhaled annoyed following suit.

"Go right in. I have to go get something from my room and I'll be right there," he replied pointing behind him.

"Alright, hurry up man. I could be lounging with the rest of the guys but I'm here helping you out, remember that," he replied walking into the training room.

"Yes, what would Sean do without you," Kadmiel replied shoving him forward as she followed with Abby on her hip chuckling.

Sean waited for a second than stared at his watch. He surveyed the room before turning to me with a smirk.

"Tim," he replied sending my heart in my throat. "I know you're here."

I crept lower trying to hide myself as he walked over to me and tapped on a nearby table.

"I'm a feel sense and I have a memory like a computer," he replied. "I never forget faith energy so I could feel you from the minute I entered. I'm guessing your using Sarai's invisibility trait, but it doesn't matter. There is nowhere in this room you could hide where I couldn't feel you."

I took a deep breath and released the bending light. He smiled as I slowly appeared.

"Why are you in here?" he replied with light hearted chuckle.

"It was kind of an accident," I replied embarrassed and afraid of the consequences of being caught. "I was looking for Jacob's room and for some reason your door allowed me in."

He scratched his chin and walked over to the door expecting it.

"Well, it's not hard to do," he replied. "It's all smoke and mirrors. These doors usually identify using a friend or foe algorithm, so if you're not a threat to the occupant. If what you say is true, and you truly did make a mistake and believed this was someone else's room than it's not hard to believe it opened for you."

I nodded thinking it over.

"So, I believe you when you say that you walked in by mistake. The question now is, why are you still here?" he replied pressing me.

I scratched the back of my neck not really knowing how to respond without sounding like the biggest scum bag known to man.

"Yeah, I'm sorry. I was worried about Pete. I was trying to see if I could...if I could maybe find some information to help him out," I replied.

He cut his eyes at my words.

"So, you were looking to cheat to get an advantage," he replied.

I swallowed hard looking away with my heart beating a mile a minute. His words made me feel like I was half a person.

"I guess so," I replied embarrassed.

He smiled trying to hold back his laughter before bursting into a chuckle. His actions caught me off guard. I didn't know if his action were that of a guy putting me on or making fun of me. I stood staring as he raised his hands apologetically.

"I'm just joking with you," he replied.

His words calmed me as I smiled trying to save face. I shook my head embarrassed but happy he wasn't mad.

"So you're not mad?" I replied trying to check to see if things were really how they seemed.

He shook his head.

"Am I happy to see you here? Of course not, but I can understand. If I saw what happened to your legionmate today and had to worry about my best friend possibly facing the same thing I would probably do what I had to do to prevent it as well. I may not have gone this far but who knows," he replied placing his hands in his pockets as he spoke.

I couldn't believe he could be this good of a guy. I stood nodded in disbelief.

"So, what happens now?" I replied willing to deal with whatever punishment he saw fit.

He shrugged and pointed to the numbers on the top of the door.

"Remember those numbers and don't come here again," he replied. "Other than that, don't worry about it. I'm not going to say anything."

I nodded with a smile.

"Gotcha, thanks, and I really am sorry," I replied walking to the door still embarrassed.

As I approached the door Sean called out from behind me.

"And Tim, don't worry about Pete, regardless of the situation, I can incapacitate him without putting him in a coma," he replied. "He's a strong and brilliant fighter, so I can't promise it won't get hairy, but I'm not Kaddy, it won't go that far."

I nodded appreciating his words.

"Thanks Sean, you're a good guy," I replied feeling peace from his words.

The worry that had dwelled in the pit of my stomach since Beth's match had vanished. I was actually excited to see Pete in a true gentlemen's battle. I trusted Sean's words wholeheartedly.

"Thanks, but it doesn't take a good guy. It just takes someone who still understands what it's like to be human," he replied. "And a Christian."

I nodded not fully understanding what he meant. I really didn't care. I was just happy it wasn't going to be a blood fest again. I gave him an acknowledging salute as I exited. He smiled as I disappeared in the light.

UMPH! I appeared in the hallway knocking Danielle over.

"Tim," she replied staring at me surprised. "Where have you been?"

I helped her to her feet.

"I went into the wrong room," I replied dusting her off.

"Oh, is Pete with you?" she replied.

"No, I thought he was with Jacob, Luke, and Uriah," I replied more asking then telling.

She shook her head surprised by my response.

"No, they thought he was with you," she replied.

I tensed up at the sound of her words. Where could he be? I thought retracing the events that had transpired minutes earlier in my head.

"He isn't with me. The last time I saw him he was leaving the Medcorps," I replied.

She looked at the floor thinking for a second than shrugged.

"This doesn't make sense," she replied shaking her head. "Let's go find your brother."

I agreed trotting with her. We walked up to the door. It scanned us as I tapped my foot impatiently. The light covered me, and I ended up on the other side of the door. I stood blown away with the suite. It looked like a palace. I walked around staring at the walls in awe.

"How did they get this?!" I replied pointing in no direction in particular.

She shook her head annoyed.

"Never mind that. Let's just find the boys," she replied. "That's not important right now."

I stared around like a kid throwing a temper tantrum internally as we walked the huge palace like inside. It had more rooms than I could count. It looked like one of the mansions from the magazines. It had pure golden walls with pearly white tiles on the floor. I stared out the window. It sat on a cliff side looking over a beautiful ocean waterfall drop. I couldn't believe it. There room made ours look like a motel suite.

"Jacob," Danielle responded turning a blind corner. "I found your brother."

As I approached the whole legion was standing in the middle of the simulator room. Sam trained while the rest of the legion looked worried standing around. They perked up at the sight of me.

"Tim," Zech replied running up to me. "We thought a wrath demon got you."

"Yeah, that or maybe you were lost...you know because you're stupid," Jo second.

Zech bowed him hard causing him to recalibrate.

"I'm sorry, I mean we thought you got beat up," he replied with a fake smile.

"Thanks for your concern," I replied not sure how to respond.

"Move you two," Luke responded nudging the boys to the side.

"Tim, where were you?" Jacob responded checking me up and down.

I sighed not wanting to go through the whole story.

"I came from the hospital and went to the wrong room," I responded. "Well, it was kind of more than that…I sort of tried to eavesdrop on the Alpha Beta Legion and got caught."

Jacob sighed throwing his hands in the air in anguish.

"Tim," he grunted.

"What, it was fine, Sean was the only one who knew, and he was cool about it," I replied trying to calm him down before he started. "He even sort of gave me his word that he wouldn't hurt Pete."

Luke's eyes opened wide as he stared at me like I was the world biggest idiot.

"So, you snuck into the guys room and begged him not to beat up your friend….so lame," Luke replied piling on with an exhausted sigh.

"No, I didn't," I responded.

"So, what did you find?" Uriah asked cutting me off.

"Well, nothing really," I replied embarrassed.

"Wait, what does that mean?—nothing really," Jacob pressed.

I sighed coming clean.

"I actually I didn't find anything at all," I replied. "I just heard a conversation between that kid Kel and the two girls, Abby and Kaddy."

"Abby?" Danielle replied bashfully.

"Dude, I know you're a kid but, man, you do some stupid things," Jacob replied shaking his head. "Do you realize you could have cost Pete his trial if that kid would have turned you in? Do you ever think before act? Just once…I'm serious, just once.

He looked like he wanted to swat me like a fly. I ignored him with a grunt as I scanned the room.

"Whatever," I replied. "Anyways, none of you know where Pete is. I mean, are you sure he isn't in our room or back at the hospital with Eve?"

Uriah shook his head.

"No, we tried all those places. We asked Eve in the hospital and Luke transported to Sai's room," he replied. "We can't find him."

I shook my head picking my brain trying to think of where he could be.

"I'll go and check the hospital again," I replied. "Maybe he's gone back since you checked."

"Why go all the way back there?" Luke replied. "We'll just contact Eve from here."

"No, I need to check some other places on the way," I replied. "You can give Eve a heads up, but regardless, I going to check the grounds myself."

They all nodded as I turned to leave. Danielle hesitated for a second than responded.

"I'll go with you," she responded bashfully.

I wanted to ask why, but she looked embarrassed enough so I just ignored my suspicion.

"Sure," I replied not really knowing how to respond.

"We want to go too?" Jo added.

"Noooo," Danielle let out sarcastically extended her response. "Maybe one but both of you are not coming."

"Jo you go, I'm going to teach Sam some more moves anyways," Zech responded.

"Okay, see, no problem," he responded with a gushing smile.

"Okay," I responded.

Danielle rolled her eyes as we turned to leave. It was good to know they were coming. They knew a lot about the Heaven Realm and I was going to need a crash course to find Pete in enough time for him to get good practice before his trial. The clock was already working against us as it was.

"So, do you know where he is?" Jo replied tilting his head as he spoke.

I lowered my head and readjusted my bag before turning to him dumbfounded as we walked.

"If I knew where he was there would be no need to look for him?" I replied dismissively.

"Oh, yeah," he replied.

He seemed to be happy just doing anything other than sitting in his room. He walked bouncing with every step as Danielle seemed distant. She stared around the lobby in a haze until I caught her attention.

"Do they allow you out of the hotel during the trials?" I replied turning to her.

She shook her head as she continued to survey the layout.

"It has to be approved by the council technically, but unless it's a true emergency. I.E., the second coming of Jesus, they don't approve anyone," she replied.

Jo was still wearing his gold-and-white trial robes, with one strap of his backpack from earlier in the day over his shoulder.

"Where do you think he is?" he asked.

We rode the elevator and walked in silence for ten to fifteen minutes and the awkwardness was at an all-time high. I ignored the two of them looking out the window trying to cut some of the tension. I could see the city from the hospital windows that looked out on it. It was beautiful. The gateway we noticed when we first arrived was considerably smaller. There was a golden expressway that cascaded rolling through it showcasing a beautiful countryside on the far northern side of the city. It looked so peaceful and organized, a stark contrast to the chaotic hustle and bustle of Angel Haven.

"I have no idea where he is. We've checked in all the places we thought he would be," Danielle replied.

Danielle stared at a holo-screen that she switched on after we walked out of the elevator. I didn't bother asking what it was. I assumed it was some type of honing device.

"You're his friend right, Tim? You should know," Jo continued. "I mean, you two are like brothers. If it was me, I would know where my brother was."

I stared at my watch tapping it like a brute caveman. I shook my head slightly embarrassed. I knew it was sad, but I was tempted to lie just to save face, but it just seemed wrong considering the setting.

"That's because it would be impossible for him to ever lose you," Danielle pressed. "Seeing as you two are always locked at the hip."

"We're separated now, so, ump," he gestured grunting immaturely.

"Yeah, and it's killing you," Danielle replied causing him to stop and think about it for a second.

"Well, he's my brother," he replied with a playful smile.

Danielle rolled her eyes before turning to me.

"Tim, I hate to say it, but maybe he's right. I mean, you have known each other your entire lives," she replied. "You can't think of a place. Obviously, you don't know a place here, but typically, what type of place does he generally like to go to?"

I shrugged then thought about the question for a second. I tapped my foot for a second or two and perked up just as I was about to give in.

"Is there a library here?" I asked turning to her.

She took in my words with a blank expression before turning back to her holo-watch. She thumbed through an invisible screen before turning back to me with a smirk that fell between a satisfying and arrogant smile. I paused not really knowing how to respond until she finally replied.

"Got him," she stated.

I nodded with a smile of my own.

"Okay, let's go," Jo replied sprinting toward the elevator.

Danielle exhaled exhausted trying to grab him before he sprinted off, but he was too quick.

"Jo," she replied narrowly missing him. "Slow down."

He shot down the hall narrowly missing several droids before turning around to respond.

"I'll be fine," he protested offended.

"Jo, look out!" Danielle yelped.

WHAM! I gasped as he crashed flush into a group of kids. I shook my head noticing who it was right away.

"Hey, kid," said a boy picking himself off the ground angrily.

It was one of the Alpha Beta's. Jo smashed into a kid I recognized from the trial banquet and narrowly missed Abby. He knocked dirt off his pants angrily staring at Jo. He reached up and grabbed him with one hand.

"Put me down," Jo replied.

He slowly stood up holding Jo extending him like he was a torch. I stood watching not knowing what to expect, but knowing I had to react.

"Hey, kid!" I shot forcefully. "I'm sorry he ran into you, but he's a kid. A kid in my legion. Meaning, his problem will become yours if you don't put him down."

He smirked in my direction. I noticed a faint bit of light energy fluctuation in his spirit. He was powering up. I gasped on the inside not fully understanding how I was supposed to handle the situation.

"Make me put him down," he replied his eyes clearly beginning to power up.

FLASH! I flash-stepped forward snatching Jo from his grasp. He looked around surveying the layout dumbfounded until he finally located me. He smiled staring at his hand pleasantly impressed before stoicly turning toward me in a threatening manner.

"Don't do that again, Eli," he warned staring at me angrily.

I pushed Jo behind me in a shielding motion as I stepped forward.

"Keep your hands off my legion mates and that won't be a problem," I shot back anticipating further conflict.

"Move, Tim, I can handle this nug-nutso," Jo replied.

I blocked him just as he was about to power up.

"Jo, don't," I replied. "You don't need to do anything that's going to get you disqualified. You still haven't done your trials."

He whimpered disappointed before shooting a sneer in the kid's direction.

"It was an accident, Benjamin," Danielle cut in. "Let's not make it more than that. We both have trials and there's no need to get disqualified over something as stupid as a kid mistakenly bumping into you."

Abby tensed at the sound of her words. She stared at her like she was looking at a ghost. The atmosphere between her and Danielle was cold. Danielle tried her best to not look her in the eye as she spoke, but the awkwardness was apparent in both of their faces.

"Danielle, you have reason to talk. You know you don't give two craps about this kid. What are trying to prove? When have you ever cared about anyone other than yourself?" Benjamin fired. "You stuck up brat. This has nothing to do with you. Go call one of your daddy's guards and leave the fighting to the real prospects."

Abby raised her hand stopping him in mid-sentence.

"That's enough, Ben," she demanded. "Let's just go."

He looked toward her with an offended glare before nodding obediently. He gave one last childish sneer before turning away.

"Abby," Danielle replied catching them as they turned to leave.

Abby stopped without turning around as Ben continued down the hall peaking back for a second before ignoring the exchange as he headed to the elevator.

"What?" Abby replied coldly.

Her demeanor seemed to cut Danielle as she hesitated before continuing.

"Look, what I said that day, my words," she muttered bashfully. "I was wrong. I was hurt and I didn't know how to deal with...things...I felt you were going to desert me and leave me all alone again...it isn't an excuse for what I said, and even if you hate me forever, I just want you to know,

I didn't mean it. You were a great friend and I shouldn't have said what I said. If I could take it back I would."

Abby stared at the floor blankly. It was hard to get a read on her emotions from where we were positioned. She continued to stand with her back to the girl.

"It's too late, Dani," she replied. "You've had years to tell me that. In fact, I waited for years to hear you say it, but the truth of the matter is, I know you well enough to know how you think. Yes, it's possible that you are contrite about what you said to me, but, it's also likely that you see me as a target and you're messing with my head. It's what your father taught you and what you taught me. Always be the smartest person in the room, right? Control the controllable. I'm sorry, but I don't trust those words after all this time. Especially amid the chaos of Light Guard Trials. Before I would have known better, but now, I just don't know."

She paused staring at the sky. Danielle nodded acknowledging her words.

"I know, and I wish I could prove it to you somehow," she pleaded.

Abby turned staring her in the eyes for the first time.

"You can," she replied. "In all my years doing this I have never met an elemental as good as you are. You're the best. I know that, but these guys don't. If you end up in the final face-off against me, respect me enough to give it your best. The only one that can bring the best out of me is you. I need to make it into the academy, and you can help me by letting me see how good I have really gotten, afterwards we can talk about the past, but as for now, stay away from me, that's all I ask."

Danielle nodded as she turned to leave.

"Okay, you have my word," she replied wiping thin tears from her eyes.

Abby seemed visibly emotional as well. It was a passionate exchange that seemed to give Danielle a bit of closure. Abby nodded as she headed toward their elevator as Ben stood waiting on her.

"Are you okay?" I pressed as Danielle seemed visibly shaken by the exchange.

She nodded exhaling as if the weight of the world was lifted off her.

"Look, just head back to your room. Jo and I will head to the library and meet up with Pete," I replied as Jo stared at me happily jumping up and down.

"Yeah," he replied yelping like a hyena.

"Are you sure?" she replied composing herself.

"Yeah, we've already found him. You've done your part," I replied with a smile. "And for what it's worth...th-that was pretty cool...I mean, you must really care about her to let down your guard like that."

She smiled with a nod.

"Wouldn't you do the same for any of your friends?" she replied.

I hadn't thought about it like that. I couldn't imagine being on the opposite side of Pete or Sai in a competition as violent and important as this was. The resolve it would take. I didn't envy her position at all. Now Abby's words rung more clearly. She wasn't only telling Danielle to give her best, but she was explaining the dilemma she was in as well. It was an impossible situation for both of them.

"Yeah, I understand," I replied empathetically.

"Well, thanks for understanding," she replied giving me a hug. "Get Pete ready, I need to sort things out, but I'll be okay. I just need to find a nice soft couch and just mellow out for a little while. Tell the guys I'll meet up with them tomorrow."

"Okay," I replied.

She grabbed her medallion as it lit up.

"Wait, you can use those things here?" I replied.

She smiled holding it out with an exhausted look on her face.

"So, you've been using the elevator to get around," she replied. "Makes sense, no wonder that droid was so friendly."

"Yeah," I replied looking away bashfully. "He's okay, though."

"Really, a droid?" she replied. "You even became friends with a droid. What is with you? Do you find a way to befriend any and everything you come in contact with?"

I shrugged humbly. She smiled extending her medallion in a demonstrating fashion.

"Yeah, it's only shut off for the pre-trial stuff, and once activated you can only move inside the resort, but other than that it works a lot better than the elevator," she responded with a smile. "See ya."

She gave me a pat on the shoulder as she disappeared. Jo stood looking me over holding his medallion in one hand.

"I thought we were only not using these things because you wanted to search everything yourself," he replied. "It was annoying. But enough talking you two, let's go get Pete."

The boy pulled me away from Danielle in a yanking motion. I smiled shaking my head as we both waved goodbye to Danielle. I locked in on Pete's faith energy and instantly my medallion began to light up. Before I knew it, I was standing at the entrance to the library.

"Why would anyone want to come here?" Jo muttered.

We stood in front of a check-in desk with a bird nosed droid sitting at the counter. She looked like a librarian from the 1960's. She was elderly with an old vest sweater and a button up shirt. She sat at the desk looking down her nose at Jo.

"Children are not allowed unless accompanied by an elder prospect," she snarled looking at Jo like he was an insect.

"I have one old lady, sheesh," he replied pointing at me.

She stared at me then back at Jo in a disapproving manner.

"What is your business, Mr. Eli?" she replied with a rickety smile.

I forced an awkward smile in return before responding.

"Is Peter Selli here?" I asked staring around.

It looked more like an oversized warehouse then a library. A space age warehouse. There was a lighting strip that cascaded down each aisle. It was all black and a clear diamond like stainless steel. The books looked like glass frames. Students pulled them out like cd's in a deck.

"Ah-...Peter Selli, you say?" she replied squinting.

A glass holograph screen rose from the desk as she moved her hands filtering through the library database.

"Yes, Peter Selli, he is in the Mechanical Engineering section. Just a second," she replied hitting a couple buttons on the screen. "Follow this arrow and it'll lead you right to him."

As she spoke an arrow much like the arrow that guided us during our training appeared blinking inches in front of my feet. Jo moved his feet dodging the arrow like his feet were on fire.

"Young man, stop that," she replied glaring at him annoyed.

Jo shot a playful mischievous smirk as he stepped one more time just to get under the droid's skin.

"C'mon, Jo," I replied grabbing him.

"Hey," he replied as I dragged him as I walked.

"You've already almost got us all kicked out of this place once," I replied waving to the librarian droid as she stared at Jo like a stain on her beautiful utopia.

I waited until I was a safe distance away from her before I let him go. I continued to follow the arrow as it took me down a hallway knifing in and out of prospects. They all stared at me star struck as I smiled trying my best to not seem stuck up. The arrow finally halted and ceased to blink in front of a book tab.

"How do I use this thing?" I replied tapping it like a Neanderthal.

"It's a book," he replied. "You have to open it. It's like another world almost. These instructional ones are like warehouses. Pete must be building something."

"What? Are you serious?" I replied staring at him.

"Yeah," he replied. "Look."

He reached out and grabbed the book as an electric charge spark then engulfed us in a bright light. When the light disappeared, we were standing in what looked like a futuristic body shop.

"See," Jo replied pointing in a direction. "Whoa...what's that?"

I followed his eyes and paused looking at a monstrous looking robot gorilla. Pete stood on a crane like platform with a blow torch like tool. It was humongous.

"Pete," I replied squinting.

He turned around surprised to hear my voice. He raised his goggles with an apologetic demeanor.

"Hey," he replied gun-shy.

"What are you doing?" I replied angrily. "And why didn't you let us know where you were?"

The platform lowered as I stood waiting impatiently. He wore a body shop cover-all that he had halfway unzipped.

"It was sort of an accident. I was just thinking it would be nice if there was a library and next thing I know, I was staring at this book. I opened it up and I ended up here," he replied showcasing the place like a hand model.

"What is that thing?" I replied pointing at the huge robot.

He turned to it with a proud smile.

"You like it," he replied backing up as he pointed to it.

"I don't know what 'it' is?" I replied.

"Whatever it is, it's awesome," Jo added tapping on the robot.

"Hey, be careful," Pete warned. "It's not finished."

Jo pulled his hands back apologetically like the robot was hot.

"Well," I replied. "What is it?"

He smiled even bigger than before.

"Remember your fight with that kid Herschel," he asked rhetorically.

I nodded not knowing where he was going with his statement.

"Well, this is my law virt version of that," he replied. "This is Lex."

I stared confused by his words. It was nothing like Herschel's beast. It was big, bulky and metal.

"Okay, explain," I pressed looking at him.

"Well, obviously I'm not a percept virt," he replied. "But I think their ability to summon these 'beast' is a valuable asset for a thinker like me. I'm an okay fighter, but my ability to command is my biggest strength. Give me four or five of these guys and I can hold my own against anyone, even you."

I stared at him shaking my head. How did I ever doubt that this kid had something up his sleeve? He was right. If he had an army then it became a game of wits and you would be hard press to find anyone on Pete's level in that regard.

"But Herschel's beast had a mind of their own, they had instincts, they were like real animals," I replied. "This thing looks like it's an empty vessel, besides, how are you going to bring these things into a fight...look at this thing, it's huge."

He smiled holding his hand out with four pill size capsules.

"That's why I'm the only guy who can pull this off. My unique ability to control the mass size of anything I touch helps me compress them small enough to fit into these capsules," he replied holding one of the capsules between his thumb and forefinger and kissing it. "And as for the intelligence, that's where this library came into play. This place is a utopia of knowledge. I got the idea to do this whole thing after your trial. I knew that I had the ability to physically create my own war machines, but it wasn't until I got here that I was able to research the artificial intelligence that the droids used. I added my own twist on it to add battle instincts. It wasn't easy, but after a little while I perfected it. Now my war machines can take on any Percept beast and I'm the only one able to do it."

I shook my head astonished by his intelligence. He used everything. That was the Pete I knew. Every experience at his disposal was utilized, every miniscule detail dissected and perfected. He was a true genius.

"Awesome," Jo replied. "Can you make me one?"

Pete shook his head with dry in his exhaustion.

"Didn't you just hear me say I'm the only one with the ability to change their mass enough to fit them in my capsules?" he replied shaking his head. "Oh yeah, and I haven't shown you the best part yet."

I stood standing as he jogged over to the foot of the robot. He lit up until he looked like a mini star then dispersed like an electrical charge. As he did the light in the eyes of the robot lit up. I stood as the machine came to life.

"How do I look?" the robot replied moving its hands.

I squinted trying to verify if what I was seeing was what I thought it was.

"Pete? Is that you in there?" I replied.

The robot nodded to my surprise. As quickly as it came to life it fell lifelessly as the electricity shot from it and converged back into a mini star. Slowly Pete came into view as I stood shielding my eyes from the light.

"You know how us virts can break are matter down to the light level in order to travel in time," he replied walking towards me.

"I think," I replied racking my mind to remember.

He cut his eyes at me and shook his head.

"Well, we can. Anyways, light energy, as you should know, is just electricity. It's what gives us life. Therefore, I can transfer myself into my war machines anytime I want with that ability," he replied pointing behind him with his thumb.

I nodded forcing a smile not really knowing what to say. I wasn't sure I totally understood it but after the mental feat he had pulled off I was embarrassed that I couldn't even grasp a simple concept.

"Well, sounds good to me," I replied. "Can I help out?"

He stared at the robot for a short second then shook his head.

"I'll be done soon," he replied. "And what I have left over, no offense, but it'll probably be best if I do it myself. It's been a long day for all of us, and I have had a even longer one tomorrow. Let's just call it a night, and I'll see you guys in the morning."

I nodded feeling useless. I was happy he had an ace up his sleeve, but I still wasn't confident it would be enough to beat Sean. I walked over to him and gave him a high five pulling him in for a hug.

"Alright, don't stay out too late," I replied. "I'll see you in the suite."

"Ah, man, I wanted to see how you did it," Jo groaned slumping.

Pete rolled his eyes in a relenting fashion.

"Alright, follow me," he replied ushering Jo toward the robot.

Jo stared at me like he was asking for my permission. I nodded giving him the okay as he smiled from ear to ear and skipped after Pete. I grabbed my medallion and before I knew it I was stand in my bedroom. After what Pete had shown me, I should have had more confidence, but I was still nervous and afraid. Pete was game and Sean had given me his word that he wouldn't put Pete out of commission, but I had a sweeping suspicion that things wouldn't go as planned.

CHAPTER

14

When in rome

When in rome

Comment [LB]: Chapter 14

Have you ever woken up in the morning and wonder if today would be one of those days? Your alarm clock wasn't set and you overslept. You missed the bus, got to school and realize you left your backpack on the kitchen counter. It doesn't matter what happens throughout the rest of the day you just have a sneaking suspicion that things were only going to get worse. Well today was one of those days.

I stood in a daze as Sean and Pete elevated on their pods to begin their undertaking. I wondered if it was all in my head. Everything seemed to go in slow motion from the moment I awoke. Pete was already sitting on the transport when I made my way down. He nodded to me as I entered. He wasted no motion. He seemed surprisingly relaxed given the circumstances and remained that way throughout the festivities. He saluted me as he elevated standing on the platform.

"What's in this Venus resort?" Jo replied staring on in awe.

"It's not a resort, Jo," Zech replied shaking his head trying to appear mature.

"That's what the guy said," Jo responded sticking out his tongue.

"He didn't say it was a resort. He said that as a last resort they could forfeit and challenge for the relic. Man, you're stupid. It's a dimension prison were two prisoners have escaped. One has stolen the Heaven Bow," Zech replied crudely. "They've found the screws and Pete and Sean have to go and bring them in. It's simple to get."

"Shut up, Zech. Your wrong. It's not the Heavens Bow," Jo replied in a mocking tone. "They said it's the Bow of Cupid."

Zech shook his head in an annoyed manner.

"Bow of Cupid is the name the Pagans came up with after it was stolen by the Nephilim Aphrodite or Venus. It's called the Heavens Bow," Zech replied. "She gave it to her son Eros or Cupid when she was captured and imprisoned on Mattara or Venus as it was called in the old days after her imprisonment. Once he and his brother Aeneas were captured the bow was taken into custody and kept on a security facility on Mattara. They just broke out and recaptured it. That's where Pete and Sean are going now. To get it back."

Jo crossed his arms immaturely unable to respond. I grabbed my bag as Uriah, and I headed into the room. It was a surprise when Pete asked me to be his advisor. I thought for sure he was going to pick Jacob, but he said he couldn't do it without hearing my voice. I was flattered and agreed immediately. I stared at the room remembering the last time I was there and the pain and disappointment surrounding it. It seemed like it was my permanent luxury box. Uriah moved to the side and politely let me pass allowing me to go in first.

"Let's get this started," he replied plopping down in the seat next to me. "How you are doing, Pete?"

"Surprisingly nervous. Seriously, I'm fighting cupid. I'm facing something I thought was a fat baby in a diaper a day ago," Pete replied stepping into the pod. "By the way, do you get a look at Ms. Munoz. My gosh, who knew she could actually find a way to be more attractive. We're in Heaven and she still makes everyone else look average."

I chuckled as he shot through the wormhole.

"Where's Sean?" I asked surveying the wormhole.

"Right now, we have to assume he's already gotten a jump on us," Uriah replied. "From what I hear he's as fast as Jacob. I seriously doubt it, but I have to assume he's at the very least extremely fast, which puts us at a disadvantage considering you're a power anointed remnant. Getting there first will not be a likely option. Let's formulate a plan based on efficiency, not speed."

Pete and I agreed as the boy squeezed his hand in an effort to shoot forward as fast as he could. It took a minute before Pete finally emerged on the other side of the portal. He emerged showcasing a beautiful amazon looking environment with a man in a light guard uniform waiting for him.

"This isn't the Venus I know?" I replied starring at the scenery.

"Venus is in the 2nd Dimension. We can't see it from our dimension. We would be like ghosts are in our dimension if we traveled there in the physical realm," Uriah explained. "That's why every planet in our solar system looks desolate. It's because we can't see it. Similarly, Earth looks desolate from Venus's dimension."

"So, you're saying the planets in our solar system are separated by dimensions," I replied.

"Yes," he replied with a nod.

"Hello, Mr. Selli. My name is Cecil Angeles. I have the coordinates of the fugitive. He has been pinned down by a Mattaraien locals. There are a few divines who you can speak to you directly, but the rest will only see Aeneas's vessel. They will see you as their commanding officer. Your trial will be to use everything in your disposal to obtain the Heaven's Bow. God bless you and may the Holy Spirit guide you. Who is like the Lord?" he replied as he disappeared into thin air.

"No one," Pete replied with a nod.

Pete uploaded the information getting into character and calming himself.

"So, what are they expecting u to do?" I asked outload.

"I drew Aeneas, crap?" Pete griped. "Sean is supposed to be the elite one. How does he get the push over?"

"Neither one of these guys is considered a pushover" Uriah added. "Especially to prospects like us."

I went back and forth from the screen to Uriah pinging like a ping pong ball.

"Besides you are the guy who chose the undertaking," Uriah continued.

"What's the plan?" I pressed trying to not seem completely useless.

"Get the forces out of there, safely exercise Aeneas from the vessel, pound him into the dirt, and have faith he's the one with the relic," Uriah explained.

"When you put it that way it sounds so easy," Pete poked.

"Let's just get going," I replied.

A portal hole opened as Pete hesitantly stepped through. As he emerged on the other side he had transformed. The light from the other side of the portal blinded me. I was surprised to see him in the middle of a crowd of weird looking people. They were reddish pink with light blonde hair and fish eyes that shined like marbles. For some strange reason they looked exactly how I expected people from Venus to look.

"Chief, the perp has four hostages and stated he's not going to release any of them until he can get to the Blux Factory on the outskirts of the city," one of the sharply dressed police replied.

Their uniforms where a royal red but other than that they looked identical to ours. Pete was dressed more sophisticated than the others. The only thing that looked out of place was the blank expression he wore. He stood like a deer in headlights until Uriah prompted him to speak.

"Pete, say something," he sparked.

"What am I supposed to say?" he uttered via BAU. "Guys get out of here because the guy in there is a possessed demon Nephilim from their uninhabitable version of Earth. Yeah, that'll go over."

"That's why it's a trial. If it was easy then everyone would do it," he continued. "Besides, you're a smart kid. C'mon, Pete, you can think of something."

The men surrounding him were starting to notice something was amiss. They stared at him trying to figure out what caused his lapse and non-response to their initial question.

"Chief, are you okay?" one asked staring Pete in the eye.

"Oh, yeah, sure," Pete replied trying to be transparent.

The men stared at each other confused as Pete pretended to be surveying the layout.

"Yes, yes," he replied in a scruffy voice not his own. "This place on the outskirts. Did anyone ever assume that is his aim? There is obviously…I mean."

Pete stopped as if to have stumbled across an actual idea while bloviating.

"What is it?" I asked catching on right away.

"Nothing, it's just, I think I know where the Bow is," he replied via BAU.

"You think this outpost…you think that's why he wants to get there?" Uriah added.

"Yeah, why else would he want to get there so bad?" Pete replied.

"I don't know," Uriah responded. "He had to know that someone from the Guard would be out here. There's no way he would make it that obvious even if he thought he was talking to Venus Realm folk. I don't know. It seems too simple. It might be a trap."

The men looked at Pete like he lost his mind. He pondered starring off into nowhere oblivious to his surroundings.

"But you never know, I mean, isn't this guy known as the brute force dumb one?" Pete continued. "He might be that thick."

"It's your call, but I just think it sounds a little fishy," Uriah added.

"I get it, Uriah. I'm not an idiot, but there are other things to consider besides the obvious. I've gone over both scenarios. I say we take this opportunity and assume that this guy is that dumb. Sometimes battles are won by assuming the opponent's weakness," Pete lashed back.

Uriah shook his head unapprovingly.

"No, my granddad taught me to never trust Intel from an enemy that is readily given," Uriah pressed.

"Well, my dad told me to always trust my gut!" Pete fired his voice slightly raising.

"Pete, Uriah's giving his advice. That's what you asked him to advise you. Remember, you're not competing with him. You're competing with Sean, okay?" I replied sensing hostility in the air.

"We're doing my plan," Pete replied sending the instructions to us via BAU.

The upload was like a photo being flashed then a strange power drunk déjà vu feeling. Once I understood what his plan was, I realized the flaws in it, but Pete was as stubborn as an ox when he had his mind set on something. It could be extremely annoying at times, but regardless of how I felt, it was his decision and I couldn't articulate my position any better than Uriah had. It would be futile to try.

"It's your trial," Uriah uttered. "So, it's your decision."

Pete turned to the cops and proceeded with his plan.

"The sniper team head to this address. There is a magnetic field device in a warehouse. Take position on the northwest side of the building. Target the far window. The rest of the unit get to the address and barrier it off. Infantry head inside and find the device," he replied sounding like an experienced vet.

The men stared at him with blank expressions.

"Chief, what are you talking about?" one of the men replied. "What about the hostage situation? We don't know anything about this device and why does it take precedence."

Pete cut his eyes at the guy without saying a word causing him to recoil.

"Umph," he replied clearing his throat. "Yes sir, you heard him, let's move out, the Chief will meet us at the address. Let's go."

It seemed like it took forever for the hundreds of men to hop in their cars and file out. As the last one disappeared Pete stepped out of his vessel like he was stepping out of a pod. He placed his medallion around the blank faced man's neck. A light emanated from the medallion then disappeared along with the Chief. After he was gone Pete stood in front of the abandon barn-like building defiantly.

"Aeneas!" He screamed.

Soon after he spoke a man appeared in the window.

"My name is Peter Selli, I am here in conjunction with the Light Guard on the authorization of Warrant Omega-5123 to apprehend you and the Heaven's Bow. I challenge you to a Lacham for ownership of this relic and your apprehension, do you accept?" Pete replied without as much as a stutter.

As he spoke a light emanated from the eyes of the vessel. The light grew until it formed into a being standing next to him. Before I could assess the situation the being appeared standing just ahead of Pete. Pete didn't flinch as he replied.

"Do you accept, Aeneas?" he shot.

He had a feminine look to him. He had short cut hair with bangs that hung over his eye like a punk rocker. His eyes were coated with red eye liner that made him look like a girl. He had on a regular rebel uniform aside from the sleeves being gone revealing completely unimpressive bony arms. He leaned against a wood fence as Pete stood unflinching. The wind seemed to pick up as to be violently reacting to his presence.

"And just once more, who are you?" he replied propping himself up on the top plank of the fence.

"My name is Peter Selli, as I said I am here…,"

"Yeah, yeah, I got that part…Selli, Selli,…Judah Tribe, descendant of Solomon, pretty strong lines, but you look more like a upstart," he deducted cutting Pete off in mid-sentence. "What are you? A first year, nah, I don't see a house badge on that uniform of yours…so, that only leaves a prospect, so it's that time of year already…The trials, man, me and my brother have been locked up for a while."

"Do you accept?" Pete replied trying to look as confident as possible.

He ignored Pete and continued to think out loud.

"Where is my brother?" he replied before turning to Pete and acknowledging him finally. "Do you know?"

Pete glared at him intensely.

"Do you accept?" He reiterated starting to get irritated.

He wasn't the only one. The guy's whole demeanor was insulting. I was expecting a titan, but he looked like an immature punk. He was a gangly built man who looked like a guy who was pulled kicking a screaming out of the 1980's.

"Testy on that one," he replied mocking Pete. "You asked first, so it's only polite for me to answer your question before asking one of my own. So, I understand your frustrations, but seeing as this seems to mean a little more to you than to me, why don't you answer my question so we both can move through this phase of the exchange quicker, shall we?"

Pete rolled his eyes before finally relenting.

"He's also a fugitive with a prospect guardsman assigned with bringing him in. His precise location is unknown to me as he wasn't my assignment. He broke out three days after you did, and has been inhabiting a Prime Savant here on Venus. Now, do you accept?!" Pete replied angrily.

"Son, do you have any idea who I am?" he continued pressing Pete's patience to the limit.

"I just said your name, didn't I?" Pete shot back with an unflinching demeanor.

Aeneas nodded agreeing resolve with a mocking one of his own.

"Yes, but do you have any idea what I was before I was captured," he replied arrogantly. "My kingdom spanned nearly a third of the earth. I was a god."

"You were an evil coward who was a mass murderer that killed millions," Pete fired back.

"I was the champion of a nation, like David, you insignificant little snot. How dare you speak of me in such a way. I am the descendant of the Founders of Rome. Do you have any idea what I ushered in? Without my bloodline none of your governmental or societal structure would be there. We streamlined it from the Heaven Realm itself.

"You and your kind led to the destruction of God's people," Pete fired. "Earth wasn't meant to be the Heaven Realm, and your kind led to all the problems that plague us to this day."

He stared at Pete finally showcasing emotion as he stared him down.

"What do you know about what me and my kind have done for your miserable race?" he fired angrily. "Is that the gratitude you show in our presence? We pulled your pathetic race from obscurity and servitude and gave you a chance to realize your potential and become gods."

Pete cut his eyes at the emotion of his words. It was obvious he was antagonizing the situation. Aeneas became more and more agitated with every word Pete spoke. I didn't know if it was a good idea, but it was an idea to get the ball rolling, and at the time it was the best we could hope for.

"If that's the case then why did we choose to serve?" Pete replied. "Why did we choose him, Jesus Emanuel, over all of you?"

"For the same reason why you're here challenging me?" he replied angrily. "Because you're too stupid to know better. I'll accept your challenge, child, and I'll show you why I am known as the First Champion of Rome."

Pete gave a mischievous smile. He looked like a puppet master. His plan had worked to perfection, but I was still weary of it. This guy looked like an easy win, but I could feel his power from inside Pete's biorhythm and it was nothing to sneeze at, and to be honest, outside the Battle of New Angeles I never witnessed Pete partake in an actual fight. I was so nervous I was unconsciously tapping my fingers on the dashboard. Uriah turned to me noticing my anxiousness. I quickly stopped non-verbally apologizing raising my hands in a relenting fashion.

"So, you accept?" Pete replied verifying.

Aeneas didn't reply he just stared him in the eyes without a word. He hopped down off the fence he stood on.

"Could we just skip the formalities. I'm anxious to bounce your head off my boot?" he replied.

BOOM! Pete narrowly dodged a straight-ahead attack. He wasn't overly fast or agile. Pete easily parried his blow causing him to strike a nearby barn.

BLUNT! BUM! BOOM! Pete quickly attacked as the two clashed blows.

The force of the blows were like mini earthquakes. The force destroyed the terrain around them.

Pete leaped backwards dodging before collapsing to one knee. I could feel his exhaustion and it was baffling because the battle had lasted all of three seconds.

"Pete, what's going on?" I replied puzzled.

"It's this guy," he replied panting.

BOOM! Pete dodged rolling trying to get distance, but he wasn't fast enough.

"UGH!" he groaned as Aeneas punted him in the rib.

PONG! PUM! BOOM! Pete skipped across the terrain like a rock and slammed hard into the barn crumbling it on contact.

"Stttttrrrrike!" Aeneas mocked like bowler. "That teach you watch your mouth when you're talking to a god in little brat."

Aeneas gingerly walked in Pete's direction stalking him like prey. Pete fought to his feet struggling to stand. His vision was blurry. Nothing made sense. Pete was able to keep up with Sam longer than I was. He had the stamina to endure such a meek exchange.

"What's going on?" I asked frantically.

"I don't know," Uriah replied. "Pete, why did you say, 'it's this guy'?"

Pete sputtered then fell to his knee yet again.

"This guy, he's like a nuke," Pete replied. "Whenever I get near him…something about him makes me sick and nauseous."

Pete looked terrible. He could barely stand and his BAU was like a pitchy radio broadcast.

"Peek-a-boo, sonny boy. I see you," Aeneas replied lifting a piece of carnage and tossing it like a crumbled piece of paper.

ZIRP! WHAM! Without a warning he vanished and reappeared pressing Pete against a nearby wall with earth shattering force.

"Isn't it funny how children have these ideological and fanciful beliefs in themselves?" he mocked holding the boy against the wall with little effort. "It's one of the many things that separates a child from an adult. An adult doesn't make rash decisions based on impulse. They have the experience to understand consequences because they faced pitfalls which demands the respect of caution but you children…"

BOOM! UGH! He pulled back and slammed Pete against the wall again. The momentum of the blow caused the boy to wince in pain. Pete's eyes grew showcasing a look of pure pain. He could barely keep his eyes open as Aeneas seemed to be sucking the life out of him as he continued to batter him.

"We have to do something," I fired turning to Uriah.

Uriah shook his head sorrowfully.

"No, we can't, this is not our trial. It's his," he replied in a regretful tone.

"Forget this stupid trial. Pete's not going to end up in some hospital or worse," I shot back angrily.

"Tim, could you please give the guy a chance to fight his own battle?" Uriah replied placing a hand on me to calm me. "Pete's a smart resourceful kid. Give him a chance to prove it."

I ignored his words. I stared at the screen as fear and doubt filled me. After Sai and Beth my mind just didn't register the same anymore. It was slowly dawning on me. As exceptional and powerful as we were, we were still kids thrust into adult situations. We weren't kids who trained for this for years. We weren't adults who lived a long enough life to gain that experience in a normal lifespan. We were just regular kids a month and a half ago, and now here we were fighting some of the nastiest beast in existence. The absurdity of it was finally sinking in.

URHG! URHG! Pete choked trying to speak as life slowly started to drain from his body. I couldn't take it anymore. I analyzed Luke's wormhole technique until I had it down, but no matter how hard I tried I couldn't get it. I need to get to Pete and fast.

"Screw this," I replied grabbing the medallion around my neck. "This thing is a wormhole jumper, right?"

Uriah shook his head disapprovingly.

"Yes," he replied relenting lowering his head in frustration.

I grabbed the medallion. I really didn't know how to use the thing to get to Pete, but I couldn't watch anymore.

"Tim, wait," Uriah replied stopping me.

"No, I can't watch anymore," I shot back angrily. "I'm not watching another one of my friends end up in a hospital because of a decision I made."

"Oh my gosh, look!" he replied pointing at the screen.

BLAM! Just as I was about to disappear a light appeared erupting like a fire cracker sending Pete and Aeneas in opposite directions.

UGH! Pete groaned rolling over in a heap. The explosion seemed to only negatively affect Aeneas. I let go of my medallion and leaned in to get a better look. What had happened?

"Pete, are you okay?" Uriah replied.

Pete nodded scraping himself off the ground.

"Yeah, but that guy, I can't fight him. His body emits some type of neural toxin. I'm useless when he's close to me," he replied. "I have to find a way to breakdown the subatomic make up of his attack. I got to keep my distance, or I'm done for."

I looked at Uriah puzzled by chain of events. He gave me an unsure shrug before turning back to the monitor.

"Pete, what happened?" I replied in suspense. "How did you get lose?"

Pete banged his palm on the side of his temple in an attempt to clear the cobb-webs.

"I didn't," he replied surprising us both. "I thought one of you guys intervened."

"No, we didn't do anything," I replied. "He was holding you then an explosion of lightning separated the two of you. You're telling me that wasn't you?"

He surveyed the layout as if to be looking for someone else before responding.

"No, I don't know what that was but…" he rose and leaped away giving himself some distance as Aeneas started to stir. "I'm not complaining."

He reached into his pocket and pulled out his bag of capsule pills. He rummaged through the pouch before pulling out a shiny gold capsule with a red label that read DOVER.

"This should even the odds a little," he replied tossing the capsule on the ground.

POOF! It exploded revealing a robot with red and black paint. It was the exact bot I saw Pete working on the day before. It was huge almost twice his size. He pulled a chip out of his back pocket walked over and placed it in a slot just behind the bot's calf. It sputtered then started.

"Let's see him get through Dover," he replied.

He pulled his hammer from its holster with a determined stare. He gripped and extended it as walked beside the mechanical beast.

"Now game on," Pete replied getting ready.

Aeneas shook his head like he was trying to wince through the pain. He grabbed his jaw and moved it back and forth.

"So, there's a Dom here with you," he replied. "From the feel of it, a pretty powerful one."

His words threw me. What was he talking about? Was Sean there? Or was he talking about Pete. Neither were Doms. It didn't make sense.

"What are you talking about?" Pete replied taking the words out of my mouth.

"I'll show you what I'm talking about. The Dom is obviously trying to protect you. Therefore, if I smack you around a little while longer, they'll stick their nose out long enough for me to rip it off," he replied pulling off his jacket and tossing it down angrily.

I had no idea what he was talking about, but Aeneas's demeanor had become colder and more determined, but luckily, he also seemed less composed. Before he was a little angry, now he was livid, and I also sensed a bit of fear in his disposition. The power had him rattled, and he was afraid, but I couldn't understand why? Clearly there was no one there. I stared into our team barrier room and everyone was accounted for. It obviously wasn't anyone we knew, and if the person was helping Pete, why would they wait until he'd taken so much punishment before intervening.

"Try it," Pete replied.

BANG! Dover attacked high but Aeneas blocked him on contact. The presence of the beast surprised him as he fought the beast off using a wind buffer to keep it from ripping him apart.

"What is this a subatomic beast?" Aeneas groaned moving his head from side to side dodging the mechanical teeth of the bot.

BANG! BANG! BANG! BOOM! The two changed pace going at each other with mind-blowing speed that was hard for me to keep up with.

"Pete, that won't be enough. I understand you created the bot to compensate for your lack of speed and close-range fighting ability, but you'll never win. The bot isn't powerful enough to deal any lasting damage," Uriah explained leaning forward as pressed down on the intercom. "Not to mention, he can't think as fast as a true living being. It more limited than a subatomic beast."

PING! PING! PANG! BOP! BOOM! The bot was going toe to toe. It was keeping step with Aeneas, but it was obvious Aeneas was simply toying with it. Just as the two were going to collide again Aeneas disappeared and reappeared behind the bot punting it like a football high in the air.

"Close but no…."

BANG! Aeneas's head almost detached from his head. Pete swung his hammer like a boomerang smashing the demon with a direct hit.

"Awesome!" I exclaimed raising my hands.

Aeneas flew across the ground and skipped across the yard wrecking through a couple wood fences before landing in a heap in the middle of a grass field. He fought to stand but crumpled still reeling from the blow.

"I stand corrected," Uriah added turning to me with a smirk. "I should've known the kid had a plan."

Pete smiled catching his hammer with one hand like a boomerang.

"Like I said, I'm a Virt too," Pete replied. "I understand the limitations of my bots better than anyone. My plan was never to let my bots fight for me. He is simply an extension of my ability."

GRRRHH! POOM! Aeneas grunted in anguish punching the ground in anger creating a crater.

"I'm going to destroy you for that" he replied in a calm yet erupting stern manner.

Before I could blink he was gone and heading for Pete.

"Bring it," Pete replied with a smirk.

POOF! BANG! Aeneas appeared in front of Pete but before he could strike the bot intervened sending him in the opposite direction.

"Who's the one with the fanciful hopes again, creep?" Pete replied flipping his hammer like a coin with one hand.

WOOSH! WOOSH! WOOSH! WOOSH! Pete began to spin with his hammer like he was throwing a shot-put. He built so much momentum that the wind around him took the shape of a tornado.

"Try blocking this one!" Pete grunted launching the hammer toward a vulnerable Aeneas.

PUPF! UGH! Aeneas let out as the hammer collided with him. His body looked like it was about to snap in half from the impact of the blow. It sent him flipping across the field leaving a large crater were his body landed. Pete stood confidently catching his hammer with one hand as Aeneas fought out of the crater. He could barely move as he recovered from the blow.

"Impressive," the demon replied coughing up blood from the blow.

"That blow," I replied recognizing it immediately. "That bot, it fights like Sam. It's almost identical."

"Exactly," Pete replied confidently. "You know me, I use every advantage I can. I made him using Sam's algorithm. I wanted to make bots that excelled at the abilities that I lacked. Two of those areas are close range reflexes and speed. Trust me, Tim. I use everything I can to get better. All that sparring we did didn't go to waste. I uploaded Sam's practice sessions and created software for Dover based on his algorithms and tendencies, and although Uriah is right about the limitations, with me running point I can work to my strengths using them to take some heat off my weak points."

Uriah smiled at me blown away by the boy's genius. I wasn't surprised. When Pete took something serious, he went full throttle. He hated to lose and used every advantage he could to make sure that was a near impossibility.

"Do you have one for me?" I replied my curiosity peaked.

"There not clones, Tim. They just take small algorithms based on fighting styles. They are extremely generic at this point," he replied a bit annoyed. "So it's a bit of a stretch to say I even have one of Sam."

I rolled my eyes pressing him seeing through his façade to keep his advantage.

"So, do you have an algorithm based on me?" I pressed in dry pressing tone.

"Tim, what do you think?" he replied with a chuckle.

I shook my head as Uriah smiled with a shrug.

"So, what are you saying Sam's fighting styles better than mine?" I added thrown.

Pete smirked fixing his glass not taking his eyes of Aeneas for a second. He made sure to keep his distance attentive of his proximity to the downed demon down to the inch.

"Tim, this is not the time for that. Besides, Sam is the exact opposite of me. I needed someone who's strengths where the antithesis of mine, and Dover fit the bill for this particular opponent," he continued. "So, don't worry about it, because I'm not telling you a thing about what I have in the cupboard for the next time we spar."

I shook my head. There was never a wasted experience with Pete he was a pure genius. He was the same in everything he did always deducting, preparing, and putting himself in the best position to succeed. He thought of every scenario and had a plan for the backup of his backup plan. That was just the type of person he was.

"Things just got a little more interesting," Aeneas replied tossing a large wood column off of him.

"That it has," Pete replied tightening his watch in anticipation.

Aeneas leaped to his feet knocking the debris off his shirt. Pete watched him like a hawk.

WHOOSH! CLANG! Dover attacked but this time Aeneas was ready for the bot. He caught him by the neck with little effort crushing the column around the bot's head.

"Enough of you tin can," he replied lifting him into the air.

BAM! CRASH! CRASH! He tossed him like a service volley and nailed him with spinning heel energy kick that exploded the bot into dust. The demon slapped his hand storming toward Pete.

CLANG! Pete shot a hammer shot toward Aeneas who flicked it away like an annoying fly.

"You're going to have to do better than that," he replied.

His arrogance had me at odds. I had no idea if he was grandstanding or if he had somehow gained an advantage.

"Oh, yeah," Pete replied pulling out his pod container.

He tossed it on the ground as it slowly morphed into another bot. Unlike the last one that had the look of a large beast, this one wasn't as big. It looked like a robot samurai.

"Meet Slash," Pete gloated with a content smile. "Let see if you can handle all of us."

Aeneas's face seemed to showcase a worried look as he geared up.

"So, another one. He definitely doesn't look like a speed bot, so I'm not worried," he replied trying to hide his worry behind bravado.

"Well, you'll just have to find out, won't you?" Pete added confidently.

His words seemed to spark something within Aeneas.

"You can pull out a million of these bots," he replied unnerved. "I'll crack them and sooner or later it'll just be me and you."

Pete chuckled out loud.

"Who do you think you're laughing at kid?" Aeneas shot fuming.

"You...more specifically, you're statement that once my bots are gone it'll just be me and you," Pete continued. "You don't realize that the least of your worries should be these bots. As a matter of fact..."

Slowly the bots morphed and flew back to Pete's hand like they were magnetically linked to his palm.

"Pete, what are you doing?" Uriah added. "Don't let him talk you out of a clear advantage."

Pete shook his head.

"No, just like him you think I can't take this guy," he replied.

"What are you talking about," Uriah shot back. "Bots or no bots, it's still you. You built the bots."

Pete stood looking forward in a stare down with the ancient demon. It was another proud Pete moment. Pete was an exceptional talent, but his affinity for pushing the envelope at the most inopportune time was really starting to get on my nerves.

"Pete this isn't some stupid video game," I fired. "This is important, you have the guy on the rope, just finish it. Not to mention, you can't stand in his presence without getting nauseas. Did you forget that?"

"No," he replied vaguely like a stubborn two-year-old.

Uriah and I leaned back in frustration. His plan was working perfectly, and he was gambling it all for no reason other than foolish pride. He was my best friend, but I wanted to tear him apart. Pride was his weakness and Aeneas unknowingly exploited with his challenge.

"Pete, I'm begging you," I pleaded. "Just forget this and stick to the plan."

"I trusted you," Pete replied. "Why can't you just trust me?"

I shook my head at the terrible comparison. It wasn't remotely close. He was trusting me to perform at my best against impossible odds. He was asking me to trust a concentrated effort to handicap himself.

"That's not the same thing and you know it," Uriah replied before I could respond. "Kid, you said it yourself, he has an advantage what are you trying to prove?"

"Enough with the self-talk," Aeneas replied cutting into our conversation. "I can't say I agree with the stupidity of this, but I'm not complaining. As a matter of fact, I'm ecstatic."

UGH! Before Pete could blink Aeneas had him around the neck.

"Not this time," Pete replied.

BUGH! Aeneas retreated flipping back as Pete exploded in mass. He almost tripled in size. I couldn't believe my eyes. His body was like a sculpted professional wrestler. He looked unworldly. His hair grew and hung over his face like a punk rocker. I was trying to see his face, but he was bent over and it was too dark to see anything.

"It took me awhile to analyze it, but that toxin was a nerve relaxer. I'm a Law Virt I control chemicals. It wasn't hard to break it down and find a cure. I just need the time to do so," Pete replied. "Now you'll see what I can really do."

The boy stared Pete down like he was an anomaly he was trying to figure out. It was obvious he nervous. He stared Pete down obviously trying to convince himself the boy's words were just a bluff.

"It takes more than that, boy," Aeneas replied leaping back into action.

BREEENK! PAP! PAP! PAP! BAM! He landed a punch flush then quickly followed them with accurate rabbit punches. He might as well have tickled Pete as the oversized boy backhand him like he was fly sending him rocketing across the field once again.

"Impossible!" Aeneas let out landing hard across the field.

Aeneas flipped gaining control over his momentum sliding across the field. Before he could blink Pete used a time flash closing the distance between the two. He let out a black fog that shot out his mouth like a blow torch.

"Now you're mine," he shouted disappearing in the fog.

THUD! THUD! We could here Pete bounding from spot to spot inching closer as Aeneas wondered around aimlessly struggling to gain distance.

"Where are you?" Aeneas replied.

POW! Pete nearly took his face off with a punch that sent him flying into a nearby wall.

"I'm not done yet!" Pete let out quickly following up.

POW! POW! WHIRRR! BAM! Pete landed another punch then a square kick that landed flush on Aeneas's chin as he flew high in the air. Pete leaped high in the air meeting the demon at the height of his ascent and smashed him toward the surface.

"Don't ever underestimate me!" He let out hovering high in the air.

I once again turned to Uriah who stared at the screen blown away by Pete's ability. I would like to say I wasn't surprised, but I was. We sparred and I never saw this version of Pete. His reflexes were off the charts. His strikes where more vicious and precise, and adding the fog, Aeneas was a sitting duck.

"I'm going to tear you limb from limb," Pete warned shooting toward him.

THUD! THUD! THUD! Pete bounded from spot to spot once again hiding in the fog. Aeneas leaped high above the fog in an attempt to even the odds.

"Going somewhere?" Pete poked.

SMASH! He almost broke Aeneas in half with the blow.

"GAWAH!" he winced gasping in pain.

Aeneas landed hard on the ground below grimacing as he fought to his feet. Pete landed feet away from him. Aeneas crawled crab style on his butt in an attempt to get away.

THUD! He grimaced as he bumped into Pete. He had used his time and space technique to travel across the field.

"Well played," Aeneas replied staring back at the boy with pure horror yet still unable to look pass the genius of the boy's plan.

"It's me, of course it is," Pete shot confidently standing over the demon.

He had shrunk back to his normal size. At least that's what I thought initially, but before Aeneas could blink the mammoth version of Pete came into view shocking Uriah and I.

"He was bluffing the entire time," Uriah responded shaking his head. "That's another bot."

I turned to Uriah confused by his statement.

"That big one is just a robot," I replied.

"No, the small one is," Uriah replied. "And it was the perfect setup. Now, it's checkmate."

WHAM! The robot Pete cocked back with a hammer that was as big as a house. It hung over Aeneas like a dark cloud and there was no escape.

"Subatomic Art, Gravity control, Gravity Mass," Pete replied with a smirk.

"No," Aeneas let out as the hammer fell.

The ground shook from the impact of the blow. A crater the size of a mansion was all that remained as Pete's hammer returned to its normal size. Slowly the mammoth size version of Pete morphed back.

"Wait, what happened?" I asked obliviously.

Pete walked over to Aeneas who was motionlessly laying on his back. He reached for his belt and unfastened it pulling off a pouch. He rummaged through it and pulled out a long gold case.

"Awesome, you got it, you actually got it," I replied ecstatic.

Pete slowly opened the box as a light emanated from it like it was a captured star.

"Mission accomplished," Pete replied flipping it like a coin. "Piece of cake."

I gave sigh of relief as Pete smiled from ear to ear.

"What happened back there," I replied surprised.

"He knew he wouldn't ever be able to pin him down, so he bluffed. He baited him into believing he was stupid enough to give up his advantage, but the whole while he was setting him up for the kill shot. Not too bad," Uriah replied congratulating him.

"How?" I replied.

"He was too fast for me to pin down no matter how many bots I used. I only used the bots to give my body time to become immune to the toxin. Once I achieved that my plan was to obstruct his view with my fog and take advantage. Even in my tier one form I couldn't land a killing blow. He's a high-level demon. It was impossible to kill him without a strike from an anointed weapon, and he knew that. He let me hit him with my fists and bots, but he made sure to watch out for my hammer. So, I had to bait and switch to get to him. He was so confident in his speed and reflexes that he always let his opponent dictate his actions, much like you Tim. So, I backed him into a corner and pounced," Pete cut in.

"Well, you got the arrow, now what?" I replied.

"Well, now…"

BOOM! I almost swallowed my tongue as two light bodies collided with such explosion that it sent Pete flying.

"Pete!" I exclaimed.

He flipped three times before landing hard against a wall. From the moment he was hit by the light he was out. He lay unconscious as the two light bodies dimmed. I couldn't believe my eyes as the two individuals came into view. I leaned into get a closer view. I was blown away.

"Isn't that…," Uriah added. "Is that really…"

"Sai?" I replied unable to believe what I was seeing.

CHAPTER

15

One crazy mother

oen crazy mother

"What are you doing?" Uriah asked me.

"I know that energy anywhere," I replied. "I don't know how, but that's Sai. She's in no shape to be fighting."

He shook his head as I reached for medallion.

"That may be true, but you don't know if that thing will work. What if you end up on the other side of the universe, little Eli?" he warned.

"Then I keep trying until get to them," I replied defiantly.

"Or, you get trapped somewhere and can't find your way back," he shot in an angry tone.

WARP! Before he could finish his sentence, I was through the portal. The smell of the air on the other side of the portal smelled like burnt grass and cement. I stared around recognizing the scenery immediately from my time in the advising booth. I was in the right place.

"Watch out!" I heard a voice say.

KABOOOM! An explosion erupted that sent Sai flying through the air. I grabbed her and Pete just in the nick of time and dove behind a nearby barn. The explosion was like nothing I had ever seen. The shot obliterated the entire landscape. It was like a meteorite had hit the grounds.

"What in the world is that?" I replied looking back.

"Trouble," said a voice to my far right.

I turned to see Sean standing on the top of the barn staring across the field. I wasn't surprised to see him there. I was more wondering if he was there as a friend or foe.

"Sean, when did you get here?" I replied staring up at him.

"I was trying to save your friend before…your other friend…well, intervened," he replied splitting blood.

I paused as my heart began to beat out of my chest. I was worried, but all I felt at that moment was exuberance. The day Sai saw me after my day was vivid in that moment. I couldn't imagine her feeling any different than what I was feeling at that moment.

"Sorry," Sai replied catching my attention. "I didn't know. I just saw you going toward Pete and I…Sorry."

She moved to make a joke, but before she could, I threw my arms around her squeezing her.

"Tim, you're crushing me," she responded causing me to release her gun-shy.

She chuckled showcasing a smile that I lost myself in. She was my better half, and I couldn't believe had her back. The feeling was unreal.

"Just joking," she shot ignoring the eminent danger behind her.

We joked like we weren't in the middle of a war zone. Sean looked at us like we were out of our minds. He sympathized with what we were feeling in that moment, but he understood the danger we were facing better than we did. He stood paranoid as we continued our reunion ignoring everything around us.

"You want to explain?" I responded unable to stop staring at her.

She chuckled blushing as I repeated my earlier actions scooping the girl up in a bear hug once again. She stare into my eyes lovingly before bashfully averting eyes. I couldn't fight the feelings I felt for her. I set her down before placing my hand on her shoulders and pressing my forehead against hers lovingly. She teared up placing her hand on my cheek.

"Don't ever do that to me again?" I responded mimicking her words to me a month earlier.

She chuckled once again. She was overwhelmed and flattered by my reception. I moved forward placing a lovingly kiss on her cheek, but she didn't mimic my action from a month before. Instead recoiling in shock, she rubbed the spot where I kissed her staring into my eye unapologetically smitten. I expected her reaction to mimic mine. The awkward pause caused me to sputter.

"A lot better than a punch to the gut I'd wager," I shot awkwardly placing my hands in my pocket bashfully staring at the ground.

She took a deep breath before forcing my eyes to meet hers.

"Tim, I promised myself that…I promised myself…that once I could talk to you again," she paused causing me to slightly raise my brow confused as she fumbled to find the words to capsulate what she was feeling. "I wouldn't…Tim, I…"

KUPT! Sean dropped down next to us with a thud cutting her off as she grimaced in frustration at the boy's interruption.

"Sorry to interrupt, you guys. I know this is a big deal considering Sai's situation, but you have to be quiet," Sean replied. "Do you feel that?"

The building shielded us from the direct contact with the energy, so it took a second for it to hit me, but from the minute we locked on to it Sai and I dropped to a knee. It was a powerful and foul smell that seem to tear our insides apart like toxic gas. Sean helped us up and leaned us against the nearby wall as we both struggled to breathe.

"What is that?" Sai replied breathing heavily. "It's so powerful."

Sean peaked around the corner before turning back to us.

"It'll take a second for the effects to wear off, but the first contact with it is brutal," he replied helping us to our feet.

Pete was still unconscious. I shook him trying to wake him from his state, but he was unresponsive.

"What happen to him?" I replied checking his pulse.

"She happened," Sean replied pointing in a general direction. "I tried to deflect the shot, but Sai knocked me off the path. It was a phantom punch. The blow caught him full contact. There was nothing I could do. He'll come around, but it might take a while."

I nodded afraid to ask the most pressing question.

"Who hit him?" Sai intervened angrily.

"Venus," he replied once again pointing in a general direction.

His words immediately put me on alert. I looked around and saw what looked to be a burning star. It slowly settled as the burning flame slowly formed into a human form.

"Aeneas? My son," she replied falling to one knee. "What have they done to you?"

She looked distraught. She hung her head sobbing unable to control her emotions. She was a classically beautiful woman. She had long red hair and wore beautiful black and gold classical Roman armor. She carried a long sword that was as big as her whole body.

"My son!" she mourned through sobs.

ZOOOM! THUD! We continued to cower behind the barn as another individual shot across the sky and landed hard on the ground with a loud implosion.

"Mother," he replied running to her side.

He looked more feminine then Aeneas. He wore a bow and arrow pack over his shoulder and Greco Roman armor like his mother. He ran to her apologetically dropping to his knees as he spoke.

"Eros!" she grunted in an agitated warning tone that was barely above a whispered.

The vibration of her words caused the whole area to tremble violently. We all dove to safety as the barn crumble from the impact almost crushing us in the process.

"Mother…I'm…I'm sorry. I-I had a powerful prospect on my tail. I couldn't shake him…I swear. I couldn't get here," he pleaded.

SMACK! She smacked him with a backhand that nearly knocked his block off. He flipped violently sliding across the terrain before settling in a heap. He winced in pain as he fought into a fetal position.

"Mother, I-I'm sorry…please forgive me," he replied reaching his hand out in begging motion.

Her eyes became as red as blood.

"Who is this prospect?" she replied angrily.

FLASH! Before we could blink, she was standing in front of Eros. She reached down and picked him up with one hand.

"What is his name? Give it to me, and by the name of my father Zeus, I'll put his head on a spike!" She screamed livid.

GRRL! COUGH! COUGH! Eros choked and gagged as she squeezed the life out of him.

"It wasn't him," he managed whimpering out each word.

"What?!" she replied angrily. "Then who was it?!"

GRURGLE! He let out gasping for air. With the little energy he had remaining, he pointed in our direction.

THUD! HUGGGH! Eros gasped sucking in as much air as he could as she finally released him.

"That boy, the one lying on the ground," he let out still gasping for air in between each word. "I saw him through my brother's eyes. He did this."

She turned to us with a look that sent a shiver up my spine. Eros turned to her still struggling on his knees.

"I'm so sorry, mother," he replied begging for mercy.

She turned to him with no sympathy.

"You've always been a coward. A stain on the line of my father, and my mistake of allowing you to live has cost me my greatest contribution to our world. My son," she replied. "I would give your life a thousand times over if it meant I could get my son back for one second, you miserable failure," she replied angrily.

BOOOM! She extended her hand and finished him off with one power shot. Her power was other worldly, and her demeanor was cold and vicious. The visceral, cold blooded attitude she carried was beyond anything I witnessed before. It was downright evil and scary. All that remained of Eros was a cloud of dust. If she could do that to her own son, I could only imagine what she had in mind for Pete.

"No way," I replied shielding his unconscious body.

Before Venus could respond Sai shielded me.

"Sai, move," I replied angrily.

I quickly used her lightning step technique to move in front of her.

"You just got out of the hospital," I replied angrily.

"No, that's just it. I'm still in the hospital, or at least my body is," she replied walking up beside me.

"What? How?" I replied turning to her.

"I don't know. I just woke up in the hospital about a week ago," she replied. "I nearly fainted when I saw my body. I was stuck in the hospital for the first couple of days, but after I saw what happened to Beth, I had to do something. So, I followed Pete."

"So, all the times I was in the infirmary. You could hear me?" I replied.

She nodded with an appreciative smile. If the look she gave me had a caption, it would've been easy for the densest person to decipher, but at the time I just saw her as an appreciative friend. I returned her smile as she answered my question still bashfully averting her eyes to prevent herself from staring into mine.

"Yes and No. I tried everything to get back in my body, but it would just reject me," she replied almost apologetically. "The day you came in…with the trials I felt so helpless. I got desperate and tried to force my way in. It rejected me violently. That was the reason for the falling flower vase in my room that day. I couldn't capitalize on it, because the impact of it knocked me out for a couple of days. When you came to visit during the commotion you left the door open and I was able to sneak out. I followed Pete and when I saw you were helping him, I figured I might as well do what I could to help as well. Unfortunately, it seems like I just got in the way."

Sean turned to us flabbergasted by our obsession with each other before pointing at Venus with a signaling wave.

"I don't mean to cut off your conversation…you two, but uh, the crazy and vengeful Nephilim with her mind set on killing your friends is headed this way," He cut in causing us both to drop into our fighting stance.

"Get out of the way or I'll kill both of you where you stand," Venus replied coldly as she marched toward us.

WHOOM! With a flick her wrist Sai and I flew like pieces of paper in the wind. It was like the magnetic pull itself had yanked us out of the way while simultaneously sending a pulsating electrical shot through our bodies. She walked like a model down a runway as she strutted toward Pete.

BOOF! UGH! I let out as I finally hit the ground. The impact felt like a punch to the stomach.

"Tim," Sai replied writhing in pain from the impact of her fall.

I crawled doing everything in my power to get to Pete, but the shot had zapped all my strength. I watched in horror as she marched closer to Pete's unconscious body. I felt helpless as she moved in for the kill. I couldn't move a muscle. I grunted wildly unable to do anything to save my best friend.

"Get away from him!" Sai shot in warning tone.

Venus turned to her with a cold stare before continuing her march with a condescending indifference.

"Pete, get up!" I replied via BAU. "Pete, please, get up!"

Pete grunted groggily. I shook my head with a sigh. For the looks of things, my BAU had broken through to his unconscious brain. He rolled over staring up at the vacant sky trying to get his wits. He was awake, but it was obvious he was still out of it physically. She inched closer to him like a shark circling her prey as the boy fought to get his bearings.

"What's going on?" he managed still groggy.

"Pete get out of here!" Sai replied fighting to her feet.

I moved as fast as I could flashing to Pete's side with Sai appearing a second later

ZUMM! She put a hex on the both of us that made us fell like we were trapped in our own bodies. I fought to control my limbs, but my body wasn't my own. I couldn't move a muscle. I crumbled over falling to my hands and knees. Sai followed suit as Pete fought to his feet behind us.

"Let them go," he wailed angrily.

"You two mosquitos are like dogs barking at the moon. You're too stupid to understand the magnitude of what you are up against, yet too naïve to just walk away," she replied. "Stay out of this."

Pete was wobbly. He fought to gain his balance on weak knees as we were once again forced into the role of helpless spectators.

"You," she replied pointing in Pete's direction. "What tribe are you from?"

Pete ignored her words finally fully gaining his consciousness.

"What…I don't know?" Pete replied. "Who are you?"

"She's Venus…," Sai replied before her lips were forcefully closed.

Pete lowered his head shaking it regretfully.

"Regardless, it makes no difference," she replied. "Why did you kill my son?"

Pete looked toward us sympathetically then regretfully replied.

"My name is Peter Selli of the Theta Delta Prospect Legion," he responded. "It was my undertaking to apprehend your son and the Heaven's Bow. Your son became hostile."

WOOF! The ground erupted around her as she sparked enraged by the boy's statement. Sai and I rolled around the terrain being tossed by the sudden shift of the ground unable to steady ourselves.

"Became hostile! He became hostile!" she getting louder with every reply as she bubbled with anger. "Would you be hostile if you were trapped on a foreign world for over a millennium? Would you be hostile if you broke free only to be confronted by some snot nose kid for a good look on his resume?! How reserved would you be given those circumstances?!"

Pete chuckled causing the woman to star at him like she wanted to tear him in two.

"I wouldn't be," Pete replied surprisingly sarcastic and calm considering the danger we were all in. "But I also wouldn't have caused millions of people to die and be thrown into a pit of fire, also."

"Pete, what are you doing? Why are you….," I managed before she muzzled me.

"You have some nerves speaking to me in such a way," she replied fuming. "I am a Princess of Olympia. Daughter of Zeus!"

"You feel better, now?!" Pete continued pushing his luck in a mocking tone. "Lady, I could care less what you call yourself. All that matters is this warning."

BOING! The sound of his axe being unlatched echoed throughout the empty area as he pressed a button on the side of the weapon extending it.

"Listen, princess. I'm going to tell you this once. Let my friends go or I'm going to knock your head off your shoulders like a golf ball off the tee," he shot confidently.

HA! HA! HA! She laughed thunderously. Her power was ridiculous. She was easily the most powerful rebel we had faced so far. The way she effortlessly went from subatomics to elemental to physical traits was like nothing I witnessed before. She was in another league. She made everyone we faced so far seem like child's play.

"I'm going to make you regret the day you stepped on my planet," she replied her eyes turning bright red like a fire cracker.

Pete readied himself for a fight, but without our help the fight wasn't going to be long. He didn't have a chance.

"Yeah, yeah," Pete continued to mock. "Just know, you only get three moves before I make mine. So, use them wisely."

He had to have a plan. There was no way he was stupid enough to be bluffing. He had to have something up his sleeve. I couldn't think of anything he could possible do against a force like Venus. She stared at him with a look that sent a shiver up my spine.

"You have no idea the power I possess prospect," she replied. "Sadly, that'll be your undoing."

"Big talk," Pete replied.

"Is it?" she replied sternly.

WHOOSH! The atmosphere became thick almost like the gates of hell were opening as she raised her hands high over her head. The outpour of gas caused Pete to cover his mouth as a foul sulfuric smell filled the air.

"Move one," he replied before falling to his knees coughing as he spoke.

BUMPF! Sai and I rolled on the ground as she finally released us. I moved my fingers making sure I regained complete control of my senses.

"How is she able to do that?" Sai replied moving her jawed around like she had been punched square.

"It's all subatomics," Pete replied. "Your lips nerves are all cells that work through a law. Electrical impulses and synapsis to be more specific.
"

"That would have been good to know before she muted us," I responded mimicking Sai's action checking my jaw.

Slowly an ear shattering rupture sounded all around us creating a gorge the size of the Grand Canyon.

"What is that?" Sai replied turning to the sound.

It looked like the world was collapsing in on itself as the terrain around us crumbled.

"Pete, let's get out of here," I replied in awe of what I was seeing.

"No," Pete replied.

"What do you mean, no?!" I responded turning to him angrily.

"I mean we can't," he replied pointing ahead.

"Why can't we?" I asked getting more agitated.

"I don't know… that," Sai cut in pointing ahead.

I turned and stared in horror. The ground split open with a sound that rung like a gigantic brass horn. The smell was overwhelming. If it was bad before now it was three times that.

"What is that?" I replied nervous. "What is she doing?"

Sai turned to me with a look that signified the answer was something I should already know.

"You can't feel that?" she replied flabbergasted by my demeanor.

As she spoke I finally acknowledged the feeling that had been creeping up my spine since the sound erupted. It was the feeling you feel when you're walking down a dark alley in a bad neighborhood but a thousand times worse.

"This can't be…It feels like purgatory," I replied astonished. "And there were millions of demons there. How many are here?"

Pete looked at his watch as if to be preparing himself.

"I don't know, but this feels like more than a small battalion," Pete replied. "I think we've stumble into a hornet's nest."

Sai shook her head frustrated. We had gone through so much already it was hard to grasp the mortal danger we faced. Especially considering we were still being monitored by the entirety of the Heaven Realm. It gave us a level of comfort knowing that could step in if things got to crazy. It was literally the only thing that kept me even-keeled.

"More like a lion's den," she added pointing catching our attention.

I raised my hands in frustration. Vile beasts of every kind climbed from the canyon. It looked like ants climbing from a colony hill. There were so many.

"This can't be real?" Sai replied flabbergasted tone.

Venus stood defiantly floating above the crater with a smug stare that resonated like our response was expected.

"Answer this question you insignificant runt of a prospect…Where do you think hell is located?" She prodded with a look that would burrow throw metal.

We looked forward not replying as a sinister smile covered her face. I couldn't believe my eyes as beast after beast climbed from the pit of the hellish prison planet.

"What is she talking about, Pete?" Sai asked turning to him.

Pete stared forward with a look that was telling. It seemed the answer was on the tip of his tongue, yet he didn't want to speak.

"Why do you think I'm housed here?" She replied with a smug look on her face. "There are many pathways to perdition both spiritually and physically, but they all lead here. I know you can feel it. The cold shiver on your neck. That burrowing in the pit of your gut. You've probably already figured it out, and if you haven't noticed by now…"

Her speech was cold yet filled with aggression. She was a lunatic and it was obvious that beneath her insane demeanor was a cold blooded killer.

"Let me be the first to invite you. Welcome to my home… Welcome to the fifth hell!" she continued.

WOOSH! WOOSH! BOOM! Explosion of gas and fire ring out all around her. As she flexed her power.

"Stay on your guard you guys," Pete grunted in an intense tone.

We shuttered as the beast formed a battle line that seemed to get larger by the second. They stood like mindless beast without moving. It was like they were under a spell. It was almost like they were an extension of her madness. They lined up behind her. They were intimidating. They were her own personal army.

"Prospect there are dimensions to every planet in our solar system. There is the so-called Earth dimension, which you should be familiar with. It is the dimension were you humans and other non-Heaven Realm beings' dwell. The second dimension is the dimension that was created specifically for me and my kind. I'm sure you've heard our dilemma. We're not heavenly beings so we couldn't go there after we died, so your Father Yahweh created a place for us and created a dimension to jail us on each planet. A dimension that from the minute you apprehended my son you have been a part of it. The dimensional barrier created by your Father Yahweh has been their saving grace, but you…you aren't so lucky," she replied raising her hands in the air. "You see you're self-righteous arrogant Light Guard Council never explained to you that you can't apprehend a Nephilim without going into their dimension. The hell you're currently dwelling in, it so happens to be the fifth dimension of hell."

Her words had a ring of truth to me that stung. It made me analyze what we were really doing in these trials. I mean she had a point. It would have been good to know that we were unknowingly going to a pseudo pit of hell.

"Great, what do we do?" Sai replied. "We can't possibly fight these many demons!"

I turned to her confused. Through all the commotion it hadn't slip my mind for a second. From the moment I arrived I was thinking about all the possibilities that could explain why and how she was here.

"Can you technically be hurt?" I replied out of nowhere. "I mean, with you being a ghost?"

Sai cut her eyes.

"I'm not a ghost. I'm in this dimension. I don't know how it works, but whatever form my soul is currently in, I feel pain and injury here. I'm physically in this dimension…I'm guessing the same happen when you guys teleported here, but that is so not important right now," she fired. "How are we getting out of this, Pete?"

Pete looked forward scratching his head in a thinking motion.

"I don't know yet," he replied. "I'm just glad to see you. I'll give you more of a welcome when we get out of this place. As for now, I don't know enough and there are too many unknowns to counter strategize."

I turned looking for any help I could find. I tried to remain calm in the midst of the chaos. I wanted to seem confident so that my friends wouldn't worry, but in order to do so I had to block out the crazy reality that was staring me in the face. It was getting harder with every beast that climbed out of the pit.

"Where's Sean?" I replied looking around for any help I could find.

Sai surveyed the layout as well. Through all the anarchy I hadn't even noticed the vast change. Venus was right. The world I watched from afar was gone. It was a volcanic mountainous inferno. Gone was the beautiful landscape of Venus. It was now a smelling rotting cesspool of evil, and Sean was nowhere to be found.

"I don't know. That explosion separated us," Sai replied. "But for the time being we need to focus on us. We have enough problems to worry about. Let his team worry about him."

"Yeah, Sai's right," Pete replied. "Besides, she said that you had to apprehend the Nephilim to end up here. All signs point to Sean never apprehending Eros. I mean, his mother destroyed him. So maybe when Venus changed the dimension, we lost him."

His words brought something else to light. I tried to react quickly before things got out of hand.

"Uriah? You still there?" I replied.

A nervous second passed before he finally replied.

"Yes, I'm here," Uriah added. "I told you to wait, little Eli. My gosh, I told you there would be consequence. It was incredibly ill-advised to shoot off like that. It overwhelmed the faith energy threshold. You're stuck. Max and Jade are trying to get to you guys, but you're going to have to fend for yourself until they can open it back up."

I shook my head with a sigh. I turned hoping Pete and Sai didn't overhear his words, but the look on both of their faces made it clear they did.

"I appreciate the assistance, Tim, but man, you have a knack for making bad situations worse," Pete shot shaking his head angrily.

"I'm sorry I tried to save your butts," I shot.

"Yeah, thanks for doing that," Sai shot back sarcastically. "Remind me to thank you again when I'm on a torture rack in some smelly cell."

"So, what? Are you saying you would be better off without me?" I replied poking causing her to shake her head.

"No, I'm saying I'd rather have Jade and Max," she replied.

ROAR! ROAR! The beast erupted with whelps and growls that filled the evening air catching our attention and effectively ending our spat. With every disgusting beast that climbed from the abyss, the more saturated with wroth and evil the environment became. It was toxic to my soul.

"Well, no use in crying over it now," Sai added.

"Yeah, besides, I know you guys in and out. We have the firepower to hold out until someone can get here," Pete replied.

"Yeah, this is an ideal situation to show off our excellent teamwork and what friends can do if they work together," she replied in a mocking tone. "Wonder Spaz Team Unite!"

I turned to him with a cynical glare.

"I think she's being sarcastic," I shot deafly dry in my response as I closed ranks as the beast continued to surround us.

"I'm serious," Pete replied following my lead pulling Sai toward us as he moved.

My heart should have been beating a thousand miles a minute. I should have been terrified, but for some reason it wasn't. It reminded me of the Battle of New Angeles, and with everything we had been through since then had strengthened my resolve. I was becoming less sensitive to danger. It didn't affect me the way it used to, and that was scary to me. I was becoming confident, maybe even cocky.

"Well, maybe this thing will come in handy," I replied reaching in my backpack and pulling out the relic that I had earned in my undertaking.

I pulled out the newly attained relic. It shined in the night air as I swirled it and slammed it into the ground sending a ripple of energy throughout the terrain.

"Is that the relic from your undertaking," Pete replied staring at it. "Are you sure you should be doing this right now? I mean, do you even know how to use it?"

I shrugged in an indecisive manner.

"Not really, but it's an extension of my Moses staff right?" I replied. "So, let's see what happens when I put them together."

I felt around and pulled out my staff. As the two objects neared one another they began to gravitate to each other like magnets. As they connected a light emanated from them both. They liquefied and combined into a beautiful flowing light then instantly hardened into a pearly white staff twice the size of my former staff. The old wooden staff had been replaced by a beautiful long Bo. I held it out taken by its beauty.

"How did you get that?" Venus replied focusing in on it.

I hesitated not sure if I should answer. Sai looked forward intently as Pete walked up and stood beside her.

"I got it from an Atlantis compound," I replied twirling it in a mocking manner.

"That's the property of the Olympians, give to me…now!" she ordered floating high above her army.

"Why don't you come and get it," Pete replied stepping in front of me.

I turned to Pete shaking my head.

"Could you reserve the taunts for you?" I shot sarcastically shaking my head in frustration causing Pete to wince apologetically. "Don't send epically insane mourning mothers at me in the future, you know, if that is in any way possible."

She grinned showing she could showcase an emotion besides anger.

"I think I'd rather they did it for me," she replied waving in a point manner over the entire platoon of goons. "Good try, but I'm sure you are aware of Light Guard Law which states that I can't technically lay a hand on a light guard prospect under any circumstances until the time of the tribulation."

I turned to Pete who wore a telling smile on his face.

"But luckily there is nothing that prevents you from dealing with the 10th Guard," she replied.

As she finished her speech, she turned to a large goblin looking Highgate.

"Subdue them and bring me the Bo and the loudmouth one," she replied turning and walking through a portal hole.

The Highgate smiled and signal for the rest of the unit to attack. They seemed to move out instantly.

"Triple face defense," Pete barked. "Tim, you got north to southwest, Sai your north to northeast, and I'll take south."

We sprinted into position as the first wave attacked. I held the bo out in a defensive position not sure how to use it yet.

BANG! BOOM! We hit with sheering velocity as they attacked. They had us badly outnumbered, but we laid them down like they were nothing. Our skills had evolved vastly in comparison to our last battle.

"Watch out!" Sai replied darting around me gracefully.

WHAM! I ducked as she catapulted off my back catching an incoming assailant with a dropkick. Before I could blink, she was back in position.

"Duck you guys," Pete replied multiplying the length and size of his hammer.

WHOP! WHOP! WHOP! He mowed them down as he spent chopping the opposition in half walloping and sending them flying in different directions.

I noticed an attacker over his right shoulder. I dematerialized immediately anticipating his path.

BOOM! FAWP! FAWP! FAWP! I shot through Pete's body and nailed him with a blow that caused collateral damage that took out a wave of attackers close to him.

"Thanks, Tim," Pete replied still in the midst of fighting.

The more we fought the more congested things got. No matter how fast we chopped them down they just kept coming.

"Element Alpha, Lightning Command, Thunder Echo," Sai replied. "Cover your ears, now!"

Pete and I followed her command covering our ears. Her katanas lit up like lanterns as thunder erupted causing everyone around us to explode like cake batter.

SWAP! SWAP! SWAP! She moved with blistering agility and speed chopping them down.

"Element Epilson, Earth Command, Pangaea Quake," I commanded while ducking for cover.

RUMBLE! RUMBLE! RUMBLE! QUAKE! The ground around us split with an ear-splitting eruption dragging the disgusting demons back to the hell they had climbed out of.

"Let's get to higher ground," Pete replied pointing to high point on the mountainous range.

Sai and I agreed following as he jumped to the top the spot. We collapsed. I sighed starring at the army of demons still pressing in on us.

"We're not going to be able to keep this up," I replied huffing like a fat kid. "There's too many of them."

"We have to," Pete responded. "Uriah, how long will it take before they can get here?"

I could hear it in Uriah's sigh before he spoke. It wasn't going to be good news.

"Well, Tim's teleportation sent a charge through the grid. Now they have to manually find your position until the grid comes back up. There are over a million of them, so you can imagine that's not going to be easy. If you add the fact that your light energy is being blocked by the intense evil of the second hell it's going to be that much harder."

His words did little to motivate our already disheartened spirits. Pete stood up getting into position as the hellish army began to attack again. I hesitated as Sai extended a hand helping me to my feet.

"Hey, we're supposed to be hot stuff, right?" she replied with a smirk. "This is our opportunity to prove it."

SMASH! Before I could blink Pete had flattened an incoming beast with a hammer shot that made him explode like a pumpkin at a harvest festival.

"Exactly," he replied.

WHOOSH! FAP! FAP! FAP! I watched in awe as he threw his hammer like a boomerang mowing down the incoming assailants.

"Well, since we're showing off," Sai replied combining her katanas. "Element Alpha, lightning command, lightning shower."

SPOOSH! LITTER! LITTER! LITTER! She shot a lone shot into the air. We waited with baited breath as it exploded raining lighting arrows down all around us. I knew she was good, great even, but what I saw next gave me goosebumps.

"You two watch each other's back," she replied turning to us. "I'll be back."

I grabbed her in a defiant manner.

"No way," I replied. "It's not happening. Luke barely kept from tearing us apart the last time you ended up in the hospital."

She shrugged off my hand looking forward with an intense stare.

"I'm a Dom remember," she replied. "I'm ten times stronger than I was then. If you want to see how much stronger, try to stop me. The strongest will protect the other, remember?"

"I have the ability to evolve too, Sai," I responded. "You're not stronger than I am."

She gave me a stubborn stare before continuing.

"Trust me. You're going to have to prove it," she challenged. "You're not dying for me again. You'll have to end me first."

Her words were stern and passionate. I couldn't understand it. Our position hadn't been compromised. She had no reason to take the risk side was proposing. Yes, her leaving would take heat off us, but we could barely sustain a fight together. How could she possibly fight alone.

"Sai, That's ridiculous. I'm not going to fight you. We're also not going to allow you to sacrifice yourself," I fired. "And there's two of us and one of you. Right, Pete?"

Pete's expression was blank. He turned to me with an apologetic look on his face.

"Pete?" I replied unable to comprehend the rationale behind allowing Sai to take such a risk.

He sighed as if he was thinking of a way to make me understand.

"I don't like it any more than you do," he replied. "But she's right. We have to cut their numbers down. Sai invisibility gives her the best chance of surviving alone."

I shook my head defiantly.

"It's not going to happen," I shot angrily. "If you try it, Dom or not, I'll knock you out and drag you back to the Heaven Realm myself. I'm not losing you again."

"How do you think I felt on the day you went to purgatory, Tim?" she shot exhausted. "You had no other choice…right now, neither do I."

"I'm warning you, Sai. Please don't make me do this," I shot in a stern begging tone.

My eyes lit up as I spoke. Sai stared at me regretfully dropping her head in a sorrowful manner.

FAWP! Before I could finish powering up I felt a hit to the back of my skull that sent me sprawling. I turned to see Pete standing over me.

"What are you doing?!" I screamed desperately staring at Sai helplessly.

Pete leaped on top of me holding me down with his hammer before turning to Sai.

"Go, now, Sai," he replied. "Hurry!"

Sai turned to me apologetically.

"I'm sorry, Tim but it's the only way," she replied. "Trust me. I promise I'll be fine."

I felt like I was losing her all over again. To be honest I couldn't deal with going through the rest of the trials without her. It had been too long and now she was about to risk disappearing again. I couldn't let it happen.

"Get off of me, Pete," I replied powering up.

EXPLOSION! I let out a power spark that nearly took out the whole mountain peak. Pete flew high in the air. I flashed snatching him out of the air before turning my attention to Sai, but she was too fast. She disappeared before I could get close to her.

"Sai!" I screamed dropping Pete with a thud. "Why did you do that?!"

I wanted to tear him apart, but with the beast bearing down on him, I had to focus my attention or Sai's sacrifice would have been for nothing.

"I told you why? It's the best plan to get us all out of here. You're so adamant about us trusting you. Try giving us the same luxury, Tim," he replied knocking the dust off his pants as he stood up.

"Forget that crap, Pete!" I replied lividly still fuming. "This is not some video game. I don't care if it was the best plan. It was too risky. It's Sai!"

BOOM! Before I could finish my speech a lightning strike erupted taking out a battalion of attacking demons. The strike was so powerful it sent me and Pete flying. I watched in awe as a silhouette in the lightning revealed Sai.

"Sai?" I replied unable to believe her power.

POW! FAP! FAP! FAP! BAM! She mowed them down. Her punches were quick. Before one assailant dropped another was feeling a blow. It was amazing how good she was. My jaw was on the ground.

"Tim, get ready," Pete replied placing his hand on my shoulder.

He swung his mallet like he was gearing it up for an attack. I nodded powering up. The annoyance in the pit of my stomach was still there, but I swallowed it in an attempt to do what was in the best interest of getting us out of there in one piece.

"Let's go," I replied summoning power that surged through me.

QUAKE! The beast cowered as the mountains around them began to shake. I hated the plan, but I would destroy myself before I let them lay a hand on Pete or Sai. The opposition had no idea how powerful I could be when I had to be. My back was against a wall, and the only way out was through them.

BOOM! My punches seemed to explode the volcano of emotions erupting inside me all over the face of a nearby rebel. I leaped into overdrive hitting the ground running giving everything I had. We fought valiantly until it felt like our bones and cells weighed a million pounds. The fight had been waging on for nearly an hour. We hit them with everything we had. The beast took their lumps and kept coming.

"Elements Delta and Epsilon, Wind and Earth command, wind boulder barrage," I commanded so exhausted I could barely get the words out.

The ground erupted as I swung the wind like a sling shot sending comets of boulders peppering as many of them as I could. It did little to cut their numbers, but I didn't care. I had one sole purpose, and that purpose was getting me and my friends out of that hell in one piece.

"Tim, don't break formation," Pete warned.

PING! WHAP! WHAP! WHAP! He threw his extended mallet trimming them down. It was futile. None of the blows seemed to stick. They would just rub off the blow climb back to their feet and leap back into the fray.

ERUPT! CRUMBLE! CRUMBLE! I moved the mountain once again making the foundations crumble all around it. We were running out of room to maneuver.

ZAAAAP! BOOM! Sai appeared smashing a line of them before disappearing again. We were woefully outnumbered, and our reserves were running low. We fought bravely, but we were surviving on our will to protect each other alone.

"Sai, get back here. It's not working," I replied. "Let's retreat to a different peak, and regroup."

FAP! PLUNK! PLUNK! Pete nailed at group of attacking rebels with a spinning mallet throw. He landed, turned, and smashed two more with the ricochet of his swinging weapon before holstering it on his back as he retreated.

"He's right, Sai," he replied backpedaling as I followed suit. "It's a bust. Get back. The divide and conquer has served it's purpose. We don't have enough room to split up anymore."

Before I could move my mouth to reply she appeared falling to one knee. Her hair was matted to her head soaked in blood and guts. She looked as a exhausted as Pete and I were.

"Well, what are we going to do?" she replied holding her side taking exhausted breath as she spoke. "We can't keep this up. The longer it takes the better it is for them."

Where were Max and Jade? We had been fighting forever. My body felt heavy and the constant maneuvering had me mentally shot. We had really stuck our noses in it, and there was no way out.

WASHHOOOH! An explosion erupted just above us. They scouted our motives and beat us to the spot.

FLASH! I grabbed Sai and Pete and diverted our trajectory to a nearby mountain ledge.

"They're getting smarter," I replied. "That was close."

Pete shook his head as we backed up into formation leaning against each other. I could feel their weight they were more exhausted than I was. I felt like I was the only thing holding them up.

"C'mon you guys," I replied trying to support them. "Don't give up. It can't be too long now."

"We've been fighting for over an hour," Sai groaned collapsing. "I just need time to regain my strength."

Pete fell to one knee as well.

"I know…me too, but we can't…they're cornering us in," Pete disclosed. "They're going to come in for the kill with their heavy hitters soon."

I nodded knowing what I had to do.

"Sai, hide Pete," I ordered. "And get to the top of that peak. I'll stay here and fight until Jade and Max get here."

They both shot to their feet at the sound of my words. Sai looked at me in a begging manner shaking her head vehemently.

"No way," Sai replied putting on a strong face.

"She's right. Sai's actions were a part of a strategy to buy time, and it worked, it bought us valuable time. Yours is just a sacrifice. It's not going to happen," Pete replied. "We're not going to leave you."

I exhaled to exhausted trying to build the energy to argue my point as I continued.

"Whether you stay down here, or you disappear, at some point I'm going to be all by myself. We should use this time for you guys to regain your strength. You can come back and save my butt if Max and Jade haven't shown up before that," I argued. "Your right, it is a sacrifice considering how little I have in the tank. I won't lie about that, but I'm the reason we're stuck here to begin with. I'm not letting you guys take the fall for my mistake, besides, it's the best plan we have."

Pete shook his head defiantly before Sai's angry look gave way to a tirade.

"Like I said, it's not going to happen," Pete replied calming Sai as she nodded in agreement. "They're about to send a kill squad this way, and whether we are worthless or not, you don't stand a chance. You'll buy us seconds at best. You want to help us, then don't make us watch our best friend get the tar beat out of him. We may not be where we were an hour ago, but we'll at least go down together."

I objected with a shake before relenting. I needed to conserve my energy, and waging a losing battle would only waste more time. There was no way I was getting them to back down and leave me alone to fight a demon army.

"Just get behind me and back me up," I ordered as they both nodded. "Don't enter the battle unless you have to."

They both begrudgingly agreed.

"Here they come," Pete replied.

FLIP! SWIFT! SWIFT! SWIFT! A group of assassins attacked. The one-eyed cyclops beasts landed as if they were teleported. They stared us down like hungry beast cornering their prey. I nodded accepting the challenge as I shooed Pete and Sai behind me.

"They're going into a delta defense," Pete replied analyzing them right away. "The one in the middle is the strongest. Take him and cripple their defense."

"Right," I replied flashing into action immediately.

VANISH! SMASH! I dematerialized through the front line and face palmed the point man with violent force that took his head clean off his shoulder.

"Element Alpha, Light command, Solar flare," Sai replied.

FLASH! An explosion of light blinded the remaining front guardsmen.

BLAST! BLAST! BOOM! I shot a light energy blast from my palm taking out the distracted assailants before sending a wind palm blast into the ground. The momentum sent the rest of the legion flying in various directions.

"How can he even fight in this state?" Sai uttered still recovering from using her powers. "I'm a Dom and I can barely stand."

Pete stared shaking his head in awe.

"You should've seen him during his trial," he uttered balancing himself exhaustedly on hand. "The kid is a cyborg. He took out an ocean floor full of Dinosharks the last time he was exhausted. Made his record-breaking game against Lincoln Springs look average."

Sai stared at me admiring me as continued fighting with everything I had left in me.

"That good, huh?" she shot staring at me proudly.

FLASH! Pete nodded mimicking her demeanor as I flashed in front them blocking out of breath. I had unreal reserves, but I was starting to feel the effects of putting my body through such a battle.

"You guys okay?" I replied putting up a façade.

The Captain Highgate stood high above the beast. He looked at me like I was an oddity he was trying to understand.

"This is absurd. He shouldn't be able to stand," he replied moving his hand signaling for the beasts to cease attacking. "Boy! What is your name?"

I inhaled catching my breath before replying.

"Tim…My name is…Timothy Eli," I replied defiantly fighting to catch my breath.

He stared scratching his stubby beard. He had a Mohawk with a mullet like pony tail. Like most highgate vampires his skin was deathly pale. The look suited his ice-cold demeanor as he continued.

"Makes sense, an Eli," he replied with a tiresome smirk.

BAM! EXPLOSION! Before I could blink, he hit me with a shot that sent me hard into a nearby mountain side. The shards from the hard rock cut me left and right as I burrowed into the terrain of the mountain.

"AHHHH!" I let out as the weight of the mountain began to collapse in all around me.

My body felt like it had been sent threw a meat grinder. I struggled with everything I had crawling to get back to the summit of the opening as the weight of the mountain began to squeeze in on me with every inch.

"Pete, Sai," I grunted in unfathomable pain as I fought to get back to my vulnerable friends.

I stared in horror as I finally made it back to the opening. Sai lay unconscious as he cradled Pete's lifeless body in one arm.

"No," I replied trying to power up.

I dropped my head unable to muster a single spark of energy to help Pete.

"AHHHH!" I let out as an electric charge shot through me.

He grinned from ear to ear shaking his head.

"Don't waste your time, boy," he replied. "That was a subatomic blow. Your nervous system is rejecting you. You think because you and your friends have a little bit of natural ability you've kinged this game, but what you don't realize is your playing tic-tac-toe while we've learned to play chess. There are so many intricacies, techniques, and combinations that only experience can bring. You fumble in the dark swinging at any and everything. We watch laughing whilst waiting to strike at the most opportune time in that very same darkness you navigate through blindly. Smile, you've been outclassed, boy."

I struggled to remain conscious as he walked toward his army mocking me with a flippant turn on his will.

"No, I won't let you, AHHH!" I managed trying to power up again before another shock set in.

I watched as it seemed everything was slipping away from me.

"Give him…"

BOOM! I felt energy that seemed to sizzle everything around me like bacon on a hot plate. Something or someone landed with a volcanic yet elegant impact. I slowly felt the effects of the demon's blow dissipating. I could finally move. I flipped on my back still lacking the energy to summon light energy as I gasped in pain.

"Tim, you okay?" I heard a voice call out.

I turned to see Sean standing between me and the Highgate. I was startled for a second. Then, with the last of my energy, I crawled over to Sai and shielded her lifeless body. The Highgate seemed almost intimidated before switching to a stale smile.

"And you're the cavalry, I take it," he replied turning to his men.

The crowd of beasts burst into laughter. Their laugh seemed to fill him with confidence.

"The Light Guard in their infinite wisdom sends a child. A child to take us out," he mocked sarcastically.

Sean ignored them turning to me once again.

"Tim, you okay?" he replied helping me to my feet.

I nodded unable to understand how he got there as my spinning head and aching body fought to hold me up.

"Yeah, I'll be fine. I'm just shot. Really my biggest concern is Sai and Pete," I replied. "I got to do something."

He nodded sympathetically.

"How did you get here in the first place?" I continued stumbling.

"It took some doing, but nobody knows realm code like me," he replied with a confident smile. "It's sort of my forte'."

I looked at him like he was pulling my leg.

"What is realm code?" I replied.

"Realm code is the frequency in which a dimension exists. It's the mathematic law that houses and separates each dimension. It encompasses distance, time, and subatomic frequencies. I won't bore you with the details. Just know there are billions of combinations. My father is a part of the Light Guard Explorer Corps so I pretty much spent the better part of my time here studying realm code. I know it like the back of my hand. I'm one of the best, if not the best prospect on the docket at this stuff," he replied. "But I'm thinking I out did myself on this one. I think I even beat the Light Guard elite here."

"HEY!" the highgate cut in seething. "I was speaking to you, boy!"

Sean slowly turned his attention to the demon for the first time.

"I'm sorry are you talking to me?" Sean replied politely.

His response visibly threw the horde. They all looked at him like he was a freak until the demon finally responded.

"Yes, I'm speaking to…"

"On second thought, shut up," Sean replied calmly.

The highgate struggled to speak as I watched unable to believe what was going on.

"I get it. I don't need to hear anything else," he replied walking like a teacher chastising a class. "I really would have like to have shown up, kicked cupid all over the yard, and left with the relic, but I knew that would be stupid. It would be stupid because there was no way I could be sure that he had the relic. So, I figured I'd chase him until he led me to Aeneas. I figured from there it wouldn't take me long with Pete's help to take them both out, but as luck would have it, my fellow prospect was a little better than I had anticipated. He beat me to the punch. But I smile now, because here I am, and there it is. And here I was thinking I was going to have to fight Pete for it. Not something I was looking forward to. Not that I didn't think I could win. That wasn't the problem. The problem was hurting a fellow guardsmen…but luckily, you guys were stupid enough to butt your nose into our business. So, I guess I'll just have to bask in the prospect of taking it from you instead."

The horde of beasts looked on unable to comprehend what was going on. I was also struggling to understand how a kid my age could be so powerful.

BAWHAHA! The horde once again broke into laughter as the head highgate still struggled to speak.

WHAM! Before I could blink the demon seemed to flinch. I never saw Sean move, but with a mere flicker he was standing with Pete in one arm. He dropped him and flipped the arrow up and down like it was a lucky coin.

"Who are you?" the demon replied shaking uncontrollable.

Sean cut his eyes at his words.

"That should be the least of your worries," he replied starkly.

SHAKE! KABOOM! He shuttered then exploded into a million pieces. I couldn't believe my eyes as the rest of the horde cowered as Sean turned to them with an icy glare that even put me on edge.

"So, who's next?" he replied with a mischievous smirk.

ROAR! ROAR! ROAR! The horde let out running toward us. I readied my staff for yet another battle barely able to stand.

"STOP!" a voice thundered sending ripples through the atmosphere.

ZAP! KABOOM! KABOOM! Max and Jade finally arrived landing with explosions that sent aided the shockwaves that were already quaking throughout the battlefield halting everything and everyone in their tracks. Their power was unreal.

"Peter, Tim, Sarai," Jade replied searching immediately.

He searched before finally finding us. He took a few steps then stopped surprised to see Sean.

"Sean, how did you get here?" Jade replied thrown.

Sean quickly changed his demeanor losing the icy stare that sent chills threw the horde minutes earlier.

"It's a long story," he replied still flipping the arrow.

As Jade and Max approached the horde retreated into the ground like they were standing in quick sand with varying whelps and roars. I stood in fighting stance until the last one disappeared then fell to my butt happy it all seemed to be over.

"It took you guys long enough," I replied taking a deep breath.

"Yeah, sorry about that, but you've got to understand a hell realm code is probably the most complicated code in existence. It takes time," Max apologized. "Well, at least it's supposed to."

Sean raised his hand sarcastically.

"Hey, I just got here myself," he replied.

Jade walked over to Sai. He energized her using light healing. She rumbled for a second or two then awoke in a daze.

"What's going on?" she replied.

She sputtered than leaped to her feet prepare to battle once again.

"Tim, Pete!" she replied surveying the layout frantically.

"I'm fine," I replied raising my hand in a sarcastically embarrassed tone. "Let's just hope the same can be said for Pete."

My words prompted a continued search before she finally found Pete.

"He'll be fine, but in his condition, he won't be able to challenge for the relic. Knowing how hot blooded you earthborns tend to be, I won't risk waking him and trying to talk him off that ledge. That being said, seeing as he probably won't be overjoyed to hear he lost the trial, it'll probably be best to wait until after we get him back to the hotel before waking him," Jade replied.

Sai nodded before finally noticing Sean.

"Ah, hi," she replied looking at me with a suspicious gaze.

"Hi," he replied with a smile extending his hand. "Sean."

She hesitated then returned his shake with an awkward smile that fell between flattered and confused.

"Sai," she replied bashfully. "I would ask what you're doing here, but I'm sure it has something to do with that arrow you're carrying."

I walked over separating the two. I was proud to call them both friends in that moment. I leaned as they both playfully supported me.

"You don't know the half," I added. "Let's just say it's a good thing he showed up when he did. I mean, he really saved our butts."

He looked away humbly embarrassed.

"Well, thank you, Sean. Whether you were doing it for your mission, or to help a fellow guardsmen, the Light Guard appreciates your assistance," Jade replied as dry as unbuttered morning toast.

"Yeah, thanks," Sai replied looking him in the eye with a smile.

He nodded returning her smile with a smile of her own.

"Anytime," he replied continuing his nervous nod. "I appreciate the gratitude, and I don't mean to be rude, but my legion is kind of waiting on me."

"Oh, by all means," Max replied.

He nodded punching some numbers into his watch as a portal slowly appeared.

"Thanks again, Sean. I owe you one," I replied sincerely.

He shook his head holding back a grin.

"Don't mention it," he replied. "We may be on different legions, but in the end, we're on the same team, right?"

I nodded once again unable to believe someone so powerful could be so cool. He was the complete opposite of Jacob. His power was on Jacob's level, but his personality was reminiscent of my own.

"I couldn't have said it better myself," Jade responded with a nod.

He raised his hand in agreement waving to us as he disappeared through the portal hole. Max tossed Pete over his shoulder as we prepared to leave. As we shot back through the portal hole, I filled Sai in on everything she missed. It was another end to a long trial. We had done three, and so far, I was the only one who won. All the gusto we came in with was starting to dwindle. These guys were good, and all the results so far showed they were in another league in comparison to us. The results were the last thing on Jacob's mind. He stood staring me down like he wanted to send a bolt at my head as I approached.

"I'm done," Jacob replied exhausted. "I mean, what are the chances that you would be directly responsible for yet another situation where you almost get half of your friends wiped out while trying to help them. Is it me or do you love to do impulsive stupid things? Do you realize if you just would have listened and focused, half of the problems we've run into would have been pieces of cake."

I ignored him tossing my bag on a nearby chair. I looked for Eve, but she was nowhere to be found.

"Yeah, Yeah," I replied ignoring him.

He cut his eyes at me.

"Tim, I know we're in the Heaven Realm, but if you yeah, yeah me one more time I'm going to knock you into next week," he replied in a warning tone.

I quickly changed my demeanor cowering as he walked toward me.

"Alright, Jake, just calm down," I replied chuckling as I used the table as a shield.

He threw his hands up surrendering as he turned back to the arena. The demeanor had to be off-putting considering the circumstance, but I was too happy about Sai's appearance for anything else to register.

"Would you look at this?" Luke replied shaking his head. "We're getting our butts kicked."

AHHH! YAYYY! The crowd roared as Sean hoisted the arrow high above his head. He humbly bowed as we watched like sore losers.

"Well, at least Pete was accepted into the academy," Danielle added trying to be positive.

Luke stared at her with a blank stare.

"Don't get me wrong, that's all good, but what difference does it make for the competition," he replied. "I mean, we're getting slaughtered. Have some pride."

"I do have pride. You would know that if you had brains," she shot back.

"You okay, Tim?" said a voice from behind me.

I turned to see Sam, but he seemed different. He seemed humble almost nervous. I guess he had done the math. With Me, Beth, Pete, Uriah, and Sai out of the equation it only left the twins, Eve, Luke, Jacob, Danielle, and him. The numbers were thinning out and I think he knew it.

.

"Yeah, I'm fine," I replied.

"You were awesome!" Zech gushed plopping down next to me.

"Yeah, awesome," Jo seconded. "But that Sean kid was better. Do you really know him? I mean, are you guys friends?"

"You traitor," Zech replied. "Tim was just tired. He could kick that kids butt any day, right Tim?"

I ignored his statement and continued to stare at the frenzy going on inside the stadium. I wasn't used to being on the losing side of anything. It was a weird feeling.

"Um...I still think Tim's the best. I'm not a traitor, I just think Sean's cool," Jo responded.

"Yeah, well, that's still lame," Zech shot back.

"Shut up, Zech, no it isn't!" Jo fired back.

The two tussled as I rose to my feet and headed toward the barrier.

"What does any of this mean?" said Sam causing me to turn to him.

He lowered his head staring out at the crowd bashfully.

"I don't know. What do you mean by 'this' ?" I replied.

"I mean, for us," he continued catching everybody's attention in the room. "We came here with all these expectations, but if we keep losing then...I don't know, faith is supposed be so key to our power, right?"

"Yeah, spit it out," Luke replied unnerved.

"Oh, sorry," Sam responded. "Well, it seems like the smartest thing to do would be to believe we're going to win. It's hard to do that with us bickering and putting each other down. You guys are right. We are losing, but we haven't lost. We should be using this time to build our faith or something."

"Seriously," Luke replied. "Faith is not something you can control. If it was everybody in the world would have it. Believe me, I know. It's a practice. We're not down because we want to be. We're down because we have bad faith, well, at least some of us do."

"Well, that's his point," Jacob intervened. "And he's right. We shouldn't be arguing with each other. We don't know how to build faith just yet, but we definitely don't need to be tearing each other down."

We all nodded accepting his words. I didn't really feel like it applied to me. I turned to the middle of the arena as the festivities were winding down.

"Yeah, Jacob's right, especially considering our present company outside Tim are the ones on the chopping block," Danielle added. "And looking at how we've performed it's not going to be easy to muster up the faith we need to swing the momentum."

"Well, Pete had a plan before Captain Save-a-lot came to the rescue?" Luke replied sarcastically.

"What?" I replied oblivious.

"Right, Jacob?" he replied turning to Jacob.

I cut my eyes at his words preparing to be bored to death by another way for him to blame me for some imaginary problem that he construed to make me look bad. He ignored Luke for a couple of seconds before finally relenting.

"Yes, please share how yet another thing is my fault," I poked agitated.

"What?" Jacob replied cutting his eyes showcasing a threatening slight hem of light around his pupil.

I straightened up quickly as he shook his head and continued.

"Believe it or not, I didn't want to further showcase your idiocy. I have to believe sooner or later it's going to reflect poorly on me," he replied showing some resemblance of a personality.

"Jacob, c'mon," I pressed. "Get to the point."

"Look, it's just a hypothesis I came to after looking over Pete's kiosk," he continued.

"Kiosk?" I responded.

"Yeah, it's like a BAU catalog. Everything we do or say is cataloged. Here in heaven it's how they keep tabs on everyone in the Heaven Realm," he replied staring out at the roaring crowd. "Anyways, something didn't sit right with me when I watched Pete today, so I decided to check his catalog. He spent hours building in that library and those three bots he showcased wouldn't take close to that long. I did some further digging and with the anointed metals Pete was using, there is no way those supplies were used on those two bots. There is no way. I also watched the way he fought. He purposely reserved his strength like he was preparing for something."

I thought about his words and replayed the entire fight using my ability and every cue Pete used his fighting style. Jacob was spot on. He was holding back. With the commotion of the battle I must have missed it.

"So, case and point, if you didn't butt into the fight and lock the portal, Light Guard security shows up and Sean and Pete battle for the relic," Luke replied butting in. "Instead, the dimension locks causing Pete to get knocked out and causes you guys to forfeit his chance at a duel. I don't know about you, but if I was Pete I would be pissed."

I shook my head not even wanting to think about the ramifications of our decision. Did we really just rob Pete of the chance to pull off an upset? I had little time to stew over the question as Jade and Max appeared with Sai who looked a little worse for wear.

"Long time no see, Sis!" Luke replied running up to her and scooping her up and she blushed bashfully.

"Luke, put me down. I'm almost thirteen years old. Stop treating me like I'm in preschool," she shot trying to hide how she enjoyed the boy's embrace.

Luke placed the girl back on the ground as the two shared sympathetic stares before I cut in.

"How's everything working?" I replied scanning her.

"Fine," she replied pushing Luke away. "I'm fine, as long as Luke stops acting like um a porcelain doll."

She fixed her shirt as the rest of the gang hugged and greeted her.

"So, what was it like," Danielle replied. "You know, the whole multi-dimension situation."

"I'll explain it later. We have more pressing issues," she replied pointing toward the big board.

Danielle slowly turned as the board lit up and flipped. It felt good to not worry about being chosen, but judging by the way things had been going so far, it seemed like I was in more danger watching than I was when I was actually participating.

"C'mon, please let it be Jake," Zech replied. "We need to win."

We all stood in suspense as the tile finally stopped showcasing Evelyn Timila. I shook my head in frustration. Here we go again. The crowd erupted as the tile stopped.

"Crap, we lose again," Jo responded quickly.

"Hey, that's my girlfriend you're talking about," Zech fired.

"She's my girlfriend," Jo replied.

"Your girlfriend, you just said she was going to lose," Zech shot back.

"I said we're going to lose," Jo explained.

"Yeah, we're going to lose because you believe she's going to lose, stupid," Zech shot again.

"Shut up, Zech," Jo responded.

"You shut up," Zech replied.

I looked over at Sai who was casing the room looking for Eve.

"Where is Eve?" she replied turning to me.

Luke turned to Danielle who snapped out of her trance and explained.

"Oh, sorry, yeah, she went back to the hospital to watch the trials with her sister. She said she wanted to be by her side when she awoke," she explained.

As she spoke the big board went black then broadcasted a live video feed of Eve next to her sister bed. She looked caught off guard by the sudden exposure. Her eyes went dim as a banner on the television read TIMILA HAS CHOOSEN HER CHALLENGER.

"Turn it on," Luke replied turning to Jade and Max. "I can't hear anything with the crowd going crazy."

Jade's eyes lit up as he created a viewing orb in seconds.

"Yes, it's true. We have the first Naqam match," said Bruce Davis as the credits were running. "It looks like this already fantastic battle just took another interesting turn. I'm Bruce Davis with Mel Michaels and we'll see you bright and early for day four of the Light Guard Trials. Good night everyone."

We all stood trying to translate his words before Sam finally spoke.

"What's a Naqalm?" he replied with a dull look on his face.

"A 'Naqam' is a duel match where a prospect challenges another prospect who has already gone through a trial. I'm sure you guys can guess who Evelyn chose," Max replied with a disappointed headshake.

"Kadmiel," I replied annoyed. "Man, what is Eve thinking?"

"She's thinking about revenge, duh," Luke replied.

"Well, let's hope she's not," Jade replied.

"What do you mean?" Jacob responded.

"Well, if that is her reasoning then it cancels her merit for a duel," Jade responded. "By admission she would be forfeiting the match."

"Are you serious?" Jacob continued. "Can we switch and make her pick someone else?"

"No," Jade replied shaking his head apologetically. "Unfortunately, once it's done it's done."

"Man, Eve is such a hot head. Seriously, this is retarded. She's going to cost us another match whether she admits this about revenge or not. Did you see that girl? She mopped the floor with Beth. Eve's better, but c'mon, she doesn't stand a chance against that girl," Luke added.

I shook my head and grabbed my bag. I had to talk to her. I know the situation with Beth had her heated, but this was not only dangerous, but it was unbelievably selfish. We all saw what that girl did to Beth? She was brutal, and to put us through that again was wrong.

"Where are you going?" Jacob replied as I grabbed my bag.

"I'm going to talk to Eve and check in on Pete," I replied pulling out my medallion.

"Wait, I'll come to," Sai replied.

"Me too," Sam shot. "The old gang back together."

He shot next to Sai with super speed and gave her a one arm hug laying his head on her shoulder before moving his lips toward hers in a playful manner.

"Sam, I know you're happy to see me, but if you're lips so much as graze mine you're going to have to reattach them, " Sai replied grabbing her medallion and shoving him. "Stop playing around."

He chuckled as he fumbled around looking for his medallion.

"Wait, hold up, let me get mine," he sputtered grabbing his medallion as we waited impatiently.

"Tell Eve we said thanks for forfeiting our win whether she wins or loses," Luke shot turning toward Jacob for a co-signing statement. "Oh, yeah, and try to not get my little sister knocked unconscious again you two."

I ignored him as my medallion lit up. I peered through the portal door. I could see Eve sitting next to Beth who lay unconscious in her hospital bed. I walk through startling her.

"Tim, I was so worried. My gosh, I don't think I'm going to survive another one of these…trials. I think I blew one of these monitor screaming at the monitor," she replied rising and giving me a hug before turning to Sai as a tear appeared as emotions erupted from her. "Hikari."

She turned as Sai leaned in and gave her a hug.

"I should kill both you guys," she replied. "I thought you were done for. But it's good to see you're okay. I checked on Pete a few minutes ago. He should be coming along any moment now. They're just doing some last second tests to make sure he's fine."

Her demeanor made things even harder. I swallowed hard preparing my words trying to think of the best way to say what I was thinking.

"Yeah, that's good," I replied almost mumbling. "How's Beth?"

She shrugged her shoulders.

"I've been trying to communicate with her ever since Sai appeared, but I'm getting nothing," she continued with a smile.

Sai looked at me then turned to her like she didn't want to be the bearer of bad news before taking a deep breath and continuing.

"I heard the doctor say my case was a special case. I think it had more to do with the fact that I was a Dom or something," Sai replied.

"Yeah, that's exactly what it was," said Pete entering the room catching everyone off-guard.

"Pete," I replied turning to him.

"Hi, good to see you guys got out of there," he replied with a dim smile.

I took a deep breath and prepared to apologize before he could even say anything.

"Yeah, look, I just want to apologize for not giving you the chance to..."

"Forget about it," Pete replied cutting me off.

I stood staring at him in total shock. I had never known Pete to take someone underestimating him so well. I couldn't believe my ears.

"Are you sure you're the Pete I know?" Sai poked giving him a hug. "Or am I still in some alternate universe."

"Yeah, Yeah, but the way I acted in that battle. I was an idiot. I've been thinking about it ever since I got up. The last thing I remembered was seeing you being bounced into a mountain and Sai taking a wicked blow, but all I could think about was the fact that I was going to lose. That scared me. The first thought wasn't about you or Sai's well-being, it was about the fact that I was about to lose the stupid relic. I remember you said when Sai first got hurt that I was starting to take this thing too serious. You were right. This whole thing was a selfish attempt for me to live up to the legacy our parents left behind. We're here in the Heaven Realm and I'm still trying to outdo my father. I guess I got carried away. And I owe both you and Uriah an apology."

I sputtered not knowing what to say as everyone in the room's attention turned toward me.

"Sure, don't mention it. I'm just glad you're okay," I managed giving him a hi-five.

"Yeah, and I'm pissed you guys didn't invite me," Sam replied. "I mean, I would have destroyed more of those demon creeps then either of you."

"Shut up, Sam!" Sai and Eve replied simultaneously.

They both started laughing at the coincidence.

"Man, it feels good to have my partner in crime back," Eve replied tongue and cheek.

"Hey, Pete what were you talking about when you said Sai's ability did it," I asked turning to him.

"Oh, well, yesterday I was researching the subatomic makeup of Doms. You know, for my bots, and once I got back here it just made sense," Pete replied.

"What made sense?" Sam added.

"Sai's situation. Think about it, a Dom evolves and adapts after every battle no matter what the situation, right? So, just consider the implications of her injuries. If her soul was damaged, then what evolved."

"My soul," Sai replied.

"Exactly, it's the reason why your soul seemed to evolve to the point that it was the exact replica of your body. It's the perfect way of preventing what happened at the festival from ever happening again," Pete continue. "Your powers are amazing."

"That's genius," Eve replied. "I never thought about it that way."

Sai nodded her head agreeing with Pete's hypothesis.

"Okay, Okay, but enough distractions, didn't we come here to tell Eve she was being an idiot," Sam cut in with the delicacy of a bull in a china shop.

Eve's eyes fell at the sound of his words as if to be hiding embarrassment.

"Nice, Sam," Sai replied putting her hand on her head.

"What?" he replied obliviously.

"Look, I know you guys think this is about what she did to my sister, but…" Eve replied catching us all off-guard. "It's about the way she fights. Think about it, every time we face these guys, they have the element of surprise. We've never seen any of them in action, and because these people have documented everything we've done, they have unlimited tape on us. All we have are some cruddy BAU images that are generally shown from the point of view of people in the midst of fights themselves. We finally have someone that we've seen. Someone we can prepare for. I'm telling you, I can beat her."

Her words seemed sound, but over the past month I was starting to understand her mannerisms. There was something that just didn't sit right with me, even if the things she was saying made sense.

"Okay, if you think so," I replied still unsure.

"Yeah, we have to start trusting each other, right? Why not start with you?" Sam added raising his hand. "I know you can beat her."

Eve smiled at his words giving him a hi-five.

"It sounds good to me," Pete replied. "Everything you said is the absolute truth. It'll be fun to have an actual game film to breakdown. Not just hypotheticals and perceived mannerisms. It'll be fun."

I nodded acknowledging their words.

"Well, let's get started," Eve added grabbing her bag. "Sai and Tim, I'll need your abilities to train. Sam, you and Kadmiel have a similar fighting style, so I'll need you as well. Pete you can help me strategize."

"Sounds like a plan," Pete replied. "Let's do it."

"You know I'm always down to fight," Sam replied.

"I'll need the chance to get back in the swing of things anyways," Sai added.

Eve batted her eyes at me melting me like a popsicle.

"Let's go," I sighed lighting up my medallion.

I shook my head as they all disappeared through their portal holes. I couldn't shake the solemn feeling that this wasn't going to end well. I looked at Beth's vacant expressions as she lay lifeless, yet she still showcased a solemn feel that seemed to foreshadow the upcoming storm. Like I had done since I first started on this journey, I sucked it up and did what was asked of me.

CHAPTER

16

Lion
Vs
The lamb

Lion vs the lamb

KABOOM! I dived out of the way as a bolt ricocheted against a nearby mountain edge.

"Watch out Sai!" I replied patting down the flames.

"Sorry, she's fast," she replied helping me up.

I knew Eve was good, but she was better than I remembered. Her technique was flawless. She moved so gracefully and was so formidable that Sai, Sam and I could barely contain her.

"You really think so?" She added slowing down.

"Gotcha," Sam replied striking.

BOOM! WHIFF! OOF! Eve elegantly sidestepped his blow like she was doing a pirouette. She landed a punch to Sam's stomach that almost knocked his breath out.

"Man," he complained falling to one knee.

"Okay, that's enough," I replied falling to my butt. "We've been at this for hours."

Pete walked over raising his hand signifying he agreed. I was so beat. After a battle like I had been through I probably should have been in bed resting, yet here I was pushing my body even further.

"Okay," Eve replied walking over to me. "You okay?"

I nodded as she paired with Sai and they both pulled me to my feet.

"Thanks you guys," she replied with a smile. "I appreciate it."

"No problem," Sam added. "We're a legion, that's what we're supposed to do."

Pete joined the rest of us as we headed to the girls living area. As we did Danielle sat on the couch relaxing looking at television.

"You guys finally finished," she replied. "I thought I would never be able to practice. Especially with Eve going tomorrow. I thought she would take longer than usual."

"Oh, sorry," she replied. "It's all yours."

"Thanks," Danielle replied rising from the couch. "I'll see you guys in a few."

We all looked surprised by her statement as Eve bashfully avoided eye contact and headed for the kitchen.

"You guys want something to eat or drink," she replied trying to change the subject before we spoke.

"Pizza," Sam responded raising his hands.

"Yeah," I second.

"Yeah, me too," Pete added.

"Okay, sure," Sai relented.

"Okay, pizza coming up," Eve replied. "I finally think I got this Heaven Realm S-frequencer figured out."

Danielle squeezed past us and headed into the training room slamming the door behind her as Eve disappeared into the kitchen.

"Beauty and work ethic," Pete replied drooling.

"Who, Dani or Eve?" Sai poked. "Someone's got a bit of a crush, eh?"

Pete's eyes fluttered as he showcased a dense smile.

"What?!" he responded. "Neither."

An awkward silence ensued as Sai shrugged her shoulders and followed Eve into the kitchen. Sam and I looked at each other trying to hold back our laughter. Pete exhaled and flopped on the couch.

"You just destroyed an ancient patriarch and took on a horde of demons from the spawn of hell, and you still can't muster the courage to speak to that girl," I added shaking my head. "Are you kidding me?"

Pete ignored me flopping on the couch as Sam and I followed suit. Sam grabbed the remote and turned up the volume.

"Hello, and welcome to Entertainment Tonight. The Light Guard Trials Edition. I'm your host Ellen Lago and boy do I have some hot news fresh off the presses. Sources say that love has erupted in the confines of our favorite legion. It seems that two of our favorite, well, lovable losers have become closer since entering the Heaven Realm. Sources say that the two legionmates were caught sharing an innocent kiss in their agents office," said the lady as soon as sound could be heard.

She had long candy red hair. It was up in a bun. She wore a dress with gold ruffles on the shoulders and silver pieces glittered off the white of the dress. Her words had caught me like someone showing your baby picture in the middle of mixed company. I was so embarrassed. It wouldn't take a scientist to figure out who she was referring to. I stared forward not even wanting to turn my head.

"You think you know a guy," Sam replied. "I guess you were trying to show ol' Pete here how to do it the right way."

"Sam, if you don't shut up I'm going to squash you," Sai replied catching us all of guard.

I slowly raised my head as embarrassment filled me. Pete's face looked hurt and betrayed at the same time. I fumbled to speak as Eve stared at me then turned to Sai.

"What are they talking about?" Eve asked turning to Sai.

"Eve, I promise was nothing," Sai replied with an annoyed sigh. "I was congratulating Tim and we accidently…kind of…kissed."

"How do you accidently kiss?" Eve pressed emotionless still trying to act like it wasn't a big deal. "Not that I care, it's just weird is all."

"Yeah, same here," Pete added visibly annoyed. "I just find it weird that two friends can accidently kiss."

"Sai's right," I muttered. "She was trying to peck me on the cheek and I just happened to be turning."

"How unfortunate that must have been for the both of you," Eve jabbed. "May I ask what you were congratulating him about, friend of mine?"

I looked at Sai and we both froze knowing we couldn't reveal the reason without telling Sam why he was really recruited to Revelations. I played mental gymnastics to come up with an explanation, but there was nothing I could say that would be believable. Sai expression showcased a similar dilemma.

"We can't really say," she finally relented.

"What? Why?!" Eve continued angrily. "You don't find it the least bit weird that you guys accidently kissed, when you were trying to actually kiss. And the explanation you give us asks us to believe it was all because you were congratulating him for a secret good job he had done that you can't share with the rest of us."

"I never said it was a secret," Sai shot back.

"Well, why can't you tell us then?" Eve shot back.

"It was an accident, okay?" Sai continued. "Ryan leaked this crap because he's trying to work some angle for publicity. We were supposed to tell you guys about it, but between the festivities, and me being knocked out, I guess we just forgot."

"Once again another coincidence," Pete replied turning to me.

"Look, it's the truth," I replied. "Ask Jacob, he was there."

They looked each other over and relented. Eve swayed from foot to foot impatiently as an envious look covered her face.

"Well, do it," she replied catching me off-guard.

"You want him to call Jacob?" Sai replied. "You really don't believe us."

Eve cut her eyes at the notion.

"It's not about belief, it's about knowing for sure," she shot back.

"This is so stupid. Besides, I thought you didn't care?" Sai fired back.

"I don't. It's just weird that something like this could be going on behind all our backs, that's all," she continued fumbling over her words.

I sat not knowing what my next move was. I stared at Pete. I knew the situation wouldn't be resolved until there was conformation on both sides.

"Fine," Sai replied her eyes lighting up immediately. "Jacob."

There was a baiting second before he finally responded.

"Yeah, I know, it's about the report," Jacob replied cutting her off. "Is Tim's little girlfriend upset?"

"I'm not his girlfriend!" Eve fired.

"She's not my girlfriend!" I replied at the same time as she did.

"Yeah, sure she's not," Jacob provoked in monotone mocking voice. "What do you guys need?"

I looked to Sai who rolled her eyes as she continued.

"Tell them about the whole situation," I replied. "Ryan, the accident, everything."

There was another second of awkward silence before he finally responded.

"Yeah, it was an accident. I guess, I didn't actually see it, but I know Sai apologized immediately. They figured you guys would be pissed and juvenile about it so they didn't want to go along with it, but after some persuading from Ryan they finally agreed," he replied.

Eve and Pete seemed to bashfully look away humbly embarrassed at the same time. I shook my head in and I told you so type of manner before Luke cut in killing my minute of triumph.

"Just for reference, Tim, if you put your lips on my little sister again, I'm going to toss you out of one of these windows," Luke cut in sarcastically.

"Shut up, Luke," Sai replied. "It was an accident."

"I know, but just in case," Luke replied. "You guys have a nice night."

"Idiot," Sai replied.

Eve and Pete stewed stubbornly before finally turning apologetically.

"Sorry, I guess it's the stress of this trial. It's got me on edge," Eve replied in a low stubborn voice covering her face embarrassed. "Regardless, I'm sorry."

"Yeah, me too," Pete added. "I guess I was caught off-guard by the whole situation."

"It's cool," I replied quickly putting it behind me.

Sai cut her eyes showing a stubborn side of her own before finally relenting.

"We've wasted enough time on this stupid stuff," she groaned. "Let's get some sleep and put this whole terrible day behind us."

"What about Pizza?" Sam added in an upset tone.

"Well, eat it in your room," Sai fired.

"Yeah, yeah," Sam added grabbing his bag.

I followed suit as Pete pulled a tab out of his bag.

"You're not coming with?" I replied taken back.

"No, I'll be along shortly," he responded. "I still have to go over some strategy with Eve and Sai."

I powered up my medallion. I nodded heading for the portal door with Sam as the three huddled on the couch as the television blasted in the background.

"Could you guys do me a favor and turn that crap off," I replied. "We don't need more negative stuff coming out. We have enough problems."

Eve chuckled as she reached for the remote and turned it off. I still got a weird vibe from her. She took Jacob's story, but I still had a hard time believing that she or Pete bought ours. There was a weird tension that didn't dissipate with Jacob's corroborating words. It just felt awkward. I wore a fake smile as I waved goodbye. I walk through the portal hole to see Sam walking toward the training room.

"Training again?" I replied still unable to believe his stamina.

"Hey, if you got it, do it," he replied in old Sam fashion.

"Flaunt it," I replied shaking my head humorously.

"What's a flaunit?" he replied oblivious.

"No, flaunt it," I replied. "The saying is if you got it, flaunt it. It means if you got it show it off."

He thought about it for a second then smiled.

"Okay, well," he replied. "If you got it, flaunt it."

I nodded with an approving smile as he headed for the training door with a salute of his index and ring finger. I shook my head in disbelief once more than headed to my room. I took a quick shower and brushed up before hopping into bed. I was so tired I think I almost fell asleep before my head actually hit the pillow. It seemed like I closed my eyes for a second before I was stirred out of my sleep.

"Welcome to WINK 7's Crossfire debate show," said a voice jarring me awake. "I'm your host Tyson Everbay and this is Rapid Fire at 7."

I jumped looking around like a crazy man before I turned to see the television shining like a beacon in the darkness of the room. It shined like a star in a gloomy night sky. I looked around the room paranoid before grabbing the remote and turning it off. I took one last surveying look then went b?" sack to sleep cautiously. Hours passed as I slumbered before Eve's training finally ended. The girl waited until she was sure Pete was gone. Danielle came along plopping down on the couch as the two girls sat on opposite sides of her.

"Where's the love in this place?" she responded staring at the girls' demeanor. "My gosh, I figured I'd be surrounded by bliss and friendly love considering Sai's situation. You guys seem colder than my drink."

The girls jostled uncomfortably before shrugging.

"I don't have a…" Eve uttered before Dani cut in.

"C'mon, guys, what's going on?" Dani continued to press sympathetically.

Eve took a gulp of her water in attempt to kill the awkwardness. Sai stubbornly refused to broach the subject even though she was largely the reason for the coldness between the two girls. She spent the majority of there sparring only speaking when Eve asked her direct question. Eve largely thought the tension was based in her presumptuous accusation, but she couldn't understand why Sai was taking things so personal. She sighed in a relented fashion continuing.

"Nothing, I…I was jealous, and I jumped to conclusions," Eve responded bashfully. "Sai, I want to apologize…I shouldn't have jumped to the conclusion that you and Tim would feel the need to lie about something that stupid…I just…I know you and Tim have been close all your lives. I have no right to butt in and try to dictate or make you feel weird about your relationship."

Sai nodded accepting the girl's words with a level of guilt before Danielle broke in.

"I don't want to speak on things that I don't fully understand, but Sai, are you sure there's nothing there?" She shot with a slight wince. "I don't mean to be forward, seriously, it's none of my business, and I know I don't know any you well enough to make assumptions, it's just, you didn't see that kid when you were out. It was like a part of him wasn't there. He won't say it, but even your brothers are convinced the kid is too immature to realize he's crazy about you."

Her words caused Sai to blush uncontrollably as the girl scrambled to find an appropriate response before giving into her anger about the situation.

"Yeah, that's because they're idiots. They've been saying that nonsense all our lives," Sai fired quickly replying seething. "They can't see past our genders. If what happened to me happened to Jacob, Luke would've been in the same condition, and he knows that. Look at how you feel about Abby. Eve is distraught over what happened to her sister as well, but no one bats an eye. It's just sexist to assume two people who grew up spending every waking moment together can't be friends with a strong bond because they don't share a gender. It's funny no one ever question's Tim's relationship with Pete, but he has to constantly defend his relationship with me because we don't share the same gender. It's the epitome of ignorance. I'm not going to try hide how special Tim is to me and it's my business what that bond means. Nobody has a right to define it, but me. I don't owe anybody an explanation because it's nobody's business. He is the most important bond in my life. He's my best friend and there is nothing inside of Father Yahweh's will that I wouldn't do for him. It is what it is. But this, it makes it so one stupid mistake is going to taint nearly thirteen years of friendship with some weird childish crush label. I hate that. Tim has always been that way with all his friends. Everyone else gets that without dissection, but now, Tim and I have to tip-toe around everything we do because of this ridiculous story. We always had effortless chemistry between us. I'm scared that now he…or we are going to question everything we do. I'm scared it's going to change the bond between us, and I don't think that's fair. It makes me so mad."

Eve lowered her head taking Sai's words as a direct shot at her. Her demeanor finally broke through Sai's stubborn stance as she finally turned to her long-time best friend.

"I guess I should've just said that. I shouldn't have sulked around like a brat. Honestly, I appreciate your apology Eve, and I'm sorry I didn't say something sooner. It was just foolish pride. I guess, with Ryan serving us up on a plate I was defensive. I hated having to defend myself against such ridiculous tabloid garbage…I guess it just got to me. Looking back on it, I think these trials have us all on edge," Sai gave in walking over to Eve and hugging her. "Whatever the reason, you got enough on your mind right now."

Eve returned the girl's hug.

"Thanks, Sai," she responded rising to her to feet as the two girls' released their embrace. "And trust me, you don't have to worry about your dynamic. Aside from the fact that Tim is oblivious to most things that are going on around him, you guys have a bond that transcends ignorant people like us. That kid loves you. Take it from someone who wished he looked at me with a tenth of the passion he looks at you with. Friendship label withstanding, it's going to take more than that to stop you two from laying your lives down for each other and…making the rest of us feel…jealous of the bond you have."

Sai lowered her head unable to fight back a smile as Dani placed a consoling hand on her shoulder.

"Sai, Tim is a great friend to me, but unlike the bond between you two…he knows how I feel about him. I wish he didn't, but he does. We don't have a relationship that is built outside of our attraction. I'm not blind. It's obvious he has feelings for me, but it's hard not to get jealous when I see him showing those same feelings for someone, he claims is just his friend. It's disheartening. So, when things like that happen, I can't fight how it makes me feel. I can accept him falling for someone else, but it's more embarrassing to not hear it from him first. You heard Jacob, people around us assume stuff about us, it makes me look like a fool. I feel like a fool. It's not an excuse, but maybe it's a pledge of temporary insanity."

Sai accepted her words with a chuckle as the girl turned to leave.

"Where are you headed?" Dani asked sitting forward.

"I saw a report earlier today on that girl Kadmiel. It gave me a hunch. Pete said they have some material for research in the library. I still have an hour or two before I have to shut it down. I figured I'd finish my training there," Eve added with a wave of her hand.

Sai smiled waving as the girl made her exit. Meanwhile, I slept for hours, but to me it felt like moments. I jostled in my bed as the light of a holoscreen television awoke me.

"We're here with Agnus Hall the author of the book, *Where did they go? And why we can't follow?* It's In stores now," replied the host catching my attention. "Also joining us is Arn Gates the chief operating president of the A.A.R.M and Dylan Matthews director the new documentary In Layered Sight: The truth about the December 21st Disappearances. I like to welcome you all. Now let's get to our rapid-fire debate."

I walked over to the television and looked it up and down whacking the side.

"Is that really the best you got," said a voice I recognized again. "You can stop rain for crying out loud, and a slap on the side is your most thought out plan of action."

"Michael," I replied exhausted. "Can you ever just make a normal entrance?"

He laughed out loud.

"Is it really that bad?" he chuckled. "I must've caught you a bad time."

I dropped my head selling my exhaustion in my demeanor.

"You have no idea," I replied. "We're getting our butts kicked, Eve thinks I'm in love with my best friend, Pete thinks I'm in love with the girl of his dream, Jacob and Luke are being jerks, and I can't seem to get through a day without being totally mentally or physically exhausted. In a nut shell, you've not only caught me at a bad time, you've caught me in a bad sequence of times."

Michael nodded sympathetically.

"I told you this thing wouldn't be a picnic," he gloated before turning to the television.

He pointed at the holoscreen as he raised the volume on the screen catching my attention. The participants were in the midst of a heated debate. An old slightly portly lady seemed angry why the other two guys as they looked at the audience with smug looks on their faces.

"100,000 out of 100,000 of the people who we've contacted with direct knowledge of their missing loved one's religious affiliation have all stated that the missing person was a Christian. Everyone. That is not a coincidence. That is empirical data that supports a possible conclusion that science is ignoring out of sheer arrogance."

The men chuckled to themselves like they were adults listening to a child give a dissertation.

"What is so ridiculous about that?" she replied annoyed.

Arn Gates smiled shaking his head. He was a weird looking guy. He had a receding hair line that seemed to be a few months away from him being bald. He wore an expensive suit with a small thin red tie. He gave arrogant a new meaning. He wasn't just arrogant. No, it was more of a mean-spirited arrogance that seemed to seep through the television.

"What's ridiculous is not the belief in doing a sound scientific study. The problem is the belief that scientific study means jumping to whopping conclusions based on a factor that could have various meanings," he retorted. "Yes, it is possible that all these people abducted could have been Christian, but that doesn't prove that there is a God. It just proves that people who believe in a God have been abducted."

"Alien abduction," She shot back falling back in her chair exasperated. "That's more plausible, an alien abduction. You can't be serious."

His face turned stern at the sound of her words as if he wanted to kill her on the spot.

"I never stated in any form, shape or fashion that the abductors were alien. That being said, there is far more evidence in our past that supports aliens then evidence that represents a God," he continued. "Look at the old relics of the past. The ancient writings. History is filled with people who misunderstood powerful beings and assume them to be Gods."

"What if they didn't misunderstand? What if they were told by these people that they were Gods?" She retorted passionately. "Why are we so arrogant in our understanding of our ancestors? They had technological marvels like the pyramids, and we have no idea how they completed them, yet we treat them like they were idiots dragging their knuckles and smacking walls with rocks. Why do we assume that they weren't smart enough to tell the difference between what was normal and what was extraterrestrial? They had sophisticated systems of governments, irrigation, and plumbing systems that were well before there times. They recognized kings, princes, and normal people. Why would they assume and called these entities Gods unless they were given that label? And why all of a sudden did one God seemed to just dwarf all the others. Tell me that?"

The man stumbled unable to speak trying to think of a good response.

"Yeah, there's a God, Agnus, "he fired back condescendingly. "That's why there are things like cancer, death, and violence."

She shook her head.

"I'm not a religious person," she replied. "But even I can realize that it's not that cut and dry. My daughter, who disappeared on that dreadful day. She meant the world to me, but that doesn't mean that I protected her from every peril. I couldn't without taking away her free will, the very thing that made her who she was. The only thing I could do is teach her. All I could do is leave her a set of guidelines that taught her how to protect herself. If she chose to disregard those set of rules? She opens herself up to follies of the risk that those guidelines protected her from. It's the same with us. There are guidelines in the bible…"

"Mrs. Hall, have you ever read a bible?" The host replied annoyed.

"No, but I know people who followed the rules within a bible," she shot back. "And I know there are rules and guidelines in it that we classified as old fashion until we run into the consequences that would have been avoided if we had just followed those guidelines. I'm sorry, but people who obey the bible don't kill and hurt people, that is usually done by people who don't."

"What about the crusades, salem witch trials, and things of that sort? There are plenty of instances of people who follow God committing heinous atrocities," Dylan cut in angrily. "That is complete crap."

The lady smiled shaking her head.

"Dylan, I have to disagree. Go look at the records and you will find that in both of the examples you put forth the vast majority of the people killed claimed to be Christian. So, your example doesn't dispute my claim. It actually strengthens it. Even if I ignore another glaring coincidence, you just said they follow God. How can you be someone who kills and hurts innocent people yet still follow and obey a book and a God that states that you shouldn't," She shot back. "Once again, I'm not a religious person, but that's an oxymoron. Wouldn't you say?"

The two men seemed infuriated by her words.

"For a person who claims to be non-religious you seemed to be pretty inspired by what religious people believe," Gates replied in an insinuating manner. "I wouldn't want to mistake you for a disrupter of the peace."

A fearful look replaced the smug grin on her face.

"No not at all, sir," she replied as the other two men looked on with sick satisfaction in her submission. "I'm simply a scientist looking for a reason and a way to see my child again, that's all. Please forgive me if it sounds like that. I just feel like the bible might have given us an insight on what's going on right now if it wasn't burned."

The man looked at her with an offended sneer and shook his head.

"Well, Mrs. Hall, I think you and your husband should spend less time looking for bibles and more time looking for actual tangible answers," he shot with a sneer that looked like he wanted to tear her in half.

The lady nodded lowering her head like a subject instead of an adversary. The dynamic of the show had shifted. There was no longer a debate of ideas. It was hard to watch as the host uncomfortably shuffled his papers. I turned to Michael as he snapped his fingers turning off the tube.

"What was that?" I replied. "And why did you wake me up in the middle of the night to see this?"

177 | P a g e

Michael slowly rose to his feet.

"Tim, you guys are losing sight of your purpose here," he explained. "The Light Guard Trials…the pomp, and gaudy extravaganza of it all. It means nothing. The light of the world is gone. I don't care if you guys end up with one house that accepts all of you and it's the worst house in the academy. The point of this whole thing is to get you ready for the worst war in Earth or Heavens history and you guys are prime players. Realize this stupid thing is a formality, you're not fighting to be your parents, or superstars. You're fighting for people like her. People who are being pulled to the Father but are prevented from accepting the Savior because there is no one to lead her to him. You and your friends will be the catalyst for that event. Without you, her and everyone like her will be destined for the pit. Now I understand you and your friends are just kids, but you have to focus on the true objective, not egotistical opinions of yourselves."

"Why are you telling just me this?" I replied reflecting on his words introspectively.

"I'm not," he replied. "I'm here to tell you something is going on under your nose that needs your immediate attention. And you are the only one who can help, just you and no one else."

He pointed toward the training room causing me to leap out of bed.

"Sam," I replied putting my pants. "Is he okay?"

He nodded raising his hand.

"He's fine technically, but I don't know how long he will be if he keeps doing what he's doing," he replied coyly.

"Well, what is it?" I shot.

He shrugged vanishing before I could press him more. Freaking angels, there manners were crap. I finally got my shoes on and shot out the door.

"Sam!" I screamed sprinted toward the training room.

I leaped from the top of the stairs to the first floor in one bound. I hit the door without slowing down.

"Sam!" I repeated panicking.

WHOOSH! I dodged as a raging flame exploded nearly burning my face off.

"Tim! Get out of here, now!" Sam screamed catching my attention.

I watched staring in awe. The entire room was an inferno. The fire emanated from Sam. It was the weird white flame. It covered his body. I closed the door using my cat like reflexes just as the flame reached me. I narrowly dodged exposure to the freaky looking flames.

"Sam?" I stuttered in disbelief.

"Tim," Sam replied bursting through the door.

I looked at him then down at my body. He fell to one knee patting me down like I was a helpless burn victim. He had a worried look on his face that made him look like he was out of sorts.

"Are you okay?" he replied.

"I'm fine," I replied forcing his hands off. "What are you doing?"

"Are you sure?" he replied unable to believe my answer.

His demeanor was eerie. I couldn't understand it. I could control fire. He had witnessed me do so countless times, so I was really confused by his concern that an accidental fire could do me any harm. It was odd. I just stared at him with a confused stare and nodded cynically.

"Yes, Sam, why wouldn't I be?" I pressed raising a brow in confusion.

He looked at his hands then back at me like he couldn't believe what was happening. He fell to his butt and covered his head like a huge weight had been taken off his shoulders. Now I was really confused. I couldn't think of a proper way to broach my concerns about the way he was acting.

"Are you okay?" I asked raising my brow.

He exhaled staring at the ceiling as a grateful smile covered his face. He put his hands together in a praying manner exhaling in relief.

"Sam!" I grunted loudly. "Would you tell me what's going on, dude. You're freaking me out, right now."

He gathered himself mentally still nodding involuntarily. I shook my head impatiently trying to prompt him to speak. He took another prepping second than finally continued.

"I'm sorry," he replied emotionally. "I shouldn't have been using it in here. It's just…I thought you were sleep. I would have never…"

"Sam, you're talking in circles, why would I need to be sleep for you to practice? What aren't you telling me? I thought you said you couldn't control that white flame?"

He shook his head embarrassed.

"I…I wasn't being totally honest when I said that," he continued in a timid tone.

"Am I not speaking English, here? Why are you talking in code? Sam, Friend name Tim asks question to you. Sam, tell Tim why boy nervous about fire?" I replied imitating a caveman in an angry voice. "Stop playing the name game and spit it out."

Sam sighed deeply before continuing.

"I can summon the white flame, but when it comes out I can't control it…at least not completely. Really, it's closer to barely control. It's like it takes over my reflexes. My emotions rage then I black out. If can stay calm I can control a small amount of it, but the longer I use it the less control I have over it," he revealed staring at the ground as he spoke.

"What do you say 'it' like that?" I continued to press approaching him and kneel in front of him. "You talk about the fire like it's alive or something?"

He stared at me with a look that revealed a fearful emotional breakdown.

"I don't know why, but it feels...it feels alive?" he replied visibly showing an anger that I had never seen in him.

"How?" I replied.

"I can't explain it, but once it comes out," he continued hesitating like he was afraid of thinking about it. "It's like it tries to take over."

He stopped gathering himself once again. He stared around the room in an effort to make sure we were the only people in the room before he continued.

"I think...I think that's what led to my brother...you know?" he explained unable to finish his statement.

I shook my head sympathetically.

"Dude, there's no way you could remember that," I replied trying to knock him out of the funk. "You were too young."

"C'mon, I don't claim to be the smartest person in the world, but I didn't have to see it first hand to piece things together, besides...I heard my housekeeper talking about this weird flame that burned down the old house. At first, I thought she was just a little of knocker.

"Rocker," I corrected out of habit.

He shook his head annoyed by my interruption before continuing.

"My gosh, rocker...anyways, she was always doing weird rituals and things around the house. Santa Rita or whatever she called it," he continued without any prompting. "She was always putting garlic and stinky oils all over the house. At the time she was just trying to protect me. She said there was a demon thing-spirit that took my brother. She said she was my Godmother and it was her job to take care of me. I was more than happy to accept, you know, after the foster home or what not. I was just happy I wasn't alone anymore. I was too young to question her, so I believed every word. I prayed day and night to prevent that demon from coming back. I was afraid it would take me the next time it showed up."

He stopped with shaking his head solemnly.

"Marcia, then, she was like my protector. She was like a real aunt in a lot of ways," he replied showcasing a concealing smile that failed to hide his rising negative emotions. "I couldn't eat, sleep, or walk unless she was with me. I spent so much time alone in those foster homes. She was the first person that truly showed me love and compassion."

He paused as his smile disappeared.

"Then like that, everything just got bad," he replied with a cold stare.

I could see the anger in his eyes as he spoke. It reaped of hurt and betrayal that was deep seated. I was terrible in situations where I was supposed to be sympathetic with guys. I never knew what to say. I assume most were like me. I never took pride in sympathy. It always made me feel weak and patronize. I was warring with that assumption about Sam, so I just sat like a deer in headlights listening and fumbling for words.

"What happened?" I replied.

"I don't remember most of what happened. I was sleeping the entire time, or at least I thought I was...maybe I was just blacked out," he continued pausing like he was reliving the incident. "All I remembered was waking up and being ice cold. My ceiling was gone, and snow was everywhere. It looked like a snow bomb had gone off. I looked for Marcia everywhere, but when I got to her, she almost climbed the wall trying to get away from me," he replied saddened with every word. "I can still remember the look on her face. She kept calling me diablo, and I couldn't understand why."

I paused still unable to put forth any words of encouragement. I was twelve years old. No matter how advanced I was, I wasn't equipped to deal. What did I know about something like this? What could I say? He continued as I stood trying to look sympathetic as atonement for my poor support skills.

"I looked down and noticed my body," he continued visibly shaken by his recounting of the story. "I was covered in the same white flame that came out in our battle. I don't know...maybe it was my emotions. I was pretty freaked out from the sight and I think it amped it up. It started to grow. She shielded herself screaming…she was screaming so loud and I couldn't do anything to help her. I tried to control the weird stuff coming out of me, but It happened so fast."

He hung his head in anguish before raising his gaze.

"I blacked out and when I came to...," he paused.

Throughout the story his voice never cracked. He didn't cry or look to be holding back any tears. He just looked defeated. I didn't know all the things he had gone through in his twelve and a half years of life, but he had the composure of a battle tested veteran. It was eerie to watch.

"What happened?" I replied.

"She was dead," he replied. "Frozen into this black statue. The authorities showed up. They obviously couldn't explain what happened, but I knew I did it. I couldn't understand how. I never saw the flame again, but it haunted me. It was a distant memory until our battle. It just shot from me again. I saw it, and I knew it was me. My brother, my godmother, they were gone and after what happened in our battle, I had no doubt I was the cause. Ever since we fought those demons I could feel it every time I trained. I've tried to suppress it. It didn't matter how many times I fought it off. I feel it all the time now. It's like it's waiting for me to lose control again. I knew I had to get hold of it. I don't want it to slip out of my control. I didn't want it to hurt one of you. Jade gave me some tips. I figured I wait until I was alone to test them out. I thought you were sleep and Pete was gone so..."

"Wait, Jade knew about this?" I asked surprised.

"Yeah, he walked in on me?" Sam continued. "I almost took his arm off."

His words piqued my interest.

"What do you mean took his arm off?" I replied.

"This flame is like white hot ice," he continued. "Whatever it encounters freezes. We were training and one day I got frustrated and it came out. It scared me because I couldn't put it out. Jade tried to stop it using the light energy thing, but it rejected the light and blew his arm to shreds."

"I didn't notice," I deducted trying to remember Jade missing an arm.

"He repaired it...or at least as much as he could. You can't really tell because it was close to a month ago, and it's almost fully healed now, but he has a huge scar. He still says he can't control light energy fully with the injured hand," he explained. "I ask him about it all the time. You know? I guess I still feel kind of guilty."

"So that's why he stopped you from using it?" I asked.

He waited for a minute contemplating whether he should talk before continuing.

"I don't know the righty science-y way to say it, but he said it wasn't natural. He said it wasn't elemental or light energy. He said he didn't know what it was, but it was too dangerous to tap into without knowing it's limi...limitations? I think that's what he said. Anyways, he scanned my body after it finally went away and said something was wrong with it. I felt fine, but he said my spirit bio-rhythm was off. Kind of like you with your ability, he told me to refrain from using it until he got more information on it," he continued.

"Okay, so why were you using it now?" I replied.

He hesitated bashfully before continuing.

"Well, we need it to win," he replied. "...and that flame, I figured if I could control it maybe I could use it."

"I thought it tries to control you?" I replied confused.

"Well, it does but it also empowers me. It makes me feel more powerful than I've ever felt. You saw me at the Battle of New Angeles. I mean, our backs are against the wall. I'm going to need all the help I can get," he replied. "I'm afraid. I don't want anyone else to get hurt. I want to be able to help like you and Sai did."

I nodded in agreement understanding his sentiment.

"Well, what if I help?" I asked hesitantly. "You know, using my ability in all. I might be able to see how it works."

"No way," he replied.

"Why?!" I replied. "You said it yourself, we could use it."

His brow frowned at the sound of my words.

"Yeah, but not at the expense of turning you into an ice sickle," he fired. "Didn't you hear me before? My brother and god mother died because I couldn't control this thing. I'm not about to put anybody else in danger. I tried to control it. I failed. That's it."

I exhaled frustrated. This power could be an ace in the hole for us. If we could harness its power, maybe we could turn the tide in this battle.

"You don't know that. Besides, didn't you say that Jade healed himself?" I replied almost pleading.

He nodded in a relenting fashion.

"Okay, well there you go," I continued. "If something happens, you can take me to the Med Sector."

"Yeah, no. I'm not going to put you in the hospital so the media can have more things to hate me for," he responded. "No thanks."

"C'mon, you said it yourself, we need this," I replied. "I'll put myself in a glass barricade with a fire layer inside. At the first sign of danger I'll blow dodge, no harm, no foul. C'mon, let's just try it."

He hesitated before finally sighing a relenting sigh. I understood he didn't want to do it, but it was desperation time. We were going to lose unless things changed for our squad, and fast. We came in thinking we were overmatched, and we had no idea how right we were.

"Alright," he replied. "But first sign of danger no matter what it is, blow dodge."

I nodded in accepting his terms. He exhaled still hesitant about the whole situation. He reluctantly followed me as I opened the door to the training room. I couldn't believe the scene. The effects of his power were still present. Everything was frozen solid. I tapped the icy interior as an ice chunk fell and exploded on the ground.

"Cold burning fire," I replied. "That is so cool."

Sam showed a bashful smile before punching some letters into the keypad. The room slowly changed to our former practice ground. I looked to him with a nostalgic smile as he nodded signaling he felt the same way.

"Man, it seems like so long ago," he replied. "It seemed like yesterday we were landing here stumbling through the pass."

"Yeah," he replied with an agreeing chuckle.

His demeanor switched to a determined one. He nodded trying once again taking in air and exhaling in effort to calm himself.

186 | P a g e

"Alright, do your thing," he replied signaling that he was getting ready to start.

"Okay," I responded closing my eyes. "Element Gamma and Epsilon, Fire and Earth command, Crystal barricade and fire wall."

The ground rumbled as a crystal barricade emerged from the ground. Once it was completely sealed I released my light energy creating a mini ozone layer.

"Okay, get to it," I replied sweating from the heat inside the barricade.

He nodded closing his eyes as he powered up. He waited a second in attempt to ignore the doubts creeping in his mind.

WHOOSH! His eyes burst into flames like two nuclear stars exploding. The transformation was instantaneous. He was right. His power spiked at levels that were beyond Aphrodite. It was unworldly, but there was a fierceness to it that sent chills up my spine. It was so raw and wild. It drop from meek to powerful every other second. It was so unstable.

"Okay," he replied. "This is the part where I generally have consciousness. The more I try to control it the less consciousness I have so I have to be careful. I'm going to try to push to the first level."

I nodded preparing myself.

WHOOSH! WHOOSH! WHOOSH! The energy pulsated like a heart exploding. Slowly the light around his eyes enlarged. The light seeped from his eye sockets and melted into his face. I could feel the ice building up on my barrier. I focused in trying to figure out what was going on.

"Oh, my gosh," I grunted summoning more to compensate for the power I was feeling.

I couldn't believe my eyes. The energy that surrounded Sam was like nothing I felt before. Light energy in the environment mutated into electricity. Faith energy burned from inside our bodies until we were covered in energy, but this energy was different. It looked like a energy was literally climbing inside of Sam and melding with his spirit.

"Sam," I replied worried. "When did this flame start?"

"I don't know. Why?" he replied struggling to control the energy as it fought to overtake his own.

I was sure he couldn't see it. As a matter of fact, I don't think anyone else noticed it. This power I had was weird. It was almost like I was looking at a literal ghost. It was in the shape of a huge lion and it looked ferocious.

"Well, that energy, you're right, it's not coming from elemental or subatomic control," I continued in awe. "It's like a...it's like a spirit."

His eyes grew big at the sound of my words.

"What?!" he replied.

KABOOSH! I watched in horror as the light took over his body after the sound of my words. Sam lost control. I was in a world of trouble. It was all the intruding spirit needed to take over. The spirit's energy swallowed Sam's energy until Sam was covered in the spirits energy.

"UGH!!" Sam let out fighting to regain control.

His body began to morph. His hair changed into a long lion's mane and his body grew fur until he was covered. I could faintly see Sam still putting up a fight, but he was fading fast. I had to do something.

SHATTER! The crystal barricade around me exploded into a million piece. I cowered as the shards of rock flew by me like sand.

"This is ridiculous," I replied cowering.

As I prepared to be frozen instantly. I was surprised to see that the energy layer I had was withstanding the environment. I couldn't believe my eyes. I looked myself up and down. I turned and watched the carnage as the power of the spirit ravaged the room around me.

"Are you kidding me?" I continued. "Sam!"

I couldn't believe it wasn't affecting me. The power was beyond anything I had seen since I arrived in the Heaven Realm. It was beyond just ridiculous. More surprising, was the fact that it wasn't effecting me at all. I couldn't understand how. I looked myself over trying to figure it. I couldn't believe what I saw.

"What the..." I replied staring up in awe.

My entire body was covered by a spirit similar to the one Sam had, but it was in the shape of a lamb. It glistened so bright it seemed like I was walking in the eye of a burning star. It melded with my spirit perfectly. It was such a congruent meld that I couldn't tell the difference between my energy and it. I look to the spirit, but it was more like a presence then anything. It felt so powerful and I felt so powerful with it.

"Tim, get out of here," Sam managed just before the spirit began to take total control.

"Sam, stay with me," I replied confidently. "Don't black out!"

Inside the spirits presence I felt invincible. It was beyond even that. I walked toward him. I flexed feeling the spirits power surge through me as the light covered my body. He fought a little longer, but he was out on his feet. Within a second or two he collapsed as the spirit took full control.

BOOM! WHAM! The spirit exploded with elemental power. It slammed me hard into a nearby wall knocking the air out of me.

"Sam," I wheezed out of breath. "Sam, wake up!"

His eyes were vacant. Nobody was home.

"It can't be controlled," said a voice that seemed to come from inside me.

It was the spirit. It had to be. Somehow it was communicating from inside me.

"Is he being possessed?" I replied willing to try anything.

The spirit was silent. As I did Sam stood up looking like a hybrid between a lion and a bodybuilder. He looked amazing. But it wasn't Sam. It just stood as power exploded from it. His eyes found me as a predator like glare covered his face. It was obvious this thing was looking for something to destroy.

"Is Sam there?" I asked hoping I could prompt a response from the silent spirit.

"The spirit can't be controlled," the voice inside me repeated.

What did it mean? I looked down as the light around me turned into a beautiful pearly white wool. Power flowed through me. I closed my eyes as the spirits words became clearer.

"The spirit cannot be controlled, but it can be contained. The lion needs the lamb," said the voice.

Its words sent me into a déjà vu like mode. Where had I heard that before? I racked my mind trying to remember.

WHOOSH! BOOM! Without warning Sam attacked. He was beyond fast. But with the power that flowed through me I was able to see everything so clearly. I dodged exploding using the energy I had around me to deflect him. I made sure not to hurt Sam, but I knew I had to incapacitate spirit.

"Sam, wake up!" I screamed.

"The lion and the lamb," said the voice. "The lion needs the lamb. The lamb needs the lion."

What is it talking about? I had no time to react.

"Sam," I replied as he geared up for another attack.

WHOOSH! OH NO! I gasped as he seemed to appear right in front of me. There was no way I could block or evade the blow and with the power I felt it was all over for me if he made contact.

"Stop!" said a voice that seemed to scream from inside of me.

Sam stopped hanging in limbo floating in mid-air. The spirit slowly dissipated before Sam fell hurdling back to the ground.

SLAM! He landed with Earth shattering force. I shot to his side using flash step as the spirit around me dissipated.

"Sam," I replied shaking him.

He groaned and sputtered before snapping up with a panic look on his face.

"Tim, get out of..." he blurted before stopping as he realized where he was. "Tim…what…what's…you're okay."

He looked me over with a grateful smile that seemed to tell his feelings without him saying a word. He was happy to black out and not come back to a corpse.

"I'm so sorry, man, I tried to control it," he replied pausing as something occurred to him. "Wait, how did you...this place... did...I mean, this place is a war zone. How did you survive?"

I paused trying to thank of a way to respond in which he would understand.

"Look, I don't really know. All I know is I think this power I have and the power you have is somehow connected to each other," I replied. "Regardless, this power of yours, I think you can control it."

"No way," he screamed. "Do you know what that was just like? It was like reliving every terrible thing that has ever happen to me. I'm never doing that again. Seriously, Tim, look at this place. Can you imagine what would happen if I used it in a stadium filled with people? No, they hate me enough. I'm not giving them more of a reason to keep me out of the academy."

"Sam, it's about more than that. I think this power of yours maybe the key to understanding my own power," I replied.

He shook his head adamantly.

"I'm not doing it again, Tim. I promise you I'll win, but I'm not using that thing. It was weird enough when I thought it was my own power, but if this is some spirit, Jade is right. Maybe we should hold off on using it until we know what we're dealing with. I mean, we did bring our Earth born bodies here. There's no telling what we brought with us," he continued.

"I know, but you didn't feel this thing. We've been around evil before. We've fought it. This spirit, it was different," I shot. "I think your attitude toward this spirit is the reason it's not melding with you. You're afraid of it."

"Tim, No!" he shot angrily. "I'm done with it. Just leave me alone, okay?! I should have never done this to begin with. It's just God's blessing that someone didn't get hurt. I'm not tapping into that power until I know it's not going to hurt anyone else."

He looked away regretfully as he fought to his feet. He stumbled as he walked over to his jacket. He grabbed it and stormed out.

"Sam," I replied as he continued not looking back.

"What the?"

As he opened the door Pete was coming in.

"What happened in here?" he replied looking the place over.

I paused not really wanting to explain. I rose to my feet trying to figure out what I was going to do next as Pete continued to look this place up and down like it was a crime scene.

"Nothing," I responded storming past Pete.

"Tim?" he replied confused.

"Nothing, Pete," I reiterated heading up the stairs. "Sam and I just had a spat. We're cool though, he just woke me up and we had some words about it."

Pete stared at me inquisitively still inspecting the room as I disappeared up the stairs. I hesitated as I walked past Sam's door. I went to knock, but I knew it wouldn't make a difference. Sam was adamant and things were too fresh. Nothing I said would change his mind after the emotion of the last incident still present. I had to give it time. I shook my head as I pulled my hand back and headed to my room. I pulled my clothes off, tossed them in a bin next to the bathroom, and crashed on my bed. I was minutes away from going back to sleep when the sound of a knock on my door caught my attention.

"Yeah," I replied agitated.

"Tim, are you and Sam okay?" Pete pressed.

"Pete, we're fine, I promise. Don't worry about it. You've had a long day. Go and get some sleep. You deserve it. Besides, we have another long day tomorrow," I shot climbing under the covers myself.

There was a second of silence before I finally heard his feet thumping down the hall. I sat up for another ten minutes just staring up at the ceiling. Was that why Michael sent me down there? Was this power good or evil? Thoughts flowed through my mind as I tried to make sense of it all. I threw the covers over my head and forced myself to lay down. I fell to sleep living yet another eventful day behind me, but I soon found out the day was the only thing I left behind. The eventful agenda and drama surrounding it was attached to me like a bad stench.

CHAPTER

17

On the

Eve

Of battle

On the eve battle

"What's up with you two?" Said a voice knocking me out of my trance.

The whole ride over on the transport I hadn't spoken. From the time I left my room I felt like I weighed a thousand pounds. The original adrenaline of the situation must have been carrying me because the moment I awoke my body felt heavy and I was sluggish.

"What?" I replied ignoring the obvious.

"What do you mean, what?" she replied mocking me. "You guys are slugging around like zombies. What happened last night?"

I looked over at Sam who was sitting at the back of the transport. He looked worse than I did. He sweated like he had a terrible fever and looked worse than I felt.

"I don't want to talk about it?" I replied too tired to explain.

"Well, if you're not going to talk about it at least stop acting like you're hung over," She retorted. "Eve's about to get into the biggest fight of her life and you and Sam are acting like you could care less."

"Sai, who cares?" I replied in frustrated tone.

My words caught the attention of everyone around me aside from Eve who sat in the front with earphones on.

"What?" Sai replied squinting like she was ready to explode.

The report from the night shot through me. It gave me such a realistic view of the trials and how much of it was pomp and glamour.

"Who cares?" I repeated defiantly without my voice raising at all. "This whole stupid competition is dumb. There are people in the real world who could be going to hell. The last thing on my mind is this competition. I don't care about it."

They all looked at me surprised by my words.

"Did you have another vision or something?" Uriah replied.

"No, he's just a brat," Jacob cut in. "I swear you are more emotional than these little girls."

"Shut up, Jacob," I fired back.

"Does it have something to do with the argument you and Sam had?" Pete added.

"Argument?" Sai replied staring a hole through me. "Were you guys fighting?"

Sam's attention raised at the sound of Sai's words. He gave me a pleading look begging me not to speak.

"No," I replied relenting. "Look, Michael showed up last night."

Sam's attention and demeanor changed along with everyone around me.

"What? When?" Sai added.

"Last night. He woke me up. He showed me a news segment where they were talking about the way things are back in the Earth Realm," I explained. "He chastised me saying that we needed to stop focusing on the stupid trials and pay attention to the reason we're really here."

"What was the news story about?" Pete pressed.

"Just, there are a lot of lost people and they're looking for answers," I replied. "And we aren't there to give it to them."

Jacob's demeanor changed. He almost seemed embarrassed as he slumped back down as we pulled up to the stadium.

"Wish me luck," Eve replied throwing her bag over her shoulder oblivious.

She was completely oblivious to the conversation going on around her. She seemed relatively normal and abnormally confident considering the fact that the girl she was fighting had put her sister in the hospital with extreme prejudice. We all nodded not wanting to alert her to the growing situation as she rose to exit.

"Tim," she replied bashfully. "Could you walk with me? Just until I get up to the entrance?"

Sai eyed me like if I said anything but yes she was going to punch me into another dimension. I rolled my eyes coyly and put a smile on as I rose to follow her. What a difference a month made. Just one ET month earlier I would have given my right arm for an opportunity to be able to coherently spend time with Eve, but now I was basically being pulled kicking and screaming.

"Good Luck, Eve," Danielle, Sai and Sam all said at varying times.

She nodded as we stepped off the transport. I looked up at the rainbow sky taking a second to embrace the world around me. It was so peaceful. It was so beautiful. There was no sun just an everlasting light that had no origin.

"Tim," Eve continued hesitantly.

"Yeah," I replied.

"Look, I know you're a little annoyed at me," she replied apologetically.

I looked at her completely confused about what she was referring to. I quickly changed my demeanor to save face.

"I am?" I replied coyly.

"Well, yeah, I know I haven't been friends with you that long, but I can tell you have been a little out of it all morning," she replied. "Considering you haven't spoken to me, I'm guessing you're still angry with me about last night."

Until she brought up b the incident from the night before I hadn't thought about the last time we spoke.

"Eve," I replied getting ready to come clean.

"No, seriously, I understand," she replied cutting. "I was being immature. I mean, it's not like were dating or anything like that."

She gave me an urging and hopeful look that I fell to pick up on because of the cluster of statements. She cleared her throat after a lasting second than continued.

"I know that, but you obviously know how I feel about you," she replied almost taking my breath away with her words.

"What?" I mustered unable to believe her words.

"I mean, I asked you out. I get then you were shy about things then. I guess things have changed since then. Don't you think? Maybe, just a little," she continued embarrassed by my none reply.

"Oh, ye-yeah, you mean how you feel about our friendship," I managed. "When you said…I thought you meant…but yeah, our friendship has changed."

She looked at me confused by my response. Then smiled pulling her hair behind her ear.

"I'd like to think we're good friends now," she replied. "I shouldn't have acted so jealous when it came to you two. You've been friends for a long time and I guess at times I feel jealous of that."

I nodded still reeling and trying to come back around after the initial excitement. My heart was in my throat.

"Well-um," I replied choking on my words. "You don't have anything to be jealous about, I guess. We have plenty of time to get to know each other and…"

I swallowed hard finally growing a backbone. This was the opportunity I had been waiting for. If it killed me I was going to take advantage of this chance.

"I know we're a little young," I replied getting ready to say the words I had been trying to work up the nerve to say for a little under a year. "But my dad said he met my mom when he was about our age. I'm not saying…I mean, I like Sai as a friend and I'm not…I mean, I never liked anybody before so I'm not totally sure what the difference is but…well, I think I know the difference."

She smiled an assuming smile that gave me a little more confidence.

"What are you trying to say?" she replied with a smile that melted me.

I paused to gather myself once more then took a deep breath and continued.

"I'm saying I want you to be, like, my girlfriend," I replied. "Yeah, I think I want you to be my girlfriend—girl…friend and person."

I cringed not even able to look her in the eye as I spoke. I wanted to turn around and walk away.

"You think you want me to be your girlfriend like person?" she replied with a joking smirk that made me feel even dumber.

I nodded looking at the ground as my very being crumbled. I would have rather taken another punch from one those demon spawns at that moment.

"Sorry," I replied trying to save face. "Just forget it."

"No, no, I won't forget it," she mocked raising my head and starring me in the eyes.

She smiled and planted a kiss on my cheek. I almost swallowed my tongue as my heart began to beat out of control.

"I won't forget it because it's one of the cutest things I've ever heard ," she said staring into my eyes lovingly. "Are you really asking me to be your girlfriend?"

I nodded bashfully.

"Tim Eli is asking me to be his girlfriend," she replied looking in the air smiling from ear to ear.

I couldn't believe her reaction. I thought I was terrible at hiding how I felt, but she acted as if she had no clue.

"I thought…I mean, the way you acted I thought you knew I liked you already," I mumbled.

She fumbled bashfully before shrugging in a relenting fashion.

"I thought maybe…but the way you act with Sai, I mean, it's hard to tell sometimes," she replied.

I rolled my eyes agitated by the constant accusations. It had been incessant. I shook my head in agitated manner.

"Why does everybody say that?" I replied with a frustrated sigh.

"Take a wild guess," she replied in a matter fact type tone.

"What do you mean?" I replied still oblivious. "Sai is my best friend, nothing else, Eve. My gosh, you guys are really starting to agitate me with this."

"Sai said something similar last night," she replied raising her hands in surrender. "I get it. I just…I don't have a bond like that with…you know a boy. It's odd. Most boys generally only talk to me when they have a crush on me. To be honest, before this, I didn't have one male friend. I guess, it's going to take some time for me to get used to."

"Don't worry about it. It's really not you. It's Jacob and Luke. They've been saying it since we were small kids. It was hard enough ignoring it when it was just them. Now the whole freaking Heaven Realm is in on the joke," I angrily grunted.

I realized the opportunity I was letting slip as I looked into her beautiful brown eyes. She was beyond pretty and I couldn't believe she actually liked me. I kept waiting on a lever to pull dropping me back in to reality. It was an other worldly experience. She showcased a look that matched mine and deep down she felt the experience was as surreal as I did. I fought the butterflies swirling in my stomach and bravely entered her space bashfully lowering my head as she smiled in a flirtatious manner at my actions.

"Regardless, that aside, I will officially answer your question," she replied locking fingers with me as we both stepped forward closing the small distance between as I wrapped my arms around her. "I would love to be your girlfriend—like person."

I chuckled acknowledging her joke. I had no idea what to do next. I held her staring into her eyes lost in her beauty.

"Okay, so what do we do now?" I replied turning to her. "How does this work? What are the rules?"

She shrugged then stood for a second thinking about the question.

"I guess the same thing we've been doing except more relationship—like," she assumed with a snicker. "I mean, we can walk and hold hands and stuff, and....kiss...I guess...if you want to...if that isn't too forward."

I almost buckled at her words. The thought of kissing her made my heart skip with excitement. I chuckled as my nerves started to takeover.

"Have you...you know, ever kissed someone before?" I managed causing her face to turn red with embarrassment as she shook her head no.

"Have you?" she responded timidly.

"Just, Sai," I responded before grimacing as my gaffe.

She chuckled causing my heart to slow.

"Have you ever intentionally kissed someone?" she continued playfully.

I mimicked her actions from before. I shook my head bashfully lowering it. She placed her hand on my chin and forced me to look her in the eyes as she slowly moved her lips toward mine. It was like I was living out my greatest fantasy from Angel Haven as I met her actions pressing my lips into hers. Her lips were soft and the act melted me as I maneuvered around to her cheek kissing her again as we embraced each other in a hug.

"How was that?" she whispered in my ear exhaling like she just downed her favorite milkshake.

I wanted to say it was the best thing I ever felt, but truthfully it wasn't. The kiss was a culmination of close to two years of unrequited affection for the girl. It was amazing, but I would be lying if I said it made me feel the way the kiss Sai and I shared in the office made me feel. It just didn't have the same electricity as the haunting and confusing first kiss. It was more than enough to confuse me. I pushed the feelings away as the difference between my first real kiss, and this one.

"It was amazing," I uttered with a chuckle.

She rested her head on my shoulder as if she was trying to find resemblance peace before the chaos. I tried to block out the thought of her being hurt like Beth as long as I could, but the prospect had me nervous. I squeezed the girl not wanting to release her to be hurt.

"I'll be okay," she whispered sensing my heavy heart.

I nodded releasing her as she kissed me once more causing me to lowered my head in an embarrassed manner.

"Okay," I replied holding on to her hand.

"Well, whatever happens, we'll be together, right?" she replied squeezing my hands and pulling me toward the arena. "But for now, I'm Tim Eli's girlfriend and that's enough for me."

It felt completely weird initially. I thought there would be a different overall feeling, but everything felt the same as it did before. I followed as she released my arms and began to talk to me as she walked backpedaling.

"I can't wait to tell Sai," she replied. "Ignoring the fact that I might be in the hospital tomorrow, this is the best day of my life."

"M—mine too," I replied shaky.

"Yeah, I can tell from your tone," she replied mocking me.

I lowered my head as we entered a crowd of people.

"Oh, sorry," I replied apologetically. "It's just hard to be happy when my girlfriend could be lying in a hospital bed in an hour."

"Thanks, for the confidence, Tim," she responded.

I stared at her a little irked by her demeanor. It was like she wasn't taking the danger seriously.

"Eve," I uttered pressing her to stop giving me a hard time.

"I'm just joking," she replied laughing.

WHACK! I recoiled as she smashed into Kadmiel. The girl stood purposely blocking her way into the entrance in an attempt to intimidate the girl. Eve quickly turned around and recoiled sternly staring at her.

"Watch where you're going, Theta," she replied in a cocky tone. "I wouldn't want you to get hurt before I can put you in a hospital bed next to your sister. You know, twin beds for the twins. Wouldn't that be sweet."

Her words seem to light a fire under Eve as I could physically feel her faith energy rise as she stared at Kadmiel sternly without a reply. Kadmiel smiled as she tossed her bag over her shoulder shaking her head unimpressed as she entered the arena. Eve's energy slowly went back down as the girl disappeared into the double doors.

"I almost forgot why I'm here," she replied looking determined as she stared at the arena.

"Are you okay?" I replied. "I mean really?"

"Yes, I'm fine or I think I'll be fine," Eve replied. "I have my best friend and my boyfriend in my corner. What could go wrong, right?"

I gave her a cynical look accepting her invitation to be in her box. She gave me a hug and turned taking a deep breath and before entering the arena.

"Eve, please be careful. I can't let what happened to Beth happen to you. I won't," I shot causing the smile to drain from her face as she gave me an affirming nod before she disappeared through the portal.

"Good luck," I replied like a worried parent.

I was focused on the real world, but regardless of how I felt about the trials, my friends were in danger and that was something I had forgot about in the midst of my anger with Sam and the glitz and glamour of the event. I watched her as she disappeared into the arena. I felt a hand come down on my shoulder snapping me out of my gaze.

"Me and you," I heard a familiar voice say. "We're Eve's hired help this time around. This is my first time so you're going to have to walk me through this stuff."

I turned to see Sai standing with a smile and initially of feeling guilt filled me and I couldn't explain it. She was beautiful as usual, but the way the light hit her face as I turned made her look like an angel as she smiled. I turned away as I replied afraid that she would sense how in trance she had me in that moment. I quickly composed myself before moving to lead the girl through the portal hole.

"It'll be my pleasure Miss Hikari," I replied with a nod and a smile.

She looked surprised by my demeanor leaning back in a mocking manner. She stepped back and looked me over like she was checking to see if it was actually me.

"What?" I replied playing coy.

"What happened?" she replied looking at me with an intrusive stare than at the vacant spot Eve exited from.

I wanted to tell her, but if it came out at that point, I would have had to sing it as good as it felt to say Eve Timilla was my girlfriend.

"Nothing," I replied bursting.

"Tim," she replied in a demanding tone.

"I'll tell you later I promise, but right now, we have to help Eve with her trial," I replied deflecting the conversation.

She stared at me with a stubborn look before finally relenting.

"Well, whatever it was, it did a lot for your morale," she replied walking up to the door and opening it before stepping to the side and letting me enter.

I was caught between feelings of worry and euphoria. I was happy that I could say my two year goal was accomplished. I couldn't wait to tell Pete and Sam. I was bursting at the seams, but at the same time Kadmiel sounded ruthless and she didn't look like she was going to hold her punches like she did with Beth and that prospect had me terrified.

"Well, it put things in perspective," I replied.

She glared at me one last time with a prying stare before rolling her eyes in a relenting fashion.

"Regardless, it's good to hear," she replied sighing.

I turned to see the rest of the legion hot on our heels along with Jade and Max. They talked among each other not even noticing us as we went ahead of them into the arena.

"After you," she joked continuing her concierge imitation opening the door with a playful bow.

I shook my head and returned the favor when we got to the isolation room. She smiled tilting her head graciously.

"See, it's not hard to not be a jerk," she poked.

"Ha, ha, ha…just get in the room," I shot back.

The opening ceremonies again seemed to drag on as Sai and I sat waiting impatiently. I sat leaning in my chair with my feet on the dashboard interface.

"Tim, put your feet down," Sai replied slapping my boots down.

"Excuse me, mom," I replied.

She shook her head chuckling to herself as I leaned forward playfully resting my head on my forearm pretending to be sleep.

"Wake me up when it starts," I replied.

She cut her eyes at me playfully offended.

"You haven't seen me in days, and this is how you react to being locked in a room with me for a few minutes," she joked. "And I had such high hopes after you showed up to my bed side."

Her words brought me back to the initial feeling I felt seeing her lying unconscious on her bed and my face showcased as much. She showed a regretful demeanor than quickly apologized.

"I'm sorry," she replied with a grin. "Too soon?"

"It's fine. It's just I never knew how much of who I am is wrapped up in my relationship with you," I muttered staring forward to kill the awkwardness of the moment. "I was lost without you."

She chuckled blushing flattered by my words.

"What can I say? I love you, kid," I responded forcing myself to look her in the eye so that she understood that the depth of my words were serious.

She stared at me unable to respond initially. She composed herself turning back to the screen unable to hold back a smile.

"I love you too, idiot," she shot bashfully melting under the seriousness of my stare.

I chuckled playfully amused by her awkwardness about me being so affectionate. Eve and Kadmiel finally appeared on the screen as the crowd cheered loudly. Sai and I exchanged looks that signified the changing of dynamic as we turned to the screen.

"You ready, Eve?" Sai asked.

Eve took a deep breath calming herself.

"Yeah, I'm fine," she replied.

Kadmiel laughed mockingly looking Eve over.

"You're even scrawnier than your sister was," she replied. "Let's save time and you a lot of pain and just forfeit the trial. Either way this thing is ending with us going up 3-1."

Eve stared her over without saying a word. She pulled her twin dagger pistols from their holsters and stared them down before pointing them at Kadmiel.

"This isn't Earth sweetie," Kadmiel replied mockingly. "You're going to need more than just cold steel."

As she spoke she began to power up to her first stage.

"Well, we'll see won't we," Eve replied her pistol still aimed at the girl.

WHOOSH! Eve focused her pistols on a blur as Kadmiel disappeared and shot toward her.

"Stay on your toes, Eve," Sai warned.

POW! BANG! BANG! BANG! Eve fired shots at Kadmiel's trailing blurs but she wasn't close to hitting her.

BOOM! BANG! BANG! BANG! BANG! Kadmiel swung leveling a nearby pillar as Eve narrowly dodged still firing from the hip as she barreled rolled out of the way.

"I'm coming, princess," Kadmiel warned.

BLOCK! BAM! BANG! BANG! Kadmiel rammed into Eve with a shoulder charge that sent her flipping. Eve was so agile that she righted her ship and fired downwind as Kadmiel tried to capitalize.

"Great Job, Eve," I encouraged on pins and needles.

Kadmiel wiped the dust off her armor as she smiled staring Eve down impressed with her speed and reflexes.

"So, you're not as pathetic as your sister after all," Kadmiel continued to mock.

I thought she bought seconds at best. I had no confidence in Eve's chance against this girl. My heart was beating faster with every second that passed.

"You have no idea," Eve shot back catching us off guard.

WHAM! UGH! She changed direction with speed that was unworldly and blasted Kadmiel with a blow that almost knocked the teeth out of her mouth. Kadmiel let out a gasp that made me cringe. Her body bounced and landed into a nearby pillar as the girl grimaced fighting to understand what happened. The power Eve struck with was on another level.

"That was for bumping into me in the hallway," Eve replied pointing her guns at Kadmiel as she walked toward her like a predator stalking its prey. "I was getting some pretty important news at the time and you almost ruined it for me."

Sai looked at me with an inquisitive stare before turning back to the battle.

"Bravo," Kadmiel replied wiping the blood from her mouth.

WHOOSH! BANG! BANG! BANG! BANG! Kadmiel disappeared as Eve fired shots at her.

Eve surveyed the layout using her extended pistols as a scope searching for Kadmiel.

"So you're hiding now?" Eve replied. "I know you're not afraid of scrawny little ol' me."

WHAM! Eve dodged as Kadmiel took another swipe at her smashing into the ground with a looping punch that leveled the terrain around her. Her speed and reflexes were off the chart. Kadmiel was visibly frustrated as she surveyed the ground looking for the girl, but Eve was like a flicker of electricity.

"I'm going to hurt you for that?" Kadmiel replied knocking the rubble of her shoulder. "I don't run and I don't hide from anyone."

She surveyed the ground as Eve appeared across the way in a flicker with her pistols still extended. To the untrained eye her pistols were useless, but I knew better. The shots obscured Kadmiel's dash just long enough for Eve to predict her moves. It was so genius, and with Eve's natural fighting skill we had no real advice to give her. She was holding her own, all on her own.

BANG! BANG! PING! PING! Eve fired lighting her up with shots ricocheting them off of Kadmiel's armor.

"You're a fast-little thing aren't you," Kadmiel replied shielding herself.

SWRRLL! Eve let out a whistle that dropped Kadmiel to her knees.

"Heads up," Eve replied.

PWUGH! Eve appeared in front her in a crouching stance socking her with an uppercut that nearly knocked her head off. Kadmiel soared high in the air from the impact smashing hard into a nearby pillar.

"That was for calling my scrawny," Eve replied standing defiantly still pointing the pistols at her.

Eve cautiously approached Kadmiel's landing spot with her pistols still aimed at the girl. Seconds passed as everyone in the crowd cheered. We waited impatiently anticipating what was coming next.

"You little!" Kadmiel exclaimed in a deafening tone.

RAWWH! The pillar exploded as Kadmiel appeared her hair was glistening. It took her the full fight to use her anointed skill against Beth. It didn't take her long to realize she didn't stand a chance against Eve without it. She exploded as her hair grew signifying she had gone to the next level. Her power seemed to suck the life from Eve as she got distance and collapsed shielding herself behind a nearby pillar breathing fast suffocating breaths.

"Where are you?" Kadmiel screamed throwing a pillar like it was weightless.

"Eve, stay hid?" Sai replied.

I shook my head in awe. Her power was unreal. The ground cracked under her feet with every step that she took. Her hair had grown substantially since her power spike. It was too soon to say if Eve was outmatched or not, but judging by Kadmiel's faith energy and experience, it was apparent Eve had an uphill battle at the least.

"Thanks for the genius idea," Eve replied peaking around one of the pillars. "What's your next string of advice, block the next time she throws a punch?"

"Don't tell me you're hiding after all your big talk and boasting?" Kadmiel replied stomping and surveying the layout.

Oddly there wasn't a spike in Eve's biorhythm. She was suspiciously calm although she played a dishelmed demeanor to Sai. I knew better because of the extra touch sensory trait I had. She was like a rock in the midst of all the chaos around her.

"Please tell me you have a plan?" Sai shot.

"Yeah," Eve sighed pulling her pistols from their holsters.

BANG! BANG! PING! PING! Eve fired shots at Kadmiel that the ultra-powered girl swatted like flies.

"Hopefully that wasn't it," Sai added placing her hand on her forehead in a worried manner.

UGH! Eve let out. Before she could Kadmiel appeared blocking her way with a devious smirk.

"Hi, sweetheart. Remember me," she antagonized standing confidently blocking the Eve's path. "I told you I'd catch you."

"Yeah, well, seeing is believing," Eve shot back with a regret-filled playful smile.

WHAM! A sickening sound a punch turned my stomach as Eve moved to retreat in the opposite direction.

"Eve!" Sai let out.

KABOOM! SMASH! BOOM! Kadmiel swatted her with a blow that sent her flying like a bullet through about three or four pillars. She flipped wildly before slamming against the stadium wall and collapsing in a heap on the ground.

"Eve, Are you okay?" I added.

"Seriously, Tim?!" Eve let out exhaling in a pain-filled groan. "I just got smacked through about four walls before hitting a stone barrier. Other than that, I'm just peachy. How do you think I'm doing, Tim?"

UGH! Eve spit blood and wipe the remaining blood from her mouth. I stared at Sai afraid to intervene for fear of saying something stupid. Me and Sai added little to no advice to the girl. The truth was Eve and Beth fighting styles were vastly different and the advantages of Beth's versatility weren't at Eve's disposal. I could tell the girl was growing impatient with us giving her little to nothing but moral aid since the duel started.

"My gosh that hurt," Eve replied struggling to her feet.

WHAM! EXPLODE! Eve narrowly dodged as Kadmiel went for a knockout blow obliterating the wall directly behind her.

"Shut your trap, girl!" Kadmiel responded standing next to the spot her power explode through.

POW! POW! BANG! BANG! Eve let out shots that ricocheted off Kadmiel's armor.

"GRRR!" Kadmiel let out shooting towards Eve.

"Eve, watch out!" Sai exclaimed.

It was too late. Before she could move Kadmiel was restricting her passage in a manner identical to the way she did before.

"Eve, don't!" I warned predicting the girl's move before she made it.

CLUTCH! She flashed in front of Eve grabbing her around her wrists holding her up by her arms like she was a baby.

"My gosh, your hard girl to get a hold of," Kadmiel chuckled as Eve fought to free herself.

UGH! SWIFT! Eve sent a knee into her throat causing her to let go before light stepping to the other side of the arena.

"Eve!" I exclaimed seeing Kadmiel's path immediately. "She's still…"

SWIFT! BAM! BOOM! Before Eve could prepare for the blow Kadmiel had struck with a shoulder block that sent her skipping like a stone in a pond. She pinged off the ground then hard into a nearby wall landed on her side in a heap.

"OUCH!" Eve let out writhing in pain as she rolled over to a crawl.

"Eve, shake it off, she still coming," Sai replied.

Kadmiel stalked her in a mocking tone as she crawled trying to regain her bearings.

"Is it too late to admit I was wrong?" Eve continued coughing up blood once again.

"Eve, will you stop joking around!" I shot forcefully. "Do you realize this girl is trying to seriously injure you? Did you miss that?"

Eve grimaced once again spitting blood before wiping the remainder of it off her mouth.

"Trust me, Tim, I've noticed," she shot mimicking my words from days earlier.

I sighed frustrated with her actions turning to Sai with a irritated head shake before Kadmiel tipped off her next attack

"Eve, look out!" I ordered a second too late.

Kadmiel grabbed her and slammed her into a nearby wall.

BANG! BANG! PING! PING! Eve fired at point blank range as Kadmiel moved her head from side to side dodging each shot.

"Give me this?" Kadmiel replied snatching her pistols and tossing them to the side.

"Element Alpha, Light Command, Solar Glares," Eve light out.

POP! POP! POP! Eve let out a firecracker like light display in point blank range of Kadmiel's face in a last ditch effort to get away. Kadmiel recoiled from the explosion dropping Eve in the process. I didn't know if the girl was going by the flight of her seat or if it was stuff she had planned, but she was resourceful. Every time it seemed the girl had her dead to rights she would pull something out of her bag of tricks to give her more time. It had me on edge, but up to that point, she hadn't taken much damage.

"Great Job, Eve, now get some distance," Sai urged her.

But Eve to our surprise she landed on her knees like she was powerless. The attack seemed to be all she could managed. To me it made no sense, that move was child's play and Eve was one of our powerful team members. She had reserves that shouldn't have been dented by such a meek attack. None of it made sense to me. Her demeanor also was off-putting. It was like she never took the fight serious. She pretended to be following my lead, but Eve and I handle conflict different. I was more laid back naturally. Eve was pure carnage when she was angry, but from the start she was taking the fight like it was a sparring session. She reserved most of her anger toward us and did little more than provoke Kadmiel. I watched trying to make sense of things as Kadmiel exploded more angry than ever. She grunted angrily surveying the layout as her hair grew longer and her power exploded to an even higher level.

"Still got some fight in you, huh?" she replied walking over to Eve. "You're sister did too. We all saw how that ended."

HEAVE! BLAP! BOOM! She grabbed Eve by her armored shirt and tossed her. She crashed into a nearby pillar then flopped awkwardly into the other side of the arena wall.

"Eve," Sai replied visibly angry.

AWWW! Eve grunted rubbing her back before flipping over and resting helplessly.

"Eve, you have got to get up and get some distance," I ordered panicking as she lay writhing in pain.

This girl was a loose cannon and her teammates stated she had a violent temper. I could only imagine what was in store for Eve if she lost her head.

SWIFT! BOOM! Kadmiel leaped into the air landing hard on the ground inches away from Eve's down body.

"This all could have been easy," she mocked cracking her knuckles. "I didn't want to put someone else in the hospital, but you brats are the thickest chicks on the planet."

WHAM! AWWW! She punted Eve like a rag doll as Eve let out a blood curdling grunt. She bounced across the sand before rolling into a heap about a hundred yards away. My heart went into my throat afraid I was going to have to witness another vicious beating. Eve lay exhaling holding her arm before fighting to her feet.

"Awe, did I hurt your wittle arm?" Kadmiel replied chuckling to herself.

"I'm going to hurt you for that?" Eve replied cradling her visibly broken arm.

"You're still talking?" Kadmiel replied exasperated. "I've beaten the tar out of you and you're still talking."

"Why..."

BOOM! She leveled Eve with a punch that nearly took her head off.

"Don't..."

WHAM! She hit her with another.

"You..."

BOOM! She continued with another.

"Just..."

WHAM! She fired again as Eve's head flew from right to left with every blow.

"Shut your mouth," She finally finished as Eve collapsed face first.

She grinned as she stood over Eve confidently.

"I told you I was going to put you in a matching hospital bed with you sister, didn't I?" Kadmiel continued picking her up by her hair as Eve writhed in pain. "I'm a girl of my word."

SWIFT! AWWWW! We watched in disbelief as Eve snatched a handful of hair in a blaze of speed that was beyond even Kadmiel's. Kadmiel dropped to one knee in pain grabbing at Eve feebly as she shot past her.

"Oh, yeah, I forgot about you saying that," Eve replied tossing the hair in the air like confetti.

"Eve?" Sai replied in awe. "How did you do that?"

Kadmiel stared at Eve with a demeanor that seemed to beg the same question. Eve tossed her hair back exposing her face. It was spotless, not a mark on it. After the beating she had just taken it was an amazing sight that sparked cheers from the crowd that was deafening.

"Let's just say I wasn't Mrs. Goodwin's favorite for nothing," Eve replied standing in a rejuvenated stance. "I played lead two years in a row. You don't do that without learning a few tricks about acting."

Sai shook her head with a chuckle. I had spent most of our drama days sleep in the crowd, but I would awake occasionally to take a rare chance to stare at Eve without suspicion. I soaked it up, maybe to the extent that I missed the point of the play to begin with, so it wasn't surprising that I didn't get Eve's reference right away.

"Bull," Kadmiel fired infuriated. "There no way you could have taken my blows at tier 3. There is no way. I've decapitated A-Class rogues with those blows."

Eve chuckled.

"See, there is something about us twins that you may or may not know," Eve continued catching our attention. "We're alike in more ways than you know."

Kadmiel's fist clinched as she stared at Eve like she wanted to tear her apart.

"Yeah, right, you and that flake are nothing alike," Kadmiel continued.

"That's my sister!" Eve replied showing an anger that exploded for the first time causing a faint navy blue light to leak from her eyes.

Kadmiel cut her eyes realizing she had finally cut into the sarcastic demeanor Eve had been showcasing from the beginning of the fight. I sat back realizing every intuition I had was right. I knew something seemed off about the whole fight. Now it made sense. Eve was playing possum the entire time and I had no idea what the reasoning for doing it was. Eve calmed herself showcasing a fake smile as I sat forward hoping for a plausible explanation for why she would make us believe she was being beaten.

"We are alike. I may not be into books and computers...or maybe I am...or I used to be...regardless, we share the same traits. The only difference is my sister while smart is nowhere near as cunning or shrewd as I am. In retrospect I am as smart as my sister but nowhere near as nice," Eve warned staring the girl down with a look that I saw once before.

The look was the look I saw in Eve's face the night before Beth's duel. It was the face she showcased before she completely lost control of her emotions. It was on display, and the BAU vibes I was picking up were so cold they terrified me.

"Yeah, right," Kadmiel replied showing a slight bit of concern in her voice. "You're bluffing."

Eve smiled in a mocking manner.

"Am I?" Eve replied running her hands over her face showcasing its flawless condition. "Every step you've taken, every move you've made, I have been one step ahead of. Every advantage you thought you were gaining was putting you exactly where I needed you to be. You idiot."

Kadmiel had a response to Eve's words that sparked a physical reaction that put me on edge. Even with the girl's awesome power the confidence and anger emitting from Eve had me more on Edge. I turned to Sai as she gave me a look begging for insight on what's going on. Before I could respond Kadmiel cut in.

"What did you say to me?" She replied snarling.

Eve clinched her fist staring at Kadmiel with an unflinching glare.

"Don't worry about what I said, that doesn't matter," She replied with extreme vitriol seeping out with every word. "Hear what I'm saying. I'm going to beat the crap out of you for what you did to my sister."

"Eve stop it!" Sai replied. "You said this wasn't about that."

Eve cracked her neck in a cold manner as she stared at the girl begging for her to make a move.

"No, I said I challenged her because I thought I could beat her," Eve replied.

I turned to Sai shaking my head in disbelief before pressing down on the intercom.

"No, you said this wasn't about your sister," I fired. "Eve, you lied to us and you lied to the council. You're going to forfeit the match."

Eve exploded with power until it looked like her body was covered in an inferno like fire. I said earlier that I had no idea how powerful she was, but this, this was on a whole new level. I thought back to our training and Jade's words after Eve revealed that she was able to tap into her abilities in the physical world. He said that she had to be exceptionally powerful, but I never expected this. I could actually feel her power and it was extraordinary and her anger seemed to be feeding it. Even Kadmiel seemed shaken by the girl's immense power. I thought back to the

Hannoch Simulation and the display she put on with only five percent of her power, and all I felt was panic. Eve was proned to go over the edge in normal situations. I could only imagine what she had in store for someone who violated and humiliated her sister in the way Kadmiel did. She stood staring the girl down as she responded to our accusations.

"I didn't lie, this isn't about my sister," she replied as the flames began to change exploding into a blue-ish orange blend. "It's about me!"

"How is she doing that?" I asked staring in awe.

"It's her sound elements. It amplifies her other abilities," Sai replied. "I knew she was amazing, but she purposely held this back from me and Pete. She cook this up on her own. My guess is she didn't want us interfering with her plans. Man, Eve!"

Sai stared at the girl helplessly as she absorbed all the sound all around her as her power continued to climb. Kadmiel was to ignorant to realize the danger she was in. She laughed at the sight trying to hide her earlier reservations in an attempt to seem confident.

"Do you really think this is what Beth would have wanted?" Sai continued trying to talk sense into her.

"Right now, I really don't care," she replied emotionless. "It was my job to protect her. I should have done something, and I didn't. I let her get beat half to death."

"Yep, and the same is about to happen to you," Kadmiel replied pulling out her sword.

I rolled my eyes in frustration at the girl's stupidity.

"My gosh, these two are like peas in a pod," I shot in frustration. "She's as bad as Eve."

"Is that so?" Eve replied stretching her neck now showcasing a steady stream of rage.

Before we blinked she regained her pistols. Kadmiel stared at her and chuckled arrogantly.

"You are fast. I'll give you that," She mocked with a laugh. "But that won't be a problem once I go to tier 4."

Eve powered up even higher.

"And what? You expect me to sit by twiddling my thumbs while you do it," Eve shot.

SWIFT! SLICE! AWWW! Eve shot slicing another piece of Kadmiel's hair dropping the girl to her knees before she could even think about powering up again.

"You little pest," Kadmiel replied grabbing her hair wincing in pain.

"What's going on?" I asked oblivious to what was happening. "Why is Eve targeting her hair?"

"It's her Achilles heel," Sai replied.

"Her what?" I replied.

"Have you ever heard the story of Achilles, the demi-god," Sai replied before answering her own question by staring at the dense look on my face. "Don't answer that...He was a demi-god who had a weak spot on his heel. It's where we get the term Achilles heel or the member the Achilles tendon. Like Achilles us Doms have a weak spot that is vulnerable to attack. It's a fail-safe in case we ever rebel or turn."

"So, you're saying Kadmiel's hair is her weak spot?" I deducted. "I think Jade said something about that during our training, but he said you guys guarded that secret with your lives. How did Eve find it?"

Sai shrugged apologetically.

"I don't know I wasn't here," Sai replied. "I didn't see the last fight."

"It was big mouth over here," Eve broke in. "Her big fat mouth. She let it leak when she bragging about putting my sister in the hospital so it was hard to ignore. She let it slip that she was Nazarene or Nazirite. You know like Samson."

Kadmiel's jaw clinched at the sound of Eve's words.

"She said she took pride in your Nazirite heritage. It sounded familiar to me, so I went and looked it up and the story of Samson stuck out to me. You know the hot head whose power was linked to his hair. Sound like someone you know?" she mocked pointing her pistol at the girl. "Judges 13:7 'You will become pregnant and give birth to a son. You must not drink wine or any other alcoholic drink nor eat any forbidden food. For your son will be dedicated to God as a Nazirite from the moment of his birth until the day of his death.' From that point on I knew it was linked. I went back and looked at your battle with my sister and I noticed that every time you went to another level the length of your hair grew. You were pegged from that moment on. The beginning of the match was a ploy. I took a snippet of your hair to see if it actually weakened you, and my assumptions were confirmed each time. From that point on I pushed you so that you could keep feeding yourself power thus making your hair longer and easier to target. Like I said before, every step you took, and every move you made put you precisely where I wanted you to be."

"That's impossible, my hair is fortified solid gold light energy. The only thing that could pierce it is condensed light energy, or a lightning bolt," She said fuming.

Eve smiled deviously as Sai and I shook our heads not knowing if we should be angry or impressed. She pulled her remaining pistol from its holster bringing both the guns together in a showcasing manner.

"Oh, that," she replied mockingly surveying the pistols. "You remember that whole wine thing from the passage. Well, these pistols happened to be dipped then crystallized in the Heaven Realms most expensive brand. Not that the price matters or anything, but I am a girl who tends to look for the best."

Kadmiel fumed as she stared her down.

"You little earthborn scum," she replied dashing at her.

DODGE! SLICE! WHAM! Eve sidestepped her like it was child's play ducking under her outstretched blow and slicing her hair as she countered with a shoulder blow sending the helpless girl into a nearby pillar.

"Like I said, every time you think you're getting closer, you're right we're I need you to be...and that's three steps behind me," she replied walking over to her with hair blowing in the wind.

The crowd was no longer cheering. There was a deaf silence as Eve ignored the scene and continued toward Kadmiel.

"I am Kadmiel Bahir, a true Nazarite," she replied. "I will not embarrass my family by losing to an earthborn unknown with no extraordinary heritage."

BOOM! SLICE! KABOOM! Kadmiel exploded in power but before anyone could blink Eve was clipping yet another strand of her hair. As Kadmiel dropped to her knees once again as Eve finished her off with a roundhouse that almost snapped her in half.

"Yeah, Yeah, Yeah," Eve replied coldly mocking the girl. "I really don't care."

She crumbled falling to her hands and knees as Eve stood over her with a cold-blooded look in her eyes.

"No one can withstand my blows. How could you do it?" Kadmiel replied fighting to her feet. "There's no way."

"Genius, I'm a sound user," Eve replied glaring at her with an emotionless demeanor that gave me that creeps. "I started training with Uriah the minute we got here. After a couple of lesson with him I learned to control external sounds. Everything in existence has a sound wave. Uriah taught me to control the sounds around me, but even he had no idea how well I learned what he taught me. Even the most experienced sound users don't know how to control sound in real time. Most are time or precept virts. They don't have the traits to pull it off. At least not at my level. But even with my heightened touch and reflexes it was a struggle. But eventually I got it. After a couple days I could stop a butterflies wings from flapping without disturbing its flight."

KUPT! She mocked the girl kicking her over mirroring the scene with Beth days before. She trailed the girl as she fought to stand.

"Controlling an unsuspecting hot head was elementary. Your punch gives off a slight sound vibration that I simply used as a buffer. Add in some opportune dramatics, physical acting, a little bit of fake blood, and it wasn't hard to conceal the fact that none of your blows ever touched me. I just needed you to believe they did. The more powerful you became the denser the sound wave became. Do you get it, yet, genius? It's just like you told my sister, you never had a chance."

"Yeah, and I'm going to crush you like I did your sister," Kadmiel replied shooting toward Eve yet again.

WHAM! Eve caught her in mid-flight with a leaping front kick. Kadmiel exploded off of her boot like a soccer ball of a strikers toe.

HORRRRN! A Siren exploded causing everyone in the stadium to groan.

"Man," Sai replied flopping in her seat annoyed.

"What? What's going on?" I replied oblivious.

Sai shook her head.

"The Validity of the Duel has been challenged," she replied.

"What do you mean? Is Eve being kicked out or something?" I pressed.

"No, it's about whether or not the trial will be forfeited," she answered solemnly.

"So, is the trial over?" I questioned.

Judging by Eve's demeanor it wasn't. She exploded in power. A blue orb appeared in front of her as she stood unaffected by the sound of the horn.

"This is for electrocuting my sister to force her to give in," she replied sending an orb toward her.

ZOOM! WHAM! BOOM! AHHHH! The orb hit Kadmiel's lifeless body with shattering impact that sent her flying into a nearby wall causing the girl to howl in pain.

"Eve stop it's over," Sai replied standing up.

"She wishes," Eve replied powering up for another attack.

SWIFT! ZOOM! BOOM! Eve rocketed herself into the air like a missile then plummeted toward Kadmiel landing with pulverizing force. Kadmiel coughed up blood as Eve turned her heel and flicked Kadmiel's lifeless body to the side like gum off the bottom of her shoes.

"Eve, I said stop!" Sai warned as Eve geared up for another attack.

Tears streamed down Eve's eyes as power seemed to surge all around her.

"Sai, you didn't see what she did to my sister. She could've just beat her, but she didn't just do that. She embarrassed her and tried to force her to give in. No!" she uttered booting the girl into the air once more.

WHAM! WHAM! WHAM! WHAM! She went into overdrive mimicking the attack Kadmiel used on her sister pulverizing the girl's lifeless body as we watched on in horror. I could understand why Eve was doing what she was doing and a part of me wanted to see the girl get what she deserved, but after stumbling in on the Alphas I realized the girl was a person with flaws much like Eve. It humanized her. I couldn't fight the sympathy I felt for her.

"Eve, what does this prove!" Sai shot angrily screaming into the intercom. "Whether you do this or not, that still happened!"

"Where are the proctors?" I shot turning to Sai.

"The siren signals the validity will be challenged afterwards. It doesn't stop the match. They still have to wait until one combatant can't compete," Sai explained staring at Eve in a begging manner as Kadmiel's body landed with a hard thud.

Eve landed seconds later marching toward the girl again.

"That's enough, Eve!" Sai responded. "Just finish it."

"I'll finish it when she says she gives up," Eve shot stalking the girl with an emotionless demeanor. "Isn't that what she tried to do to Beth? Embarrass her for doing nothing more than trying. Do you know the damage she's done to my sister? No, she's going to pay for that if it's the last thing I'll do."

SWIFT! SWIFT! BOOM! As Eve shot in for her next attack Sai exploded through the nearby wall. Before she could strike Sai shot in her path shielding Kadmiel.

"Stop!" Sai standing in direct line of the girl's path.

Sai wasn't moving and Eve wasn't stopping. This wasn't good. I stood not knowing what to do.

SWIFT! WHIF! I stood an awe as Sai suddenly shot toward Eve.

BOOM! The paths collided. I had no other choice. I had to react. I didn't have time to think. I shot toward the exploded dust cloud. I paused in my tracks at the scene. When the dust settled Sai stood cradling an emotionally distraught Eve. The girls were in an embrace as Eve sobbed on Sai's shoulder like a broken child.

CHAPTER

18

Power

Of the

three

power of the three

The cold air in the courtroom like council room had me uneasy, and if I was feeling this way, I could only imagine what Eve was going through. Everyone was sitting on pins and needles as well. Pete and Sai sat on opposite side of me with Sam sitting next Sai. Jacob, Uriah, Danielle and Luke sat in the pew behind us. The place like everything in the Heaven Realm was pearly white with statues of important figures littered around the courtroom. If I wasn't there under such bad circumstances, I would probably have taken the time to enjoy a tour of the place. The council sat discussing among themselves as the atmosphere on the court had become unstable.

"The prospect knowingly challenged using deceit and malice," said Councilmen Uriel. "And normally that is not only grounds for a forfeit, but it is usually ground for the prospect to be disqualified and taking out of consideration for admittance into the Light Guard Academy."

"This guy is so annoying," Pete added shaking his head frustrated.

I turned to Eve not wanting to think about what the councilmen words could mean for our legion. I strummed my fingers on the pew as we sat behind Eve. Sai leaned forward. I know a part of her wanted to jump over the barricade and give Eve a huge hug. As it was, she just sat biting the nail on here thumb with a worried look on her face.

"Hold off Councilmen Uriel," Abdiel added.

"Yeah, let's not make this personal attack on this council," added Councilman Mikell.

The air around the room was thick. Eve stood gun shy watching as the councilmen argued back and forth. Maxiell stood defenseless. I couldn't imagine what his defense for Eve could be. What could he say? Eve had stated it on live broadcast. There was no going back. The rest of us were on pins and needles as the men decided whether to forfeit the match and make our already unsurmountable chances worse.

"Why?" said Kiel Landon. "The circumstances are obvious. The girl intentionally mislead the council so that she would have the opportunity to settle a vendetta. If that isn't the letter of the law nothing is."

"Yes, that may be true, but there are circumstances surrounding the situation that must be considered," added Councilmen Mylingiel.

He pointed in Eve's direction like a prosecutor laying into a defendant. He wore a robe that made him look like a heavenly vampire. He wore a high eccentric collar that looked like a Vegas show guy. His hair was slick back in a horrible attempt to make himself look prestigious. He looked so cheesy. Any other time I would have normally cracked up from the sight of him, but I ignored it, more focused on the conflict at hand. I was overtaken by the tensions of the situation.

"This guy's a clown," cut Zech chuckling.

"Yeah, a clown," Jo seconded.

Landon stared back at me with a look that was usually reserved for my teachers when they chewed me out, but the look was way more forceful.

"I am surprised we are not considering throwing the entire legion out," Landon continued. "It surprises me that a council as prestigious as this one continues to allow these Earthborns to ignore our customs and rules. It's disappointing to say the least.

His words caused a stir among our legion. I sat quietly as the rest of legion whispered disparaging marks under their breath. As brazen as he was in his critique there was a sting of truth to his words. I mean, we were far from the most respectful guest in regards to following the rules and regulations. Showing up to meetings late, being unprepared, constantly breaking protocol and procedure. Honestly, we were literally the only legion which has had a non-competing prospect physically attempt to intervene in nearly every single match.

"Is this guy serious?" Luke added.

"Shhh!" Danielle ordered covering her lips with her finger. "You have to admit he has a point."

"Well, yeah, but he doesn't have to be a jerk about it," Luke objected.

Sai shot an objecting glare before Jacob seconded Danielle's sentiment.

"Have some respect for this council and for me," Landon replied turning to us.

His expression took Luke back as he stared at him like he had lost it.

"This council and your so-called host may allow you to run amuck and make spectacles of yourselves, but I will not allow it in my presence. Respect this court and cease your bickering in an official Light Guard Council meeting."

We all stared around looking at each other not really knowing what to say. He had a point, but once again it was lost in the way it was expressed. Jade turned to him with an angry glare while Max ignored him whispering something to Eve discreetly.

"Man, this guy is smug," Danielle added via BAU.

He smirked before being interrupted by Abdiel.

"Seeing as you are so versed on Light Guard etiquette, I shouldn't have to tell you that it's rude and in bad taste to chastise the members of an opposing legion. Especially in the presence of what you so generously described as a prestigious council," he fired.

"Ha, burn!" Sam added before being bowed hard by Sai. "Ouch, what?!"

She shook her head embarrassed as Landon cleared his throat embarrassed. Abdiel continued sending a covert wink toward me. I smiled happy to see he didn't agree with Landon or at the very least he didn't think the same way.

"We're not considering throwing the entire legion out because there is no precedent, or reason for it," Abdiel snapped. "Do not attempt to sully the reputation of this council by assuming we would give anyone preferential achievement. That being said, we are also not going to be bias based on the opinion of an opposing headmaster."

The group nodded pleased by Abdiel's reaction. I was still uneasy as I tapped my feet nervously. Sai placed her hand on my leg motioning for me to stop. She smiled as I nodded in her direction.

"She'll be fine," she replied.

"What is with those guys," I asked Jade via BAU.

He sighed and then tried to keep a straight face as he replied.

"Landon used to be a council member awhile back. Abdiel's position to be exact, but after a while he was voted out by the people. I'm pretty sure you can understand why. Afterwards he started the Alpha House and has actively bumped heads with the council ever since," he replied. "Once again, I'm sure you can understand why."

I nodded once more as Landon smiled weirdly turning to Abdiel. He rubbed me the wrong way. He seemed like he just didn't belong. I stared at the back of his head as he continued smugly.

"I just want justice under Light Guard Trial law. Nothing more, nothing less," He replied. "As Head Councilmen I will defer to your judgment."

Abdiel turned to Eve with a disappointed look on his face. It seemed like the whole thing was a task he would have rather not have to endure. All in all, he seemed to be on our side, but his hands were tied. It was obvious it wasn't going to end advantageously for us. He shook his head sorrowfully then turned to Eve as he continued.

"Ms. Timila, in your own words, do you feel you deceive this council in presentation of your motives behind why you challenged Prospect Bahir?" Abdiel replied sternly.

Eve looked at all of us sadly then lowered her head still wiping the remains of her tears as she continued. It had been almost an hour since she had broken down, but the dried remains of her tears were still visible. I leaned forward not knowing what she was about to say. I waited impatiently nervous about what the outcome could be.

"Sir, I apologize and ask for forgiveness," she replied ashamed. "Yes. I apologize, but my angle wasn't to lie or disrespect this council. I was just naïve and arrogant. I thought that I could keep my anger toward Prospect Bahir and channel it into beating her, but the truth is, at the time I challenged her, I knew there was a possibility that I could've subconsciously wanted revenge. It was confirmed when I saw her for the first time. I knew then that my anger was the reason. It got the best of me, and I know now why I truly challenged her, no matter what lies I told myself. I purposely ignored those hateful feelings. So, while I did not intentionally lie to this council. I did purposely hide the reservations about my intentions for challenging prospect Bahir, and for that I apologize, and I ask for your forgiveness."

Abdiel sat back with a disturbed look as he looked to his fellow councilmen. He had a looked that revealed reservation that probably proceeded the hearing. At that point, I really didn't care about the trials. Whether she lost or won was inconsequential. I didn't want to lose her. I didn't want Eve to get kicked out. I had grown so attached to her. Now I couldn't imagine being in the legion without her.

"Eve, I appreciate your apology, and in this realm, if you ask for forgiveness, it will be given. That aside, Light Guard law is set by Father Yahweh and the Christ. It is absolute. we will convene than respond accordingly," Abdiel replied with a sympathetic smile.

Eve nodded as a huge barrier lowered restricting access to the Council. Eve broke down once more as Maxiell consoled her. Sai and I leaned over the pew patting her on the back. The rest of legion sat on their hands waiting for a decision. It was minutes, but it seemed like an hour as we sat waiting. The barrier slowly raised revealing the council. Eve rose along with Maxiell almost like a defendant waiting on a jury's verdict.

"I'm sorry for the delay, but we understand the care and thought that must go into this decision," Abdiel replied in an apologetic tone.

Eve nodded respectfully taking a deep breath as he continued.

"Ms. Timila, we have come to a decision," he replied.

My heart beat fast and my palms were sweaty as I gripped the pew in front of me. It felt like I was on trial. I rocked dropping my head almost covering my ears paranoid about what the outcome would be. Eve once again nodded as he laid things out.

"We have decided that because you have shown contrition and the ability to thrive in the Light Guard Academy, we will not revoke your prospect status. We will grade you on the ability you showed in your trial, which if I may say so, was extraordinary," he replied with a staggered smile.

Eve returned his smile with an appreciative smile of her own. Abdiel and a few of the other councilmen showcased agreeing smiles before he continued.

"Unfortunately, it was overshadowed by the malice and deceit you used to showcase it," he continued. "That being said, it is with regret that all the cunning and skill you showed will be all for not as the match will be forfeited because of the false pretense in which it was proposition."

His words had a two pronged affect. I was happy to see that Eve wouldn't be disqualified but to hear that we were now down 3-1 was a letdown. The rest of the legion seemed to feel the same as the showcase looks of controlled and disappointed gratitude. I raised my head and took a sigh of relief as Eve nodded.

"That was a relief," Pete whispered in my ear.

I nodded in agreement as he continued.

"Count yourself lucky. If you were a normal Heaven Realm citizen, you would have been disqualified. Luckily, after their discussion it was decided it would be unfair to hold you to the standard of recruits who have lived and abided in our realm for years," he continued. "Taking into account that you are considered young even by Earth Realm standards, it would be unfair to punish you in such a way, but this is a onetime deal, so to the rest of you, this is not only a warning for her, but for all of you. There are consequences for all the decisions you make, and they won't be lenient, so make the right one."

We all nodded. With that everyone said their courtesy goodbyes and headed toward our transport. The media was waiting as the portal door opened. Eve lowered her head as they peppered her with questions.

"Ms. Timila, will you be answering questions?" they all asked in varying ways.

"This child is in no shape to be answering any questions. She has been given a waiver and will not be doing a post-trial press conference. I apologize and we will receive the next trial participant on our transport," Jade replied covering Eve as we maneuvered our way through the fans and media.

I finally breathed a sigh of relief as we enter the transport and the door closed behind us. I sat not really wanting to speak. To be honest I don't think anyone else did either. My guess was they were all on pins and needles about the next trial. I wasn't but maybe I should have considering how terribly the last two had been.

"3-1, its over," said Zech tossing his bag. "I would have never gotten on this legion if I'd known we were going to get embarrassed like this."

"Yeah, it's one thing to lose but to lose…," before he could speak.

Jade motioned for him to stop.

"Don't say that," he shot. "We are far from out of it. Not one of our Doms have fought yet. We have plenty of opportunity to even the score."

"Exactly," added Max trying to pep us up. "Besides, even we don't win. It's not the end of the world. All the prospect so far have passed. Tim with an 11, Beth with a 8, and Both Pete and Eve with 10's. That is amazing even if we don't win, and it's also enough for the legion to qualify. All we need is for one or more of you to get a 7 or higher and were gold. Of course, we won't be able to choose our house but that's alright too."

UMH! Jacob interrupted clearing his throat catching everyone's attention.

"Well, that would be great, but there's only one problem," Jacob stated looking out the window. "Either we all get in or none of us do, remember? You stated earlier that Sam will more than likely not be an automatic qualifier based off of his showings in our earlier battles. Therefore, if Sam doesn't compete or we don't win, he doesn't get in. Am I right?"

His words sent a pause throughout our group. We had been so focused on winning the trials that we had completely forgotten about Sam. Well, some of us. Jacob's words sent us all crashing back to Earth. I had only been thinking of the competitive advantage of Sam not competing. I never stopped to think about what Max and Jade had explained earlier. Sam had to compete, or we had to win. We all assumed we would win so we never thought of the consequences of what would happen if we didn't, but now that possibility was a very real one, so much so, that I would go as far as saying it looked like the most likely outcome considering our present hole. Everything changed. There was a very real possibility that we had to either drop Sam or decline our invitation to the Light Guard Academy.

"Yes, that is correct," Jade replied trying to act confident. "But we have the utmost faith in God's plan. Either Sam will be chosen and exceed, or we will win."

The faces around the room were looks of shell shocked individuals. It looked like they were fighting a skeptical dilemma as they stood speechless. Especially Sam. He stared out the window as if to be ignoring the conversation entirely.

"You hear that Sam?" Sai replied turning to Sam.

He nodded barely moving his head.

"I'm going to destroy whoever they put in front of me," Sam replied. "Watch, you'll see, and when I'm done you guys will have to admit I'm

239 | P a g e

the best, even better than both my cousins. Then, I'll be the best, not Jacob, not Tim but me. I'm going to be the first Human Arch. I said it and I meant it. I promise."

His words were met with politely skeptical looks. I didn't know how to respond and before I could my attention was caught by a message that ran across one of the screens on the transport.

"What?!" I replied staring and pointing at the screen at the same time. "Turn up the volume."

Jade slowly raised the volume as we all watched in awe. In huge letters on a banner across the screen the letters read ABA's LOWELL CHALLENGES JACOB ELI. Were they serious? Was this a joke? They have the competition in the bag, and they challenge our strongest member. I turned to Jacob along with the rest of the group. His eyes went vacant for a second and then returned. We all knew what had happened without him saying a word. I turn to the screen dying to hear his score.

"Well, you are not going to believe this," said Mel smiling like he was trying to contain his excitement. "If the reports I am getting are accurate...this is amazing we may have an extraordinary bit of news to share with our viewers."

He waited for a second as if to be still getting information via BAU as we all sat on the edge of our seat for the news that we all pretty much assumed was a given.

"Yes, it is official, we have just received word that we have indeed just recorded the first ever perfect score!" Mel continued.

The crowd erupted so loud that we could hear the roar outside of the stadium. The cameras showed closed up of fans with looks of pure admiration and surprise. On the bus the feeling was the same. The legion went bonkers with Luke jumping all over Jacob as the rest of legions mouths lay on the floor.

"Wow!" Zech gleamed jumping up and down.

"Yeah, that is so awesome!" Jo seconded.

I looked at Sai as she stared at Jacob like he was entity from another dimension.

"Are you serious?" she added turning to me and Eve.

Danielle shook her head unable to grasp the reality of what had just happened.

"Can't say um surprised," Uriah added patting Jacob.

I didn't share in their jubilation. I was paralyzed realizing a very familiar feeling. It rocked in the pit of my stomach like a violently wave. It was pure anger. I stared out the window trying to quell the jealous feelings inside of me. After all I had done and all the strides I made, I was back in the shadow of my older brother. How could I ever match something like that?

"What were they thinking?" Pete added. "What could possibly be the strategy behind challenging possibly the best prospect ever? All they needed was one more win and Sam was there. I just don't get it."

As he spoke Jade raised his hand pointing at the television.

"I think you're about to get your answer because a reporter just asked Jacob's challenger Jermel Howell that exact question," he relayed catching all our attention.

The boy looked gun shy. He was around the same age as me with frizzy brown hair and brownish red eyes. He stood next to a man who he shared a slight resemblance although the man had darker hair. From the start I could deduct this guy didn't seem like the type of guy who was confident enough to take such a risk. His shoulder slouched as he huddled almost hiding behind his speaking orb. His eyes wondering nervously.

"Well, my father and I...we felt it would be an opportunity for me to show how great the Alpha House is. We want the best, and we fight the best. No easy victories," he replied. "With us having the final two challenges we figured Jacob would be a great opponent to showcase my skill against."

The crowd chuckled coldly as he spoke. As one of the reporters spoke up.

"I mean, you can't be serious. This isn't just any prospect. This kid is possibly the best prospect we've ever had. You were scored at a 9. There had to be more of a method to your madness other than showcasing your skill, because if that was the case, why wouldn't you put yourself against someone who…in all honesty you had an actual chance against."

His words seemed to spark an angry reaction as the man next to him sat forward.

"Are you insinuating my son doesn't have the ability to beat an Earth-Born rookie with no pre-trial training?" the man continued. "You can't be serious. This Jacob Eli is extremely talented, but like him my son has been trained by the best trainers in the Heaven Realm. Prospect Eli is extremely talented, but he's also woefully inexperienced. Besides, whether or not my son wins is irrelevant. It is his aim to put on a show to represent the brilliance of the Howell family extends beyond our industrial pursuits."

"Who is this guy?" Luke asked staring at the screen.

"Real Estate Mogul Yusel Howell," Max continued. "His family has owned the largest Renovations firm in the Heaven Realm for millenniums. They reside in Quadrant Rho-Theta-Tau-Mu-Delta-Beta."

The kid stood like a deer in headlights as his father continued to dig his grave deeper and deeper. I looked over at Jacob who wore his usual poker face. He was as calm as a cucumber as he sat staring at the screen emotionless.

"I thought there was no money. How can someone be a mogul?" Eve asked turning to Jade.

"Resources are endless, but there is still currency. In the Heaven Realm it doesn't translate to power or control like it does on Earth, but it does lend itself to prestige and recognition. Howell's family is one of the richest families in the Heaven Realm," Jade explained.

"Well, he's acting like a world class jerk. I mean, it's obvious it wasn't that kid's idea to challenge Jacob, it was his," Sai shot angrily.

Jade nodded empathetically.

"Be that as it may, it's still a plus for us," Max added. "And after all we've gone through the past couple days, we needed one."

I nodded trying to take as much positive as I could as the transport screeched to a stop. Outside waiting at the hotel was a mob. All we could see was a sea of lights, cameras, and people. We all threw on our hoodies like bullet proof vests and prepared to unload off the bus.

"Keep your heads down and keep moving," Max ordered.

"Yeah, we have the waiver," Jade continued. "No question need to be answered. Let's just get to our designated rooms and try to get back to normal."

I nodded zipping my jacket up.

POP! As soon as I stepped off the bus light orbs popped flashing hot light in our faces. They acted like I didn't exist as there nearly threw me out of the way to get to Jacob. I was the little brother of the town superstar once more. I covered my head and bullied my way through the crowd as they screamed questions at Jacob. It seemed like forever before we finally ended up back in the hotel lobby. I shook my head unable to believe the spectacle.

"Jacob can I have BAU signature?" said a voice from behind me.

It was another prospect and I turned around to see another sea of prospects standing in a crowd to greet us as we entered the lobby. It was insane. How big of an achievement was this. We all looked around as the frenzy was at an all-time fever pitch high.

"Jacob"

"Jacob"

The crowd was closing in on us. Jade motioned for us to go to the elevator as he and Max blocked them off.

"Please, he has a big day tomorrow," Max explained blocking off a wall of prospects as we entered the elevator.

We all sighed staring at each other in disbelief as the elevator door close.

"What is going on?" I replied shaking my head. "When did this turn into a groupie meeting spot?" Sai chuckled.

"Well, you heard that Mel guy. This isn't an everyday thing, and here in the Heaven Realm it's all about experience. It's the one commodity that isn't shared evenly," Danielle explained. "And how many can say they were a part of something that historic, I mean, really?"

We nodded acknowledging her words still coming down off the rollercoaster of events.

"So, what's the plan of action?" Uriah continued focused on the particulars as usual.

Uriah stirred for a second staring down at the sea of people watching him before responding.

"I want to train with Tim," he replied not looking at me as he said the startling statement.

Everyone looked at him like he had lost it. I stared him trying to understand the selfish motive that I was sure was somewhere in there hidden.

"Are you sure?" Luke replied. "No offense to Tim, but he is just a kid. I mean, are sure you don't want someone who you could somewhat go toe to toe with?"

Jacob shook his head before Luke could even finish his statement.

"No, Tim is the strongest elemental on our team. This guy is supposed be some hot shot elemental, so Tim can give me an insight on some of the techniques is all," Jacob replied. "Besides, we've sparred enough over the past couple of days."

They both nodded in agreement. Which I sort of saw as them living me out to dry. Didn't I have a say in this equation? The last thing I wanted was to be stuck with Jacob for a night. But as it was, I smiled and tried to act neutral about the situation. Jacob turned still looking out the window as he leaned against the wall of the elevator. It was going to be a long night.

I was tired and a little burnt out. The last thing I wanted to do was spar or do any type of training with Jacob. I shrugged my shoulders and leaned against the back of the elevator unable to hide the disappointment on my face.

"Okay, it's you're trial," Luke replied.

"How you doing Eve?" Sai asked.

She still appeared to be a little shaken from the day's events. She stood staring out at the sea of people moving about underneath us.

"Yeah, I'm just a little embarrassed is all," Eve replied. "I was just so mad."

Jacob turned to her with a consoling glance as Danielle put her arm around her.

"As pious as we try to be, we're all still human. As Jesus said we don't battle with flesh and blood, but against principalities. He could have easily said we battle against principals, because those same powers govern our principles of right or wrong. My father always said nothing corrupts free will like justification. We can justify anything, and once it's justified it's a free ticket to do as we will," he replied showing a level of care that he never showed to me.

Luke joined Jacob, Sai and Danielle placing his hand on her shoulder.

"Yeah, we're not angry with you, mostly because none of us could say we wouldn't have done the same thing given the opportunity and circumstance," Luke added. "So in a way, your actions we're representation of all of us. I think that's why that Abdiel guy responded the way he did."

Eve nodded acknowledging their words. It was weird to me. To think a little more than a month ago we all barely knew each other, but it seemed like with every day that passed the bond between us seemed to grow stronger and stronger.

"It's still annoying we lost though," Sam added.

I ignored the conversation mostly going in and out alternating between listening and thinking about the annoying task that lay ahead of me. I wasn't looking forward to it. I started to move toward Eve, but before I could Pete stopped me.

"You okay?" Pete shot via BAU.

I turned to him with a telling stare before I replied.

"What do you think?" I shot back. "I don't want to spar with him. All he's going to do is boss me around and criticize me the whole time."

Pete couldn't help but show a playful smile which he covered by staring down at his feet covertly.

"C'mon, maybe it won't be so bad. I mean, you got to admit he was pretty cool during your trial, and you have to admit some of the things he says about you are true," he expressed still his best to be non transparent.

I raised an eyebrow at his statement, all but revealing to everyone who was paying attention that I was in a conversation. Luckily no one was paying attention. They were too focused on Eve to pay attention to either of us.

"Thanks," I replied surveying the elevator to make sure.

He tapped his foot and looked at the ceiling in a terrible attempt to be transparent.

"I'm sorry but you know what I mean," he continued. "Tim, you are a highly blessed individual. You always have been, but Id be lying if I said you don't take advantage of those talents from time to time. Seriously, are you trying to say you really can't understand why he says some of the things he says?"

I gave him a blank expression without replying. It was obvious he had a point in what he said about me, but let's be serious, he didn't criticize anybody else the way he did me. It was just because I was his little brother, and Pete couldn't understand that plight. He just saw things from a non-emotional analytical point of view and everybody agreeing with him constantly cutting me down in front of everyone was starting to run thin.

"What are you guys talking about?" Sai intervened via BAU.

Her words literally stopped another tantrum that was going to kill the whole dynamic of the group hug session going on in the elevator at that moment.

"Is it that obvious?" I replied.

She covertly cut her eyes still consoling Eve.

"Well, not really but I know you two," she replied.

Yeah, that could have been true, but I thought what was more telling was the obvious looks I was giving Pete and the terrible job he was doing of selling the conversation outwardly, but that could have been my paranoia.

"Well, if you do know us, then you should know what we're talking about," I replied jokingly.

"Maybe it won't be so bad," she replied.

Pete finally looked at up at the sound of her words.

"That's what I said," He chimed in.

As they spoke the elevator finally stopped on our floor. Everyone stood for an awkward second as the doors of the elevator opened then slowly filed out. Jacob turned to me just as I moved to exit.

"Tim, take some time to rest. We'll meet up in an hour or two," he replied.

I nodded narrowly catching his words among the chattering in our BAU. I tried to look as normal as possible as all the faces on the elevator slowly turned to me.

"Okay," I replied happy to hear at least we were on the same page about something.

As we all exited Eve hung back.

"Thanks you guys," she replied. "I'm going to go sit with my sister. I figure if she's anything like Hikari, she'll want to hear about what happened."

Sai turned and joined her.

"Yeah, I'll go with you," she replied stepping back into the elevator.

"Me too," Danielle replied following Sai's lead.

They gave awkward smiles as they punched in buttons on the elevator.

"Okay, we'll see you guys later then," Sam replied.

We all waved as the door closed. Before we could turn around Jacob, Luke and Uriah had already gone ahead and were heading toward their rooms.

"I guess we'll see them later," Pete replied sarcastically. "Why are teenagers like that? I mean, they act like since they're older there is no need to be respectful."

"What do you expect?" Sam replied. "They're probably super nervous about the trials. They're trying to get as much training in as they can. You guys have done it already. You don't have to worry. They're probably just scared, you know."

I don't really remember the travel back to our room. It was all a funny haze. We entered our room and as usual I headed to my room to sleep, Pete headed for the lab and Sam headed to the training room. I fell to sleep before my head hit he pillow, one again mentally, physically, and emotionally exhausted. I drifted off instantly. It was a peaceful sleep, but as you can probably guess, it was short lived. I felt a pulling sensation then a voice jarred me from my sleep.

"Timothy Eli," said a voice faintly.

I awoke to the sound of cricking pipes and dripping water hitting me in the face. I recoiled shocked surveying my surrounding. I threw my hands up annoyed.

"Can't I have a moment of peace?" I grunted angrily slapping the wall next to me.

I had done it again, but at least this time my surroundings were familiar. I remembered the place immediately. It was the place I had heard the voices the first time I teleported.

"Timothy Eli," said a voice catching me off-guard.

I slid up against a nearby wall. I was so afraid. It took a second for me to realize how stupid it was to be hiding from someone who obviously already knew I was there.

"What?" I replied reaching for a weapon.

I had nothing on my hip. I had no armor. I was wearing the same clothing I had on the day I died.

"I mean you no harm, Timothy Eli," said the voice. "Please I've brought you here to speak with you."

At the sound of his words I rose and cautiously walked toward the sound of the voice. The halls were slimy and wet. I crept through the hallway cautiously stepping through the muddy passageway. It looked like something out of a mid-evil story.

"Come with me, Tim," said a familiar voice as I came around the final corner.

It was Michael. I couldn't believe it.

"Michael?" I replied. "Was that you calling me?"

He shook his head as he motioned for me to fall him.

"It's wasn't me," he replied. "I'm here to make sure everything is on the up and up. We've only done this once before. It was during the alpha generation cycle. They chose a man named Enoch. He became the first and only man they've ever asked to speak on their behalf.

His words were making me uneasy. Michael was normally so carefree. Now his demeanor was stoic and serious. He led me toward a cell that was surrounded by Guardsmen. Michael acknowledged the men as they opened the door and allowed me in. As I entered, what I perceived to be an angel sat bent over at the waist with his head hanging between his legs.

"Hello, Timothy Eli," he greeted startling me.

"Hi," I replied still gun-shy.

He slowly raised his head and glared at me with eyes that were as black as coal. I recoiled as he raised his hand reassuring me he meant no harm.

"How's the Light Guard Trials going for you?" he continued like we were old friends.

Michael stood between us. He spoke with heavy emotional gravity. He sounded defeated in a way that made me feel sorry for him. I moved to respond, but before I could Michael cut me off.

"Semyaza!" Michael warned angrily. "Ask him the question so we can get on with this. Like I told you before, I am not at all comfortable with this, so until I can be sure of your motives, I will not allow this meeting to continue."

He raised his hand in an apologizing manner as Michael stared darts at him.

"I'm sorry, Michael," he continued raising his hands in a surrendering manner. "Timothy Eli, do you remember this place?"

I nodded not knowing the purpose of the question.

"Yeah, I think I was here a couple of days ago," I continued surveying the place as I responded.

Michael turned to me. He his exhaled in a frustrated before placing his hand on his head as he asked a question of his own.

"And when you were here what happened?" he asked staring at me.

I stared at him trying to understand why it was so important. I shrugged my shoulders expressing a level of ignorance. The man's refused the raise his head and the longer the conversation went the more off-putting his demeanor was. I answered Michael's words still wondering why the angel was so apprehensive about showing me his face.

"I don't know really. I just remember waking up here. As soon as I got my bearings I heard voices...Two people arguing," I replied turning to Michael to get assurance from him that things would be fine.

Michael sighed at the sound my words.

"What were they talking about?" he replied.

"It sounded like…It was like one of them was trying to get the other one to do something," I replied. "I was confused by the whole thing. I had no idea what they were talking about. I just heard something about sons and a war."

Michael stared at the ceiling like my words were the last thing he wanted to hear before forcing Semyaza to continue with a point of his finger.

"Was his voice one of the voices you heard?" he asked.

"I think so," I replied. "His…and I also heard one of the voices call the other voice Semyaza."

Michael nodded at the sound of his words. Then signaled with the movement of his hand for Semyaza to continue. Semyaza nodded and turned to me.

"Timothy Eli, do you know who I am?" he replied looking me in the eye.

I turned to Michael for conformation before continuing. He nodded giving me the okay.

"Well, kind of, Max, Hanz, and Jade explained a little about you and your legion," I continued. "You're the guy who was a part of... or the leader of the watchers, right?"

He nodded acknowledging his words in a manner that showcased a heavy guilt as he rocked back and forth.

"Exactly, that is true," he responded nodding as he spoke. "I was the head of the legion your people refer to as the 'Watchers'."

I nodded still somewhat hiding behind Michael as the angel finally raised his head showcasing dark black eyes as he spoke. His eyes were like the rebel demons. I backpedaled causing Michael to place a sturdy hand on my shoulder calming me.

"I can read your actions Timothy Eli," he responded. "You're wondering why you're here? You're wondering why you're here talking to me?"

I stared at him without replying before Michael unsheathed his sword. It seemed to grow on his side from nowhere.

"I warned against that form of BAU," Michael responded in a warning grunt.

Semyaza raised his hands in a begging manner.

"Michael, I used no form of BAU," he defended pleading. "I watched Adam's people for hundreds of years. I know how they think. That's all I meant by the statement."

Michael closed his coat concealing his weapon as it shrunk back to the size of a pouch. He nodded signaling for him to continue. His demeanor threw me. I had never seen Michael like this before. He was so cold and emotionless with the man. He was uncomfortable for the first time since I met him.

"So is it true, young Timothy Eli?" he asked looking me in the eye. "Do you want to know how I got here?"

I looked around the room at the guards who looked to be terrified as they stood at the gate as if they were worried something could be coming at any moment. I swallowed hard and took a deep breath before nodding my head.

"Great, because it will be a great segway into why you're here?" he replied with a smile that put me on edge. "I know you've heard the legends, but I think it's time I told you the true story of The Watchers."

He paused for a second composing himself before continuing.

"Timothy Eli, in order to explain our story, in a sense, I'll have to first explain your story," he continued.

I furred my brow at his statement unable to fathom what he meant. I looked to Michael who gave me a calming nod.

"What do you mean my story?" I replied confused.

He chuckled outloud at my naïve nature. I stared at him unmoved as he continued.

"Well, I know the story of man," he continued. "And you're a man, aren't you?"

I stopped to analyze the question. Technically he was right in terms of species, but I had a few people who would fall over themselves to breakdown every way I fell short. Namely my soon to be training partner and big brother Jacob.

"I guess technically," I replied.

He shook his head with another chuckle as Michael stared at me with a look that tried to bait me with a protecting smile, but I could see he was still worried. His gaze bounced from us back to the entrance and it made me uneasy.

"Well, not a mature man but you're a man all the same," He replied smiling. "Am I right?"

I shrugged my shoulders than nodded hesitantly.

"Yeah," I relented.

"Well, Adam your father," he replied.

"How do you know my father?" I cut in.

Michael shook his head exasperated.

"He's not talking about your father Adam, Tim," he replied placing his forehead in his hand

I turned to him confused by his phrase.

"Oh, well what Adam is he talking about?" I replied.

He stared at me blankly then sighed.

"Take a wild guess," he replied shaking his head. "Semyaza can we pick this up? Tim is a very literal and impatient kid. Think about what you say or circles like this will be a permanent part of our conversation."

I stood like a deer in headlights as the two exchanged glances. Michael wore an impatient scowl while Semyaza nodded in agreement as he continued.

"I was referring to the father of man. Adam, the first man. He was a friend of the angels. He was our brother," he replied staring at Michael as he spoke.

Michael showcased a soft glance just before his face fell to the floor in a sympathetic manner. Semyaza turned to him seconding his demeanor.

"Adam was like our little brother in every sense of the word," he continued. "We taught him everything. He was the darling of the Heaven Realm then. Everything was one. We all knew him. We all knew why Father Yahweh created him. He was the new race. It may sound amazing to a short-lived race like yours, but we angels were used to it. Father Yahweh made new creations all the time. It was nothing out of the ordinary. Every now and then he'd bring his creations and let us see them.

We gushed and were in awe every time he did. Like proud brothers we were honored to see every new addition to the family. But from the moment we met Adam we knew he was different?"

His words left me wondering as I spoke reflexively without thinking.

"Why?" I replied. "What was different?"

He looked at Michael with a look that made it obvious he was asking for permission. Michael stared away never making eye contact with Semyaza as he spoke.

"Well, in short he was one of us," Michael replied.

"I'm super confused right now," I replied surprised by Michael's words. "Adam was an angel."

Michael turned to me impatiently sighing unhappy about having to explain something else.

"No, Tim," He replied irritated. "I just meant he was made in God's image like us. He had the breath of God in him. He was the first creation of his kind."

His words piqued my curiosity as I stared at him.

"Why...why did that make him special?" I asked confused. "I mean, I thought all God's creation had a part of him in them?"

I turned to Michael as I spoke, but before he could reply Semyaza broke in.

"Yes, his light, but not his breath Timothy Eli," he exclaimed using his hands for effect. "Think about it? What is more powerful than the breath of God? It's his word. So, Adam was the first creation to have the ability to speak with the authority of the breath or word of God."

Michael stared away once again his gaze going back to the entrance.

"It instantly made him the most powerful being in creation," he replied staring me in the eye. "But then he was just a boy. He didn't understand it. To him he was just our little brother. We all knew there was a special plan for him, but we never knew what plan was. All we knew was Father Yahweh was pleased with him and wanted us to watch over him. Even before Adam was created, Father Yahweh decorated his home world more beautifully and extravagant than any home world he ever made. It was like watching a proud father creating his son's nursery."

He smiled as if to be reminiscing on it.

"When it was perfect and good, he created Adam. He spent years having Adam name any and everything on the Earth giving him supreme authority over it making anything he said law. He made every animal male and female, but Adam was alone," He replied continuing. "Adam being the only one of his kind wanted someone like him. Father Yahweh heard his words and decided to make him one, but he knew it would be too dangerous to make someone exactly like Adam. Father Yahweh in his infinite wisdom knew that there would be conflict so he decided to make Adam a companion of what your people use to refer to as smokeless fire or what you know as electricity, but instead of dust like Adam, she was made from the deep soil of the earth."

His words led me to an understanding that I deducted within seconds, but like I did with most times I ended up at the wrong conclusion.

"Eve was made of light," I blurted.

He stared at me with his dark pupils almost squinting in anguish.

"No, Lilith was," he replied. "Lilith was."

I stared at Michael who was already shaking his head in frustration.

"Who is Lilith?" I asked confused.

Michael sighed before turning to Semyaza who continued.

"If Eve is the mother of the living on earth, Lilith is the mother of the dead," he continued. "She was also a gigantic bratty annoying child that was a pain in the butt of every Angel that had to watch her."

He shook his head in the exact opposite manner to the one he had when thinking of Adam.

"Why?" I continued to press.

"Well, let's just say she refused to listen to anyone," Semyaza continued. "Us, Adam...no one."

Michael stared at the entrance as he interrupted.

"That could have had something to do with the spoiled brat who watched over her," he cut.

I turned to him at the sound of his words.

"Who?" I asked.

He cut his eyes immediately.

"Lucifer," he replied. "The great deceiver, son of the morning...please, he's a selfish petulant child."

Michael's face was brimming with disgust that seemed to weigh down his entire demeanor.

"Wait, Lucifer, as in the devil," I replied.

Semyaza nodded as he continued.

"You never wonder why he was forced from the garden," he continued. "Unlike the rest of us, he never agreed with Father Yahweh's decision to make a being like Adam. He actively hated and envied him from the moment he was asked to see him as his superior. Mainly because he knew what it meant. He was one of the highest-ranking members in the Heaven Realm, but the thought that Father Yahweh loved any race more than us infuriated him, and like a child whose father brought home the new baby, he was jealous. Next came the temper tantrum in which he rebelled taking a third of our brothers with him."

He gripped the bed he sat on firmly as he spoke visually agitated absorbing his words. Michael stood kicking at the floor with his hands in his pockets.

"But who am I to speak right?" he replied turning to Michael.

Michael nodded empathetically.

"But I digress, Lilith under Lucifer's tutelage became more and more defiant. When Father Yahweh finally intervened, she fled. Father Yahweh wanted to fill the earth, but before he could allow Lilith and Adam to create seed, she defiled herself with the dark beast of the field," Semyaza continued.

I frowned at the thought.

"Wait, you mean?" I replied disgusted.

Semyaza nodded finishing my thought.

"Gross!" I shot sickened. "That's so gross."

Michael chuckled snidely.

"My thoughts exactly," he seconded.

"So, what happened?" I pressed.

"Well, Adam was obviously upset," he replied. "And Lilith knew that she and Adam could never be together again, but the love she had for Adam never subsided. The two were raised together. It broke her heart to lose Adam. He was the love of her life. She rebelled against all form of control and she finally went too far. She wasn't clean, she like Lucifer couldn't enter the Garden and worst yet, her union created abominations, or what you refer to as demons. She corrupted Father Yahweh's perfect world. Lilith Gone and Adam alone we all knew that something had to be done. Adam was a wreck. He walked around the Garden sad so Father Yahweh decided to create someone he thought would be perfect for Adam."

"Eve," I chimed in.

Michael stared at me with an inquisitive gaze that led me to believe he got right away why I was so quick to answer the question the way I did.

"Yes, Eve," he replied.

Semyaza stared at us both for a second than continued.

"Eve, unlike Lilith was made from the very body of Adam. She loved him with a love that we angels never witnessed outside of our love for Father Yahweh," he continued. "She was so beautiful and caring. She was like no other being we had ever met. She was a perfect complement for him. Unlike Lilith she was loyal to him. Which made her an obvious target for Lucifer to go after?"

His words gave me pause.

"So, you're saying he like...liked Eve?" I cut in.

He turned his head slowly.

"He wanted someone who was loyal to Adam," he replied. "Who or what it was, that was inconsequential. It was about taking everything from Adam. He perceived Adam was the reason everything was taken from in his eyes. He wanted retribution. It was his contention that he would test every blessing given to Adam to prove he wasn't more worthy than he was. I'm pretty sure you're familiar with the story."

I nodded remembering the story that had been told for thousands of years. The story of the fall of man.

"That wasn't about taking Eve it was about taking everything?" he continued. "Eve was just a means to an end. Unlike Adam, Eve didn't know Lucifer's energy, at the time, she really didn't know about anything. She was left alone, and Lucifer knew she was naïve. He targeted her at a time where she was vulnerable. He pretended to be an angel of light.

Since Eve didn't know there were bad angels it was an easy ploy. He knew Adam loved and trusted Eve, so he found a way to control her. It was the only way to get to Adam."

His body tensed up at the sound of Adam.

"So how?" I pressed. "I've always wondered about that?"

He stared me in the eye as he continued.

"With doubt?" he replied shockingly. "Doubt is the father of lies and sin. It's Lucifer's biggest asset, his creation. The fruit he presented brought the ability to decipher freewill. Doubt is the only thing that calls for the analysis of right and wrong. It's the catalyst of sin. Think of every sin. Lying, cheating, stealing, lust...it's all based in doubt. Whether its doubt of loyalty, ability, means, or authority, doubt is the fall of man. Sins are just the fruits of the labor. Money is obtained through stealing, lying, and cheating to control circumstance. Lust built on the back of insecurity is the way we confirm our worth both physically and emotionally. It all comes from low self-esteem and a lack of faith. Lucifer knew this was the only card he had and he played it. He took one of the most powerful beings ever created and turned him into a self-conscious, insecure, worry ridden, anxiety filled and faithless mess, with a compliment who was worse than him."

Michael shook his head as Semyaza continued.

"In that apple was a science. Lucifer created a disease that attacked the physical and spiritual immune system. It was what created the barrier that stymies your abilities and severed you from the Heaven Realm. It separated the will of the flesh and the will of the spirit creating an unbalanced divide. The flesh could no longer survive feeding off the spirit. The infused doubt needed to be quenched. Fear, anxiety, and insecurities attacked the flesh through the very same receptors that you now understand controls your faith-based powers. So of course, Father Yahweh instituted the barrier to prevent Adams children from destroying yourselves, but in doing so, all the things that you once had control over, you now didn't. The world that bowed to him no longer had a master. It became wild and unpredictable. It was filled with as much doubt as Adam was. Lucifer took advantage of this. He met Adam after he was exiled and asked him to give the fallen creation to him. He was an arc and convinced Adam he could control it. Adam gave in mostly because he falsely assumed he would be taken back to the Heaven Realm eventually. He didn't understand the effect that decision would have on his children. Eve if he was gone, he children would have to live in this world."

His words angered me.

"Why?" I asked. "Why would he do that?"

He sighed shrugging his shoulders in a helpless manner.

"Adam wasn't the same Adam from the Heaven Realm and Eden. He was filled with doubt, and so was Eve. He and Eve were constantly under attack from Lilith, especially Eve. Lucifer was constantly lying and deceiving Adam filling him with doubt about Father Yahweh's love for him and unwillingness to protect him. Adam knew this wasn't true, but the doubt in his brain couldn't let him be sure. So, after years of torment he finally agreed. He said he would lease the planet to Lucifer if he promised to protect Eve from Lillith. The girl was pregnant with his first child. He figured it would allow her to rest while he did penance to gain forgiveness from Father Yahweh," he continued explaining things. "He figured that without Eve he had a better go at it. She was slowing him down because of her physical weakness. All in all, he accomplished his goal. With the help of the Archangels, Father Yahweh forgave Adam and once again allowed us to protect him. Eve returned with her son to meet Father Yahweh from the first time since her exile."

I nodded knowing the significance immediately.

"Cain," I replied under my breath.

He nodded in agreement.

"Exactly, it was obvious from the moment we came across him that he inherited the disease. We all were saddened as we knew what it meant. This disease was a part of Adam and Eve, and now we knew it would also be a part of their children as well," he continued annoyed. "It was heartbreaking. After a couple more births we were all but sure that this disease couldn't be cured. It was a very hard time for Adam who was convinced his seed would forever be cursed...Then they had their next child."

"Abel," I replied.

He looked at me with a smile.

"Timothy Eli, do you happen to know what that name means?" he asked.

I shook my head as Michael intervened answering the question.

"Breath, A breath," he replied in saving grace type of tone.

He smiled starring at Michael.

"Exactly!" Semyaza replied excitedly. "Exactly, he was the first being since the original Adam. He didn't have the disease. The breath of God, the word of God dwelled with in him still...untainted! He was the first light in a decade of darkness. He was the legacy Adam was waiting for. We rejoiced. Adam had hopes of redeeming the New Heaven and Earth. Throughout the hoopla and circumstance, we all forgot that there was another son."

Michael turned to me with an empathetic glare.

"I'm sure you can empathize with why that would make someone mad," he poked.

I nodded as Semyaza continued.

"Yes, but Father Yahweh was always considerate of Cain, but he understood the monumental task ahead of him. Cain didn't understand this. He couldn't understand why he was always so monitored and not allowed to do things Abel could. Father Yahweh knew Cain had to control his emotions or sin would overtake him, but Cain was too young to understand this and by the time he became a man the anger that built inside of him became resentment for his brother. The final straw came when it was decided that Abel would inherit the Earth after Adam passed on. Cain was livid because he was the older brother. He didn't understand the reasoning because he never knew the dangers of sin. He understand why Abel was chosen. He didn't understand what his brother not having the disease meant. He didn't understand Lucifer and his demons could not influence his little brother with doubt. Abel had the ability to protect his sisters from Lucifer, but Cain was filled with anger. He felt he was the only other man, if he got Abel out of the way then it would be his inheritance. Once again, I'm sure you've heard the story."

His words gave me weird feelings. It was so easy to demonize Cain without understanding the whole story. I could understand the mindset of being forgotten to the point that at times it seems you didn't exist. But what he did put in anger in my stomach that seemed to travel to the pit of me. It was an anger I couldn't understand.

"So, the light or breath of God had once again been extinguished and the only other man had been soiled with murder. Cain was gone and Adam and Eve were beyond themselves with worry even though Cain was covered by the mark of God," Semyaza continued. "He was distraught over the death of his brother, but it was done. After his exile his children filled the earth and a war began between the children of Cain and the children of Lilith. Adam and Eve watched as the child they once loved created children who fought the armies of Lilith and Lucifer with physical assault knowing they couldn't harm them receding them to the dark recesses of the Earth once again claiming the Earth for man. Cain returned believing he had redeemed and shown that Father Yahweh had made a mistake in not making him the inheritor forgetting the very reason he was able to conquer the Earth was because of the mark bestowed upon him by Father Yahweh. It was then that he found out his mother was pregnant again. We all rejoiced when it was discovered that it was another boy, but our rejoicing slowly dissipated when we discovered he like Cain had the disease."

My countenance fell at the sound of his words.

"But something was different about him," he continued. "The doubt affected him differently. He had freewill and doubt, but he chose to do what was right. It wasn't because he had to, he did it ecause Father Yahweh said it was the best thing to do. And when Father Yahweh asked him why he chose to listen to him even though he didn't have to. Seth said, 'I was made in your image and you said I should'. His words filled not just us, but Father Yahweh with a feeling we hadn't felt since Adam."

I could tell their emotion just by the look on their face. It was like remembering an old good friend.

"Cain wanted Seth to follow in his footsteps, but he wouldn't. Seth always followed the word of God. When Adam passed on he left his protected land and inheritance to Seth. Cain was crushed. Unlike Adam and Seth he wanted to prove Father Yahweh wrong rather than ask for forgiveness. A notion and passion he no doubt got from Lucifer who revealed to him that it was he who protected him during Eve's labor not Father Yahweh," he continued. "He had Cain convinced that the one thing keeping him from his inheritance was his brother, but Cain refused stating he would not take another brother's life after the pain of the last time. Lucifer quickly manipulated him into believing his offspring would be the true inheritors, and even though Cain refused, after he passed his children were not as hard to convince. After his death they started a war with the children of Seth that waged on centuries."

I nodded trying to remember all the things that were said. He clinched his hands showing visual disdain that made me uneasy.

"That is where my story comes into play," he replied sighing loudly.

"You're talking about the downfall of you and your legion, right?" I asked.

He nodded. His eyes no longer filled me with fear, but now gave off a more destitute distant look. It brought out feelings of sympathy one would get when looking at a blind man.

"I, like Michael, was trusted to make sure Seth's children weren't wiped out by Cain's offspring. This was mandatory. The war between the two families wasn't even. Cain's children had learned secrets of war while Seth's children were peaceful and forest dwellers who wanted to follow

Adam's lead. They felt an obligation to protect the earth. Their aim was to restore balance to the planet. They had the ability to fight using the light art, but they weren't killers. They were spiritual people that wanted to save the world, and that included the souls of the children of Cain," He continued. "But Cain's children were completely consumed by their desires and gave in to their most carnal instincts. They were warriors, they systematically searched and destroyed all of Seth's children. It got so bad the Children of Seth had to go into hiding to prevent extinction. Sadly, the world wasn't big enough. No matter where we hid them the Children of Cain found them and brutally massacred them. Seth protected them as long as he could, but he realized before he died that Cain's hesitation wouldn't be shared by his children so he foresaw the fall out that followed Cain's death. He knew running wasn't going to suffice. He, unlike Cain, was there when Adam passed."

His words were foreign as I stared befuddled by his statement.

"What do you mean?" I asked pressing him.

He turned to Michael who once again gave him a permissive nod.

"The story that is in your bible is not the end of Adam and Eve's story?" He continued. "Adam was the first being God created that had to die with doubt. So, while on his death bed, he called all his children and grandchildren together and for the first time he had Eve explained who Father Yahweh was and why they were no longer in the Garden. He explained why he and Eve were no longer able to travel to the Heavenly Realm. When he finished he sent Seth to beg for forgiveness on his behalf and give his father his dying wish of his favorite fruit from the garden. Seth battled all types of beast and beings to get to the Garden and once there he spoke with Yahweh and begged on the behalf of his father. Father Yahweh forgave Adam and upon his death he was taken to the Heaven Realm along with Abel. Soon after that his mother Eve passed on to the Heaven Realm. They became the first members of the high council in the human quadrant, but on Earth, me and my group was left in charge of making sure Seth and his family were not destroyed by Cain's family. Each Angel in our legion was in charge of a woman by order of Michael under the advice of Seth."

I turned to Michael at the sound of his name. He turned to the entrance in a coy attempt to look away. I turned back to Semyaza more entrenched into the words he was about to say.

"Michael…and Seth to an extent, they trusted us to watch over the women until a boy could be born to wife them, and for a time there wasn't a problem. It worked to perfectly until Seth's granddaughter Diana came along," he replied shaking his head.

"Diana?" I questioned. "It sounds so familiar. I've heard that name before…"

"She is fairly well known as the goddess Diana," He responded causing me to nod. "She was also known as Rhea the mother of the most powerful Olympians."

Before I could reply he continued.

"She was so beautiful. The only thing close to her was Eve. I never felt attraction before. I didn't understand the pull of the heart. I didn't understand the obsessive thoughts and dominating feelings that arose from such an attraction. She was a wise woman. She understood the effect she had on all men. She was another Lilith. She was supposed to be married several times but refused. She never felt any man was good enough for her. As she rebelled, she became more and more provocative in her tempting of the watchers in my legion. As a result, a majority of my legion mates couldn't watch over her because they said she would purposely tempt them, so I was constantly changing her watcher until I finally had to take over myself. Immediately she had me drawn in. Years passed and we became closer and closer until I was sure for the first time that I was in love with her. I wanted to be with her like Adam was with Eve and I didn't think that could happen. When I went to excuse myself based on these feelings several of my legionmates disclosed they were in similar situations. They said why should these women who are not marrying be by themselves for the rest of their lives, and why shouldn't we be able to have someone to love," he replied in a pleading tone.

Michael turned to him at the sound of his words.

"Simple, because you weren't made for that purpose. It wasn't about being alone. It was jealousy and a sense of entitlement. Lucifer may have been more upfront with his feelings, but they were the same as yours. Don't masquerade your feelings as human because they weren't. You just convinced yourself that you were in love and infatuated with this woman. You weren't. You were jealous and you took advantage of the trust that was given to you by me and Father Yahweh. Don't sit here sweetening and romancing your motives to Tim, because your actions were equal to pedophilia in my eyes," He fired showing visual agitation.

Semyaza face scrunched at the sound of his words. He showcased an anger toward Michael for the first time since I had been there.

"Michael, you're so perfect, right?" he shot. "Who are you to tell me what I feel? Maybe it was jealousy, or entitlement, but you left us here to watch over them without ever letting us know the dangers."

Michael shook his head laughing.

"I left you here because I trusted and had faith in you. There was no danger to disclose. The only danger was the danger you created," Michael replied. "You knew that sin was a possibility because you were in a world leased by the creator of the very disease. You let your guard down because you were away from Father Yahweh and let Lucifer lull you and your legion into a false sense of security. You believed that you had the free range to do as you please and you exercised that right. It was you."

Semyaza lowered his head in an ashamed manner.

"So, what happened?" I asked turning to Michael.

Michael turned to Semyaza as he continued.

"I took Diana as my wife on the word that the others would join taking women as their wives," he replied. "But I never understood that the situation was a set up. Lucifer had infiltrated my legion and it was simply a ploy to corrupt our legion and inevitably Seth's offspring. My legionmates taught their wives light art creating the first witches. We found and punished them, but we couldn't harm humans. So, the witches began to teach others creating wizards of the same ilk. Things became worse. These men were not like the woman. They began to use these skills in their war with the children of Cain. Seth who cared about the Earth he inherited understood the effects of using these arts would have on the world."

I stared forward feeling serendipitous goose bumps on my neck thinking about the implications.

"As you now know, dark arts require sacrifice. Witches and now wizards were sacrificing earth elements, animals, and human blood to attain the light energy they needed to make their spells work," he continued. "These spells corrupted their souls, mutating them mortifying Seth's line along with Cain's who had long been corrupted by the rebel angels long ago. Then…things became more corrupted. My legionmates began to have children with their wives creating the hybrid beings you know as Nephilim. These beings were beyond evil. Calling them bullies would be mild. They were almost two to three times the size of normal men when they reached maturity, and usually learned the dark arts from my watcher legion personally. It was hard to keep them in line, but we were able to quell them because they weren't very powerful because they were the product of lower level angels. All that considered, they still were able to cause crippling damage to both the children of Cain and children of Seth. They were both targets, but it was manageable enough that the Heaven

Realm was unaware. I see it at the time, but I was only seeing the grassroots of their master plan. You see there were thirteen Master Class Angels in my legion. I was one of them, and Diana and Lucifer's end game wasn't to create hybrid beings. Their master plan was to create the next great race. Diana seduced me and I was the first to have children. I understood they were too powerful to allow out in the world, so I kept family from the rest of society caged away from the world at our Olympus compound. My actions earned me the nickname that would remain. The name Cronus was what I was know as to the people. The name was a term that meant to cut off or keep away. Diana hated this, she wanted them to take their place as the new race. The new leaders of Earth. I explained to her that to do that would put us in direct opposition because the inheritance of Seth was what I was sworn to protect. Over the years she had become more and more powerful learning the dark arts from Lilith and Lucifer to better perpetrate their plan. I was so in love with her and I trusted her like Adam trusted Eve. I never thought she would ever betray me, but I had no idea she had already forfeited her soul to Lucifer for immortality and to learn the dark arts. She became pregnant and kept this away from me until the child was born. She gave me a subatomic clone while she allowed the real one out into the world. I went utterly blind for the majority of the years until finally I heard that there was a Nephilim who was more powerful than any the legion had ever faced. I went to meet him and I was surprised to not only see him, but the rest of my children as well. They had enslaved the children of Cain and referred to themselves as the Olympians named after the compound where I had kept them. With my powerful lineage, faith energy and Lucifer's subatomic training, they were more than formidable, but that didn't matter to begin with. They were my children. I couldn't fight them.

Years passed and it was no longer Cain's offspring vs Seth's offspring, it was now human vs Nephilim, or as they began to call themselves, gods. Diana had become my nemesis, but by this time there was no way to go back, my brethren had succumb creating more and more beings like my children to the point that they overran the Earth. There were more Nephilim than men. I knew the death and destruction that prompted prayers to Father Yahweh would reach back to the Heaven Realm. I expected a swift reaction. In all actuality, I wanted them to come, I had put myself in such a deep hole and I had no way out. When Michael finally arrived, I was so relieved that I was willing to accept whatever punishment Michael or Father Yahweh found appropriate. Michael arrested me and my legion and placed us here because he wanted us to watch as our children destroyed each other. The rest of the story you know. The world needed to be cleansed so he set aside Noah. "

He paused gathering himself. I was still sputtering confused as to why I needed to hear the story. I didn't get it's correlation to me. Hearing how this war between two brothers shaped the world I knew was unsettling. I stared at the enormous guilt at the man's feet and I found it hard to find sympathy to outweigh the anger that was prompted from the carnage and death that he brought upon my people for some carnal lust. I juggled both emotion as he ran his fingers through his hair before continuing.

"So, hearing my words Timothy Eli, do you pity me?" He said staring at me.

I looked at Michael who was still staring at the entrance almost ignoring the conversation before turning back to him.

"I don't know," I replied. "I guess what you did was bad…really bad, but to be honest I don't know."

Before I could finish my words he interrupted me.

"I understand," he replied. "I've only asked one human that question from this very cell over two millenniums ago."

I turned to him with curiosity.

"Who?" I asked curiosity peaked.

"Enoch," he replied. "His name was Enoch… he was my friend. Timothy Eli, do you know who Enoch is?"

I shook my head no as he continued.

"Enoch was a very special man," he explained smiling exuberantly. "He was like Abel. He was born without the disease. The first one since Abel, but what was more important, he was the man who let us know the secret to the disease Lucifer created. There were always three. The disease had three in every generation."

I stepped closer to him.

"What do you mean by 'three'?" I replied.

"Each generation there are the three catalysts. There is a seed of Abel, Cain, and Seth to prophet each generation," He continued. "So, the disease had a controller of the soul, a controller of the flesh, and a controller of them both. These three individuals arise to lead there people in each generation. The Cain population is most vast with about 8 of out 10 humans being born falling in that category. The next is the Seth population at about 1.9999 out of every 10 humans born. The Abel is about .0000001 out of 10 people. The catalyst of these three people is special because they are the ones who will decide the fate of each generation."

His words were starting to become evident as he continued.

"What do you mean?" I pressed.

"Do you know of the two witnesses of revelations?" he replied.

I shook my head no once more.

"And I will give power to my two witnesses, and they will be clothed in burlap and will prophesy during those 1,260 days. These two prophets are the two olive trees and the two lampstands that stand before the Lord of all the earth. If a anyone tries to harm them, fire flashes from their mouths and consumes their enemies. This is how anyone who tries to harm them must die. They have power to shut the sky so that no rain will fall for as long as they prophesy. And they have the power to turn the rivers and oceans into blood, and to strike the earth with every kind of plague as often as they wish. When they complete their testimony, the beast that comes up out of the bottomless pit will declare war against them, and he will conquer them and kill them," he continued. "These two men are the one chance of hope. The children of Seth have been taken. They are the pre-rapture Christians. What's left over, or more specifically, the people you and your legion are battling for, those people are the Children of Cain that will choose Father Yahweh over the Lucifer. These men are going to be the final sacrifice for these witnesses."

"So, who are these witnesses?" I asked empathetically.

He looked me in the eyes with an unnervingly weird stare.

"Enoch and Elijah," he replied with a woeful sigh.

His words were relieving as I exhaled happy to hear.

"Well, where are they?" I replied. "And I thought you said there were three."

"There are, but understand, just as the Christ has his witnesses, so does the anti-Christ," he replied. "He exercises all the authority of the first beast in his presence. And he makes the earth and those who dwell in it to worship the first beast, whose fatal wound was healed. He performs great signs, so that he even makes fire come down out of heaven to the earth in the presence of men. And he deceives those who dwell on the earth because of the signs which it was given him to perform in the presence of the beast, telling those who dwell on the earth to make an image to the beast who had the wound of the sword and has come to life."

As he finished his words an eerie feeling filled me. The energy was toxic and it over took me quickly as I fell to my knees. A voice echoed catching my attention as Michael turned to me signaling for me to keep quiet.

"Funny running into you here," said a Man with long black hair.

It was obvious he was an angel, but the way he was acting threw me. His mannerisms and the way he walked was different. Outside of Michael, the majority of the angels were robotic in their mannerism, but this guy was different. Michael signaled for me to follow him via BAU as he turned to leave without saying a word.

"Brother, Michael, not even a chastisement for old times sake," he replied in a mocking tone.

Michael cut his eyes as we walked past the angel. I snuck by him getting the impression he couldn't see me as he never even turned in my direction. Michael's warning made it abundantly clear that I was invisible. I just had to be quiet. It was obvious Michael was trying to smuggle me out without this guy knowing and I figured it would be smarter to follow his lead and ask questions later.

"I hear you guys have picked the legion to stop me," he replied stopping me and Michael in our tracks. "I hear they're getting their butts kicked so far in the Light Guard Trials, and after all the hoopla too, but what can I say about a legion you put together."

"Why are you here?" Semyaza shot angrily.

He gave Semyaza a cynical glare then replied.

"Oh, I was just trying to let you know we got the old gang back together. All your children are back with dear ol' mommy," he continued. "As much as I know you hate hearing about my current bow, and your ex-wife Diana, I just had to share the good news. So, that's all. I can see I'm not wanted here so, I'll make myself scarce, but I'll definitely give your family your regards."

He winked at Michael as he created a wormhole and step through it. As he disappeared the guard closed the cell door as Semyaza approached the bars.

"Michael, be sure to let my friend know that the story I told him is very important. He should find these people. His future depends on it," He replied. "Tell him it's all in the Nephilim Testament."

I turned to Michael who was nodding as we were enveloped in light. I didn't even blink and I was standing in the middle of my room.

"Michael, what was he talking about?" I asked turning to him. "And was that guy?"

He shook his head emphatically.

"It was too risky to go there. I knew I shouldn't have…" he barked to himself.

"Michael?" I pressed.

"Tim, my job is to make sure you're trained. I can't intervene beyond those parameters. That is why I took you to Semyaza. There are things about your world you need to know that I can't tell you, but I shouldn't have taken that chance. It was too risky. That man was an angel, as I'm sure you could tell, Lucifer…it was Lucifer."

My eyes almost jumped out of my head.

"You had me in the same room as the Devil," I shot angrily.

He raised his hand in an apologetic manner.

"Unfortunately, yes," he continued. "You and your legion need to know this stuff. You have forever to learn the Heaven Realm, but your obligation is the Earth Realm. There are factors here that you need to understand that I can't tell you because it falls out of the laws set up to protect you. I'm only able to help you in matters of training. The rest is in the word."

"Can't I just do like a BAU upload or something?" I shot.

"No, the Bible is not Heaven Realm law, it's Earth Realm law, it isn't here," he replied reaching into his bag. "Here take this. Use your teammates to decipher the message Semyaza gave you and seriously think about what you learned tonight, alright."

I nodded as he walked over and placed his hand on my head like my father used to do. I started to object and tell him I wasn't a little kid, but there was something wrong about saying that to a guy who's a couple hundred thousand years older than you that seemed to cause an argument to lose its validity.

"I'm sorry. I wish I could stick around and help you sort this stuff out, but as I said I only get a small amount of time to interact with you. I have to go, but seriously, Tim. Take care and I'm rooting for you okay, kid?" he continued with a smile as he disappeared.

I went to fall on the bed, but before I could I heard a knock on my door.

"Hey, Tim, Jacob is ready to train," screamed Sam from the other side of door.

Through all the commotion I had almost forgotten Jacob. I sighed and peeled myself of the bed. It was like the knowledge of the history of our world was a heavy burden that was weighing me down. Like with everything that had been heaped on me before, I forced it to the back of my mind, struggled to my feet and kept it moving.

"Yeah, Yeah, I'm coming."

CHAPTER

19

Girls night out

girls night out

I could feel the heat of Jacob's stare as I walked through the door to the training room. The whole Legion was sitting on the sideline waiting for me with impatient glares as I walked past them. It was highly unusual considering no one cared about my training before. I placed my bag next to Sai who was giving me an empathetic smile. I tried to consciously look away, but her stare was burrowing into side my face like a laser.

"What?" I asked cracking a relenting smile.

She giggled breaking her glare.

"Why are all you guys here?" I asked shaking my head.

They all looked at each other showcasing waning glances before they all shrugged their shoulders at varying times.

"To be honest, to watch you get your butt kicked," Luke shot. "But mostly we want to see what Jacob's got, because as you may or may not know, none of us have ever seen him fight."

His words caught me off-guard as I tossed my hoodie over my bag.

"Are you serious?" I continued tightening my shoelace. "You're kidding right? I mean, he said you guys sparred."

Luke turned to Uriah and Danielle.

"Well, we did, but none of us ever actually saw him while we were fighting?" Uriah replied. "Even with my time manipulation his speed and dematerialization made him impossible to find."

Luke smiled nodding in agreement.

"Yeah, we figured maybe if we saw it from a viewing perspective, he would be easier to see. These guys just overheard us talking and joined us," he added.

As he finished his speech Jacob frowned turning to Luke with a playful sigh.

"C'mon, Luke get these guys out of here," he shot.

Luke stood up at the sound of his words raising his hands in a begging manner.

"C'mon, Jake," Luke complained. "Let's us enjoy the show."

Jacob stood at him with an unrelenting stare.

"This is serious," he replied before finishing with a sighing command. "It's not a game. Now get out."

Luke and the rest of the legion grumbled at the sound of his words.

"Alright, move out," Luke replied in a parody drill sergeant type manner.

As they all got up to leave Jacob broke in once more.

"Zech, little man, you can stay," he replied. "We can continue your training and I can use your help."

Everyone stopped at the sound of his words. Zech dropped his head in a sulking manner as the rest of the team walked out. Jo stood in awe.

"Can I stay too?" Jo asked.

Zech stopped turning to his brother in a sympathetic manner.

"Just go ahead, Jo," he explained. "This is boring stuff. I'll meet up with you later to play video games."

Jo waited for a second as if to be contemplating Zech words before cautiously nodding and walking out. I stood trying to understand the dynamic and how different it was from what I was expecting.

"What is this Jacob?" I shot angrily. "I thought it was just me and you."

Zech sighed at the sound of my words.

"Yeah, and I don't want to do this anymore. I'm still sore from last time you were training me," Zech shot.

Jacob walked over to him and put his hand on his shoulder like a big brother. Obviously, it was something I wasn't used to him doing with me. I stared at them slightly peaved as he continued.

"C'mon, Zech, just help me out for a little awhile and I'll show you that technique from the last time. I promise," he replied.

Zech's face lit up at the sound of his words.

"Really!" he gushed. "Are you serious?!"

Jacob confirmed his words with a nod.

"Just help me train with my little brother, and I'll help you train yours," he continued.

Zech was nodding ecstatically at this point. I shook my head exhausted by the exchange impatient and little jealous to be perfectly honest.

"Okay," Zech replied still glowing.

Jacob turned to me and it seemed like the compassion drained from his face the minute his eyes met mine. I rolled my eyes as I turned to speak cringing thinking about his next words.

"You ready to get started?" he replied dry before finally noticing my demeanor for the first time. "You okay? You look terrible."

I shook my head.

"I'm fine, it just seems like that because…Michael kind of showed up again?" I responded with a relenting sigh.

My words caused him to squint as walked over and sat next to me. Zech followed suit skipping over next to me and plopping down.

"The coolest things happen to you!" he gleamed swaying from side to side.

I glared at him without saying a word.

"So, what happened?" Jacob pressed.

I sighed before I relented and continued.

"He just took me to this Semyaza guy," I replied.

Jacob looked like he wanted to throw something as he grew with anger.

"Are you serious?!" he grunted. "'Michael did this? Why would he…I mean, are you sure it was Michael?"

I stared at him with a cold stare.

"How dumb do I look, Jake?" I replied. "It was Michael."

He sighed and gestured for me to continue.

"Did anything happen?" he shot his voice slightly concerned.

"He told me the backstory of pretty much everything. You know, the three catalysts, the witnesses, and the Anti-Christ, but he didn't get to finish telling me who the third catalyst was because Lucifer showed up," I replied regretting spilling the beans the minute I finished my sentence.

The look on his face at that second made the other look appear meak in comparison to the look he gave me after my words.

"You have got to be kidding me?" he replied.

I shook my head frustrated.

"He didn't see me," I shot. "Michael blocked me."

He put his hands in his face and sighed before turning back to me.

"That doesn't matter. He still could have sensed you. Lucifer like Michael, is an Arch. I trust Michael's judgement, but it was still dangerous." he replied shaking his head. "What did he tell you about the witnesses?"

He gave me a weird look that made me feel like his question was coming from a place of understanding. It was like he was gauging how much I thought I knew with how much he actually knew.

"He just said they were Enoch and Elijah, but he didn't tell me who the third catalyst was," I replied. "He just said something about the Nephilim Testament and finding the witnesses."

My words sparked a responsive glare.

"What's the Nephilim Testament?" Zech replied.

"It's Lucifer's Bible," Jacob responded.

"Wait, the Codex," Zech replied.

Jacob nodded non-verbally answering as Zech continued.

"But I thought that was just a bunch spells thrown in with the bible," he pressed.

"Yes, that's partly true, if you're reading it in the physical realm. If you read it without the spiritual barrier bogging down yours senses, it's the story of Lucifer and what he believes will happen in the final days. It's his plan. His battle cry. Essentially, it's the rules he mapped out to test…well, us. It pretty much lays out the plans for his demons, Nephilim, and rebel angels," Jacob explained. "Regardless, Tim, did he say find the witnesses, or find out who the witnesses are?"

I shook my head agitated.

"No, he told me who the witnesses were. He said it was Enoch and the prophet Elijah," I replied flippantly. "He never told me who the devil's witness was."

"No, that's not what he meant?" Jacob sighed. "Enoch and the Elijah are not like…when he said these three catalysts did he explains how they worked?"

I shrugged not knowing for sure what he was aiming for. Once again it seemed like he was trying to gauge how much I knew. I didn't get the feeling he was asking because he genuinely wanted insight on something he didn't already know. It was unsettling. I fumbled trying to phrase the question in a way that would satisfy him.

"I guess, I think he said they were the leaders of their people," I replied.

He shook his head throwing his hands up finally meeting his wits end.

"It's like the more I hear the worst it gets. You know what? Don't tell me anything else?" he replied standing up. "We'll deal with it later."

I nodded as he walked toward the middle of the floor. As I did Beth, Eve, Danielle, and Sai were pulling out sleeping bags after transforming their suite into a party ready palace. Eve got a bit of good news when she visited the Medcorps. She was overjoyed to see her sister up. Pete and the rest of the girls met up and had spent the hour or two I was sleeping to catch the girl back up. It was then Dani suggested a party to celebrate Sai and Beth's recovery. For once, neither one of their heads were on the chopping block and they were more than confident Jacob was going to walk through his trial against Howell. To them it was finally a night off. The girls agreed overjoyed to finally have a day to just relax and have a good time. Dani scooted in happy to mingle with girls around her age for a change. It was comforting to finally be in what she perceived to be a normal teenage dynamic. As chaotic as the days had been the nights were some of the best times of her life. Over the relatively short amount of time she spent with Eve and Beth, the three girls had grown close. When Sai returned, she genuinely felt like she was part of a sisterhood. She was on cloud nine as the girls finished up a romantic movie making gagging noises.

"Eve, my gosh, that was horrible," Sai uttered tossing popcorn at the girl as she cowered chuckling.

Eve tossed popcorn back at the girl as Beth and Dani joined in. The girls laughed enjoying themselves as Eve responded defending her decision.

"Look, Miss Hikari, some of us mere mortals have our guilty pleasures," Eve responded. "What's wrong with wanting to see a beautiful well-told love story?"

Sai stuck her finger in her mouth imitating a gag.

"Mostly because they're crap. Most of them have idiotic premises that no one outside of a four-year-old would or should believe. And that is including this movie. Yeah, real believable. This super handsome guy meets some random girl, and in what, two days he's risking his life and showing his undying affection for her? It's poisoning kids into believing this ridiculous notion that love is like a virus you catch. It's so irresponsible," Sai cut in causing all the girls to boo and throw popcorn at her.

Eve continued arguing her premise as Sai cowered.

"Sai, why are you so cynical when it comes to relationships? I promise, Dani, she's been like this since we were in elementary. Ever the cynic, spouting her Debbie-downer statistics. Can the rest of us just enjoy a terribly written, horribly acted, and highly unbelievable tale? I mean, maybe some of us want to believe in the soapy girly stuff," she cut chuckling as Dani gave her a hi-five seconding her words.

"Preach, sister," Dani cut in causing Beth to laugh. "I spent most of my nights with Abby doing the same thing. She was just as pessimistic. Let us dream of a world where men named Bryson Everhart come in and sweep us off our feet?"

Sai rolled her eyes playfully agitated as she continued.

"Oh, c'mon. Name one guy who looks like this," she replied snapping her finger causing a life-size lasting image of the star of the movie to pop up. "Name one guy like this dude…this guy is beating them off with a stick, but he's going to find some slightly above-average girl and fall for her to the point that he's going to risk his life in at most a couple of months in most cases. It's mental. That's crap. We've all been around guys that look like this guy, and they aren't mister perfect. In my experience, they're the exact opposite. Most of them get girl's without putting much effort into it. None of them are rolling out the red carpet or dying for chicks they barely know. Most of them ditch a girl as soon as they get bored, and or she becomes more of a headache then the next prospect in line."

Her words seemed to cause a solemn feel to wash over the room. Sai picked up on it. She relented with an unapologetic shrug.

"Ouch, my gosh. Who's spurned this chick?" Dani shot causing Beth and Eve to chuckle as Sai playfully shoved the girl.

"No one. Miss perfect doesn't date. She says adolescent relationships are a waste of time," she continued pretending to be fixing imaginary glasses speaking like a professor. "Ninety-four percent of teens believe in love. A study by nerdy guy at prestigious school says eighteen percent of both male and female adolescents inevitably say that the experience of dating was a negative one...and blah, blah, blah, blah."

Sai chunked a pillow at the girl as she batted it down playfully. Dani waited until the spat between the two girls ended before breaking in again.

"I don't believe it," Dani shot. "I think there's a bleeding heart under that icy coat, and I'll prove it."

Sai gave the girl a cynical stare pressing her to continue.

"Let's play a game of last guy standing shall we," she shot pointing at Sai in a warning manner.

Sai and Eve both sat forward attentively as Beth slowly followed suit. She reached on the table behind her and grabbed a water bottle.

"Beth, can you do the honors?" she shot holding the plastic bottle in a pinching manner.

Beth moved her hands causing the plastic bottle to transform into a glass one. She thanked the girl with a playful bow before dramatically placing the bottle on the ground and spinning it. It slowed before landing on Beth.

"If you're looking for a kiss, I think you've woefully misinterpreted the vibe of the room," Beth cut in causing the girls to chuckle as she bashfully lowered her head.

"No, it's a game. You tell us the trait of your ideal guy, and based on the guys we know, we cross off boys until we land on the perfect guy for you," she responded turning to Sai and Eve as they both instantly blushed. "Once we've done that, you'll tell us if we are right or wrong, but there's a catch. A catch I will tell you about after you finish telling us about your ideal guy."

The girls went to object, but before they could Dani continued raising her hand cutting them off.

"Beth, what are the traits of your dream guy?" she shot over Sai and Eve's objections.

Beth sputtered showing a bashful demeanor as well. She turned to Eve and Sai asking with her eyes if the girl was serious. When she realized the girls were reluctantly going along with things, she sighed and continued.

"I don't know," she shot shrugging.

"C'mon, Beth. Nobody's going to judge you. We're just having a little fun is all. It's not like our choice forces you to get married. It's just to show chill veins over here that there are plenty of good boys out there," she shot with a playful wink that caused Sai to shake her head.

She was nervous about the girls end goal, but she didn't want to show it. She continued to play along even though everything in her wanted to stop the game before it started. She jostled uncomfortably as Beth responded.

"I...Dani, seriously, I don't know. I mean, nice, smart...really smart, actually. Someone that I could do the things I like without boring them, you know?" she responded. "Obviously, I would want him to be good-looking, but it also wouldn't be the most important thing. I just really want someone I would be attracted to. In all seriousness, I want someone who is patient with me. I want someone who truly respects and cares about my thoughts and convictions. And, I want someone I can follow without worrying about the decisions they're going to make."

The three girls stared at Beth then stared at each other cynically before turning back to the girl with playful dismissive indifferent expressions.

"So, we can strike out anybody who's name isn't Pete, right?" Eve cut in causing the room to erupt in laughter as Beth bashfully tossed popcorn at her sister.

Dani nodded seconding Eve's words as she snapped her finger. As she did a holographic scene scrambled through pictures shocking the girls.

"Wait a minute, this an actual game with scientific BAU data?" Sai pressed hesitantly.

Dani nodded as the picture stopped blinking showcasing an envelope. She moved her hand in a pushing manner causing the envelope to float to Beth.

"Now, we won't read it. It's for your eyes only. This randomizer uses relationships severity and the BAU consciousness of every boy in the Realm and it spits out a name just for you. All you have to tell us is whether we're right or wrong."

Beth nodded grabbing the envelope and playfully opening it. Her eyes squinted as if to be making sure she was reading things right. She turned to Dani in a pressing manner.

"And this thing…it just picks random names, right?" Beth pressed. "You're just joking with us about the BAU stuff?"

Dani stared at Eve and Sai quickly shaking her head as if she was begging them to trust her.

"No, it really does have an analytical mapping of algorithms that predicts past, present, and future behavior patterns. The results showcase the person with the highest percent chance of lining up with everything you stated you were looking for in your ideal husband," Dani shot. "But forget all that, just answer the question. We got it. It was Pete, right?"

Beth stared down at the paper like she was sadden by its content before shaking her head no as perplexed as the three girls watching her were.

"Okay, now you have to tell us," Eve pressed picking up on her demeanor.

Beth eyes shot to the girl quickly shooting down the notion.

"No way," Beth uttered eviscerating the paper in a small show of fire.

Dani raised her hand stopping Eve's actions.

"Nope, that's one of the rules that makes it fun," Dani shot placing her hand on the girl's shoulder proudly. "It's her choice, and we can't press her. That's against the rule. The best part is if you say no and place the paper back, it's erased from your memory as well. Isn't the Heaven Realm awesome?"

She said her words in a provoking manner as Eve and Sai sulked childishly. Beth immediately reversed time as Dani chuckled at the girl's display knowing it would make the curiosity in the other two girls all the more insatiable. They stared at Beth in a pleading manner, but the girl refused to adhere to their whims as she pushed the envelope back into the randomizer. It sputtered then disappeared. Beth exhaled happy to have the weight off her shoulders as the two girls stubbornly groaned knowing they would never know the girl's secret. Dani reached over and turned the bottle one more time. It sputtered then landed on Sai as Eve smiled exuberantly.

"This I got to hear. Who is good enough for Miss Perfect," the girl cut in.

Sai rolled her eyes as the girls continued to press her burrowing into the girl with impatient eyes. She sighed exhaustedly before giving in to the kids wishes.

"Real. I want someone who is real with me. I always want to look at them and know that I'm looking at someone I know. I want them to feel comfortable enough to trust me, and I want them to be someone I can trust as well," she responded staring down obviously embarrassed as she continued. "I want someone who respects and accepts me for who I am. I want someone who sees me as their equal with the understanding that I'm allowing them to lead my family because I chose to follow them, not because they're a male."

The girls truly took in her words. No one laughed they all just stared at the girl captivated with her insight at her age as she continued.

"I won't someone who cares about me as much as I care about them," she continued fidgeting with her fingers as Dani showed a mischievous smirk as she continued.

"Oh, you mean someone who would die for you, go bezerk on a minotaur within an anointment barrier for hurting you, and walk around half-dead visiting your unconscious body," Dani shot causing Eve to uncomfortably fix her position on the floor as Sai blushed uncontrollably.

Sai shrugged awkwardly before lowering her head without a reply. Eve picked up on the girl's emotions through her extra sensitive touch and a part of her felt guilty. She held back the news about our relationship because she wanted to speak about things when she and Sai had a chance to talk in private, but the situation was becoming more awkward by the second. She moved to speak but before she could Sai cut in.

"Yeah, Tim's an awesome guy, and yes, he does do all those things for me, but he does it as my friend. Which is cool. If I'm being honest, I don't think he sees me in that way. Our relationship has just always been so chill and easy. I love the kid," Sai uttered blushing as her voice betrayed the calm demeanor she was trying to portray.

Eve lowered her head now fidgeting with her hands.

"So, you do like him then?" Eve pressed letting her eyes wonder before forcing her eyes to confront the Sai's surprised gaze.

Sai's words gave the girl pause about our relationship. At that moment, if the girl stated she did have feelings for me, Eve would've end things, but unfortunately, instead Sai said words that set in motion a chain of reactions that would send ripples throughout our legion. Sai sputtered embarrassed by Eve's words before shaking her head adamantly.

"No!" she shot squinting angrily pretending to be frustrated to cover up her earlier vulnerable look. "I would say the same thing about Pete, or Jacob. They all have those tendencies. I'm just pointing out…"

"You have got to be kidding me? I'm such an idiot," Dani shot covering her mouth. "You have a crush on Jacob, don't you? That…It makes so much sense now. My gosh, I don't understand how I could've missed it. My gosh, you practically go to mush whenever the guy speaks directly to you. You're always sticking up for him whenever Tim says anything about him. The constantly chiding your brother for mentioning your age and making it seem like your so much younger. The complete ignoring of the obvious affection shown by your dreamy best friend. The annoyance at being romantically linked with Tim, especially when the accusation came from your older brothers. You're literally waiting until you get older because then your age won't mean so much. It's all there. My gosh, this…I thought you were crushing on Tim, but you…you've got your eye on another Eli."

Sai looked like someone dashed her with cold water as Eve stared at the girl begging to know if the Dani's assumptions were founded. Deep down it would be easier if that was the case, but Sai quickly shot down the notion.

"Wow, you pull a muscle with that reach?" Sai shot cynically. "Uh, no. Nice deductions, but…just no. Jacob? Seriously, you think I have a crush on Jacob?"

Dani returned her cynical stare with one of her own.

"C'mon?" the girl shot in disappointed tone. "You're saying everything I just said was imagined?"

Sai moved her head up and down slowly in mocking manner.

"Believe it or not, no one's mistaking your skills with Uriah," she continued placing a hand on Dani's shoulder. "Jacob is like my mentor. When we were younger Tim and I saw him as our mark. The truth is his opinion and recognition mean a lot to me, but saying I go to mush is reaching. The defending him is generally more about Tim than it is about Jacob. Tim's animosity toward his brother is brought on by his frustration with constantly being compared to him, at times that frustration can cause Tim to unfairly blame his brother. The age thing is more about the way Luke treats me. You more than anybody should understand. Luke sees me as his kid sister, which causes him to be overprotective. The guy found a letter a kid wrote to me in my backpack and the next day he was jacking the kid up at the local arcade for saying hi to me. He's completely crazy.

It's like he doesn't get that I'm getting older and he doesn't have to treat me like I'm five. And the Tim thing, I explained that, and what I said was the truth. So, to make it abundantly clear so that there are no misconceptions, I have nothing resembling romantic feelings for Jacob. Just admiration for the Christian and person he is."

Dani gave a disappointed sigh before Eve cut in ready to finally unburden herself.

"So, you're saying you don't like Tim, Jacob, or Pete? Romantically, I mean," Eve questioned nervously.

Her words caused Sai to sputter mimic her manner. Sai shrugged her shoulders unable to lie.

"I can't say…" she paused stopping herself from lying with a relenting sigh. "Honestly, with Jacob and Pete, um no."

Her heart beat out of her chest as she fumbled to find the correct way to phrase what she was feeling.

"Tim and I…it's so complicated," Sai spoke barely over a whisper causing Beth and Dani to chuckle.

She shoved Dani playfully as the girl shot a vindicating smile. The girl's defense mechanism kicked in causing her to cover as soon as she could.

"But no…I…I…I can't say I like him. Romantically, I mean," she said telling a truth and a lie at the same time.

She purposely phrased her words as to not lie, but she regretted them immediately as Eve's face perked up.

"So, if he was to…say, ask someone out. Would you think that person was the worst friend in the world if they said yes," Eve responded wincing with a begging smile.

Sai's eyes widened at the sound of the girl's words.

"No way," Dani shot covering her mouth. "Tim asked you out?"

Eve nodded turning to Sai who showed a smile and exuded a genuine happiness that calmed the girl's psyche. She was sure Sai was holding back feelings for me, but her best friend's BAU made it abundantly clear that it was in her mind. Sai was genuinely happy and the feeling filled her with exuberance as she nodded as Sai and Dani tackled her dumping popcorn on the girl in celebration.

"Why didn't you tell us?" Sai shot smiling from ear to ear. "No wonder he was acting so weird when I arrived."

Eve smiled overwhelmed and pleasantly surprised her friend didn't resent her relationship.

"I'm sorry. With everything that happened during and after my trial it just slipped my mind," Eve responded.

"I'm guessing you said, yes?" Beth pressed.

Eve hesitated shy in her response as she slowly moved her head up and down.

"That's awesome, Eve," Sai uttered. "It's been a long time coming. I know how long you've been waiting for this. It's great."

Eve's heart stopped as she finally felt the hint of sadness in the girl's spirit that she expected initially. She lowered her head as she could feel the sadness growing in her best friend with every passing moment. She felt guilty and she wanted to tell Sai why, but she couldn't without revealing to the girl that she was hiding a secret that she was afraid could end their friendship.

"Sai, I don't want to mess up your friendship with Tim. I don't want to step on your toes. If you're not comfortable with this, I promise, I'll end it. I don't want to…"

"Eve, he asked you because he wants you…you know, in his life. Of course, I'm not happy that my best friend is going to have a girl in his life that will more than likely change our dynamic. I'm also not happy that you are going to have Tim and it may change our relationship as well, but I'm happy for you because I know how much this means for you. I'll get used to it. Tim and I have our bond, and you and Tim have yours. They'll just evolve a little is all," Sai continued obviously holding back emotion as she once again nervously fidgeted her fingers to kill the awkwardness.

Dani moved up placing her arms around the three girls pulling them in for a group hug and a lasting image.

"Let's celebrate the occasion, girls. The first one of us to have a boyfriend is pretty big stuff," she shot as the girls smiled into the camera orb as it flashed.

The girls continued to take pictures as Sai noticed the BAU scrambler moving. She covertly scooted over to the machine as it stopped. She quickly snatched the envelope placing it in her pocket as the other girls continued to take lasting images.

"C'mon, Sai," Dani shot as the girls laughed loudly.

Sai forced a smile and made her way over to the group as I continued my nightmare experience of training with Jacob. Zech skipped over to the center of the training room following my lead. I sat down and took a second to rest dreading another highly combustible situation.

"Get off your lazy butt, Tim," Jacob groaned in a warning manner.

I cut my eyes in his direction. I reached in my bag and grabbed my water bottle.

"If you don't get up in the next five seconds," he grunted walking toward me angrily.

I raised my hand dropping the bottle.

"Alright, alright, calm down...I knew this was going to suck...I mean, why did you choose me anyways?" I shot making my way to him. "I thought you hated me?"

Jacob sighed showing a hint of regret.

"Why?" he responded. "Why would I hate you?"

I shrugged my shoulders not wanting to respond as I swallowed hard in an annoyed manner.

"Listen, I don't hate you. I hate things you do," he said illustrating his emotions with his hand movements.

I responded like a true little brother lowering my head embarrassed and little proud to hear him say it. He stared at me awkwardly not knowing what to do before continuing.

"Do you remember about a year ago?" he replied. "After that game against Lincoln Springs."

I nodded agreeing. It was my first game after my granddad died. I remember that game like it was yesterday. The emotion surrounding it. I looked away as a lump came into my throat. Jacob rocked back and forth not really knowing what to do with his hands as he stared me down.

"That game…if you knew how proud dad was of you that day," he replied smiling. "Tim, you are an extremely talented kid, but your propensity to not care about…you, is beyond me. Do you remember why you did what you did that day?"

I nodded becoming sad thinking about the circumstances.

"Yeah, I promised dad I would break your touchdown record for Gramps," he replied. "I wanted to cheer him up after Gramps passed. It was the only thing I could think of to help him get out his funk."

He nodded acknowledging my words.

"You had my record by half-time," he replied. "Eight touchdowns in one half. You couldn't be stopped that game. You know why? Because for once in your life you had focus and purpose. You could have done that every game if you wanted to. Why don't you? Because you walk around feeling sorry for yourself, crying, complaining, and wanting everything to be easy. It makes me so angry. I ignored it for the most part because it was your life and your talent to waste, but now, I can't. We have hundreds of thousands of people depending on us. I can't let you rely on your natural ability and just run through something this important with the same immaturity you do with everything else. So, yes, I ride you harder than the rest of them, and I do that for three reasons: first because nobody goes into autopilot like you, and I mean no one goes into autopilot like you…"

He paused like he wanted to kick himself for his following words.

"Second you have talent like nothing I've ever seen before. Third, and most importantly, you're my brother, and with mom and dad gone, you're my responsibility. I'm going to protect you even if it's against yourself, and I'm not going to apologize to anyone for doing things the way I choose to do them," he replied passionately. "Dying for Sai, going to purgatory to get Luke, you name it, time after time you sacrifice yourself for others. You have no regard for your own well-being because you always feel as if everyone would be better off without you. I'll admit that I may have something to do with that, but whatever the reason, I have to protect you from you and that's what I'm going to do starting today. That trial was the last gamble I'm letting you take."

He stopped pausing before continuing.

"What do you think the key to your ability is?" he asked squinting like he was piercing through me.

I shrugged then replied.

"My need to outdo everybody," I replied more like I was asking than telling him.

He shook his head.

"Tim, your ability doesn't come from your need to outdo everyone," he replied. "Now, your ability to understand things and counter is a gift from God. It's just a natural ability that you have, most Eli's do, we're natural fighters, it has nothing to do with your ability though. Your true metaphysical ability comes from your need to protect everyone. Whatever you have to do to protect the people you care about, you'll do, that's why your metaphysical ability works the way that it does? The phantom or unconscious learning of powers seems to happen when you're doing what you need to do to protect the rest of the legion. That's why you can't prevent yourself from doing it. A metaphysical power is the function of the soul self. It's the subconscious will of the soul. The very essence of who you are."

He pressed his finger in my chest as he spoke. I couldn't believe I never thought of it in that way. Each time I gained a new power trait I was protecting someone in the legion. It made perfect sense why I could mimic certain powers, yet others I couldn't. I nodded as he spoke agreeing he had a point to his words. I still thought he was a jerk, but it reminded me why I still loved him so much. He was my brother, and as annoying as he could be, he always looked out for me. In many ways, it's what made him a good older brother.

"That's why I wanted to train with you," he shot. "Because I wanted to help you understand the key to your power."

I nodded as I spoke.

"What is it?" I inquired.

He turned cracking his knuckles as he spoke.

"It's understanding the need to protect yourself like you do others?" he replied. "Once you understand how to value protecting yourself, you'll be able to protect others, but first you have to gain faith and self-confidence. You'll never be able to master your ability if you're constantly feeling sorry for yourself believing everyone would be better off without you."

I looked at him and all I felt in the pit of my stomach was jealousy. He figured out my power in days. I practiced with Jade for weeks and neither of us could understand it, and here he was holding a seminar on it like he created it himself. I nodded slightly bitter.

"So, how do I do that?" I replied.

He turned to me with an obvious provoking glare.

"By getting better," he shot. "The better you get, the more your confidence will grow. The more your confidence grows, the more vital you see yourself being to the welfare of the people you care about. It's that easy."

I nodded cherishing the irony of it all. The person who was giving me the most important key to being better than Jacob, was Jacob himself. He signaled for me to follow him as we headed to the center of the floor.

"Listen, you and Zech are going to spar. I'll teach you both and as I do so I'll study the elementals style," he replied.

Zech nodded as I hesitated before finally relenting.

"Don't go easy on me, "Zech replied bowing ceremoniously.

I stared at him for a second then returned his bow with one of my own. I didn't really know what to expect, but if it was to help, then I was willing to do whatever Jacob needed.

"Okay, let's go," Zech replied dropping into his fighting stance.

As he did so his body began to change covering itself with an icy exterior that matched his white hair.

"How are you able to do that?" I asked trying to mimic his technique. "Whenever I do it my vitals kick and my body cells go haywire. Not to mention, you're not even an elemental. How can you control wind and water to create solid ice? I thought Doms only had one element."

He smiled bounding from foot to foot.

"Well, that's because you still have your earthly body, but even if you had your heavenly body, you wouldn't be able to do this. It's a technique my family has honed our bodies for years to do. Seeing as I'm a Dom, my body adapted this way. Besides, lightning at it's core is cold, not hot. So, when you think about it, I don't have ice, it's my own lightning element, and I'm the only who can do it. My brother can do fire, but that's easy because he's an elemental cheater, but he can't absorb it into his cells like I can. I'm the only one who can do that," he replied proudly. "But hurry, I don't' want to talk anymore."

BOOM! Before I could blink he was heading for me.

"Wait a second, Zech?" I replied quickly responding to his attack.

DODGE! ICE! I dove as I created an ice wall barrier to intercept him.

CRUSH! He burst throw it absorbing it into his armor like it was glue.

"C'mon, your Timothy Eli," he said continuing to charge.

"Well, how am I supposed to hit you?" I replied angrily.

BLOCK! KICK! PUNCH! BLOCK! I countered each of his punches and kicks not wanting to hurt him.

"I said don't take it easy, it's the only way I'm going to get good enough to teach my brother," he shot swinging for the fences.

BLOCK! I blocked one of his kicks.

DODGE! I dodged a countering sweep.

WHAM! I leaped over his extended leg and hit him with a spinning back kick that sent him reeling.

CRUSH! He hit a nearby tree before forcing himself off the ground and clearing the cobwebs still smiling from ear to ear.

"Okay, you got me. Keep it going!" he replied charging at me again.

"Zech," I groaned turning to Jacob in a pleading manner.

He watched surveying us like an instructor walking from side to side getting in position to dissect every move.

"He's weak on his left side, Zech, charge right and wait for an opening when he's vulnerable on his left. He won't be able to recover," Jacob instructed staring me down as he spoke.

I stared at him angrily objecting to his words.

"That's not true," I shot.

"Okay, then prove me wrong," he shot back.

CLASH! SHATTER COLLIDE! He sent a cold blast that I intercepted with one of my own. He was following Jacobs's instructions keeping me off balance on my right side.

CLASH! BLOCK! BLOCK! DODGE! BLOCK! He was on me hard I tried to compensate but his speed was as good as anyone I had faced since arriving, and for a kid his age it was saying something.

BOOM! He kicked into my high block with bone cringing force. I slid trying to catch my feet as he continued his attack.

"I gotcha," he replied attacking yet again.

WHOOSH! I did a spinning wind kick shot that caught him in midair and sent him flying in the opposite direction like he was fired out of a bazooka. His feet kicked as he landed with a thud across the field. He dusted himself off and prepared for another attack.

"Man, wow, did you see that, Jacob? He's like you," he replied.

He stopped as if something had just occurred to him.

"Okay, I think I got a plan for you," he replied springing back into action.

ICE SHOT! ICE SHOT! ICE SHOT! He was sending ice blasts at me faster than I could block them, and each blast was more powerful than the last one. The little midget was really starting to agitate me. The impact of his shots obstructed my view as fog filled the air becoming thicker with every blast, and before long, I lost sight of him.

"Element Gamma, Fire Command, Inferno," I commanded.

WHOOSH! I erupted as flames exploded clearing the fog around me. I powered down as soon as the fog dissipated but Zech was still nowhere to be found.

"Gotcha," said a voice from beside me.

WHAM! I turned into a punch that sent me flying.

"Told ya," Jacob poked as I flopped uncontrollably.

As I gained control of my body I turned to him rubbing my sore jaw in an agitated tone.

"No, you didn't. He didn't hit me on the left side, it was my right," I shot back peeling myself of the ground fixing my sights on Zech.

"Wait for it," he replied.

I turned to him with an inquisitive stare.

"What are you…?"

WHAM! Before I could finish my words I was floored with a high kick to the side of my head that popped so loud I thought I was going to go deaf. I flipped awkwardly from the momentum of the kick until I flopped into a heap on the opposite side of the floor. I grimaced wincing from then pain before I punched the floor in frustration as I fought to my feet.

"Jacob, why did you kick me?!" I screamed. "You didn't tell me it was two on one!"

He stared at me shaking his head.

"That wasn't me?" He shot chuckling. "Trust me, if that was me, you'd be sleeping right now."

I surveyed the room angrily.

"Then who was that, Jo?!" I screamed out for blood. "Show yourself!"

A chuckle rung out at the sound of my words.

"That wasn't Jo," said a voice from behind me.

I spun around as Zech was walking toward me.

"Yeah, it was just me," said another identical voice across the room.

I shook my head as the person behind the voice came into view. It was Zech or a replica of him. The clone was identical to the Zech standing next to me.

"How?" I replied. "There are two of you."

He nodded with a smile as his eyes lit up and the other replica of him turned into light and was absorbed back into his body.

"No, just one," he replied. "It's my metaphysical trait. I can make copies of myself. My brother can do the same thing. Jade says it's because we depend on each other when we're in tight spots, and something about twins being able to split apart and create duplexes of ourself. I think."

I nodded wanting to kick myself.

"I may have needed Jacob's help, but I got you," he replied smiling from ear to ear.

I nodded unable to believe the kid had actually gotten the drop on me because Jacob just had to intervene once again.

"I can't take credit for anything," Jacob replied shocking me. "Especially considering the things I said about Tim were completely bogus."

His words caused us both to turn toward him confused.

"What?" Zech replied.

I stood aghast waiting impatiently for him to continue.

"I made up the crap about Tim being weak on his left side," he replied. "Tim's left side was actually his stronger side."

Zech stomped his feet at his words.

"So, you were trying to set me up?" he replied slighted.

Jacob shook his head in response as he continued.

"I was trying to illustrate to both of you how powerful the mind is in combat. I took a strength Tim had, and a handicap that you had, and I swapped them by simply intervening with a modifier," he replied proudly. "Zech, you had the belief that Tim was head over heels better, and Tim had the belief that he had to take it easier on a smaller kid. All I did was implement doubt into the equation and it worked to Zech's benefit and your detriment."

"Wait, what?" I replied understanding exactly what he meant but being coy out of embarrassment.

"Simple, I gave the impression that I was evening the odds. I took something you both had belief in, and I used it to change your outlook on the battle," he continued. "In this case, you two believed in my superiority. You blindly believed that I knew you two better than you knew yourselves. Doubt crept in just long enough for you guys to exceed your limitations, and in Tim's case, question them. Once it was done, I just sat back and watch which was stronger; faith or doubt, and as always faith won out."

I stood blown away with the amount of things I learned from my brother in the thirty minutes I trained with him, and it made me sick. Where did he get his ability? How was he so smart? It was maddening. The whole time he was playing both of us like puppets on a string.

"This is my point, when you have faith it doesn't matter what the odds are if you have faith in the person who tells you how to overcome those odds. Our powers are based on faith. Doms we are the ones with the shrewdest faith, we're easy to convince and stubborn to change. Which makes us easy targets because we become proud and angry when what we believe is challenged. As a child of God, it is a blessing, but people like us outside the faith are also the hardest to convert to the faith. What make us so powerful is our unwavering stubborn faith because it is the most powerful thing in all creation. We are designed in the image of David and like David, we are powerful. Our vices will overtake us because we become proud. Now Virtues have faith as well, but their faith is based on facts. They are centered in them. They analyze the facts, weigh their options, and go with what makes the most sense. Their power is based on knowledge, because the more knowledge they gain, the stronger their faith becomes, but in the same sense, knowledge or more specifically, knowledge or doubt is there Achilles heel. It's why they are only as smart as the knowledge they have. Doubt eats away at their power, so they constantly needs facts to build it back up. They are designed like Solomon, and like Solomon, they are powerful geniuses, but their weakness lies in the same knowledge they covet. It's simple really, the more knowledge you gain, the more knowledge you need to maintain the power, and as doubt creeps in, knowledge becomes corrupted. You guys, the elementals are the wild free ones. You guys choose to have faith. It's not because you feel you have to, or because the facts tell you it's right. You guys are all about feeling. Your faith is gain through experience, which is why you become stronger and stronger over time, because unlike us, your limit isn't predetermined, and like Virtues you guys don't generally lose faith in God, you may be stagnant, but for the most part, you don't waiver because of the experiences you have builds your strong faith in God. This makes you guys infinitely powerful. You're made in the design of Moses, and like Moses you guys are powerful mouth pieces of God. You guys hold more power than the other classes because you have the ability to connect with the people around you. The problem with that is, like Moses, you guys have such impressive abilities that those that follow began to have a hard time distinguishing the blessing from the blessed. They start to put their faith in you, and not the word or power of Father Yahweh."

I nodded able to understand the similarities in the comparisons he drew in all of us. It showcased how we all fell neatly into the characteristics he illustrated, and once again, it made me sick to my stomach to think about the jump he had on me from a mental standpoint.

"What you guys have got to realize is," he continued. "The key to power is Father Yahweh and the Savior Emanuel Jesus the Christ. We are Father Yahweh's chosen people. We are his children. There is nothing we should ever believe we can't do, and we shouldn't believe there is anybody with stronger faith. And if there is no one with stronger faith, there is no one stronger. We are the best because we believe we have more faith in Father Yahweh and the Christ then any being in this realm, and if that is the case, we are unstoppable if we believe the word. Zech you overtook Tim because like a Dom it was easiest to convince you that you could. Tim you were easy to convince negatively, because doubt clouded the unknown. You stayed stagnant. Overcome them, both of you. Zech don't accept limitations, and Tim believe you are as talented as that kid I saw that day you made Dad proud. I promise you two will become powerful.

Now, Tim, suck it up and don't hold back. If you guys do that then maybe I can get a look at the way an Elemental targets a Dom, and get something out this whole thing."

I nodded as Zech and I powered up for another showdown.

BANG! We both locked in as our power raged. We gave it everything we had for the next couple hours. When it was all said and done neither one of us could stand. I saw limitations Jacob described and I wished that I could change things, I couldn't, but he did give me faith that I could gain a stronger bond with Father Yahweh and the Christ over time. Zech on the other hand seemed to take Jacob's word in stride. He was a beast to handle after Jacob's words, bringing more validity to his outline. We both sat sucking wind as he walked over to us.

"So, you guys work on what I told you?" he replied. "Tim, teach your friends what I said, and Zech do the same with your brother. Do that, and we'll do better, trust me. We can still win this thing."

I believed him as I smiled at him for the first time since I arrived. He returned my smile with a pet on the head. As annoying as I thought our session would be, I was happy I got a chance to do it. I got a better insight into my brother and to a lesser extent the rest of my legion. I had forgotten about the situation with Michael, I knew that chapter was far from over, but I tried to focus on the things at hand without ignoring enormous tasks that lay ahead of our legion. For now, I was proud of my brother for helping me and Zech the way he did. I would have like to see him fight, but I guess I just had to wait like everyone else. I was expecting a show, but even I had to admit in my assumptions about how his match would play out I had grossly underestimated my remarkable older brother. I grabbed my medallion and sparked it up to leave, as I did, Pete was taking a breaking for helping Sam trained and almost tripped over Sai as exited the room. He sputtered catching his balance before chuckling as he reached his hand out placing it on her shoulder to steady himself.

"Sorry, Sai, I…" his heart dropped at the sight of tears in the girl's eyes. "Sai, my gosh, what's going on? What happen?"

She leaned her head back against the wall and turned away from the boy in a remedial attempt to hide her tears. She relented as the tears wouldn't stop. She covered her mouth letting her emotion out as Pete hugged her consoling the girl.

"Sai? Seriously, what happened?" Pete begged as she released the boy before once again wiping the tears from her face.

She paused to gather herself. She wanted to unburden herself, but she also wanted to be careful about what she disclosed. She brought her knees into her chest and wrapped her arms around them. Pete hesitantly began to rub her back as she finally proceeded with her explanation.

"Have you ever felt, embarrassed, stupid, and unattractive all in a one-minute span," she responded causing the boy to stare at her like she was insane for insinuating she could be anything but perfect.

Pete didn't know how to respond, so he sat continuing to console the girl allowing her to continue. She chuckled sorrowfully in a way that cut the boy to his core before continuing.

"I'm such an idiot," she shot once again lowering her head allowing grief to overtake her. "Have you ever been in a position to grab the one thing you've always wanted, hesitated, and then had to watch it slip away not knowing if that chance would ever come again?"

A time emanated in the boy's brain immediately. He blushed uncontrollably as the girl leaned her head on his shoulder. He hugged her as his heartbeat sped up from the closeness of their embrace.

"Sai, I don't know what happen, but stupid and unattractive aren't the words anyone would use to describe you," Pete cut in causing the girl to find his gaze in a manner that caused him to go into recovery mode. "I mean, if…they were…saying you weren't good looking. I don't…I mean, I do, but…"

She forced a snicker and gave him a consoling pat on his chest.

"Pete, I get it. I know you don't like me," she shot lowering her head causing the boy to grimace kicking himself. "But I appreciate the words all the same. This is so embarrassing. I thought I could hide using my invisibility, but I was too stupid and emotional to find a place without through traffic."

Pete placed a reassuring hand on her shoulder shaking his head.

"Sai, you have nothing to be embarrassed about. We're friends. I'm here if you need someone to talk to, but if it's something embarrassing that you don't feel comfortable telling me, that's fine too," he responded nervously fixing his glasses as the girl stared at him with appreciation.

She leaned her head on him once again as his heart warmed.

"I don't know what I would do without you, Pete," she responded sighing deeply as she finished the sentence. "I ask myself all the time, why can't all the boys be like Peter Selli?"

She chuckled bashfully as Pete leaned over bringing the girl in closer as the two embraced each other. In that second, every pain she had was gone. All she felt was comfort and she was immensely thankful for the moment of clarity to regain her bearings.

"Thanks, I think you're amazing too," he responded loving every second of their embrace.

The smell of her hair was intoxicating and the feel of her soft and delicate skin against his gave him goosebumps. It was now. There was no better time. He took a deep breath and decided to go for it with his heart in his throat.

"I hope you don't mind. I just need my best friend a little while longer," she continued with a bashful chuckle.

Pete smiled embracing the most intimate embrace the two had ever experienced.

"It's fine, take your time," he expressed nervous barely able to get it out.

His heart was beating so fast he was afraid she would feel it. He knew he couldn't waste another moment. He had to act before she cut him off again. He closed his eyes going for broke.

"Sai, I…" he managed before the sound of the girl's room door opened catching their attention before he could get the words out.

"Sai?" Dani uttered stepping into the hallway.

She paused covering her mouth as she backed away apologetically.

"Sorry, I didn't mean to interrupt," she shot with a poking wink.

Sai and Pete quickly release each other as Sai realized the suggestive position they were in. She rolled her eyes in frustration as the smile on Dani's face grew.

"Dani, this isn't at all what you think," she shot placing her head in her hand in a frustrated manner.

Dani continued to poke the girl with a provoking smile as Sai stared at her forcefully unrelenting in her stance.

"You're elation about Beth's…ah, wrong assumption is making more sense by the second," Dani cut in. "Here we were wondering where our little anti-love project was, and we had no idea you were proactively getting the job done."

Sai shook her head as Pete blushed uncontrollably.

"First, Pete and I are friends. Nothing else," she protested apologetic to Pete in her demeanor as she continued. "I'm so sorry, Pete."

Dani continued mercilessly throwing fuel on the fire of their embarrassment.

"Yeah, that looked real friendly," she shot sarcastically. "It's perfectly normal for two friends to sneak out and set up a secret snuggle session."

"Will you stop talking so loud?" Sai objected forcefully whispering signaling for the girl to lower her voice. "Dani, that's not what happened."

Dani gave her cynical look before respectfully whispering as she remembered Beth's feelings for Pete.

"Then, what was it?" she responded pressing.

Sai was stuck between a rock and a hard place. She moved to fall on her sword for Pete's sake, but before she could Pete cut in.

"Sam and I, we were training. I just happen to step out. I'm guessing from your words Sai was hiding from you guys, and we kind of just ran into each other," he cut in saving her. "We just started talking about…you know, how we feel about everything we were going through, and she kind of got a little depressed is all."

She stared at the girl sympathetically taking Pete's words with a level of guilt before raising her hand apologetically.

"Oh, I'm sorry, Sai. I wouldn't have joked if…"

"It's fine," Sai assured the girl cutting her off. "Just don't tell the guys. The last thing I need is another Sai sympathy session and ruin the vibe of the night. Just give me a second, and you guys can use me as your love drug guinea pig the rest of the night."

Danielle nodded hugging the girl before waving bye to Pete. She disappeared into the room as Sai turned to Pete with a loving chuckle.

"Pete, thanks," she shot staring at the boy beaming with admiration and love.

He lowered his head bashfully. He moved to speak, but before he could Sai was already moving toward him. She planted a kiss on the boy's forehead that melted him as his eyes met hers.

"I know you don't have those type of feelings for me. I promise, I get that…Pete, you are always…I'm sorry, I am, it's just, I'd be a lucky girl to have a boyfriend half as sweet as you," she responded staring into his eyes once more before giving him another peck on the cheek. "Now, wish me luck. I am ninety-percent sure they're angling me toward Sam, but I figure I could make a plea for Zech or Jo on the grounds that I could mold them."

Pete didn't hear a word of her joke, but he managed a playful smile through his blissful haze as Sai backpedaled amused by the boy's vacant stare. She rolled her eyes in defeat exhaling before vanishing into the room leaving the boy standing in the middle of the hallway on cloud nine.

CHAPTER

20

This is your life

This is your life

"Tim!" Pete shot beating on my door.

I grimaced looking at the clock before forcefully sitting up and groggily walked across the floor and answered the door.

"Pete?" I asked shielding my eyes as the sudden exposure of the hall light blinded me.

The boy walked around me beaming. I sleepily followed him into my room. I sat at my computer desk while sat on my bed. He smiled from ear to ear.

"I can literally die now," he responded falling back with extended arms.

I rubbed my eyes and yawned exhausted before leaning back in my seat.

"I'm guessing at some point you're going to tell me what has you so happy. If the rings under my eyes aren't a big enough indicator, I'm hoping it's sooner rather than later," I responded prompting him to continue.

"Oh, sorry," he chuckled sitting up.

He rubbed his hands together before exhaling shaking his head still in a state of disbelief.

"She kissed me," He gushed happily moving his hands up an down with a chuckle.

His words quickly knocked me out my funk. I sat forward immediately pressing the kid.

"Who?" I pressed blown away.

"Sai," he responded leaping to his feet.

His words caused my heart to beat out of my chest. I stared at him with a feeling in the pit of my gut that I wanted gone, but at that moment, I was confused, and I needed clarification.

"Sai. Sarai…Hikari. She kissed you?" I pressed needing to confirm the unbelievable story.

"Yeah, well, it was on the forehead and cheek, but she practically said she would love it if she had a boyfriend like me," he continued. "Can you believe it?"

I shook my head unable to congratulate the boy because of the confusion from his story.

"Wait, can we go back?" I asked annoyed. "You're all over the place."

Pete calmed himself nodding trying to quell his euphoria.

"Sorry. Yeah, where do I start?" he responded fidgeting excitedly. "Well, Sam was driving me crazy. I stepped out to get away from him, and I just ran into her. She was...she was crying."

His words caused my eyebrows to furl in confusion.

"Sai, was crying?" I pressed concerned.

He continued explaining the entire incident, both the highs and lows. When he finished he was still beaming.

"Pete, from what it sounds like...and I promise I'm not trying to rain on your parade with this, but it doesn't appear like she was on the same page as you on this thing," I uttered feeling like a heel.

I wanted to tell him the kiss meant as much as he thought it did, but the truth was, Sai actions screamed a lack of infatuation that Pete's obsession with the girl caused him to miss. I didn't want the boy to get his hopes up for nothing.

"I'm not an idiot, Tim. I get it, but even if that is the case, I have at the very least a sign that she could see me in a romantic capacity," he gushed. "I think your plan worked. Dani mentioned something about her being wrong about Beth's relationship, and she literally said, she felt like she missed an opportunity and she may never get the chance again. It worked."

He leaped up hugging me happily nearly kissing me as I politely gave him a congratulating pat. I exhaled once again unable to understand my fear for the boy. I had a need to tell him the risk and it was like I couldn't stop myself.

"Pete, I understand you're excited, but we both know about Sai's thing for Jacob. It's hard to believe it could be gone so abruptly," I pressed causing him to shake his head vehemently.

"I know we don't believe her, but she did say she didn't like Jacob. It's a good possibility we just assumed her admiration for the guy went deeper," he responded with a shrug.

I nodded taking in his words with a sorrowful gravity that I couldn't understand.

"Regardless, did she ever tell you why she was crying?" I cut in yawning once again.

"No, but I think it had something to do with some letter she had in her hand," he responded with a shrug.

"A letter?" I followed up.

"Yeah, it had your name on it actually," he responded scratching his head. "She said something about them pushing her to date or something. Maybe them proposing you to her was the straw that broke the camels back. She said she felt stupid and unattractive. It was similar to the day a couple years ago where I choked and loss my chance with her."

He lowered his head stopping himself not wanting to exposed the secrets he and the girl shared.

"Sai, she's more sensitive than she lets on. She just hates for people to see it. My guess is that's what happened. I didn't press, so it's the best I can do," he continued. "All I know is, I'm going to keep it up a little while longer. Just until I'm sure."

I nodded as a part of me felt relieved. The guilt for that feeling was overwhelming as the boy patted me on the back pumping a triumphant fist.

"I'm sorry for waking you, Tim. I just had to come and thank you," he responded walking out the door as he finished his sentence.

I stared in a haze. I was upset by Pete's words and I couldn't understand it. Sai was my best friend. Pete had a crush on her for as long as I knew him. I should have been overjoyed, but all I felt was depression and I couldn't wrap my head around the rationale behind the negative feelings I have. I finally had Eve. Sai and I were friends. In our relationship there wasn't any confusion about that, but the truth was, no matter how often the girl stated she didn't have romantic feelings for Jacob, I knew her. He was the one and only boy I saw her act strange around, and our battle with the Jinn all but proved it. The Jinn specifically said they tracked the girl using her lust and Jacob was the only other person besides Luke with the girl. Nothing made sense. Listening to Pete's words, I couldn't make heads or tails of anything. It took me a while to get to sleep as I tossed and turned wrestling with feelings of guilt and depression throughout the night until my alarm clock awoke me. I took the extra time usually reserved for watching the light guard trial analysis and slept. I got ready and shot out of the room making a b-line straight for the transport dodging by reporters as I made my way on the transport. I stood in an awkward position. Both Eve and Sai had open spots next to them arms I was genuinely confused about which one to sit by. Normally it would've been Sai, but now with my relationship with Eve I was torn. Eve made things easier as she marched over and hugged me.

"Morning, Tim," she greeted happily.

She showcased a smile that ensnared me. She kissed me on my cheek moving her head to the side just enough to for me to get a glimpse at Sai. She quickly she in comfortably jostled angling her view away from us. I blushed still falling between guilt and embarrassment.

"Dani needs my help with an elemental technique. I just wanted to make sure I greeted you before I went in to help her," I smiled still smitten with the girl as she gave me another hug before heading to the training room.

Pete and the older guys were camped in the back talking strategy. I sat down next to Sai. She continued to stare out the window ignoring my presence.

"Well, good morning, Miss Hikari," I shot trying to break the ice.

She turned toward me with a look that fell between indifference and annoyed. It surprised me as she nodded instead of speaking before turning her gaze back to the window.

"Sai? Is everything okay?" I responded nervously.

She continued to stare out the window obviously holding back emotion as she responded.

"Tim, why didn't you tell me you and Eve started dating?" she responded surprising me.

It was last thing I expected to hear. I fumbled to answer her apologetically.

"Oh, that. I'm sorry, with the trials and Eve's hearing it just slipped my mind," I responded. "Truthfully, I forgot."

She covertly rolled her eyes showcasing frustration at my words. From the position of her head I couldn't see it, but I did pick up on the tension in her shoulders as she continued.

"You forgot?" she responded with a scoff. "It never occurred to you that dynamic might change things between us. There is nothing in you that felt I would want to know that."

Her words sounded heavy and at the time even I was mature enough to understand the double meaning in her words, but after Pete's story my mindset had already filled in the blanks.

"C'mon, Sai, I was going to tell you," I responded defensively. "But seriously, you have to admit it not the most important thing going on in our lives right now."

She chuckled facetiously turning back to me showing visible disappointment in her eyes as she continued.

"Our bond is important to me, Tim. I know it shouldn't be as important as it is, and it shouldn't be on my mind in the midst of this crazy rollercoaster ride we're on, but the truth is, it is. I can't see how you don't get why? I don't know how you could just change that bond and think it wouldn't affect me. I know you miss obvious things on the regular, but there was a part of me that thought I was more important to you," she continued vaguely spilling her soul.

I sat trying to piece together her words in an order that made sense. Of course I should have taken in account how getting a girlfriend would change the dynamic of our relationship, but I had every intention of telling Sai.

"Sai, it won't affect our relationship. I promise," I responded placing my hand on her shoulder.

She jerked away placing a shielding hand between us in protest.

"Tim, if you believe that then..." she paused stopping herself.

She paused giving me a pleading look almost begging me to understand what she was trying to say, but it fell flat with the understanding I had. Especially with the addition of Pete's story.

"Just forget it," she shot with a sorrowful sigh.

It was obvious she was holding back tears as she stared out the window once again.

"Sai, why are you taking things so negatively? I messed up, sure, but you're overthinking it. Honestly, with the way you're acting it's almost like...you're jealous or something," I blurted almost begging the question then asking it.

She turned to me with a squinting offended glare.

"Jealous?" she responded with a chuckle. "Why would I be jealous?"

I shrugged with a dense passive look on my face.

"I don't know. You tell me," I continued lowering my voice so we wouldn't be overheard. "Pete said the thought of the girls putting us together frustrated you to the point that it made you cry last night. I'm sorry, Sai. No one is good enough for you, and there's nothing wrong with having principles that you live by, but I'm not dumb enough to see why no one measures up. The rest of us aren't as thick as you think. I'm happy you want to remain single until you get to an age where you can go after the love of your life. I wish I could do that with you, but that's not what I want."

She stared at me thrown by the accusations.

"That wasn't what happened, Tim," she shot angrily.

"So, they weren't trying to match you up with people last night," I pressed.

"Yes, but…" she managed before I cut her off.

"And they didn't end up frustrating you with the thought of the two of us being…you know, more than friends," I pressed angrily. "And it wasn't just me, was it? Everyone they chose you turned down, didn't you?"

"Yes, Tim, but it wasn't because I…Pete, he made the wrong assumption. I wasn't upset over that. I was…" she shook her head stuck between the truth and appearances pausing as she rubbed her temples in frustration.

I stared around subconsciously continuing mindful of the volume of my voice.

"Sai, I don't know what our bond means to you, but I promise it means a lot to me. I wouldn't do anything to jeopardize it. I don't want things to change between us, but I also understand at some point it will. We're getting older, and I know you don't plan on dating anytime soon, but that doesn't mean you don't want to. I just wish you would just stop with the tomboy act and admit how you feel...you know, about boys. You have eyes. You have attraction to a boy. I don't know why you won't just come out and say it. It drives me crazy," I responded pressing the girl before leaning back uncomfortably as I finished my sentence.

She nodded aggressively leaning forward continuing to whisper as she responded.

"Well, maybe if this boy gave me any indication other then vague mixed signals I'd have the courage to do that," she shot furiously.

"Oh, c'mon, why would he? You're invisible to him unless he presses you on an issue or he needs something from you. You're so good at hiding behind this façade. He would have to be a mind reader to recognize which signals are mixed," I whispered forcefully meeting her anger with my own.

She stared at me scoffing offended by my words.

"What do you want me to say to that, Tim?" she shot angrily.

"I don't know…maybe the truth for a change. If you want to make believe you're too mature for an adolescent relationship that's fine, but if you have a crush on someone you should let that person know, because there are other people who may be collateral damage that don't want to sit around waiting to be heartbroken," I fired thinking of Pete immediately. "Those people don't deserve that."

Sai leaned back sighing instantly thinking of Eve as guilt filled her.

"Tim, you really think that's an easy thing to do?" she shot turning to me with an exaggerated chuckle. "Have you ever stop to think I want to? It's more to it than that. This could forever change the relationship I have with…this person. If I tell him how I feel…I'm afraid…I'm afraid he won't feel the same. If that happens, the relationship we currently have will never be the same."

I nodded sympathetically accepting her words.

"Sai, he'd be crazy to pass up the chance to be with someone like you. Trust me. I know how special you are, and…as annoying as it is to say, my brother is too smart to overlook someone as amazing as you," I shot chuckling.

She chuckled along with me before stopping herself as my word finally sunk in.

"Wait, what did you say?" she shot turning to me with a confused look on her face. "Did you say you're brother?"

I chuckled placing my hand on hers in an assuring manner.

"Like I said, I know you," I responded with a smile. "You obviously are holding back feelings, and my guess is your jealous that Eve and I are moving forward and you'll be stagnant in your own situation. I get that, but I'm not going to leave you high and dry. I promise, nothing's going to change. We're still the dynamic duo. Where I go, you go. Eve's my girlfriend, not my best friend. That bond isn't going anywhere."

She shook her head moving to respond but before she could the transport stopped catching our attention.

"Tim," she whispered urgently trying to speak as Max stood cutting her off.

She grimaced angrily as my attention turned to the angel. She desperately waited for a lull in the commotion to speak to me again, but Jacob chose me and Zech to be his advisors causing us to leave immediately. I gave her a wink as I turned to leave. She returned my gesture uncomfortably unable to clear the air with our new audience of people around. I exited so used to the routine that I completely ignored the crowd as I made my way to the barrier and into the advising room.

"It's awesome in here," Zech responded surveying the layout.

The cold feel of the stadium matched the look on Jacob's face as he made his way to the center of the stadium. The crowd was at a stand still waiting as impatiently as we were to see what Jacob could do. The only one who looked unamused by the moment was Howell. He stood downwind with a look that fell between nervous and scared. I felt for the kid, and at that moment I could tell, he knew he was in over his head. The whole time the referee gave them the briefing he stood staring at Jacob trying his best to make eye contact, but the entire time it was painfully obvious he was intimidated.

"This is so cool?" said Zech spinning in his chair next to me.

"C'mon, Zech," I complained annoyed. "We can at least pretend we have a reason for being here."

He looked at me like I had a screw loose.

"What? He doesn't need us," he replied still spinning in his chair. "This kid is about to get his butt kicked."

I turned around as he leaped out of his seat and started running around the room. As powerful as he was, it was hard to see him as a child, but now it was annoyingly obvious.

"Zech, sit down," I replied. "Stopping playing around in here. You might break something."

I couldn't understand why Jacob chose us to begin with. I know it wasn't much anybody could advise Jacob on, but at least Uriah and Luke could have given him something. We were just watching, well, I was watching. Zech was playing.

"I wonder what this does," he replied surveying an incased button.

"I don't know, but the anti-anointment metal lock is giving me strong vibes it shouldn't be touched," I replied exasperated.

He looked at me with a mischievous smile.

"But you can open it," he replied in a pleading manner.

I cut my eyes at him. I was beginning to understand the annoyance of having a little brother.

"Zech, come sit down, the match is about to begin," I commanded turning toward the screen.

"Why doesn't anybody ever do an undertaking?" he replied plopping in his seat. "I like undertakings, but outside of you and Pete, no one did one. If I get picked, I'm doing one. I don't care if I win or lose, because even if I lose, I'll beat whoever wins the relic anyways."

I rolled my eyes as he continued like a with all the annoyances of a hyped up kindergartener. As he did Jacob and Howell nodded signaling the beginning of the match. I sat forward intently as Zech flashed causing his seat to spin. When it finally stopped he stared at the arena impatiently waiting for the match to start.

"Here we go!" he exclaimed slapping the console.

"Finally," I expressed leaning back.

Jacob stood in his stance unflinching as Howell backed up. He forced a stern stare, but it was laughably done. Everybody in the stadium could see the kid was afraid. The two of them stared at each other for a lasting minute as if to be trying to psyche the other out. Jacob didn't flinch as the kid reached and pulled out a boomerang from its sheath. Just as Howell went into his fighting stance Jacob raised his hand to stop him. The kid stood startled for a second then lowered his weapon.

"What?" he replied raising his hands annoyed.

Jacob walked toward him calmly as Howell watched him suspiciously.

"I've watched you fight…you're a good fighter," he explained stopping as he started his speech. "I think the Light Guard Academy would be better served to have you, so, to make sure you get the proper platform to showcase your ability, I'm going to give you a choice. You can forfeit now and withdraw you're challenge giving you the opportunity to participate in the possible trial duel in the event that there is one."

Howell began to laugh at the olive branch in a disrespected manner.

"Who are you to…"

"I'm not finish," Jacob replied cutting him off.

His eyes lit up at the sound of his words causing Howell to drop to one knee. His power was crippling. I could see it rippling through the stadium as people fainted and dropped like flies.

"Whoa!" Zech replied smiling as he turned to me. "Awesome, just his faith energy did that!"

I nodded staring forward as Jacob stood over the kid like a parent scolding a child.

"You're second option is to hit me with everything you got for five minutes, and at the end of those five minutes, I'll end the trial," he replied powering down.

As he powered down Howell stumbled to his feet. He stared at Jacob like he was looking at an anomaly he couldn't crack.

"How? What are you?" he replied staring Jacob in the eye.

Jacob cut his eyes as he turned his back.

"I'm a Christian," he replied walking back to his spot. "What are you?"

As he spoke an envious glare appeared on Howell's face. He pulled his boomerang from his back infuriated.

"I wanted to fight you, but if you're stupid enough to just sit there, I'll just have to show you why taking me lightly is a bad idea," he shot.

SWOOSH! He threw his boomerang.

BOOM! It circled and danced in the air for a couple of seconds. It caused an air pocket that swirled until it formed a mini tornado.

BOOM! It sputtered for a second then crashed and collided into near by pillars.

"Did you see that, Tim? He created a tornado with his boomerang," Zech gushed.

SWOOSH! The boomerang was connected to him like a magnet.

SWOOSH! It returned to his hand as smile grew on his face.

SWOOSH! He tossed it at Jacob once more creating another small tornado. As quickly as he caught the boomerang, he was sending it back. The arena was covered with small tornadoes destroying everything inside it.

"Scared yet,?" he questioned staring at Jacob. "You sure you don't want to rethink things?"

Jacob stared forward unmoved by the events going on around him.

"You're funeral," Howell replied. "Converge!"

As he finished his words all the tornados begin to move in unison. They cut across the terrain with one single path. The tornadoes converged until they created one large and massive tornado. Jacob stood downwind unflinching as he watched the massive monstrosity spinning out of control heading straight for him.

"You wanted the best I got?" Howell continued confidently. "Well, here you go."

BOOM! The tornado crashed into Jacob with stadium shaking power. The intimidating tornado was bigger than anything I ever attempted in my limited time as a remnant. Jacob wasn't lying. This kid was powerful, and with the way he used his boomerang to create the tornadoes, it was obvious he was transferring his anointment into it. It was obviously a metaphysical trait. I didn't know if it would be possible to obtain the trait. I didn't know if which theory was right. Jacob's theory about sacrifice being the key, or Jade's assumption about my will to outdo people. The truth was, both allowed me to obtain traits. I didn't know which method was the key, but I knew had to remember the trait for either one to work. Just in case I somehow got a hold on the ability in the future. It might come in handy later.

"Jake, you okay?" I asked unable to see him as the tornado raged on.

There was no reply. It just raged on for a couple of seconds before Howell chuckled and moved his hand causing the tornado to disperse. As he did the crowd watched in awe. Jacob was nowhere to be found.

"Hmph," Howell added chuckling proudly. "I guess I over did he. I must have sent him out of the stadium."

FLASH! Jacob appeared within ear shot standing right behind him as breaking the boy prideful exhibit.

"4 minutes," Jacob warned.

SWOOSH! FLASH! Howell swung around swinging at thin air as Jacob reappeared across the field. He spent around swinging like a wild man. It was almost like he was fighting a ghost as he swung wildly at the air as Jacob watched him from across the field emotionlessly.

"3 and half," Jacob shot signifying his position to Howell.

Howell grunted pulling out a second boomerang that was identical to the first as he turned to my brother in a threatening manner.

"Okay, no more games, Element Alpha, Light Energy Command, Static charge," Howell commanded extending his hands causing the boomerang to spin like two small fans.

ZIP! The static electricity around him sparked wildly until it looked like he a thousand electric arms that extended throughout the stadium.

ZIP! He moved his hands causing the spinning boomerangs to spark like two tiny lightning bolts.

WHOOSH! He powered them up until they flickered loudly creating a lightning storm.

"Okay, catch this," he threatened tossing the boomerangs.

BOOM! Howell sent his hands forward in a striking motion sending the boomerangs toward Jacob. They settled high above his general area like a storm cloud.

CRACK! CRACK! Static electricity rained down like lightning sparking all around Jacob. He stood stoicly. His arms were crossed in front of his chest as he moved around the arena appearing and reappearing in different spots.

"Where are you!" Howell screamed frustrated.

He continued to send strikes toward Jacob, but no matter how fast he sent them, Jacob just dodged them like child's play.

"Three minutes," Jacob replied light stepping across the field appearing behind him once again.

ARRRGH! BOOOOM! He exploded with energy like a bomb trying to obliterate everything in its vicinity. He was angry and unstable as the electricity became a part of his armor in a manner similar to the twins.

"Who is this kid?" I asked turning to Zech.

Zech stared forward kicking his feet back and forth like a kid with ADHD.

"He's my cousin?" He replied not even looking at me as he spoke.

I stared at him waiting for him to elaborate.

"What?" he replied shocked by my demeanor.

I stared at him irked by his dismissive words.

"Don't you think I should have known that?" I fired staring him up and down.

He perked up at the sound of my words.

"Oh, well, now you know?" he replied smiling obliviously. "Besides, I don't really know him. My father and his father are brothers, but I don't see him much because our fathers don't like each other. I think they were in the same mogul business or something."

I gave a nod as I watched the boy continued to absorb the solid elements scattered around the arena into shield. I turned to Zech pressing him.

"So, that's why he can use that technique?" I asked causing the boy to smile from ear to ear.

"But he's a cheater like Jo. He's an elemental," he shot proudly sticking out his chest. "That's why Jacob wanted me to train with him. He wanted to see how our family technique worked. And I'm such a nice person I said okay. Pretty good thing to do, huh?"

"Yes, you're selfless nature inspires me, Zech," I mocked with a sarcastic sigh leaning back as the boy smiled ignorantly.

I turned back to the center of the arena ignoring the boy as the battle raged on. Howell continued to send shots at Jacob who continued to dodge as sparks erupted all around him.

"1 minute," Jacob replied over the loud crash of Howell's attack.

Howell raised his hands angrily causing the terrain underneath Jacob to rise into a mountain. Jacob stood on top of it like a pirate at the helm of his ship.

WHOOSH! Howell angrily tossed fire balls toward him in a last ditch effort.

WHOOSH! WHOOSH! He frantically tossed fire balls toward the mountain as Jacob appeared in reappeared at different spots dodging them effortlessly.

"Times up," Jacob replied in a calm and controlled voice.

BOOOOOOM! The mountain exploded like it was hit by an atom bomb. The explosion was deafening. The area around the mountain collapsed at the sound of Jacob's word. There was debris everywhere. Howell stood unable to move as he watched in awe.

"You have got to be kidding me!" I exclaimed watching in awe.

When Jacob reappeared, he stood with his arm reaching over his back grasping the huge sword that lay on his back.

"I gave you the opportunity to showcase your power, now it's time for me to showcase mine," he replied unlatching and pulling the large sword off his back.

WHOOOSH! The sheer power that exploded from the moment he pulled the sword from its sheath was ridiculous. I could feel his power surge threw everything. It was glowing like a lantern in the dark. The explosion was so powerful that it crippled half the stadium sending a crack along the stadium wall.

"Awesome!" Zech replied clapping hysterically. "Jacob's awesome!"

Howell stumbled trying with everything he had to remain standing as Jacob approached. Jacob hadn't touched him. It was just his presence alone. I couldn't believe what I was watching. The closer he got to Howell the worse it became. Howell fell to his knees then crawled in an attempt to get away as Jacob walked toward him sternly with a sword that was a big as he was. I stared at him in awe. *Was it the sword? Was that what made him so powerful?* I thought the jealousy rising with every passing second. *How could he be so powerful?* I raged jealousy watching as I tried to come to grips with what I was seeing.

"This trial is over," Jacob replied flash stepping in front him blocking his path.

BOOOM! The momentum of his speed caused a wall directly behind him to explode like someone torpedoed into it. Howell fell on his stomach fighting to raise his head as Jacob continued his march toward him.

"What am I supposed to do, Dad?" Howell responded startling us. "There is nothing I can do!"

Even Jacob seemed taken back by his words. His brow raised stopping his march momentarily. Howell slowly raised his gaze and stared at Jacob in a pleading manner.

"How can you do this?" He questioned taking the words out of my mouth. "What makes your faith energy this dense?"

Jacob cut his eyes stopping to respond.

"The people in this realm are under the assumption that since you're born here you somehow have an advantage over us Earthborn," Jacob replied tossing his sword into its sheath. "In some ways you're right. We have a harder time taking the truth at face value because we are so used to the terrible things in life, but consequently, those same terrible experiences build our faith. Even though we work at a beginning deficit, once we gain our faith…it's stronger. What we lack in initial power, we gain in experience. You guys don't have the same experiences to draw upon. You can't use the same hardships we do to help you gain faith in Father Yahweh. Even though you guys believe you can do amazing things, you're limited by the same societal norms you believe makes you special. We have no idea what our limitations are because we have overcome so much already. When that is your reality, nothing seems impossible."

Howell stared at Jacob for a lasting second before passing out. Jacob latched his sword in as the crowd erupted so loud the stadium began to shake. The Earthborn section was a frenzy jumping up and down proudly. I stood with a jealousy in the pit of my stomach. It burned like a fire in the furnace of my gut. Then I got it. I could see what she saw in him. I could see what they saw in him. I could never measure up to that. It made me feel numb.

"He's so fast," Zech replied. "I never saw him. Not once."

I chuckled thinking his words were a joke.

"Are you serious?" I replied turning to him. "He was just flashstepping and dematerializing. I saw him the whole time."

He looked at me as a smile grew on his face.

"You could actually follow him?" he pressed looking me in the eye. "That's so crazy. I never saw a move he made. I just heard Jacob's voice then saw the explosions. BOOM! BOOM! BOOM! It was awesome!"

He was joking. I lost Jacob for a second or two, but for the most part I followed him. It had to be Zech's short attention span. I shook it off then grabbed my things to head out as Jacob walked toward the council to get his debriefing.

"Let's go," I commanded heading toward the door.

Zech quickly grabbed his things and trailed me outside. As we exited the room, I was bombarded by the excitement of the rest of the legion who were celebrating like we had just won the whole thing.

"Tim," Eve replied giving me a hug. "Have you ever seen anything like that?"

"Considering ninety-percent of the things I've seen in the last week would fall under that generic title, it doesn't seem to give the proper justice to what I just witnessed," I responded almost agitated as I push my way to my seat.

Before I could fully take a seat Sam, Sai, and Pete joined Eve tackling me in a group hug as Jo grabbed Zech. It was a stark contrast to the dull atmosphere from a couple minutes earlier..

"Yeah, take that," Luke echoed pumping his fist. "Whoa! Man, it feels good to finally get another one."

As they celebrated Zech pulled my shirt catching my attention. I turned to him as he continued.

"Tell him, Tim, didn't you say you were able to follow, Jacob? You actually saw him moving, right?" he replied catching the attention of everyone in the room.

I nodded not understanding the importance of the question.

"Tim, you actually saw Jacob fight?" Sai replied.

Luke, Danielle, and Uriah walked toward me at the sound of Sai's word.

"Yeah, what's the big deal?" I replied agitated. "Everybody in the stadium just saw Jacob fight?"

They all looked at me with a look that was becoming a daily ritual for us.

"No, Tim, we didn't," Pete replied looking at me like I was an alien.

"He was moving too fast," Uriah added. "He disappeared at the beginning then reappeared a couple minutes later and the kid was out."

Sam stared at me before breaking in.

"Tim's lying," he replied. "There's no way he was able to follow that. The announcers couldn't even do that."

I stared at him like he was crazy.

"Yeah, Sam, I made this up?" I replied sarcastically. "I lost him for a second when he was on the mountain, but for the most part I saw everything."

"Well, what happened?" Danielle cut in.

They all stared at me like kids waiting for a bedtime story.

"Yeah, did Jacob beat the crap out of the kid?" Luke responded.

I shook my head still trying to proceed while coming to grips with what I was being told. I couldn't understand it.

"No," I stuttered. "He didn't touch the kid. It was all his faith energy. He was just using his speed and dematerialization the entire time. Then the five minutes ended and he pulled out that huge sword on his back. The kid fainted from the power of it. That's it. THE END."

They all continued to glare at me with a look that fell between impressed and confused, but nobody pressed me. I couldn't understand why I was able to follow him when nobody else could.

"He's not lying," Uriah broke in. "I can tell from his biorhythm. He's telling the truth."

"Whoa! Yeah!" Luke exploded clapping hysterically. "Alright, Jake!"

"Amazing," Sai seconded.

"Your brother is ridiculous," Pete added.

I rolled my eyes grabbing my bag needing to get away from the love fest.

"Tim, c'mon, wait," Sai replied laughing trailing behind me.

"Yeah, we'll come with you," Eve replied chuckling as well.

Pete shook his head realizing the reason for my abrupt exit as the rest of the legion celebrated ignoring me. The crowd was exploding as I walked out of our cell angrily marching for the transport. For the first time since I arrived, I was once again, the little brother of a prodigy. The labeled I thought I escaped came rushing back with a vengeance. I walked toward the bus with Sai, Sam, Pete, and Eve. The press exploded as we exited the building only to subside when they noticed it was just us.

"It's just the little brother and his friends," said one of the reporters.

It was official. I grimaced lowering my head angrily throwing my hood over my head.They moved to the side allowing us to pass like we were nobodies. Any other day it would've been a welcomed sight after a win, but the significance of their words wasn't lost on me. I swallowed a deep seated annoyance that I was starting to realize would be around as long as I was Jacob's little brother. I walked on the bus and turned to the robotic driver.

"Can we leave?" I replied angrily.

"Don't you want to wait on your brother?" the transporter replied.

"No, do you see that stadium? Jacob's going to be here all night," I replied trying to bury my envy. "I'll catch him at the hotel."

The transporter nodded signaling he agreed as the rest of my company trailed me on to the bus. I stared out the window angrily as a crowd began to form awaiting Jacob. I could fight the deep seated annoyance that ate at me, but the truth was, as long as I lived my brother would always be the alpha. It was what it was, take it or leave it, this was my life.

CHAPTER

21

Family ties

Family ties

"Are you coming?" Pete uttered clumsily turning back to the door.

Sai stood with Eve and Sam as they all exchanged awkward glances.

"Well, we still have to do our choosing?" they replied pointing toward the stadium.

I wanted to kick myself. I was so annoyed by the circumstances it completely slipped my mind. I rose begrudgingly grabbing my bag and followed them.

"We'll be back," I replied to the transporter as they all exhaled happy to see I hadn't been completely overtaken by the selfish spirit I was acting like. "I'm sorry you guys. I forgot about your choosing."

"It's fine," Sai replied turning to walk as we headed back toward the stadium.

Sam walked without saying a word. I would have normally thought it was because he was nervous about the trials, but his demeanor was aggressive. He stared at me shaking his head a couple times. I let it go on as long as I could, but it was obvious he was angry with me. It became the pink elephant in the room as we walked. Everyone could see it and it was causing tension throughout our walk. I finally got to my wits end angrily turning to the boy.

"What's your problem?" I cut. "You got something to say to me?"

Sam stopped clinching his bag stopping in his tracks. He turned to me with an angry stare.

"Yeah, I do," he fired. "That's your brother."

I raised a brow surprised by his statement.

"Yeah?" I said trying to quell my anger. "Good deduction, Sam. Unfortunately, everyone from my dad to the lady selling popcorn at Angel Haven High knows that. What's your point? One more time, what's your problem?"

He stared at me steadfast in his anger as he continued.

"Your brother just did something that no one has ever done before," he shot angrily. "And he returns to his legion, which he just pulled from the fire for the umpteenth time, and half of the legion isn't there to congratulate him. There's nothing wrong with that picture to you?"

I stared at him angrily looking him over.

"Sam, I made a mistake. What do you want from me? I said I was sorry," I shot angrily.

He scoffed looking around at the rest of the crew shaking his head in a I told you so type of manner.

"This isn't about you," he replied. "Where you go, they follow."

I glared at him with a helpless shrug.

"I didn't ask anybody to follow me," I fired.

He shook his head showing an ironic smirk.

"You know what Tim? I don't doubt that, but it doesn't matter. Whether you accept it or not, they follow you. It makes me sick," he shot his temper running over. "Everyone follows you. In school, the football team, everywhere. You never ask for anyone to look up to you, or follow your lead. I get that, but people do. And it's all about the talent you have. The way you are. They just think you're so cool. It's all I ever hear. How everyone wants to be like Timothy Eli. How everyone loves Timothy Eli."

His words sent an unsettling feel through the legion. They all lowered their heads in embarrassment as he emptied his soul. It was obvious the boy had been holding this in for a while, but he caught me at the absolute worst time to unburden himself.

"I'm cool"?" I shot blown away by his words. "I'm cool? What's so cool about me? What, Sam?! The fact that I'm a constant mess up? How I destroy everything I come in contact with? What? The people who think that I'm this guy you're talking about, they can't know me?"

He looked around at the ground as his head subconsciously fell. The rest of the group continued to watch our spat awkwardly staring at us like it was a car wreck they couldn't look away from. Sam fists clenched as he finally raised his head.

"I'm a mess up!" he screamed catching everyone's attention.

His words were like daggers. I got his point, but it was apples and oranges. Our situations were totally different. My anger picked up as I stared around at the forming crowd.

"Beth is a mess up," he continued pointing at the girl as he spoke. "We fight to do things you guys do…with ease. We are mess ups. You're a mess up?"

He spoke his words with an offended chuckle.

"Do you have any idea how it is for us to do the most basic things, Tim," he shot staring me in the eyes angrily. "We deserve those titles. We embrace and shatter them, but you don't get to do the same…it lowers our accomplishments. You are not a mess up...man, you're a genius!"

He responded stepping toward me as Eve stepped in between us.

"Okay, guys, maybe we should take inventory of our surroundings," she cut cautiously looking around embarrassed.

Sam casually acknowledged before continuing unaffected by her objections.

"You know what's funny...you say those people can't know you, right? But honestly…that's just hilarious. I thought it was an act, but truthfully, you are the most clueless person I've ever met…News flash, those people are standing right here, right now. Go ahead check their BAU-eey thing and see if you can find one of them who doesn't feel that way, one of these people who can't know you, then tell me I'm wrong," he shot angrily pointing at my friends as he spoke.

I just stood staring at him trying my best to control my temper. I tried my best to mindful of doing anything to further hurt Sam morale, but he was pushing me to my limit. He didn't understand the predicament I was in as Jacob's brother. Worst yet, I was starting to wonder if they all saw me in that way. Did they really see me as this prodigy? I looked around at them as they all let their eyes dance subconsciously affirming Sam's words. I turned back to him livid as he continued.

"And if you have the time after you've finished checking them, check mine and see if you don't get the same answer," he replied passionately. "Because from the time I met you all I wanted to do was be as cool as you were. I trained from dusk til dawn, and guess what? They don't make it possible for people like me to do things that people like you do, and I can accept that. Do you have any idea how special you are? Do you know how many people would kill for the chance to be half as talented as you are? We all watch in awe at the things you've done and continue to do, and accept you're on another level. So why can't you do the same when it comes to Jake? Why can't you accept that there is someone that makes you feel the same way you make everyone else feel?"

He shot continue with no filter. I stared at him squinting angrily, seconds away from exploding as I stared at the gathered crowd.

"No, instead we have to watch you sulk and complain about how unfair life is. The nerve! We have to be rude because you are jealous that for once someone else has the spotlight," he accused sending my emotions into overdrive.

I stared at the sky biting my lips trying to keep the anger rushing to the surface at bay. His words sparked an anger in me like nothing I've ever felt before. It was the words I heard my entire life. My whole life the common theme was I was jealous of my brother, and I hated that narrative. No one knew what it was like to be me. I grew up idolizing my brother. I wanted to be him, and it was what everyone expected, but by the first grade, I realized that wasn't ever going to be a fair comparison. Jacob was a true prodigy both mentally and physically. I wasn't. We were so close in age, and with the small population of our town, it was hard to get out from under my brother's shadow. I accepted the fact that I was talented, and it wasn't my fault others felt I made them seem average, but I'm not their older brother. They weren't constantly being compared to me. They couldn't understand the pressure of one person making your life a prison. My demeanor and disposition were directly correlated to my experience with my brother. I was content with average because at least then I had my own identity. It beat falling short of Jacob's legend day in and day out. I realized when I did the minimum, comparisons were non-existent. They accepted my limitations and left me alone.

It saved me from the depression, Jacob left a mark on everyone he met and a standard for me to follow. When teachers and coaches come across a child like my brother, they almost craved another one just like them. As his brother, I was the perfect candidate, and they wasted no time in letting me know every way I fell short when I didn't live up to one of his many exceptional feats. It didn't matter that I did better than everyone else. I wasn't Jacob and that's what everyone expected me to be, no matter how well I did, I was a failure. Sam couldn't understand this. His history with me wasn't lengthy enough for him to grasp. Any other time I would've given him pass, but the fact that he made light of my situation infuriated me. All I got was the insult. To make such an ignorant statement in front of so many bystanders was beyond inconsiderate and I had finally met my limit.

"Are you serious?!" I replied walking toward him. "Are you saying I walked out because I want his spotlight?! You think I would ever do that! You've known me for almost three years. When have I ever cared about spotlight?!"

Sam met my eruption in anger without backing down meeting me as I walked toward him.

"When it's Jacob's spotlight!" Sam fired. "Always!"

POOSH! My power burst forward causing everyone around us to back down. My friends quickly went on high alert. I headed toward Sam with a menacing look on my face.

"Take it back, Sam!" I shot angrily.

Before I could take a step, Sai was standing in front of me and she wasn't looking to block. I knew the look on Sai's face, and she meant business.

"Stop it, Tim!" she replied glaring at me.

I looked at her like she had lost her mind.

"Sai, move," I replied dismissing her actions as an over exaggeration.

She didn't budge. She stood blocking my path. She held Sam back as he frantically worked to get around her.

"If you want to fight somebody fight me," she shot angrily. "I don't know if you want the spotlight, but I do know what you did was extremely rude, and I can't believe I followed you. Sam is right. Tim, we follow you sometimes to a fault. We should have said something. I'm just glad Sam woke us up."

I stared at the crowd surrounding around us before returning my gaze to her. My emotions caused more of my light tattoos to become visible causing more of a stir.

"Sai, are you serious?!" I pressed offended by her actions blind to the appearance of my energy tattoos.

Before I could blink Eve and Pete shot next to Sai's side shielding Sam as well. My heart dropped. What did they truly think of me? In all actuality I had no plans of ever fighting Sam. I smirked still controlling the wave of emotions flowing through me at the time.

"Do you know if I wanted to hurt Sam?" I shot through gritted teeth. "All I'd have to do is…"

FLASH! I dematerialized through them in a flash landing behind Sam with my back turned to them. They quickly turned around unable to keep up with my speed.

SWING! CATCH! Sam took a swing at me that I caught with one hand as they looked on with the crowd in awe of my power.

"I have put my life on the line for nearly everyone in this legion at one point or another. I have never asked for a thing in return. Don't you get it? I don't want fame. I didn't even want to be here. I just want what I've always wanted, and that's to be normal," I replied powering down. "You talk about my talent and how many people would kill for it, well, guess what? I'm not one of those people. I know the limitations of this talent. It isn't enough to remove the weight that is on my shoulders. Not by a longshot. My destiny was chosen the day I was born, and I'm fine with that. I'm fine just sitting in the background being the normal Eli kid. I don't want his fame. I don't want his skill. I don't want his power. I want to be left alone to fail or succeed based on my standards and my merit, but no one gives me that chance. I'd give up this power in a second if I was judged on the same scale as everyone else. I am always paired with and against my brother and I'm tired of walking around with the weight of the destiny his greatness demands. That's a weight none of you will ever understand."

Sam lowered his head as I tossed his hand to the side staring at them all disappointed.

"I have tried to be what you guys want me to be. I'm burning the candle on both ends. Every night I'm pushing myself to my absolute limit to make sure I'm here to make up for the danger I've put you guys in. I accept that burden, because it was my decision that brought you here, but I'm still human! I'm not Jacob! I don't always do the right thing. Yet, somehow, it's always what's expected of me. I walked out of the stupid trial celebration because for the first time since we've been here, I needed a second to compose myself. I need a second to focus on my mental state. I never asked any of you to follow me. You decided to do that. I didn't prevent any of you from celebrating Jacob's victory. Yet you're here blaming me for decisions you chose to make. You sit here looking down your noses at me for walking out on your hero Jacob's win. Yet, Jacob cuts me down every second he gets, and no one was ever there to be offended by his undermining of my contributions. I bust my butt for this legion, and he's always there to tell me where I fell short, and none of you are there to defend me. None of you show this sudden comradery. You laugh and make things worse. So, let me say this to appease the severe pain I've caused you. Sincerely, I apologize for disrespecting the contributions of a person that disrespects my contributions daily with no hurt feelings or rebuttals from any of you."

Sai's eyes dropped at the sound of my words. They all showed slumped shoulders as the crowd stood in silence after my words. I shook my head as she moved toward me. I raised my hand stopping her.

"Tim, we…" she managed before I brushed passed her shaking my head.

"Just save it, Sai," I shot shaking my head with my back still turned to them. "If you guys think I would attack Sam after all I've done to make up for what I did to him. You guys don't know me. You guys were powering up to fight me in front of all these people based on your perception of who I am. So stop trying to feed me some garbage about unwittingly following me. Please, you followed me, you don't follow me. You follow him and that's fine, but don't speak on my life because none of you have walked a mile in my shoes."

Even Sam seemed visibly contrite as he clenched his fist staring at the ground. An awkward silence ensued. Before Sai shook her head refusing to let things end on such a harsh note.

FLASH! She flashed in front of me stopping with an extended arm. She forced the hood off my head as she spoke apologetically.

"Tim, you're right," she sympathized calming me. "We overreacted, but all the same, whether you want to take ownership or not, we do follow you, and Sam was right. Just like you can't help people comparing the two of you, neither can your brother. Tim, he didn't deserve that, and yeah, it was a momentary lapse, but I'm not angry because you made a mistake, I'm mad because that was the first thing your mind told you to do. You are always so selfless when it comes to the rest of us, but it's like when it comes to Jacob, all you see is red. That isn't fair to him, you or us. It shortchanges you and your brother, and it puts us in the middle."

I lowered my heads taking in her words as she continued.

"And another thing, don't throw us in with everyone else. They don't know you, we do, and to those of us that care about you, you're so much more than Jacob's little brother," she shot forcing me to look into her eyes before hugging me.

"I know, Sai," I responded hugging her back.

"But you're right about us. We did what we did. We didn't have to, but at the end of the day, it's what were going to do. Whether you accept it or not, we follow you. So, keep that in mind, every mistake you make, where probably going to be on your heels making the same ones. That's the weight of your spirit and talent, not Jacob's. Jacob may inspire strangers to follow him because of what he can do, but just as important, you inspire those that know you because of what you've done. Realize when you make a decision, it doesn't matter what they think."

She pointed around at the bystanders with one hand while placing her free hand on my cheek.

"We follow you. You can't afford to make the same mistakes as the rest of us, because the mistakes you make effect the rest of us. Everyone standing in front of you, we follow you. We said we trust you with our lives. Which means, every decision you make has to consider us. Get used to that dynamic. You wanted that trust, well guess what? You got it. I don't want to hear the crying now," she explained with a snicker causing me to follow suit lowering my head with an embarrassed chuckle. "Sam snapped us all out of that funk. We should be thanking him. I'm not angry that he addressed the elephant in the room, even if the way we all handled the situation made things worse."

I accepted her words with the level of gravity it deserved. I stared into her eyes with admiration and appreciation for who she was. I twiddled with the strap on my bag before hugging her.

"Tim, go ahead," Pete cut in. "The rest of us we'll meet you afterwards. Jacob should be getting back from the council any minute. We'll just meet you at the hotel."

I accepted his words awkwardly waving feeling subconscious about our tirade in front of the small crowd of people. I knifed through the crowd and heading toward the transport. Sam wasn't as receptive to the reconciliation. Of course, he felt a level of guilt for the way he attacked me, but that didn't soothe the level of anger he felt for leaving in the midst of my brother's celebration. He rocked awkwardly for a second than walked away following the group. I contemplated Sai's words on my way back to the transport before I heard commotion behind me that stopped me in my tracks.

"It was an accident, kid," I heard Eve protest loudly. "He was chosen. He couldn't control what he was doing."

I turned to see Sam with a groggy look on his face. He was arguing with Kel who was accompanied by Abby, Sean, Kadmiel and a little girl. Things were getting testy. I started to just leave before I sighed and walked toward them in a relenting manner.

"What's going on?" I asked walking up.

They all became more reserved as I approached. Even Sean began to tense up.

"Nothing," Sai shot trying to cut me off before I got too close. "Sam was chosen."

My heart went into my throat. Even after what just had transpired my heart went out to him and that was just one of the emotions flowing through me at the sound of her words. Another was regret. The tension between us would not be a good way to start Sam's trials, and on top of that, what luck we had for him to be chosen with one person left to be chosen. It was just rotten luck for Sam. He just stood with a dreary look on his face as the volatile atmosphere around him became more and more hostile. Sai pointed in his direction before stopping in a sympathetic manner.

"When he did his BAU conference he stopped for a second and hit this guy," she replied pointing in Kel direction.

I turned to him as he stood impatiently listening to Sai explanation.

"I don't care if it was an accident," he replied. "It don't mean, squat. He made me drop my drink."

As he spoke Sean stepped in between he and Sam. He and Abby stood as a barriers with their backs to Sai and Pete keeping Eve and Sam away from Kel and Kadmiel.

"Kel, stop the crap. Let's just go," he replied angrily shoving the boy back.

"Yeah, this kid isn't worth it," Kadmiel added pulling him back.

Eve forced her way toward her at the sound of her words as Sai pushed back blocking her.

"If she comes near me, I'm going to put her head through a wall," Kadmiel warned going from mediator to aggressor at the Eve's display.

"Yeah, you had your chance, and if it wasn't for Sai you'd be lying in a hospital bed," Eve cut seething as Sai forcefully pushed the girl back.

Kadmiel surged toward Eve as Sean and Sai were almost touching nose to nose keeping the two legions apart. I stood watching like a deer in headlights.

"Stop it!" Sean screamed.

"Why don't you guys just get out of here," Pete shot.

"Why don't you?" Abby shot back.

Just as things were at a head Jade arose from the double doors like a
godsend.

"What's going on here?" he replied with a surprised look on his face.

Everyone stopped and dispersed like kids caught doing something wrong
when an adult enters a room.

"Nothing," I replied as Jade approached.

He watched as the ABA Legion walked away looking back in a warning
manner.

"Where were you guys?" Jade replied. "I've been looking all over the
place for you."

I looked away embarrassed as I could feel everyone's attention lock on
me. Jade stood in a surveying glare for a second before continuing.

"Sam," he replied empathetically. "What's the story?"

He shrugged his shoulder as laughter erupted from inside the facility
turning our attention toward our surrounding. It was coming from the
media section. They were all crowded around a monitor behind a glass
door next to the entrance.

"Let's go," Jade replied suddenly.

I looked at his eyes not really wanting to follow his orders.

"Let's go!" he said this time more assertive.

He shoved Eve forward pointing for us all to head for the transport. As he did, I turned to see the media flooding toward us. Jacob and the rest of the legion poured out of the door walking at an accelerated rate.

"What is going on?" I asked speeding up my walk to keep up.

"Get on the bus, Tim!" Jacob replied shoving me forward.

We all trotted on the bus as the transport door closed.

"Go, Go!" Max screamed as the transport pushed the bus in gear and shot off.

"Will someone tell me what's going on?" I shot looking around the transport in an annoyed tone.

They all sat quiet before Sai signaled for me to come to the back of the transport. I followed suit heading toward her.

"What?" I replied plopping down beside her.

I looked around at the awkward feel in the transport and I couldn't understand it. It was like someone had died and it was starting to make me uneasy. Sai signaled for me to be quiet putting one finger over her mouth. I cut my eyes to object, but before I could a surge of energy shot through me. It was a BAU feed of information fired into my brain like I was watching a fast action trailer. I blinked uncontrollably when it finally relinquished. I tried to come to grips with whether or not what I just witness was real.

"Did that really happen?" I whispered turning to Sai.

She nodded emotionally. Sam, I couldn't believe it. Sam had gone through his evaluation and had scored an amazing 1 out of 12. Jacob's score was as amazing as his score was disappointing. The laughter we heard in the lobby, all the commotion, I saw it all. They laughed at Sam.

"Well, what do we do?" I replied.

Just as I spoke Jade stood up catching everyone's attention.

"Even though we didn't assume his score would be this bad, it doesn't change the overall plan. We all assumed Sam would probably have to do a duel and an undertaking," he replied.

"Exactly," Max second. "Of course, we understand the disappointment on Sam's part."

Sam sat unemotionally looking out of the window not saying a word as Max continued.

"What difference does it make?" I asked.

"Well, for one, he no longer can do the undertaking alone, someone else has to do it with him and It has to be someone who has already been accepted into the academy. More importantly, it can't be Jacob because he just competed and there is a two day waiting period before a prospect is eligible to compete again," Jade explained in an upset manner.

My eyebrows almost touched the back of my skull.

"Why didn't you tell us this before?!" I replied.

This whole time I thought I was in the clear after my Trial and to have this thrown on me at this time was a little more than I could bare.

"Well, no one has ever scored so low. The average lower level prospect could apply and at least get a two. It's extremely rare to get a two. I should've seen this coming, but I was naïve. I thought Sam's heritage would be enough to suffice, but I underestimated the prejudice of some of the council members. I can't believe them!" he exploded angrily. "Even if he does make it with the assistance, there must be a trial to decide whether or not he will be accepted unless he wins his duel. It's preposterous!"

I felt for Sam, but I was also angry and confused. Now, the atmosphere on the transport made sense. The media waited behind the media line as we pulled up.

"Sam," Jade pressed leaned toward him. "You have your press conference?"

Sam stared at him without saying a word and threw his backpack over his shoulder and headed toward the door.

"It doesn't matter," he replied angrily. "I just want to kick these guys butt and go home."

We all sat watching him as he made his way off the bus. He was like a blank page. He had no emotion. He looked totally drained. After everything he went through since we arrived. It all made sense. The media launched questions at him as he cut through the crowd and went into the hotel. No one said a word. We all just sat in silence.

"Why is it always that kid?" Luke replied. "I mean, this SOC thing, is it really that bad?"

Max looked over at Jade in begging manner. Jade nodded permitting him to continue as he began.

"Look, we didn't want to tell you guys this so soon," he replied taking a long exhaustive breath. "The prejudice against Sam is in part because he is a SOC, but there are many SOCs in our society in prominent positions. Majority of times it's harder because of all the prejudice about them, but generally, once they showcase their ability, they're accepted fairly quickly."

Danielle sat forward at the sound of Max's words.

"Yeah, I noticed there seemed to be something different about the way Heaven Realm higher-ups treated Sam. The way the council members and people in the media talked about him," Danielle replied catching our attention. "I've never seen them like that so openly."

Max nodded continuing his speech.

"Yes, well, there is a reason for that," he continued. "What I am about to tell you guys you must not under any circumstance tell Sam. I need your word on this."

As he spoke he waited for us to agree. We all nodded agreeing to his terms as he continued.

"Only the most senior aged Heaven Realm residents know this. It isn't common knowledge, but there is something you all should know about him," he continued. "Well, more so, his father."

Her words caught our attention immediatley. My attenas had been up ever since we had met Sai's mother.

"See, I told you," I said turning to Eve.

Max and Jade followed up surprised.

"You know about this, Tim?" Jacob replied.

I shook my head raising my hand in a tempering manner.

"Well, I knew something was up," I continued. "You remember when Sai was in the hospital and we met her mother?"

They all nodded in succession.

"Yeah, Eve told me about it. She said something about it being weird that your parents never explained to you guys that you were related, even though they were the ones who brought Sam to Angel Haven," Sai cut in.

I nodded pointing in her direction affirming her statements.

"Precisely," Jade continued. "There was a reason for it. Sam is your blood cousin and so his brother Isaiah."

I leaned forward pulled in by every word.

"The brother that Sam killed in the fire," I replied spilling the beans.

Everyone's gaze shot to me the minute I spoke. I wanted to backpedal but I said too much to turnback.

"Wait, what?!" Eve replied.

"Sam told you this?" Jade replied in an inquisitive manner.

I sighed trying to calm everyone down.

"No, well, yes...I guess, but it was an accident," I replied. "It was that weird white flame. He said when he was small he couldn't control it. Well, he still can't really control it now, but when he was small, he said he really couldn't control it. It would happen involuntary. It was terrible. He kind of told me that one night he awoke and the whole place was on fire and they couldn't save his brother."

Everyone's countenance fell at the sound of my words. Even I had to stop and think of all the things he'd been through. I just couldn't understand how a kid could get kicked in the face as much as he did and still have such strong faith. He was such a happy go lucky kid. You would never guess he had such tragedy in his life. I never saw him pouting or making excuses. I thought back on his words to me just minutes earlier, and the sting was worse. It's why my attitude ate at him. This is a guy who hadn't had a family his entire life, and here I was complaining about mine. Compared to what he had gone through, I could see why he thought I was being an arrogant jerk.

"Man, how much can anyone take?" Uriah added. "The kid has no parents, no family, no friends, and has endured unspeakable tragedies throughout his entire life, yet he's the most upbeat and positive kid I've ever met. I mean, how?"

Jade ignored Uriah's statement and pressed me as if something I said had caught his attention.

"So, Sam believes he killed his brother?" he responded.

I nodded agreeing with his statement.

"Why?" I pressed.

He paused before relenting.

"Sam's brother isn't dead," Jade respnded.

His words floored all of us. We all looked at him in complete and utter disbelief.

"What do you mean?" Pete replied.

Jade once again rolled his eyes in a relenting fashion before continuing.

"Listen, I'll get to that, but first let me explain Sam's father to you, and it'll explain itself," he replied. "Sam's father or Tim and Jacob's uncle's name is Phillip Rothman."

His words almost made me swallow my tongue.

"Philip Rothman?" Eve pressed. "The richest man in the world. The head of the A.A.R.M."

"Are you serious?" Pete added.

"No way," Sai uttered shaking her head speaking in a gasping tone.

"Talk about a punch in the gut," Luke added.

We all looked queasy at the sound of his words. We didn't know how to react. I had known Sam for years, but it was going to be hard for me to look at him the same again, imagine if I didn't know him. Suddenly the treatment he received was starting to make since. Now the actions of the prospect at the trial celebration made more sense. Somehow he knew.

"Who is this guy?" Danielle added.

"In our realm there is a group of vigilantes that go around killing Christians and all resemblance of Christianity in our society. They've been around since the biblical days going by different names and infiltrating different sects of society recruiting until they formed an army that even our own government had to contract just to keep them in check," Jacob explained. "The Rothmans are the richest family in our world. Their a controlling part of the Council of Thirteen. They are the most powerful family in the world."

"Wow, so you guys are like princes," Zech replied.

"Us, no?" Jacob replied. "That's not how it works in our realm. Power isn't passed like that. Especially not in the Council of Thirteen."

Max cleared his throat calling for attention before continuing.

"Regardless," he cut in. "Philip wasn't always like that. You're right Jacob. Your mother's family is the most powerful family in your realm, but neither she nor her brother had any idea."

We all settled down as he continued.

"Why didn't they know?" I pressed.

It felt like a long time coming. I wanted to know about my mother for so long. I couldn't believe somebody was finally going to tell me. Jacob leaned forward attentively as well.

"Your grandmother, Natassia, the mother of your mother and uncle. She was the mistress of James Rothman. After years of abuse your grandmother became pregnant with your mother. Afraid of your grandfather's occult practices and abuse, she wanted to protect her child, so she fled without ever revealing to James that she was pregnant. It worked for a while, but with the evil forces in your world there was nowhere she could run where he could find her and when she finally gave birth to your mother she went to the one place where she knew your mother would be safe. She went to a Church during the great religious wars of the early 2050's and met a young pastor named Thomas Matthews. He protected and look after Natassia and new born child. Eventually in fell in love with the woman and took her as his wife and your mother as his child. Covered in the Holy Spirit the evil spirits in the world lost track of Natassia as she married and developed a new name. It was a chance meeting at a Southern Conference where a false prophet came across Thomas and Natassia. James had now ascended to the top of the Rothman family and now had unlimited power. It wasn't long before he tracked down your grandmother and mother. James was still infatuated with Natassia and pursued her, but she turned him down and spurned his affections. James was not used to his advances being unrequited and in a fit of rage he gave the order to have Natassia's husband killed. Once her husband was execueted he warned her that if she ever found another mate, he wouldn't only kill them, but her and Leah as well."

The more of the story he told the madder I became. I could tell the feeling was mutual as I looked around the transport.

"Soon she became pregnant again and like the first time she was afraid of the occultic practices of the Rothman," Max continued. "But this time unable to live a lie she refused and finally revealed in a fit of rage that Leah was his child in an attempt to show him the beauty of life. He acknowledged her words by stating he would groom your mother when she became old enough, but the other child had to be a sacrifice for his bid to make the high council because he wasn't about to sacrifice any of his legitimate kids. He stated he would give her 9 months and she had decide which one of her children would die. It was her choice."

My jaw clinched at the sound of his words. I couldn't believe this was my heritage. I couldn't believe that someone who was so closely related to me could be so evil. I couldn't accept it.

"Natassia prayed and prayed for an answer and because of the stress of the ordeal she decided to flee, but unlike the last time Natassia fled, the world was in chaos. The religious wars were at their height. Many false prophets had infiltrated the church at that time, and new members were no longer accepted as freely as they were before. In her state, she didn't get too far before the stress of her situation caused her to go into premature labor. With no money, no identity, and a three year old child, she died in labor," he continued. "Leah and Phillip never knew their mother and grew up bouncing from foster home to foster home never knowing anything about who they were or what happened to their parents. Leah was a beautiful girl who generally made friends quickly. She had a magnetic personality that just attracted people to her. She was a great student, athlete and Christian. Philip was the complete opposite. He was a violent and angry kid. He was constantly getting in trouble and causing problems which made impossible for he and Leah to stay anywhere. They were a package deal and she got kicked out as many homes as he did because she refused to leave him behind. As they got older, Philip only got worse. He finally did something that got him put into a boys home for two years when he was around your age. It was a blessing for Leah. She blossomed in his absence and was adopted by a well-off family in Lincoln Springs almost immediately. Once there she met your father and the rest of your parents after being adopted by Sai's grandparents the Hikaris."

I chuckled under my breath smiling at the irony.

"I guess I see why Dad was so quick to take me in," Luke cut with a smile.

"Iggy was the complete opposite of Philip. He was everything she wanted Phillip to be. She couldn't have asked for a better life," Max continued. "It was there she met Adam and Jacob, Sr. Jacob who had been a Remnant and was passing his anointment on to his son asked Michael if he could create and train his own legion to help mankind in the late religious wars. He wanted to prepare them for the Trials. Naturally, Michael agreed. Adam chose a few of his friends and it was Jacob who chose your mother and a few of her friends to round out the group. Your father, seeing her as the controlling presence of his father, actively despised her when she first arrived, but watching her loyalty and talent, he soon became infatuated with her. They trained in the Heaven Realm for years, but constantly fell short with Adam and Leah being the only ones accepted trial after trial. Finally, on the eve of Leah's eighteenth birthday Philip was released. Leah explained and shared everything she knew and learned with Philip for the entirety of his stint in prison, so when he was finally released he was an extremely experienced Remnant. Adam and the rest of the legion didn't know him well enough to trust Philip, but they trusted Leah's judgment wholeheartedly. No one could've seen what type of person Philip was."

"What do you mean?" I asked.

"Philip was an exceptional remnant, but he was a double agent from the beginning," Jade cut in.

"How?" Eve added.

Jade turned to her with a look that fell between surprised and empathetic. He sighed before turning to us in a leveling manner.

"Well, Jacob," he replied catching all our attentions. "Jacob Sr."

His words slowed my beating heart as I nodded trying to keep a calm demeanor. Jacob himself seemed to be at ease to hear Jade say my grandfather's name. Still his words were polarizing. My grandfather? What did he have to do with Sam's father going rogue? I leaned forward attentively as he continued.

"Jacob, like Tim chose a legion. He knew the risk of bringing Philip on, but he trusted that your mother would bring him over like you did with Luke, but unlike you guys, they weren't dead, things weren't as obvious or cut and dry as going to retrieve a lost soul. There was no jarring experience to judge. Philip was trained from the time he was very young. His father found him through the evil forces in your world when he entered the Juvenile center. He met his father who already knew about your mother's training. He disclose to Philip who his mother was and told him of his heritage. Lucifer turned him before your mother could get to him. Your grandfather knew how powerful your mother was because of the many double agents here in the Heaven Realm who saw her excel time after time in the trials. So, he used Philip in a plan to dispose of your mother?"

"But why just their mother?" Sai replied. "Why not the entire legion?"

He turned to her with an apologetic shrug.

"At the time, she was the legion," she replied. "And even if it meant taking out his daughter, he was willing to do it to keep his spot on the council."

He stopped shaking his head in a sorrow filled manner.

"We lost contact with the legion after they graduated from the Academy, but I always suspected he would be the downfall of that legion," Max interrupted.

"Why?" I pressed.

"Leah was as protective of him as...Jacob is of you," he replied pointing at the two of us. "She let her guard down around him and would sacrifice herself for him without hesitation."

Jacob leaned forward. I stared at him anticipating what his words would be as he opened his mouth to speak.

"So, is that how she died?" he replied bringing everyone else in.

Jade shrugged his shoulders turning to Max. He avoided eye contact as he continued.

"We don't know?" Max replied in an embarrassed tone.

"What do you mean, you don't know?" Jacob shot back angrily. "Why don't you know?"

Max stood for a second as if to be composing himself then turned and walked off the transport angrily. We all stood confused by his display as Jade turned to us in a sympathetic show.

"What's the matter with him?" I asked. "Why is he leaving?"

Jade stopped and sighed in a relenting fashion.

"He doesn't know what happened to your parents because it's classified," he replied.

"How? Wasn't he the legion's host?" Pete pressed.

Jade shook his no.

"He has the ability to but he...he's been hesitant to delve into it," he replied.

He stood as we all stared at him expecting him to continue, but he was unrelenting as he stared at us unapologetically.

"That aside, the point for me telling you guys this is to explain the reason for the bias toward Sam. The rest is classified. I can't tell you until you've graduated from the academy and joined the Light Guard so leave it alone," he replied.

He cleared his throat as we all gave varying glances as he continued.

"Sam's mother Samantha was pregnant with Sam when it all came out," he continued pulling us back.

"What? When what came out?" Luke pressed.

"Shut up so he can tell us, Luke!" Sai commanded.

"Sam's father was allegedly the chosen one of Satan. He is believed by many in this realm to be the anti-christ," Jade replied shocking everyone.

"What!" Eve replied. "Sam's father...Tim's uncle is the antichrist?"

"You have got to be kidding," Danielle added.

"That's scary," Zech replied.

The dynamic of the room was completely different. You could hear a pin drop. No one wanted to speak. No one wanted to be the first to interject. No one know what to say.

"It's just a theory," Jade replied. "No one knows for sure but from the moment it was assumed, Samantha, his brother, and Sam went into hiding. Samantha...was lost to Phillip, and the kids were lost. Both Adam and Phillip searched desperately for the kids. It didn't take long to find them. A battle ensued and Phillip caused a fire that burned down Sam's home and took his brother."

"So, the demon Sam was talking about, the one his guardian was trying to keep Sam away from was Sam's father?" I pressed flabbergasted.

Jade gave a non-verbal nod and continued.

"After the battle Sam was lost…Luckily, Adam and Leah didn't give up. They eventually found Sam brought him to Angel Haven," he responded obviously hiding something as he navigated the story.

"So, why did Sam's brother get taken but not Sam himself," Jacob replied.

"Your parents showed up in time to save his brother," Jadiel replied. "I don't know the details, but Sam has been under their protection ever since. Soon a war started between the DOL and Phillip. Angel Haven became a battlefield."

He paused in a deeply regretful way. We all watched unable to understand why.

"And unfortunately, it led to death of a lot of your parents," he finally disclosed dropping a pipe bomb.

His words were a hard pill to swallow. We all sat in shock. You could hear a pin drop. An uncomfortable silence ensued before Zech finally cut in.

"So why didn't they just let his father have him?" Zech replied.

Somebody should have said something. One of us should have objected, but no one said a word. Jade stared around with a look that fell between angry and disappointed. We were all struggling to accept Jade's words and trying our best to conceal it from each other. We couldn't understand the bombshell he had just dropped. He had basically just told the entire legion that if it wasn't for Sam their parents would be alive.

"Because," he replied angrily. "That kid didn't do anything to deserve hell and neither did his brother, so they fought to get his brother and they fought to save him. It would've been cowardly, and they can blame Sam for their problems if they want, but at least they had someone."

As he spoke his eye sparked with anger. I had never seen Jade so infuriated. He looked like he was going to blow his top.

"He had no one," he replied snapping us all back to earth. "So, I am truly sorry for your loss. Yes, lost parents, but no one has had to endure what that kid has, and if you're going to have feelings about him that mirror the short-sighted bigots in this realm, then I severely misjudged the integrity of this legion."

He stared us over shaking his head in disappointment before continuing.

"Regardless, he won't hear any this. If he does, you'll have to deal with me," he continued angrily.

A look of bewildered regret covered the face of nearly every face in the room.

"We didn't mean..." I sputtered.

"Don't try it," Jade replied cutting me off. "I have been doing this longer than you, Tim. That feeling I felt was anger and it was all aimed at an innocent kid who is more a victim than any of you. I am disappointed in all of you aside from Jacob. The BAU's I got from the rest of you who lost parents...I understand your young, but I expected more. Regardless, Tim, you will accompany him and you both are going back to Earth."

"Wait, what?" I asked surprised by his outburst. "Why me?"

Jade stared at me with a look that almost caused me to swallow my tongue.

"It's you because it requires the talent you have. Your diversity is needed because there is no telling what is required to accomplish this mission," he replied pausing in annoyed manner. "You will be going back to Earth. Understand, this is not a normal undertaking. Because of Sam's low score he was given a special mission. It is an E rank mission."

"What!" Eve cut in. "That isn't fair!"

Jacob scoffed in a matter of fact type tone.

"No, it is, a person with a one has relatively accomplished nothing, so they have to be beyond reproach. You can't just give them a run of the mill undertaking. Unfortunately, Tim's decision led to Sam's predicament," Jacob replied. "It's only right, he should be the one to help him."

I acknowledged Jacob's word. He was right. This was my chance to make a wrong right. Suddenly my spirit changed. I now was intent on making sure Sam made it. Jacob was right, this way my chance and I was going to make it right.

"Tim was nearly killed the last time he went there," Eve cut in. "What...how can they do this?"

She seemed like she was about to breakdown. Over her time training with us the three of us had developed a bond. It killed her to hear we'd both be risking our lives for the sake of some trial.

"Can we just forfeit? Why risk it? Let Tim said, who cares about the Academy. We've been trained by angels. Couldn't Jade, Max, and Hanz continue?" she cut in a pleading manner.

"Evelyn, the Light Guard Academy affords you guys domain, power, and resources we could never match alone. Is it impossible to protect the witnesses without the resources of Light Guard Academy? Of course not, but hear me when I say, the chances of success are drastically cut. Without the academy, you guys would have no right to be here. You'd be sent back to the Earth Realm. As you know, time there is different. There is no way you'd be able to put in the years of training you could here. You would have months before literal hell would be let lose and you'd be completely abandon by the Light Guard. I'm sorry, that would be suicide."

I shook my head angrily.

"If you knew that why did you let us make that promise to Sam?" I shot staring at the man blown away by his revelation. "Why did you give us the impression that we had a chance to do this without the trials?"

"Because it doesn't matter," Jade fired. "You made a promise. Honor it."

"What does that mean?" Sai cut in.

"It means get ready for the trials," he responded vaguely before angrily walking off the transport.

We all sat frustrated staring vacantly around the transport waiting for someone to speak. Once again Uriah took the lead standing and turning toward me.

"I'll help you guys," Uriah cut in standing gripping the seat as emotion ran through him. "I'll go over that undertaking with a fine-tooth comb and anyway I can help, I will. Forget the odds, faith dictates reality, right? Maybe we should stop relying on our gifts and start relying on our faith. That's why we're here, isn't it? We're the Theta Delta legion. We're the legion that had demon's in fear before we knew who we were. We're done losing. We're done being less. We hold the cards. Our faith has made these so-called experts look like fools on too many times to count.

Nothing we've done has been easy, most of it's been downright impossible, but that's what faith is. It's the faith in the unseen, and if that faith dictates our circumstance. Let's start dictating."

We all sat up attentively taking in the boys words before Pete rose inspired.

"I'll help too," Pete replied with a nod of his head.

"Let us know if you need our help," Sai replied. "It's the least we can do considering how we just acted."

"Exactly," Pete replied.

His words had breathed life into our legion as we all rosed with determined demeanors slowly exiting the transport. I walked through the crowd of reporters as they all flocked past me to get to Jacob. He signaled for us to keep going stopping to answer questions so that the rest of us could get into the hotel without a problem. I nodded in appreciation as we all trotted inside. Sai moved to the side letting the rest of they guys pass before grabbing me and pulling me next to her.

"I see you guys in a little bit," She said to Eve and Dani with a smile.

I stood thrown by her actions as Eve responded.

"Yeah, my sister has her last check up," Eve added. "So we'll just check back up when she gets her final release."

Sai nodded as Eve, Beth, and Danielle disappeared in a show light.

"Me and Uriah will go and look over the specs of the undertaking," Pete added shaking my hand before exiting as well.

Sai and I stood in place as everyone else dispersed in light. I stood confused by her actions before she finally turned to me.

"I don't like Jacob," she shot through a clenched false smile as she waved to our exiting legionmates.

"What?" I responded thrown.

"I'm not acting when I say I don't like Jacob. I promise you, I don't like Jacob," she shot begging me to believe her.

I nodded accepting her words still confused about why she felt it important enough to pull me to the side. I fumbled before pressing her.

"Okay? If it's not Jacob, you've stated on too many times to count it wasn't me, Pete or Sam," I continued. "Who is this mystery guy?"

She stared at me angrily shoving me. I winced with a chuckle as she shook her head sarcastically frustrated as she continued unable to hold back a snicker.

"Don't worry about it," she fired causing a soothing calm to come over that I didn't understand at that time. "First, don't believe everything a girl says truly encapsulates what's in her mind. Second, you used the word crush, not me. Third and final, I'll bite, Jacob, Pete, Sam…and especially you, like you said to Eve, I'm not blind. I can't help it. I think it's totally weird but I find myself being…attracted to you…not you, but boys…I mean, you specifically are attractive to me too…I know I should've let you know, but it's an awkward thing to admit. I want to wait until I'm old enough to get married, but now that I see all the…you know, good guys around me being swiped up, you're right, I'm jealous. I'm starting to wonder if they'll still be around when I'm able to pursue them."

Her words came out in an exaggerated humor-filled sigh. She lowered her head bashfully as I stood in awkward silence before bursting into a chuckle. She stared around the lobby embarrassed before slugging me in the arm.

"Tim, stop it," she shot unable to quell a chuckle of her own. "Don't make me regret telling you that, you idiot."

I continued to chuckle as she slugged me again. I smiled appreciatively goading her more before finally responding.

"Well, Miss Hikari, color me flattered," I poked staring her up and down.

She blushed once again before placing her head in her hand visibly embarrassed as she chuckled nervously.

"Sai, I appreciate you being honest," I shot walking over to her and placing my arm over her shoulders. "And in the spirit of being upfront with each other, the feeling is mutual. Pete and I talk about it all the time. Sai, you're a beautiful girl, and times it can be awkward navigating that for both of us."

I should've stopped there, but it was like the freedom of speaking and telling her the pent of feelings I had put me in a trance. I stared into her eyes as she blushed awkwardly at my candid words.

"My gosh, and that kiss," I continued causing her eyes to widen. "It was like… I tried for weeks to get it out of my head, but I couldn't. It was amazing."

She nodded continuing to let me talk. It was obvious what her aim was, but my mind was nowhere near as mature as her was at the time. I continued to speak unable to stop venting the pent-up emotions in me.

"To be honest, I should've told you immediately. Were friends, but who says it has to end there. You know…" I paused catching myself as she crossed her arms covering her mouth hiding a provoking chuckle.

I closed my eyes playfully as embarrassment filled me.

"Oh, please, don't let me stop you, Mr. Eli," she joked in the same vain as my poke moments earlier stirring my embarrassment.

I shook my head nodding accepting my punishment as she smiled in vindicated manner. I stared at her in a way that drained the humor from both our faces.

"Well, if you truly are serious about keeping this thing between us the same," I responded continuing to stare at her like we were the only two people in the room. "You should watch that smile."

She stared at me thrown by my words. I quickly fumbled trying to cover for the flub the candid vibe between us caused me to spill.

"I mean, it's a nice smile…or you have a nice smile," I responded flustered. "Which is super awkward for one friend to say to another friend, I know, but…"

I stood dying a slow death as she stared at me unapologetically smittened. We both were stuck in an awkward lull as a saving voice cut in.

"Tim," said the voice causing both of us to turn.

I turned to see Sean and almost on reflex I sighed. After what had just happened at the trials. He was last guy I wanted to see, but considering the circumstance, I would take it. I nodded in his direction as he approached me.

"Hi Sai," he greeted causing the girl to acknowledge his words with a nod before he continued apologetically. "Look, I just want you to know that what happened today, you know the thing with the guys."

We both nodded remembering the interaction from earlier in the day. He pointed behind him symbolically even though there wasn't anyone standing in the direction of his point.

"I just wanted to say I'm sorry. The guys, they were out of line," he expressed regretfully.

I nodded not really wanting to get into a discussion about it.

"Yeah, thanks...it's no big deal, we were kind of out of line ourselves," I replied.

I nodded feeling self-conscious about the abrupt way in which I knew I was going to have to end the conversation, but regardless I had a lot a work ahead of me and Sai and I had wasted enough time as it stood. I had to go.

"I wish I could talk about it, but I'm kind of in a rush," I replied throwing my bag over my shoulder.

"Okay, cool, I'll come with you," he replied. "I have something I need to ask you."

I looked at him with a look that fell between startled and taken back.

"Okay...sure," I replied not really know how to respond.

"Tim, I'm going to go meet up with the girls. It was nice to...you know, get things out. Honestly, I feel a lot better," she responded giving me a hug.

I nodded taking in the aroma of her rosy perfume. Deep down I didn't want to end the conversation there. I grimaced awkwardly releasing her as she turned to leave. I stood in a trance watching her walk around as Pete and Uriah appeared startling me.

"Tim," Pete uttered. "We have…"

The two boys paused as the noticed Sean. I continued walking toward the elevator as the three boys followed me. A part of me was skeptical of Sean's motives seeing as we were getting ready to embark on one of the most important trials of the competition. Pete and Uriah watched with suspicious looks on their faces as we approached the elevator. I cut Pete a look that told the story in a glance. I had no idea what his motive were, but the guy had been nothing short of a stand-up guy. Truthfully, Sean saved our lives at the expense of his own, and he had earned the trust of a conversation.

"Hi," he greeted speaking to Uriah and Pete as he boarded the elevator.

Pete and Uriah nodded uneasy as he nestled into the elevator.

"I know you guys are wondering why I'm here," he replied turning toward us. "But something has been on my mind since I arrived here, and to make a long story short, I'm from Angel Haven and like the majority of parents in Angel Havens my father was a protector."

I looked at Pete liked Sean was talking Chinese.

"Protector?" Pete responded.

Sean stopped surprised we didn't know what he was talking about.

"Well, as I am sure you know, Angel Haven was built by religious settlers," he responded waiting for us to fill in the blank. "Who were looking to escape religious persecution in the first religious wars of the early 2050's."

We glared at him with dense expressions before he sighed in an annoyed tone.

"Man, your teachers weren't too thorough with the history, were they?" he replied with a straight face.

I shrugged acknowledging his statement. He looked at Pete and his demeanor changed.

"Or it could have been intentional," he replied. "Maybe things changed in our generation. After your family moved out my father says a lot changed."

I looked at him like he was crazy.

"My family never moved out," I responded confused.

"Not your family, his family," he replied pointing directly at Uriah.

Uriah looked as surprised as the rest of us. Sean shook his head in frustration.

"News to me," Uriah replied.

The elevator stopped as he sighed. We walked off the elevator as he continued.

"Well, most of the stuff is in the Heaven Realm database. I've been studying my hometown for years, I know it like the back of my hand," he continued with a look that showed a slight bit of regret about what he disclosed. "Regardless, these protectors were normal earthborn people with basic light are training. My father like many, if not all the parents in Angel Haven, was a protector. They were the eyes and ears of the remnants, but that isn't my point. My point is, from the minute I knew...u know what was coming. I wanted to help. At first I thought I could possibly help in the small ways that I could, but after realizing what was at stake, I've realized that won't be enough. Those people are just as much my people as any yours. I shouldn't be a part of a legion that is striving to bar you guys from saving those people. It just doesn't seem right."

We all turned to him inquisitively at the sound of his words.

"The trial against Pete, it was eating at me," he replied solemnly. "I'm from Angel Haven. I should be with you guys, not against you."

I nodded almost involuntary as I almost heard his words before he said them.

"So, if you guys would have me," he continued. "I would like to be a part of your legion."

We all stood by in shock without saying a word for a second before I sputtered.

"Um, sure," I replied gun shy. "If it isn't against the rules?"

Pete and Uriah just stood still not saying anything. I was skeptical. Was it some type of trick? A mind game right before the trial?

"Thanks," he replied. "It's not against the rules. I was accepted into the academy I can do what I want. I met my obligation to the Alpha House by competing and winning my trial. Besides, they were never really my style to begin with. I belong with you guys. I'm an earthborn guy from Angel Haven, and it would make my father proud to see me representing his earthborn home and serving the greater good. I mean, how many people can say they saved their home world?"

We all just shook his hand not really knowing how or what we were supposed to do to cement the deal. It was an epic turn of events, but I had nothing. I was never really a people person, mostly because I never really knew how to react in emotional situations. Sean kind of half shook my hand and half-stood there as his attention turned to the door just behind us. As he did Kel arose from the room with agitated look on his face.

"Sean?" he replied. "Abby just said you were switching out on us?"

Sean turned not wanting to reply. The kid looked visually effected. He stood staring at Sean an in an exhausted stance before turning to us like we were pariah.

"I'm not switching. I'm not competing anymore. I'll still be rooting for you guys, but my fate is theirs," Sean continued visibly contrite. "I'm sorry. It's no offense to you guys. We've been through a lot together, but in the end, a lot of you guys are heaven born, and that's fine, but honestly, you don't understand how Abby and I feel. To you guys this is just a game. It's not for us. This is our home realm. We shouldn't be the ones to stop our chosen legion. I don't want that on my family's name. I just can't do it."

Kel nodded in an understanding manner, but still looked like he would sooner spit on us.

"And where is your friend?" he said spitefully.

"Right here," said Sam catching us all off-guard.

He turned to Sam and looked down at him like he was insignificant and chuckled.

"Leo's going to destroy this kid," he replied with a chuckle.

After everything I heard I wasn't going to sit by and let anyone insult Sam anymore.

"What did you say?" I replied walking towards him.

He looked at me with a look that fell between intimidated and angry. As he did Leo, and Kadmiel exited their room. I acted as if I didn't see them as I continued my march.

"Tim, stop!" Pete replied cutting me off. "I know how you feel, but if we get caught, we'll lose the competition and Sam won't be able to enter the Academy. In the end what did you really do?"

I paused wanting to punch something as I stopped my momentum agreeing with his words. Kadmiel antagonized me with a smile that ate at me and without thinking about the consequences I just reacted.

WHIFF! I blinked sending a slicing wind to her hair that dropped her to her knees.

"Tim!" Pete replied.

WHAM! Kel hit Pete with a wind blow that nearly sent him throw the hallway wall.

"Pete!" I replied leaping into action.

POP! WHAM! I hit the tall kid with a punch and finished him off with a roundhouse that left him unconscious against a nearby wall.

"Kel," Kadmiel cried storming toward me.

WHOOSH! I conjured a dense wind and with a spinning swipe I slammed her into a nearby wall with earth shattering force that left her lying next to Kel.

Leo stood staring at me focused on each movement, but before I could make a move my body seemed to stop in mid step. I couldn't move. I was stuck.

"Chill," Uriah replied.

It was him. He was using some type of subatomics. I looked at Leo and neither one of us could move.

"This altercation was a dispute nothing more, since neither one of us want our legionmates to be disqualified, we'll just keep this altercation to ourselves," he replied finally releasing us. "Agreed."

I exhaled finally able to move freely as Leo nodded scooping up Kel and Kadmiel. He turned to me with a lasting look before disappearing into their room.

"You okay?" Uriah replied staring at me.

I nodded as Sean helped Pete to his feet. They all looked at me like I was some type of freak.

"Your speed," Sam replied staring at me. "How could you do that?"

"Do what?" I replied. "I've always been fast."

They looked me over still not letting me in on the secret.

"Not that fast," Uriah added. "I wouldn't be surprised if you picked up a few more traits from watching your brother."

I looked over at them not even acknowledging his words as I turned to Sam. At the time it wasn't important. I shrugged it off turning to Sam.

"I'm going with you," I replied. "And were going to train until you make each and every one of those jerks eat their words."

CPSIA information can be obtained
at www.ICGtesting.com
Printed in the USA
LVHW030759181119
637663LV00005B/2035/P